THE GAMES ARE AFOOT. . . .

Lydia Chin discovers there's more than love on-board when she takes a cruise to find a business-man's daughter in "Marking the Boat" by **S. J. Rozan.**

A disgruntled husband hires **Parnell Hall**'s Stanley Hastings to find "The Missing Heir," but is it for love or money?

Jeremiah Healy's John Francis Cuddy looks into a case of sibling rivalry gone awry and attempts to answer the question "What's in a Name?"

Racketeer Frank Nitti asks **Max Allan Collins**'s Nathan Heller to silence a "Screwball" whose bad taste in jokes is bad for business.

And ten more stories featuring today's most popular super sleuths from The Private Eye Writers of America.

Other Anthologies
Edited by Robert J. Randisi

The Eyes Still Have It:
The Shamus Award-Winning Stories

First Cases: First Appearances
of Classic Private Eyes

First Cases, Volume 2: First Appearances
of Classic Amateur Sleuths

First Cases, Volume 3: New and
Classic Tales of Detection

The
PRIVATE EYE WRITERS OF AMERICA
presents

THE
SHAMUS GAME

14 New Stories of Detective Fiction

Edited by
Robert J. Randisi

A SIGNET BOOK

SIGNET
Published by New American Library, a division of
Penguin Putnam Inc., 375 Hudson Street,
New York, New York 10014, U.S.A.
Penguin Books Ltd, 27 Wrights Lane,
London W8 5TZ, England
Penguin Books Australia Ltd, Ringwood,
Victoria, Australia
Penguin Books Canada Ltd, 10 Alcorn Avenue,
Toronto, Ontario, Canada M4V 3B2
Penguin Books (N.Z.) Ltd, 182–190 Wairau Road,
Auckland 10, New Zealand

Penguin Books Ltd, Registered Offices:
Harmondsworth, Middlesex, England

First published by Signet, an imprint of New American Library,
a division of Penguin Putnam Inc.

First Printing, September 2000
10 9 8 7 6 5 4 3 2 1

CONTENTS

INTRODUCTION

The private eye genre provided some of the best writing and storytelling done during the nineties. We in PWA intend to continue that trend as we enter a new millennium, in both the short and the long story forms.

All fourteen of these stories are original and written specifically for this book. In several cases these are the first short stories written by authors about their series character—which means they might also end up in a future edition of my *First Cases* anthology series. Specifically, Shamus winner Terence Faherty's first Scott Elliott story appears here, Parnell Hall's first Stanley Hastings story, and Shamus winner Rick Riordan's first Tres Navarre story. We are honored to present these here.

We are sure readers will be happy to see the return of old favorites Max Allan Collins's Nate Heller, Loren Estleman's Amos Walker, Jeremiah Healy's John Francis Cuddy, Jerry Kennealy's Nick Polo, and John Lutz's Alo Nudger.

Also appearing here is Bill Pronzini's first Nameless short story in five years, and Edward D. Hoch's first Al Darlan story to appear in . . . well, more years than that.

Among the new favorites are S. J. Rozan's Lydia Chin, Gary Phillips's Ivan Monk, Les Roberts's Milan Jacovich, and Christine Matthews's Robbie Stanton.

There are eight Shamus winners in this collection and, we are sure, many future winners, as well.

Each of the authors went all-out in this collection and produced stories of the highest quality we have come to expect of them. We call these "short" stories, but these are prime examples of "long" short stories, several of which almost reach novelette length.

We have raised the bar very high, indeed, in *Shamus Game,* and we look toward the future—and the collections that follow—to raise it even higher.

Please read, enjoy and look forward to what comes next.

—Robert J. Randisi
St. Louis
August 1999

MARKING THE BOAT
A LYDIA CHIN STORY

by S. J. Rozan

S. J. Rozan's reputation continues to grow by leaps and bounds with every book. Already a Shamus winner once for Best Novel, she will undoubtedly be nominated again and again in the future—not only for novel but for short story as well.

In this story Lydia Chin's search for a missing girl takes her on a Caribbean cruise, and Lydia's powers of observation are very much in evidence.

S. J. Rozan won the Shamus for Best Novel with her book *Concourse* in 1996. Her newest novel is *Stone Quarry* (St. Martin's Press, 1999).

Marking the Boat to Locate a Lost Sword

A man was ferrying across a river. When, by accident, his sword dropped into the water, he immediately carved a notch on the side of the boat to mark the place where his weapon was lost. "What's the use of making a notch there?" the irritated ferry man asked him. The man replied, "That's the place where my sword dropped into the river. I'll jump into the water from the same place to find my sword when the boat moors." That was what he did when the boat reached the other bank of the river. However hard he tried, he could not locate his lost sword.

—from *The Discourses of Lu Buwei*

Golden sun, azure sea. Balmy breezes and the scent of hibiscus. Tiny waves glittering away to a distant and cloudless horizon. I leaned on the ship's mahogany rail, polished by white-uniformed crewmen at least twice a day, as far as I could tell.

This should have been fun.

And it might have been if I wasn't here to pick up the trail of a young woman who, I was sure, was already dead.

I didn't like the sound of it when I first heard the facts. But the case was irresistible. All my white-knight, saving-people-in-distress instincts screamed for me to take it, after Mr. and Mrs. Chu explained their problem to me. Actually, Mr. Chu explained. Mrs. Chu served tea and butter cookies in their Sutton Place duplex, straightened a room that didn't need straightening, and was silent.

Their problem was serious. It involved their older daughter, Janet. Six weeks ago, upon Janet's college graduation, the Chu family—Mr. and Mrs., Janet, and younger daughter, June—took a week-long cruise to the Caribbean.

A week long for everyone else. But Janet never came back.

"It was our second cruise on that cruise line. In fact, on that very ship." Mr. Chu, a Hong Kong-born vice president of something for a Singaporean electronics firm, spoke with controlled care, measuring his every word and the emotion he allowed it to hold. I thought Mrs. Chu, having brought us tea in a silver tea service, would sit in the brocade-covered easy chair opposite Mr. Chu's leather one, but she remained standing by the bookcase, looking uneasy, as though she was afraid there was something she had forgotten to do. She slid a bisque figure of a sailor boy a millimeter to the right of where it had been.

"Last year, when June finished high school"— Mr. Chu nodded to his younger daughter—"a cruise seemed to me the perfect graduation gift. Something we could all enjoy."

June, a smooth-cheeked, glossy-haired girl seated on a leather hassock across the deeply figured Oriental carpet, nodded quickly back, agreeing with her father that the perfect graduation gift was one the whole family could enjoy. If she'd graduated high school last year, that made her a college freshman now, on summer break. Most of the college kids I knew were wearing shabby jeans and short, tight tops this year, but June sat in her parents' living room in a plaid skirt and white blouse.

"That first cruise was excellent," Mr. Chu was saying, hands folded over his belly. "Flawless. Everything worked out so well that I chose the same ship to celebrate Janet's graduation from college."

Out of the corner of my eye I saw Mrs. Chu peering helplessly around the room for more strayed knickknacks to restore to their rightful places. She found none. I hoped, if she was looking for something to do, she might open a window, or at least turn up the air conditioning; it was stifling in there. But she didn't. Looking deflated, she slowly sat. She refilled my teacup, and her daughter's, and her husband's, and finally poured a cup for herself. She took a sip, then placed it on the coffee table. She didn't touch it again.

"The fifth night at sea was the night of the Captain's Ball," Mr. Chu continued. "My wife and I attended, and excused ourselves just after eleven. We don't enjoy late evenings."

I glanced at Mrs. Chu, partly for confirmation, partly to offer her the chance to participate in this conversation, but her eyes remained fixed on the clear golden tea in her abandoned cup as though something could be found in its depths.

"June is eighteen, so naturally her curfew is earlier than Janet's," Mr. Chu told me. I thought, curfew? At eighteen? Or at—what must Janet be, twenty-one? "June was back in the stateroom suite by midnight. Many people later reported seeing Janet dancing at the ball until a little past two. Ship's records show that she returned to the stateroom at two-sixteen."

"Ship's records?" I asked, my first contribution to this discussion since I'd thanked Mrs. Chu for the tea.

"The *Asiatic Pearl* uses a key-card system. It records each time a card is used."

"The *Asiatic Pearl*? That's the ship?"

"Yes. The flagship of the Orient America line." Mr. Chu shifted in his armchair, reestablishing his position before going on. "The ship is of Dutch registry, but the crew is largely Taiwanese. That was why I chose that line. Because of my daughters. I wanted to feel comfortable—well, you understand."

Yes, I thought, sipping my tea, I understand. Daughters are universally assumed to be safer among men of one's own race—disciplined and honorable—than among lusty young barbarians.

My mother certainly thinks so.

"But," Mr. Chu added, "it seems I was wrong."

The rest of the story was quick to tell, both because there wasn't much to it and because Mr. Chu, for all his control and restraint, clearly found this part difficult.

Janet had not been seen again.

When June awoke at half past seven—"My usual time"—in the room she shared with her sister on one side of the two-bedroom-plus-sitting-area first-class suite, Janet wasn't there. Her bed looked unslept-in, though, "It's hard to say," June told me, her voice quiet, almost a whisper. "She usually makes her bed when she gets up."

"Even on a ship?" I didn't know much about cruise ships, but I knew they were like hotels, where they had people who did that sort of thing for you.

June shrugged apologetically. "That's how we were raised."

I thought about my mother, pursing her lips at any one of my many transgressions, telling me in accusatory tones, "People will think you were raised that way." I sipped my tea and waited for the rest.

"June thought Janet had already gone for breakfast, so she wasn't concerned," Mr. Chu picked up again. "Or perhaps she was jogging. At the health club, of course. I didn't permit it along the deck, where any man might take it as his right to stare."

Of course. "Would she have gotten up that early if she didn't come in until two?" I asked.

"My daughters are quite self-disciplined."

Again: of course.

I noticed both Mr. Chu and June spoke of Janet in the present tense. Missing people's families almost always did, until they could no longer deny, or hope.

I turned to June, though the question was for them all: "Did any of you hear her come in that night or leave in the morning?"

"No," June said in her well-mannered whisper. "I'm a very sound sleeper."

"You didn't hear the door opening or anything?"

"When we were children," she whispered, "Janet used to come sit beside me when I was asleep and tell me all her dreams and secrets. She said she did it because she knew I wouldn't wake up, so they'd all stay secret."

Mrs. Chu glanced up at that, as if hearing something she hadn't known before. She did not speak.

"Is there a record of when she went out?" I asked Mr. Chu.

"The system doesn't record when the door is opened. Just when the card is used."

I'd expected that, but it never hurts to ask.

"My wife and I were not concerned, either," said Mr. Chu, abruptly picking up the story again, "until by nine o'clock we had not found Janet yet."

"We looked everywhere," June put in, as if to assure me they hadn't been neglectful of their duty. "The dining room, the health club, the pool. I even checked the kitchen."

"Why the kitchen?"

"Janet has an interest in cooking," her father said shortly.

"When we were little, she used to talk about being a chef," June told me with an anxious glance at her father. "About having a restaurant of her own. On the first cruise she visited the kitchen a lot."

"Janet graduated magna cum laude from Stony Brook," Mr. Chu said firmly. "Her degree is in business administration. She has a good position waiting for her in my firm, which she was to take up upon our return from the Caribbean."

Ah, I thought to myself, never mind. "But you didn't find her?"

"No," Mr. Chu said, a touch more softly. "We began to worry. I went to look for the ship's security officer. At about the time I found him—between nine-fifteen and nine-thirty—the gangplank was being lowered and the passengers invited to go ashore."

"You were in port someplace?" I asked, suddenly having to rearrange my mental picture.

"The ship had been docked since ten the previous evening. We were at St. Maarten. The *Asiatic Pearl* makes two port calls on this particular cruise. St. Maarten is the second."

Mr. Chu suddenly reached for his tea and, though it must have been cool by now, brought it to his lips and sipped it with determination, as though it were the one thing in the world at the moment most demanding of his attention.

I looked away from him, at the heavy furniture and deep green walls and carefully placed bric-a-brac, stopping at the large gilt-framed oil painting above the fireplace. June and, I assumed, Janet: two tall, thin, long-haired, porcelain-skinned Chinese beauties in traditional Chinese dress. I wished again for a breeze, even a New York July breeze, to bring some movement to this still, close air.

"I had to tell my story"—Mr. Chu clinked his teacup down, his jaw tight—"repeatedly. First to the security chief. Then to the first mate. Next to the captain. It was close to noon before the ship's officers instituted a search of the crew's quarters. It took much more effort, including a call to the American consulate on St. Maarten, to persuade them to allow the local authorities on board to also search the passenger cabins." He took a deep breath and moved his shoulders as though untangling himself from the coils of memory. "It wasn't a popular procedure among the passengers, but what did I care? However, nothing was found."

"Nothing?"

"No trace of Janet. Not the dress she was wearing that evening, not her shoes, not her handbag. No sign after all the searching, except in our suite, that she had ever been on that ship."

I glanced over at Mrs. Chu, sitting with her hands folded in her lap, and realized that without movement or sound she was crying. I wanted to jump up and go over, put my arm around her shoulder, make some useless comforting noise. But neither her husband nor her daughter did that, and it wasn't my place.

"Miss Chin," Mr. Chu was saying, "candidly, I must tell you I don't have a high opinion of most people in your profession. I am not pleased at being forced into a position where I must employ a private investigator, and I was surprised to find such an evidently well-bred young Chinese woman as yourself doing this work." Score one for my mom. In fact, score two. "But you come recommended to me, and you suit my purpose."

Well, that's what I'm here for, I thought.

"I want you to go aboard the *Asiatic Pearl,* Miss Chin, and find out what happened to my daughter."

So I did.

Mr. Chu booked me a first-class cabin on the *Asiatic Pearl,* leaving from Miami the next week. I packed up my swimsuit and flew down there. It was the ship's final Caribbean cruise of the season, mid-July, what with the hurricane months coming up, so I was lucky to get on it.

Especially according to my mother.

Not that I got that directly from the horse's mouth. To me, what she said, narrowing her eyes as she watched me pack, was that I should remember I was being sent on this cruise to work, and that Mr. Chu, a clearly important and powerful man, was placing a great deal of trust in me with this assignment. She added that she hoped a lazy girl like me wouldn't treat the whole thing as just a chance to lie in the sun, especially in a cabin that was considerably above my station in life.

I might have mentioned that you can't really lie in the sun in a cabin, but I just kept folding cotton blouses. My mother wandered off to call Mary Kee's mother to inquire innocently if Mary had ever been on a Caribbean cruise. That was where the words "Ah, too bad" and "My Ling Wan-ju, so lucky" came up.

On the other hand, Bill Smith, my sometimes-partner, who used to be in the navy, did not consider anything that involved a ship to be a case of good luck.

"The good luck," I pointed out to him over the

phone, moving the blouses aside on my bed so I could sit, "is that you're not invited."

"Good luck for you or me?"

"Both of us. You don't have to go back to sea, and I can have a shipboard romance with some tall, handsome sailor."

"Good luck for the sailor, then. You sure you don't need me?"

"Having you there would cramp my style."

"I meant for the case."

"That too."

He gave me some advice about seasickness and sailors, and I promised to call. Then it was back to the blouses again.

Mr. Chu was an important and powerful man, as my mother had said, I reflected as I packed, but not important and powerful enough to get any authorities to take seriously the disappearance of his older daughter.

I had asked about that at the end of our meeting in the Chus' airless living room. Mr. Chu's anger and frustration had been clear in the tightness of his jaw, which I was learning to read, and the extra control in his words.

"The St. Maarten police, after their search, claimed to have no further jurisdiction over a cruise vessel, especially where there was no evidence of a crime. No evidence of a crime!" I almost thought he was going to spit in contempt; if he'd been on the street instead of in his own home, he probably would have. "The authorities in Miami, of course, had as little jurisdiction, and less reason to become involved in a situation that took place on a ship of foreign registry docked in a foreign port."

"But someone must be in charge," I objected, realizing as I said it that I was probably wrong: in some situations, as organized and disciplined as everything seems, the truth is that no one is in control.

"Legal authority on shipboard," Mr. Chu said, "lies with the captain, governed by certain international regulations concerning activity on the high seas. Oh, Miss Chin, I have learned a great deal about these matters in the weeks since my daughter disappeared." He smiled a bitter smile. "The captain was considerably more concerned for the cruise line's reputation than for the fate of one unknown young woman. It was he who suggested that my daughter had merely left the ship, and that the answer lay on St. Maarten itself. As if she would have even considered such an action without consulting her mother and myself!"

Across the room, June looked down at her well-polished shoes. I watched her for a moment, then turned back to Mr. Chu. "Would it have been possible, though?" I asked cautiously. "To leave the ship that night?"

Mr. Chu gave me a cold look. For a moment I thought he wasn't going to answer me, but he did. "Not for passengers. Whatever crew members are not on duty may go ashore at any port call, as I understand it, at whatever hour. But the gangplank was not lowered for passengers until well after nine that morning. Janet was already missing. Also," he added pointedly, "passengers going ashore are required to give their names to the duty officer as they leave. The officer records the time of their departure and return. My daughter's name was obviously not among those on the officer's list.''

"I wonder if the crew goes through the same procedure," I said, half to myself, as I put my teacup down.

"What difference does it make what the crew does in port? Whatever befell my daughter happened on the *Asiatic Pearl*. The answer is there!" Mr. Chu snapped. It was suddenly clear to me— oh, Lydia, you sensitive individual you—that his iron self-control was stretching thin, and that maybe this would be a good time to wrap things up.

So wrap things up I did, stopping only to accept a retainer—quite generous, I thought—and pick up a few photographs of Janet from a neatly organized stack June, at a word from her father, pulled out of a drawer in the foyer for me.

"This is from the day before she disappeared," June whispered, lingering over and then handing to me a snapshot of a smiling, tanned young woman in a pink polo shirt and white Bermuda shorts.

"She cut her hair?" I asked, looking from the photo to the painting on the wall in the other room. As opposed to the painting, the young woman in the photo wore a short, artfully tousled cut. Clearly up-to-the-minute, height-of-fashion stuff, though not, I reflected, particularly good for a long, delicate face like hers. But it would probably look great on someone shorter, whose face was rounder, like, for example, me.

"She did that just before we left," June answered. "I thought, if she was going to cut it, she should make it shoulder-length, with bangs; that's such a pretty look, and Father might not have minded. But she wanted the cut a friend of hers from school had. She even took her friend's picture to the hairdresser to show him." June looked down at the photo again. "Father wasn't pleased at all. He thinks short hair looks—his word is 'brazen.' But Mother said he mustn't let his temper spoil our trip, and that Janet would grow her hair long again as soon as she started her job in his company. Father told Janet to see that she did, and no one said anything else about it."

I looked back at Mr. and Mrs. Chu, each staring silently across the living room, not seeing each other or, it seemed, paying any further attention to me or June. I wondered if that was the effect of June's soft voice and self-effacing manner, or the cause.

"Does Janet do many things your father doesn't approve of?" I asked, using the present tense myself. June wouldn't notice me doing that, but she'd notice if I didn't.

June's eyes widened slightly. "Oh, no," she said quickly. She bit her lower lip. "Well, if it's really important to her. For example, Father wanted her to go to Barnard, so she could live at home, but she wanted to go away for college. What she really wanted was to go to restaurant school, but of course he wouldn't let her do that. She finally talked him into letting her go to Stony Brook. But he didn't really disapprove, because she promised to study hard and graduate cum laude, and she did."

And, I thought, because the State University of New York at Stony Brook is on Long Island, barely an hour from Sutton Place.

"Father can be difficult," June Chu admitted. "He does lay down laws. But really, he's only thinking about what's best for me and Janet. That's why he wouldn't let her go to restaurant school. His family owned a restaurant in Hong Kong when he was a boy, and he had to work there. He hated it."

"And Janet understands that, too?"

June blinked. "Of course she does."

"Tell me, is she looking forward to her new job in his firm?"

"It's very exciting. It's an important job, especially for a woman."

Not the question I'd asked, but an answer that, I had a feeling, told me what I wanted to know.

I hadn't shared with the Chus my thoughts that day, but here, leaning on the rail as the *Asiatic Pearl* steamed out of St. Thomas, our first port of call, I had to admit that I had no reason to doubt my original hypothesis, though I had no evidence yet to prove it, either. My assumption was that Janet, who rebelled, it seemed to me, in small ways—like getting a haircut she knew her father wouldn't like—might have been looking for one last little fling on her graduation cruise before settling down to work in her father's firm at a job which was not her dream. June and Janet Chu were sheltered Chinese-American girls; the muscled Taiwanese sailors probably seemed both thrillingly exotic, and at the same time—as their father had thought—safe. Trustworthy, their sweet nothings honest declarations of attraction, maybe even love. But Janet, I was assuming, had chosen badly.

I hadn't shared this with the Chus, but it was obvious to me that Mr. Chu, at least, was thinking the same way.

Liaison with a passenger meant immediate dismissal to the crew member whose involvement is discovered. This I had learned from the *Asiatic Pearl*'s security chief, the only person on board who knew who I was and why I was there. I'd paid him a professional courtesy call the first morning, after spending the afternoon and evening we left Miami unpacking and wandering the ship, getting acquainted with my new surroundings. He—John McKay, a former Chicago police lieutenant who, at retirement, came south looking for a less exciting, more sun-filled life—was officially not pleased with my assignment.

"Anything you find," he pointed out as we sat in his cramped port-holed office, a couple of plaques and pictures on the wall, papers spread on the desk, "if it shows evidence there could have really been a crime, will make the ship—and me—look bad. I mean, we did an investigation, and nothing turned up. The official position of this cruise line is, nothing happened to that girl aboard this ship." He scratched his chin thoughtfully before he spoke again. "But between you and me? I remember her. They were on the ship last year, too, you know. Her and her sister. Pretty young kids. The older one was quiet, but kind of—bouncy, like she was holding herself in, you know what I mean? And the crew noticed them, I know they did. We don't get a lot of Oriental passengers. I think there's only two other Orientals besides you on this trip. Japanese. Cousins, I think. One's a little like you, the other's heavy. I guess it's not a big thing with you people, cruises?"

He looked at me inquiringly, but I couldn't help him; I had no idea whether it was a big thing with us people or not.

"Anyway," he went on, apparently not troubled by his unsatisfied curiosity, "these Chu girls were a lot more high-class than the other Oriental girls on board—waitresses, housekeeping staff, people like that. I saw the guys eyeing them."

"Any guys in particular?"

He shook his head. "I wish I could say I'd noticed. I've thought about it since, believe me. And I asked around. But I can't come up with anyone."

"But that doesn't mean there wasn't someone in particular?"

"That I couldn't find him? God, no. When these kinds of affairs happen, they hide it real well. The passenger as much as the crewman. The couple of times I've found one out, any ship I've been on, the passenger turns out to have been getting as big a kick from sneaking around and hiding it as from the affair itself."

I thought about tiptoeing around a cruise ship, meeting among coils of rope, hiding behind fog horns.

"Why is it," I asked, hoping to satisfy some unsatisfied curiosity of my own, "that the entire crew of this ship is from Taiwan? That seems so strange to me."

"It's not really. All the cruise lines do it this way, try to recruit a whole crew from one place. Running a cruise ship is a tough business for the below-decks crew—not like for the officers. For us it's a job, not a vacation, but we can mingle with the passengers, eat in the dining room, stroll on the deck," he said matter-of-factly. "These guys, mostly they're menial laborers. For them it's chopping vegetables, doing laundry, repairing leaky pipes. Like any nine-to-five. The difference here is, there's no bar to blow off steam in when you get off work. You can't go home to your wife and kids. And you live in a cabin with three other guys and no windows."

My eyes went involuntarily to the porthole in his office. Not much of a window, but at least some sense there was a world out there.

"They sign on for six-month stretches," Chief McKay went on. "They work six days a week. It seems to help if they're surrounded by their own. Then you have people who speak the same language, eat the same foods. A lot of times we get brothers and cousins all signing on together. It keeps them happier, and they keep each other in line a little better."

Hmmm, I thought. Or cover for each other, the way family will do.

"Well," I said, "tell me what you think happened to Janet Chu."

He gave me a carefully blank look. "I already told you: the official position is, on my ship, nothing."

"Okay," I said. "But what if there was a situation like this on someone else's ship? Just hypothetically, what would you think?"

He nodded, as though he'd been waiting—maybe even hoping—for just that question. "Now, I'm not saying this happened," he said. "But say a passenger gets involved with a crewman. Say something happens—maybe she gets drunk, falls, maybe she's hurt. The guy gets scared—I mean, most of these guys, they're supporting whole families back home on what they make here—well, you can see what might happen."

" 'What might happen,' " I repeated. "Can you be more specific?" I knew what he meant; I just wanted to hear it from someone besides myself.

Chief McKay shrugged. "There are a lot of places on this ship you could throw someone overboard, no one would ever know. I mean, she might not have even been dead when she went over, just suddenly more trouble than she was worth."

I thought of Janet Chu, the shock of the cold black water, the enormous ship looming above her, the churning wake pulling her under as she struggled to keep breathing. Maybe Chief McKay thought of her, too. He gave me a long look and said, "Anything you need, if I can help, you just tell me."

So my job, as I saw it, was to find out whom among the crew Janet Chu had been involved with. Of course, it might not have been a crewman. It might have been a fellow passenger. I doubted that, because it seemed to me at least June, and possibly even Janet's parents, would have been let in on a legit shipboard romance like that. Or it might have been nobody, and something totally else had happened. If I hit a dead end, I'd have to consider that possibility, but right now I was following the obvious path. That path led below decks, and the first place it led to, I decided, was the kitchen.

Janet Chu's love of cooking had brought her to the kitchen both times her family had sailed aboard this ship. What the security chief referred to as her "high-class" beauty, coupled with her wide-eyed interest in the work of the kitchen, could have handed some vegetable-chopper both a reason and an opportunity to strike up a conversation with her.

At the mahogany rail, I checked my watch. Three o'clock—perfect. It was late enough now that the last of the after-lunch clean-up was over, early enough that dinner preparations would be only barely underway. A good time to hit the kitchen.

Or so I thought until I got there. Pushing through the stainless steel doors from the silent dining room, I wasn't ready for the bustling, shouting, steaming, clanking, boiling, slamming, and rushing, all presided over by loud, though unintelligible Taiwanese pop music from a tinny boom box on a high shelf.

At first no one noticed me. T-shirted, aproned men slammed cleavers onto cutting boards through sides of beef, tossing bones into a simmering pot, meat into a huge bowl already piled high. A skinny guy went by dragging a bag of carrots bigger than he was. Someone yelled at someone else, got yelled at by a third man in return. Clouds of onion- and herb-scented steam billowed from giant stockpots. A waterfall roared from a faucet and a kettle shrieked.

I had stopped just inside the door, wondering what to do next, when a huge man whose blood-streaked apron barely covered his massive belly pointed his cleaver at me. Like everyone else in the room, he was Asian: Taiwanese, I assumed.

"Passenger not allowed kitchen," he told me, un-grammatically but informatively. "Sorry, you leave now."

He didn't seem sorry, but I wasn't here to pick a fight with him. I let my face fall.

"Oh," I said, "but please? I'm so-o-o interested in cooking. Especially professionals like you, seeing how you do it. A whole big kitchen like this! My friend, she said you'd let me watch. If I keep out of the way?"

Stonily, he shook his head. "Sorry, you leave now," he repeated.

Wondering if he spoke any more English than that, I sidestepped a little farther into the kitchen and raised my voice slightly, to take in a few more of the furiously chopping, stirring, scraping men.

"My friend Janet—Janet Chu, you know?—she was on this ship last year, and she said the kitchen was the best place of all. Boy, she was right, too!" I skirted the man with the cleaver, pretending not to notice the creasing of his brow as I skipped over to watch a kid who didn't look more than sixteen slicing up a mountain of potatoes. "Janet said the guys in the kitchen were the nicest guys on the ship, too." I smiled at the potato kid. He looked at me blankly, then sped up his slicing. "You remember Janet?" I asked the kitchen at large. "Her family took this ship last year, then I think this year too, but this year she cut her hair, so she looks different, but you'd know her, and she said she used to come down here all the time and I should too because it would be okay as long as I kept out of the way."

I was wandering around as I blabbered, avoiding

the guy with the cleaver, who seemed to be getting more and more mad but less and less sure about what he was supposed to do as I waltzed among the stoves and counters. I was counting on the idea that he couldn't just pick me up and throw me out; manhandling the passengers was probably worse than letting them mess around where they weren't supposed to be.

"Janet and I met at restaurant school," I said to no one in particular, "that's what we both love, I mean she cooks a lot better than I do but anyway I'd run the place, that's what I'm good at, people skills, you know, and I'd hire all these great cooks like Janet, that would be cool, huh?"

I stopped to lean over a counter and inspect a sheet of pastry dough a tall young man was rolling out, push-pull, push-pull. "And my folks said I could take this cruise, like a graduation present, because Janet's family had such a good time, I mean on the first one, I haven't seen her in a while so I don't know about the second one but I bet that was fun too, so I'm here with this friend of mine and she doesn't care about cooking but it's what I love best so I came down here to watch."

I snapped my head around as someone sizzled oil into a heated frying pan. "So this is like dinner prep, huh? I didn't expect you guys to have started dinner already but I guess for this many people you sort of have to, huh? Boy, Janet was always saying I never thought ahead enough, that was my problem in restaurant school, I mean I tried but I'm just not good with details." I giggled, watching out of the corner of my eye as the man with the cleaver made his way up my aisle.

"Well, I don't want to like get in the way or anything, so I'm gonna go, but I'll come back, like maybe in the morning. I'd totally love to see you guys make breakfast, french toast and pancakes and stuff, and those great croissants, you bake them yourselves, huh? I mean if I can get up that early, Janet always went for a jog before breakfast when we were in school but I was lucky if I made it to my early class, but anyway, I'll try. Bye!"

I yanked open the door, hurried through the still and silent dining room and out again onto the deck, feeling the eyes of the guy with the cleaver still on me.

That was okay. When I was out of sight he'd let the kitchen door close and go back to hacking through beef bones with one stroke, probably imagining they were pushy, annoying passengers.

I ran my hand through my hair, letting the sweet breeze clear the smell of onions from my head. I wasn't worried about the man with the cleaver anymore. I'd gotten what I wanted.

The man with the cleaver wasn't the only one of the kitchen workers I'd watched out of the corner of my eye while I hopped around their workplace. Each time I'd tossed Janet Chu's name out I'd looked for any reaction it got. Most of the time I caught nothing. But twice I saw heads turn, glances thrown across the room. So I'd skittered over to the place the glances had gone and dropped her name again. And the tall young man's cheeks had colored, and he'd avoided my eyes as he'd pushed and pulled at his pastry dough.

*   *   *

To me, the fact that the tall young man reacted to Janet Chu's name didn't necessarily mean my search was over. It certainly didn't mean he'd killed her. But it meant he'd known her. And that was a place for me to start.

For my next trick I needed to know who he was, and I needed to get a chance to question him. I went back to my buddy the security chief, who hauled out a book with all the crews' ID photos in it for me to go through. A half hour of careful searching later— large cruise ships, it turns out, carry crews of over a thousand—I found the guy. Han Sho-Shi, his name was, pastry sous-chef, here aboard the Asiatic Pearl with a number of family members. This was his, and most of his relatives', fourth voyage. That meant he had been on board both last spring, on the Chu family's first cruise, and six weeks ago, on their second.

Chief McKay leaned over my shoulder and looked at Han's photo. "That one, huh?"

"Did you question him when she disappeared?"

He shook his head. "I don't remember. I'll check my notes if you want. I went at them randomly. It wasn't like I had any real suspects. Remember, officially I didn't even have a crime. I just kind of stirred the pot to see what would happen."

"But nothing did?"

"No."

He did check his notes; he had not interviewed Han Sho-Shi. The randomly chosen kitchen workers he had talked to had yielded, like everyone else on the ship, nothing.

"But I'm the law," he said. "They'd had time to think about what to say to me. You caught them off guard. How'd you know she was interested in cooking?"

"Her sister told me."

"No one told me. I'd have looked into the kitchen men more closely if they had."

I thought about Mr. Chu, denying, even at a time when it might have helped, that his daughter was anything other than perfect, according to his definition of what a perfect daughter would be.

Chief McKay made a call to the ship's director of hotel services and found out that Han's shift ended at nine, after the late dinner seating had been served. That was my seating.

How convenient.

I spent the rest of the afternoon lounging by the pool, poking through the gift shop, and writing postcards to be mailed from St. Maarten, the next port of call. I watched the Caribbean sky from the deck as the early dinner seating drew to a close, and then, at eight o'clock, I went in, chatted with the people at my table, and ate yet another delicious dinner. This one featured boeuf bourguignonne and, for dessert, raspberry tarts in a flaky pastry crust.

I had arranged, through Chief McKay, to have the hotel manager ask Han Sho-Shi to come to the management office when he got off duty. That he'd been called there would not arouse the suspicions of the other men; anything from an irregularity in his paperwork to a birthday phone call from home could bring a crewman to the office. If Han had anything to do with Janet Chu's disappearance, his own suspicions would already be aroused by my trip around the kitchen, but that couldn't be helped.

Chief McKay had offered to sit in on the interview, but I declined. If Han had actually killed Janet, I didn't expect him to admit to it, in the presence of the security chief or anyone else—unless he was overcome by guilt and grateful for the chance to confess, which, luckily for law enforcement, happens more often than people imagine. I wasn't likely to be that lucky. But if he hadn't done it but knew something, whatever he did know would have a better chance of being shared with me, a civilian, non-ship-connected Chinese, than with a white ex-cop from Chicago.

And if he did know something, or had done something, and told me nothing, still this interview would stir the pot, with a different ladle from the one Chief McKay had used.

So I sat alone in a borrowed office until I heard a knock on the door. At my "Come in!" the door opened. Han Sho-Shi frowned as soon as he saw my face.

The frown meant he wasn't going to start by playing innocent, gee-what's-up with me. So I wouldn't go back into the flaky restaurant-school-pal persona with him; nevertheless, I thought my professional identity was something Han Sho-Shi didn't have to know.

"Sit down," I invited him. Frown aside, Han was a good-looking young man whose intense dark face was creased with laugh lines around the eyes and mouth. I remembered the muscled arms rolling out dough and decided he was an easy guy to fall for.

Looking not happy about it, Han Sho-Shi sat on his hands on the edge of the chair across the desk.

"My name is Lydia Chin, and I'm a friend of Janet Chu's," I said.

If he didn't speak English, that would all be lost on him, but he looked at me unblinkingly and asked, "What you want?" in English that was accented but serviceable.

"Janet took a cruise on this ship and didn't come back," I said. "I want to know what happened to her."

"Why you ask me? Only pastry chef."

"You knew her. Don't shake your head; some people have already told me." Lying in the service of discovering the truth is not a sin.

He continued shaking his head anyway. "Don't believe you."

"Her sister remembers seeing you together."

For a moment, a flash of fear in his eyes; then it was gone, as he realized that if that was true, he'd have been hauled in for questioning long since.

He gave me a small smile. "Sister don't say that."

"You knew Janet," I said. "I haven't told anyone on this ship yet about that, but I will if I have to." I let that threat sink in. "I'm not accusing you of anything," I went on in a softer voice, playing good cop to my own bad cop. "Except seeing her the day she disappeared and not saying anything." I said that as though I knew it was true. "If you tell me what you know, I can keep it between us."

Han Sho-Shi gave me a long look, and the small smile again. "You not a friend of Janet Chu," he told me.

"I know her family."

He shook his head. "Not so well."

"What do you mean?"

"Mean nothing. You don't know Janet Chu, and sister don't say I know Janet Chu. Nobody say nothing, and you stay out of kitchen from now."

With that, unceremoniously, Han Sho-Shi got up and left.

So Han Sho-Shi was calling my bluff with one of his own. I'd said unspecified "people" had already given him up; he was betting they hadn't.

We were both right, but I was righter. He'd known her. The flush in his cheeks this morning and the glances thrown his way, the fear that came and went in his eyes just now, the lack of surprise or defensiveness when he found that Janet Chu's disappearance was what he'd been called here to talk about: he'd known her.

I sat, looking at the door Han had closed behind him. If I couldn't find a way, in the next four days, to get to him, I'd have to make sure he was arrested when the ship hit Miami again, and grilled by people with some clout. Chief McKay would help me do that. In fact, that might be the smart way to go: to wait, now that I'd gotten the pot stirred up, for the pros. After all, Han Sho-Shi wasn't going anyplace.

But I hated waiting. And as my mother would have pointed out, I hadn't been sent on this very expensive cruise to spend the next four days lying in the sun.

Not that right now I had any idea what else to do. I left the borrowed office and headed out on deck, to let the soft Caribbean breeze try to get some thoughts moving in my head. The ocean was black and smooth as it stretched away from us, white and frothy where our huge steel hull cut through it. The sky was a black that was almost blue—this must be the famous "midnight blue," I decided, a color I'd seen only in my childhood crayon box until now—and the stars were sprinkled across it in a profusion that amazed me, a Chinatown kid used to seeing only the few stars aggressive enough to compete with New York's city lights. I thought about those other stars, shyer, less insistent, but maybe no less certain of what would make them happy. The warm, wide Caribbean sky seemed like a nice place for them.

As I leaned on the rail, the breeze playing with my hair, a couple pushed through the glass doors from the ship's nightclub. Dance music came out with them, escaping into the sky, maybe to visit the stars. It grew quiet again as the doors closed and the couple, tipsy on champagne and Caribbean nights, strolled along the deck. They neared me and the man lifted his hand in greeting.

"Hi, Mariko."

I turned, about to correct him, but he corrected himself. "Oh, gee, sorry," he said with a friendly smile. "I thought you were Mariko. You look like her."

His woman friend gave him a pitying look. "You'll have to excuse John," she said to me. "He's drunk, and he's not all that bright when he's sober. You don't look like Mariko at all, except you're a short Asian woman with short hair." John grinned, unembarrassed. "I'm Jane," the woman told me. I told her who I was and we shook hands. "John thinks I'm going to marry him," Jane went on, "and I might, if he learns to tell one short haircut from another."

And one Asian from another, I thought, though that might not actually be a valuable talent wherever they were from.

"Besides, Mariko's in there dancing," Jane said, punching John lightly on the arm. "In that shiny green dress. See," she said to me, with a what-we-women-put-up-with look, "he didn't notice what you were wearing, either. You know, men are idiots." She said this as if the thought had just occurred to her. "Do you think I ought to marry one?"

"I don't know," I said. "What's the upside?"

Jane looked at John as though trying to figure this out.

"I'm cute?" he offered.

Jane and I both shook our heads.

"Are you rich?" she asked.

"Not yet."

"Well, I'm not marrying you yet." She turned to me. "We're computer nerds," she said. "I do hardware, John does software. So we work together well. I wonder if that's enough?" She tucked her arm in his. "Want to come get a drink with us?" she invited. "You could help me think of reasons why I should go through with this."

I hate to see people in romantic difficulty, so Jane and John and I went off to the bar together to see if, over mai tais for them and club soda for me, we could work this out.

*   *   *

The next morning I was strolling along the deck by myself, after a breakfast of scrambled eggs, sourdough toast with marmalade, and fruit salad, which, probably to the eternal gratitude of the kitchen men, I had not gone back to watch them make. Lacking inspiration, I decided it was my duty to do the plodding work of a P.I. and go interview other members of the below-decks crew, especially the kitchen men who'd thrown the glances yesterday that had first alerted me to Han. Someone would tell me something about the relationship between Han Sho-Shi and Janet Chu. Or maybe they wouldn't. But the fact that I was talking to them would get back to Han, and that would keep the pot stirring.

In fact, I thought, let's turn the heat up under the pot. If I'm going to talk to people, I might as well start with the family Han Sho-Shi had signed on this cruise with. They were the least likely of the crew to give me anything, but Han would know I knew that, so it would make him even more nervous that I was approaching them first.

That was my plan, anyway; but as soon as I made the first move, the plan short-circuited itself.

Han's four cousins worked below decks, one in the kitchen with Han, one as a carpenter, the other two as common seamen. His sister, Han Bi-Si, worked in the shore-excursion ticket sales office. She would be easiest to find, though probably hardest to talk to during working hours. The security chief could help me locate the cousins. On my way to see him I thought I'd drift by the ticket office to check Han Bi-Si out, so when she came off work and I was waiting in the hall I'd accost the right person.

So I stuck my head into the ticket office, just another passenger wondering if there was anything exciting to do on St. Maarten. A young Asian woman looked up from a desk and smiled. When she did a whole new thought hit me over the head like a hammer.

She was pretty and thin and she wore Janet Chu's haircut.

I talked some nonsense, smiled, picked up some brochures, and backed out the door, my mind tearing down and rebuilding furiously. The elegantly tousled haircut looked better on Han Bi-Si than it had in the photo of Janet Chu, but there was no mistaking that they were identical, unless you were as unobservant as my new friend John from last night.

Which a lot of people, particularly men, were.

Out on the deck, my brochures stuffed unlooked-at into my pocket, I put it to myself this way: Janet Chu had wanted that haircut, had even taken a photo of a friend with that cut to her hairdresser to make sure she got it. She had done this right before she got on this ship for the second time.

Was the friend Han Bi-Si? And if so, or even if not, could this be pure meaningless coincidence, or was something going on here?

I thought about John, mistaking me for Mariko because I was a short-haired Asian. I thought about Han Sho-Shi and his pastry dough, and Jane and her computer hardware. I thought about restaurant school, and Caribbean nights, and an idea began to form in my head.

Mr. Chu wouldn't like it very much, but I was thrilled.

I hightailed it down to the business deck to see Chief McKay. He listened, eyebrows raised, as I explained what I was thinking. He rounded up the paperwork I needed—crew photographs and shore records—and explained to me the procedures I was wondering about.

"St. Thomas and St. Maarten are foreign countries," he said, leaning back in his desk chair. "Both crew and passengers need passports to go ashore, but it's pretty routine."

"Do you show your passport to the duty officer?"

"When you leave the ship? No, why would you? You go through passport control at the customs house on shore."

"And when you come back?"

"Same thing. Passport control's on shore. You just give your name to the duty officer when you come back on board, same as you did when you left."

"So no one gets left behind?"

He grinned. He liked my new idea as much as I did. "Ship sails with the tide. It's more so if someone gets left behind, we know who it is."

We leaned together over the list of passengers who'd gone ashore at St. Maarten six weeks ago, on the Chu's second cruise. As Mr. Chu had said, Janet was not on it.

But at half past midnight the night before, one of Han Sho-Shi's cousins and his sister, Han Bi-Si, had left the ship.

"At that hour?" I asked. "Why would they do that?"

"Probably to get a drink. Any port has a couple of bars on the docks. They go just to get off the ship. You can see, all night we had crew coming and going."

"What happens," I asked Chief McKay, "if someone doesn't report back on board?"

"Crew or passenger?"

"Crew."

"The first thing, the duty officer contacts me. Or whoever's on duty if I'm off. We alert the shore authorities."

"Does it happen often?"

"Almost never. What are these guys gonna do, they get stuck on shore? Sometimes one of them gets too drunk to find his way back, but usually their buddies look out for them. The truth is, mostly when someone doesn't check back in it's a mistake."

"What do you mean, a mistake?"

He shrugged. "Say the duty officer's snoozing. Shouldn't be, but he is. Crewman comes back drunk at half past three, staggers onto the ship, gives his name as he passes the officer, doesn't notice the guy's out like a light. In the morning, the crewman's not checked back in. Looks like a problem, right? Smart duty officer always calls down to the crewman's quarters before he rings the alarm bell to see if the guy's really here."

We checked the log to see who the duty officer had been the night of Janet Chu's disappearance. The ship's officers all rotated that job; that night it had been the purser. The security chief gave him a call, and we headed down, logs in hand.

"The St. Maarten port call six weeks ago?" the purser asked us as we all settled on chairs in his office. He was a robust, blond young Dutchman with a charming accent. "Of course. I had the night watch. Is anything wrong?" His eyebrows knit together. "That was the trip when that American woman disappeared. But she did not leave the ship that night."

We hadn't told him what we were thinking. We wanted his memory uninfluenced. "Tell me," I said, "were there any irregularities at all on your watch?"

He frowned in thought. "May I see the log?"

Chief McKay handed it to him.

"There was something, yes . . . ah. One of the girls, I thought she had not come back." He smiled, chagrined, at Chief McKay. "But of course, she had."

"Do you remember who?" I asked, almost holding my breath.

"Right here." He pointed to a log entry. "This one, Han Bi-Si."

After that, it was easy. Chief McKay and I had a long talk with Han Sho-Shi after he came off work that evening. He stonewalled at first, until we explained that we knew what had happened, and that talking to us was better than the alternative, which would involve the authorities back in Miami. Even though, to Chief McKay's unending delight, there was, in fact, no crime.

After our talk with Han Sho-Shi we talked with

his sister, and then, for good measure, with his cousins. I thought at that point about calling the Chus in New York, but some deeply ingrained sense of fairness—or rather, sympathy for the underdog—made me want to wait. Chief McKay was against waiting, but I pointed out that he'd never have solved this case without me.

"I guess you're right," he grumbled, leaning on the rail beside me. "I don't suppose you're looking for work? I could make an opening on my staff pretty easily. Not a bad life, cruising up and down the Caribbean for cash."

"Thanks," I said. "But I've got a partner back in New York, and he hates the ocean."

So he made the phone call to St. Maarten, and I spent the next two days lying in the sun. Every now and then my mother's disapproving face floated into view, but I managed to enjoy myself anyway. On the evening of the second day we sailed into St. Maarten, and the instant the gangplank was lowered for the crew, Chief McKay, Han Sho-Shi, and I were striding down it.

Janet Chu was waiting for us at passport control.

The three of us presented our passports, declared our business—"tourism"—and were waved through with no problem. Han was the last through the turnstile, but he was the one Janet Chu grabbed, hugged, and kissed.

Then, with a look at Chief McKay, she turned to me. "You must be the detective."

"Lydia Chin," I answered.

She slipped her arm through Han's, entwined her fingers with his. "I'm sorry," she said.

"I'm not the one you need to apologize to," I

told her. "Your family hired me to find out what happened to you. They think you're dead."

"I know." She didn't meet my eyes. "This was the only thing I could do."

"I can't believe that."

She shook her head. "You don't know my father," she said softly.

"He sent me here," I replied evenly. "Were you just planning to stay dead?"

Janet Chu looked up quickly. "Oh, no! I would have called them. Just another week—less, even." She looked at Han Sho-Shi. "At the end of this cruise the crew ends up back in Miami. Most of them fly home from there. Sho-Shi is coming here."

"Already have jobs," Han Sho-Shi said, speaking for the first time. "Both. Good restaurant, French side of island. Owned by cousin."

"I couldn't do it," Janet Chu said, squaring her shoulders. "Go back to New York, work in Father's firm, sit in an office for the rest of my life. When I could have this!" She gestured beyond the windows, at the starry sky and the ocean and the road along the shore. She took a breath. "Sho-Shi and I met on the first cruise, when I used to go down to the kitchen and watch them cook. Once or twice I even helped prepare meals. I loved it so much!"

"And after the cruise was over, you wrote each other?" I asked, confirming with her what Han had already told us. "And concocted this plan?"

"Well," she blushed. "Well, after we knew we wanted to . . . to be together. I got my hair cut exactly like Bi-Si's, just before the cruise. As soon as June left the dance, Bi-Si and I changed clothes. I gave her name when I left the ship, and she kept dancing. Later she stuck my key card in the door, but she didn't go in."

"What if your parents or June had been awake?"

"I knew they wouldn't be," she said, almost sadly. "They're very predictable."

"That's why Han Bi-Si didn't check back in," Chief McKay said, looking at me. "And why she was on the ship when Peter looked for her. She never left it."

Janet Chu nodded. "I've applied for permanent-resident status here. I've got a job, so I'll get it, and so will Sho-Shi. And I would have told my family as soon as I felt I could."

"You had to do all this?" I asked. "You couldn't just say, no, thanks, I don't want to work in your office, I want to cook?"

Janet Chu answered softly, "You said you knew my father."

I had no answer to that.

"Listen," Janet Chu said. "I'll call them tonight. In an hour. But first . . ."

"First what?"

She and Han looked at each other, and both smiled. "First, Sho-Shi and I are going to be married."

So Chief McKay and I spent the midnight hour in a chapel on St. Maarten, as the guests and witnesses at Janet Chu's wedding to Han Sho-Shi. Han was nervous at first about having the security chief there, but Chief McKay shrugged and pointed out that marriage was a sacred estate, and that he'd never actually caught the two of them in a compromising position on the ship, so he had nothing more to say on the subject.

Afterward, we went to the patio bar at one of the local hotels and drank champagne under the stars. Even I had a sip, swallowing the tickly bubbles, looking up at the stars, both the pushy ones and the shy ones. I had a second sip, and was going to explain to Chief McKay about the shy stars, but instead I got up and called the Chus in New York, waking them and telling them I had good news. Then I put Janet on the phone and sat back down. Janet, holding Sho-Shi's hand, spoke to her father. Chief McKay and I grinned at each other. I wasn't so sure how pleased Mr. Chu would be with my handling of this case, but I *had* solved it for him.

And anyway, my cruise was already paid for.

NECESSARY EVIL
AN AMOS WALKER STORY
by Loren D. Estleman

Loren D. Estleman won the Shamus for Best P.I. Novel with *Sugartown* in 1985 and has been nominated three other times. He won the short story award for "Eight Mile and Dequindre" in 1986 and "The Crooked Way" in 1989 and has been nominated eight other times. His total of thirteen Shamus nominations is the most of any writer. He went on a seven-year hiatus with his P.I. Amos Walker, but has come back strong with *Never Street* (The Mysterious Press, 1997), *The Witchfinder* (The Mysterious Press, 1998) and *The Hour of the Virgin* (The Mysterious Press, 1999). In "Necessary Evil" Walker must find some files which have been stolen from his office before the blackmailer can make use of them.

Rosecranz, the building super, met me in the foyer. He was the oldest thing in the place after the plumbing, and whether he existed outside it was a mystery no one had yet paid me to solve. At midnight and change he had on the same greasy overalls and tragic expression he wore at noon. At the moment it was directed at the ruins of the front doorframe, shot to splinters by a solid professional kick to the dead-bolt lock that had torn the screws from the pre-Columbian wood.

"You didn't hear anything?" I said by way of greeting.

"I had on *M.A.S.H.* It must have been during the shelling."

"Uh-huh." I didn't elaborate. Whatever the corporation that owned the building was paying him, it didn't cover acts of valor. "How many offices got hit?"

"Just yours."

"Uh-huh."

I got the rest during the climb to my floor. After the sitcom rerun had finished, he had stepped outside his office/apartment to check the front door before bed and had found it in its present condition. He'd snatched up the monkey wrench he kept around for pipes and crackheads, tried the doors to all the offices, and learned that mine alone had been forced. By then the intruders had left. He'd called me instead of the police on the theory that they hadn't changed since they put him in the hospital for attending a rally for Sacco and Vanzetti in 1922. I couldn't see any holes in the theory.

The lock to my outer office—the one with A. WALKER INVESTIGATIONS on the door—had been slipped with a credit card or a strip of celluloid. The furniture and magazines inside were undisturbed. I'd secured the door to my private brain trust with a dead bolt, but they're only as sound as the woodwork; the white gash where the frame had shattered was so worm-tracked it looked like Sanskrit.

"You went inside?" I asked. Rosecranz nodded.

I believed him, but I unlimbered the Chief's Special and poked the muzzle into all the holes and corners. A good break-in artist can hide behind a dust bunny.

Mounds of papers leaned at Dali-esque angles atop the old desk, crumples lay around the kicked-over wastebasket, the blinds hung crooked over the window. Everything just the way I'd left it when I locked up the evening before.

Everything except the two green file cabinets.

Even there they'd made a tidy job, springing the two simple bar latches that secured all the drawers, the same way every file case had locked since Eve hired Cain to get the goods on Adam. All the missing files had been scooped from the top drawer of the second cabinet, between Beeker and Day.

"Something?" The super's sad eyes had followed every movement like a dog's.

"Something." I slammed the drawer shut with a boom they heard in Alberta.

"Police?"

"Why? I've already been robbed."

He called Detroit headquarters downtown anyway, for the insurance company. I skinned him a twenty to forget all about my office when he filed his statement, and got to work.

I couldn't get to who without going through why, and why wasn't worth banging my head against until I figured out what. That meant identifying which files were gone.

With the back of the customer chair tilted under the doorknob for privacy, I sat on the floor surrounded by spiral pads and transposed my notes onto a legal tablet, focusing on the names of clients that fit the hole. As experiences go, it was about as nostalgic as cramming for a tax audit.

When I finished the room was full of daylight and cigarette smoke. My throat burned and my eyes felt pickled. I wrenched open the window, sucked in my morning's helping of auto exhaust, and sat down at the desk to place the first of many telephone calls.

It was wild goose season. Two of the older numbers were invalid. Owen Caster's machine answered, and I left a message asking him to call me back. April Berryman hung up—divorce case. I wound up with six no-answers, four new-parties-at-old-numbers, and three appointments for interviews. That was swell, provided I could think of some questions.

"Amos Walker. I hoped I'd never hear that name again."

Evelyn Dankworth met me at the Caucus Club. Her deep auburn hair and mahogany-colored eyes went with the stained glass and paneling, her tall highball with her two-fisted legacy. Her great-grandfather helped found General Motors and drank himself to death in 1930. Her parents had gone in an alcoholic murder-suicide, and after a long custody battle she had been raised by an uncle who later stood trial for drunk driving and manslaughter. These days she divided her time between Betty Ford and a clinic in Toledo where cosmetic surgeons removed the fresh-burst blood vessels from her cheeks.

"I get that a lot," I said. "I'm only bothering you to prevent someone else from bothering you worse." I told her about the burglary.

"I hired you to rescue my daughter from a cult. You didn't deliver. That's hardly a scenario for blackmail."

"You hired me to find her. When I did, you tried to pay me to kidnap her and deliver her to some professional deprogrammers you'd hired to scare the cult out of her. I turned you down because she was eighteen and an adult. I'd have stood trial for abduction."

"In any case I haven't heard from her in two years. She might be dead."

"Someone who knew about the situation might want to shake you down. That case file would help."

"You know my family history. Do you honestly think I could be hurt if any of this was made public?"

I sipped my scotch, a single malt that tasted like the smoke from an iodine factory. "I wasn't talking about blackmail. Someone might make contact with you and offer to deliver her for a consideration. A phony who got all his inside information from the stolen file."

"Very well. You've told me and I'm forewarned. May I now consider our association to be at an end?"

I said that was fine with me, but reminded her I was in the book in case she heard from someone. She climbed back into her sable wrap and left. She wasn't in such a hurry she forgot to finish her drink.

I found Chester Bliss sitting on a broken foundation on Woodward, eating his lunch in what was left of the third largest department store in the

world. He was one of the workers hired by the city
to clear away the debris after a demolition crew
blew up J. L. Hudson's to make room for a mall
or a casino or maybe just another empty lot. The
big black face under the yellow hard hat was a mass
of bone and scar tissue. He'd sparred with Joe
Louis and Floyd Patterson and quit the ring in 1962
after a kid named Clay laid him on his back forty
seconds into the third round. When he spotted me
wading toward him through the dust and broken
bricks, he put down his sandwich and took my hand
in a grip I can still feel.

"They're selling those bricks for five bucks a pop
down the block," I said when I got it back. "You
could slip one in each pocket and wait for the market to rise."

"Suckers. Bricks ain't history. My foreman said
you called. Don't tell me you found it after all
this time."

I hated to shake my head. Fourteen months earlier I'd spent a week on his retainer trying to track
down some items that had been stolen from his
apartment. The only one he really cared about getting back was the Golden Glove he'd won in 1954.
"Someone pushed in my office last night and made
off with some files, yours among them. I wanted to
let you know in case someone called and offered
to sell you back your glove."

He grinned. He had all his teeth—a testament to
how good a fighter he had truly been—but there
was no sunshine in the expression. "They wouldn't
eat out on what they got. All I own's my pride,
and they can't have that."

"The B-and-E community's pretty tight. If I turn up this clown, he might know who hit your place."

"You think?"

I shook my head again. "Not really. It's just something I'm supposed to say."

He picked up his sandwich then and resumed eating. He managed dignity without stained glass and paneling.

My third appointment showed up at the Scott Fountain on Belle Isle just as I was getting ready to leave. The gunmetal-colored stretch limo crunched to a stop alongside the two-lane blacktop that circled the island and stood there with no one stirring inside while I finished my cigarette. That was apparently as long as it took to determine there were no snipers in the trees or FBI men within eavesdropping range. The driver, six-three and two-fifty in a camel-hair coat and dark glasses on an overcast day, got out then and opened the rear passenger door.

Boy Falco gestured to the driver to stay with the car and trotted up the steps to the fountain, swinging his club foot out in a half circle with each step. He'd dropped the *d* from the end of his first name about the time of his first face-lift. Scuttlebutt said he hoped to win the sympathy of the grand jury with the illusion of innocent youth. They'd voted to indict anyway. He was out on bond pending a new trial; a witness had recanted.

"Entertain me." He stuck his hands in his alpaca pockets and leaned back against the railing.

"Aren't you supposed to shoot at my feet?"

"I forgot you're a comic. Somebody cut out my

sense of humor in the shower at Jackson. This about that stolen credit card?"

"You used the name on the card, Cruickshank, to fly to Miami and pick up a shipment from Bogotá. The client died while I was working the case, bum ticker. I proved he wasn't on that plane so the Widow Cruickshank wouldn't have to pay the bill. There was no reason to ID you as the card user."

"There was one damn good reason not to. You shaking me down after all this time."

"What would it buy me, a better coffin? No one would see it. The file walked out of my office last night. I don't want your boys coming to me in case someone calls you looking for Christmas money."

"That could be a fancy P.I. way of putting the sting on me without fingering yourself as the stinger."

I moved a shoulder. "Don't pay."

"I never do. In money." He pushed himself away from the railing. "If that credit card turns up in court, you won't."

"I thought you'd say something like that. I'd hoped it would be more original."

"The old ways are the best. That's why they're the old ways." He went back down the steps and swung his club foot into the car.

The telephone was ringing when I got back to the office. It was Owen Caster, replying to the message I'd left on his machine that morning. He was an investment broker with a juvenile theft conviction that had been sealed for thirty years. On his behalf I'd broken a couple of things in the living room of the former court stenographer who'd tried to sell him a duplicate transcript, and the threat had gone away.

"Someone else called after you," Caster growled. "He offered to sell me my file for a thousand."

I sat up. "What did he sound like?"

"I'm not even sure it was a he. It was a whisper. Twice I had to ask him to repeat himself. It might have been a woman."

"Disguise. Anything unusual?"

"Foreign accent, maybe. Probably another disguise. Tell me, do I have to hire you again to clean up your own mess?"

"This one's on me."

"I'm starting to think I should have paid the stenographer and kept you out of it."

"You'd still be paying him."

"Him, Mister or Miss Whisper, what's the difference? What's the *P* stand for in P.I., Pandora?"

"Paradox. Clients hire me to take away their grief. Most of the time I manage to do that. Sometimes I just exchange it for a different kind of grief. I'm a necessary evil at best."

"Maybe not so necessary. Call me when you sort this out."

"When I do, can I get a tip on the market?" I was talking to a dead line.

The receiver rang right out from under my hand. A jovial Chester Bliss told me he got a call after his shift asking him how badly he wanted his Golden Glove. The old fighter had danced around with the caller for a minute, but the party got suspicious and hung up.

"Man or woman?"

"Woman, I think," he said. "She was whispering."

"Did you notice any kind of accent?"

"Couldn't say. I don't hear so good over the phone. Patterson busted my eardrums good."

"Thanks, Chester."

He hesitated. "You don't suppose she really has my glove?"

"I wish she did."

"Mr. Walker."

"Did you get a call, Mrs. Dankworth?" I'd just had time to get a cigarette going. I flipped the match at the ashtray.

"Ten minutes ago. When I asked for a description of my daughter, they quoted from the one I gave you. I hung up."

"Was it a woman?"

"Certainly not. I can tell a man's whisper from a woman's, even if he was European."

"What kind of accent was it?"

"Oh, I don't know. One of those eastern countries we're always sending food to. What are you going to do?"

"Make a call."

Boy Falco was a while coming to the telephone. He didn't have one in his office above the meat-packing plant he owned on Michigan and took all his messages through the realtor next door. So far federal judges don't okay wiretaps on instruments belonging to gangsters' neighbors. "This better be something," he said.

I asked him if he got a call.

"You mean besides this one?"

"That answers my question. There's a good chance you will. Whoever copped those files has been running up his bill all day. When he calls you, I want you to arrange a drop."

"Be glad to." He sounded too pleased.

"I'm not setting up target practice for your boys. Once he agrees to the details, I want you to forget all about them."

"What if I don't?"

"Then I'll send my notes to the Federal Building."

"What do you want done with the ashes?" he snarled.

"You'll be too busy sweeping out your cell in the Milan pen to make the arrangements."

"Where do you want the drop, meat?"

"Four thirty-one Howard."

There was a long silence. "That's the DEA!"

"He'll feel safe there."

"I sure as hell won't."

"That's the idea, Boy. If your word were your bond, the judge wouldn't have had you put up half a million to stay out."

He had me repeat the details several times; writing things down wasn't his long suit. "I want those notes," he said then. "The file too, when you get it back."

"Too rich."

"I ain't asking."

"You've got enough on your plate without hanging me up on one of your hooks," I said. "You know a lot of people. A client of mine had his

Golden Glove stolen a little over a year ago. He wants it back."

"Baseball?"

"No, the other one. Boxing."

"Trophies are tough to unload. I might know a fence with a soft heart. I ain't promising nothing."

"Me neither. I may not get that file back."

"I'll make some calls."

"Don't tie up the line," I reminded him.

I killed the time browsing through the yellow pages for a locksmith whose name I liked to replace the dead bolt on my office door. The telephone rang while I was deciding between Sherlock's Home Security and Lock You.

"The puke called," said Falco by way of greeting. "It's set for seven-thirty tonight."

I wrote down six o'clock. I trusted Boy like pro wrestling. "How much?"

He snorted. "Thousand bucks in small bills, brown envelope. I got no respect for leeches in general, but I got less than no respect for a cheap one."

"Was the leech male or female?"

"Male. I guess I know a chick when I don't hear one. That whispering dodge has got hair growing out of its ears." He paused. "I think I found your glove thing. There's a name engraved on the plate. Sailor Jack Moran."

"Wrong name." I winched my heart back up where it belonged. "Wait. Does your fence do engraving?"

"Not for free."

"I'm good for it. Tell him to match the plate." I
spelled Chester Bliss's name.

I left the office in plenty of time to buy a current
TV Guide at Rite-Aid, check a listing, and call
Channel 2 from a public telephone to confirm
something. Then I drove to Howard Street.

There was a wire city trash basket on the corner
near the plain building with the flag flying out front.
I slid the brown envelope under a Little Caesar's
pizza box and walked around the corner out of the
pool of light from the lamp. I came back on the
shadowed side of the street and pegged out a spot
in a doorway across from the basket. An empty
crack phial crunched under my foot, ten yards from
the Detroit office of the Drug Enforcement Agency.

It might have been the trouble he was in, but for
once Boy Falco kept his word. In an hour and a
half a handful of people walked past the trash basket, and not one of them was packing a tommy
gun. I had a palpitation when an old woman in a
knitted cap and a torn and filthy overcoat stopped
to root through the trash, but she stopped when
she found a piece of petrified pizza in the Little
Caesar's box, claimed it, and moved on.

Seven-thirty came and went. The temperature
had dropped since sundown, and I had begun to
lose all feeling in my toes when he showed up.

He had on a shapeless fedora and a faded mackinaw over his old overalls. His breath frosted in
the air while he poked among the newspapers and
Styrofoam cups in the basket, then lifted the pizza
box, plucked up the thick envelope, tested its heft,

glanced around, and stuck it in a side pocket. He turned and started back the way he'd come, his heels scraping the sidewalk.

I crossed the street and fell in step behind him. I followed him a full block before he turned his head.

He didn't try to run when he recognized me. Instead he leaned against the lamppost, collapsing a little like a sack of old fruit. I circled around to stand in front of him and held out my hand. I had my other hand in my coat pocket with the Chief's Special, but it didn't come out. He slid the envelope out of his mackinaw and laid it in my palm.

"What is inside it?" Rosecranz asked. "Not money."

"*TV Guide.*" I put it away. "You shouldn't have trusted it. *M.A.S.H.* was listed last night, but it didn't air. A programmer at Channel Two told me the president's speech threw off the schedule. The last half hour of *Steel Magnolias* ran in that time slot. That soundtrack wouldn't have drowned out a mouse's burp, let alone a burglar kicking in two doors."

The building super moved a shoulder. "The same thing runs every night at the same time for two years. Who knew?"

"What did you need the money for?"

"I didn't. I don't." He leaned his cheek against the lamppost, sliding his hat off center. "I am eighty-six Friday. I never did nothing. Nothing since I came to this country."

"What about Sacco and Vanzetti? You were arrested at a rally."

"That was my cousin. I tell that story. I never did nothing. Nothing in eighty-six years."

"You're hell on locks."

"I smash the dead bolts with a monkey wrench. Forty years I have spent opening file cabinets when tenants lose keys."

"You shook down a fighter, an heiress, and a racketeer. That's not nothing. What did you do with the files you took?"

"I will show you."

I drove him back to the building, where he unlocked his single room on the ground floor, complete with steel desk, Murphy bed, and a teenage soap playing out in black-and-white on his ancient TV set. His tools lay in a pile on a folding table designed for lonely dinners in front of the tube.

He moved a stack of *Popular Mechanics,* and there were the manila folders in a dilapidated egg crate. I went through the files quickly. Nothing was missing.

"Comfy setup. Ralph Kramden ever drop by?"

I turned around. With Boy Falco and his family-size driver standing inside it, the room was barely big enough for oxygen. Rosecranz was watching them without hope.

"See what happens when you leave the front door open?" I said.

"You're a laugh hemorrhage." Falco's smile was dead on arrival. He was looking at the stack of folders in my hands. "Mine in there?"

When I hesitated, the driver unbuttoned his overcoat. The fisted handle of his Magnum stuck up out of a holster two inches left of his navel. I shuffled the stack and gave Falco the folder tabbed CRUICKSHANK. He riffled through the pages, paused to examine the signature he'd forged on the airline receipt—all the feds needed to tie him to the Miami drug scene—then put it back and stuck the file under his arm.

"What's it doing in here?" His tone was almost pleasant.

"I asked Rosecranz to hide the files in his place until I get a better set of cabinets."

"Thief give you any trouble?"

"Trouble's my name. I changed it to Amos when the other kids laughed."

He wasn't listening. He was looking at the super. "Whisper something," he said.

Rosecranz looked sad. "What should I whisper?"

"That's the accent." He jerked his chin at the driver. The Magnum came out.

"You got what you came for," I said. "What's the point?"

"The point is, I don't get crapped on by private creeps and janitors. Make it neat. I'll be in the car." He turned toward the door.

As he passed in front of the big man, I snatched the monkey wrench off the folding table, the same wrench Rosecranz had used to demolish the front door lock and the one to my office. It was fourteen inches long and as heavy as a handtruck; it swung practically without help. The case-steel head struck the knobby bone on the driver's wrist with a crack and the gun went flying.

That was it for the muscle. He doubled over, gripping his shattered wrist between his knees, and I stepped around him and laid the wrench alongside Falco's head, a little more gently. I didn't want to crush his skull, God knew why. He folded like a paper fan.

When I turned around, Rosecranz was covering the driver with the Magnum.

The big man wasn't paying much attention. He was still bent into a jackknife and his face was gray. Rosecranz looked as tragic as ever. The hand holding the gun was shaking. I took it from him, put it in my pocket, and drew out my own .38. I have a thing against playing with someone else's clubs. I told the old man to search Falco for weapons while I kept an eye on the driver.

Rosecranz knelt beside Falco and rose a minute later hefting a paper sack. "He had this under his coat."

I went that way, still holding the gun, and peered inside the sack. I reached in with one hand and drew out the heavy object. The engraved brass plate was riveted to the base.

"Whaddaya know," I said. "He spelled Chester's name right."

The super looked around. "Just like *NYPD Blue*."

"You do need to get out more." I reached over and turned off the TV.

"Police?" he asked.

I nodded. "Police."

"Me?"

"No."

He didn't look any happier. "Why?"

"You're a necessary evil." I put the Golden Glove back in the sack, pocketed the .38, and picked up the Cruickshank file from the floor while Rosecranz worked the rotary dial on his old telephone.

SCREWBALL
A NATHAN HELLER STORY
by Max Allan Collins

Max Allan Collins has won two Best Novel Shamus Awards with his Nathan Heller historical P.I. novels *True Detective* in 1984 and *Stolen Away* in 1992, and has been nominated six other times. He's also had one nomination for Best Short Story, for a total of nine. His newest novel in the series is called *Majic Man* (Signet, 1999). In "Screwball" Heller heads for Miami to do a favor for Frank Nitti—a man you never refuse.

Not long ago Miami Beach had been a sixteen-hundred-acre stretch of jungle sandbar thick with mangroves and scrub palmetto, inhabited by wild birds, mosquitoes and snakes. Less than thirty years later, the wilderness had given way to plush hotels, high-rent apartment houses and lavish homes, with manicured terraces and swimming pools, facing a beach littered brightly with cabañas and sun umbrellas.

That didn't mean the place wasn't still infested with snakes, birds and bugs—just that it was now the human variety.

It was May 22, 1941, and dead; winter season was mid-December through April, and the summer's onslaught of tourists was a few weeks away.

At the moment the majority of restaurants and nightclubs in Miami Beach were shuttered, and the handful of the latter still doing business were the ones with gaming rooms. Even in off-season, gambling made it pay for a club to keep its doors open.

The glitzy showroom of Chez Clifton had been patterned on (though was about a third the size of) the Chez Paree back home in Chicago, with a similarly set up backroom gambling casino called (in both instances) the Gold Key Club. But where the Chez Paree was home to big-name stars and orchestras—Edgar Bergen and Charlie McCarthy, Ted Lewis, Martha Raye—the Chez Clifton's headliner was invariably its namesake: Pete Clifton.

A near ringer for Zeppo, the "normal" Marx Brother, Clifton was tall, dark and horsily handsome, his slicked-back, parted-at-the-side hair as black as his tie and tux. He was at the microphone, leaning on it like a jokester Sinatra, the orchestra behind him, accompanying him occasionally on song parodies, the drummer providing the requisite rim shots, the boys laughing heartily at gags they'd heard over and over, prompting the audience.

Not that the audience needed help: the crowd thought Clifton was a scream. And, for a Thursday night, it was a good crowd, too.

"Hear about the guy that bought his wife a bicycle?" he asked innocently. "Now she's peddling it all over town."

They howled at that.

"Hear about the sleepy bride? . . . . She couldn't stay away awake for a second."

Laughter all around me. I was settled in at a table for two—by myself—listening to one dirty joke after another. Clifton had always worked blue, back when I knew him; he'd been the opening act at the Colony Club showroom on Rush Street—a mob joint fronted by Nicky Dean, a crony of Al Capone's successor, Frank Nitti.

But tonight every gag was filthy.

"Hear about the girl whose boyfriend didn't have any furniture? She was floored."

People were crying at this rapier wit. But not everybody liked it. The guy Clifton was fronting for in particular.

"Nate," Frank Nitti had said to me earlier that afternoon, "I need you to deliver a message to your old pal Pete Clifton."

In the blue shade of an umbrella at a small white metal table, buttery sun reflecting off the shimmer of cool blue water, Nitti and I were sitting by the pool at Nitti's Di Lido Island estate, his palatial digs looming around us, rambling white stucco buildings with green-tile roofs behind bougainvillea-covered walls.

Eyes a mystery behind sunglasses, Nitti wore a blue and red Hawaiian print shirt, white slacks and sandals, a surprisingly small figure, his handsome oval face flecked with occasional scars, his slicked-back black hair touched with gray and immaculately trimmed. I was the one who looked like a gangster, in my brown suit and darker brown fedora, having just arrived from Chicago, Nitti's driver having picked me up at the railroad station.

"I wouldn't call Clifton an 'old pal,' Mr. Nitti."

"How many times I gotta tell ya? Call me Frank. After what we been through together?"

I didn't like the thought of having been through

anything "together" with Frank Nitti. But the truth
was, fate and circumstance had on several key occa-
sions brought Chicago's most powerful gangster
leader into the path of a certain lowly Loop private
detective—though I wasn't as lowly as I used to be.
The A-1 Agency had a suite of offices now, and I
had two experienced ops and a pretty blonde secretary under me—or anyway, the ops were under me;
the secretary wasn't interested.

But when Frank Nitti asked the president of the
A-1 to hop a train to Miami Beach and come visit,
Nathan Heller hopped and visited—the blow soft-
ened by the three-hundred-dollar retainer check
Nitti's man Louis Campagna had delivered to my
Van Buren Street office.

"I understand you two boys used to go out with
showgirls and strippers, time to time," Nitti said,
lighting up a Cuban cigar smaller than a billy club.

"Clifton was a cocky, good-looking guy, and the
toast of Rush Street. The girls liked him. I liked
the spillover."

Nitti nodded, waving out his match. "He's still a
good-looking guy. And he's still cocky. Ever wonder how he managed to open up his own club?"

"Never bothered wondering. But I guess it is a
little unusual."

"Yeah. He ain't famous. He ain't on the radio."

"Not with *that* material."

Nitti blew a smoke ring; an eyebrow arched.
"Oh, you remember that? How blue he works."

I shrugged. "It was kind of a gimmick, Frank—
clean-cut kid, looks like a matinee idol. Kind of
a funny, startling contrast with his off-color
material."

"Well, that's what I want you to talk to him about."

"Afraid I don't follow, Frank . . ."

"He's workin' too blue. Too goddamn fuckin' filthy."

I winced. Part of it was the sun reflecting off the surface of the pool; most of it was confusion. Why the hell did Frank Nitti give a damn if some two-bit comic was telling dirty jokes?

"That foul-mouth is attracting the wrong kind of attention," Nitti was saying. "The blue noses are gettin' up in arms. Ministers are givin' sermons, columnists are frownin' in print. There's this Citizens Committee for Clean Entertainment. Puttin' political pressure on. Jesus Christ! The place'll get raided—shut down."

I hadn't been to Chez Clifton yet, though I assumed it was running gambling, wide open, and was already on the cops' no-raid list. But if anti-smut reformers made an issue out of Clifton's immoral monologues, the boys in blue would *have* to raid the joint—and the gambling baby would go out the window with the dirty bathwater.

"What's your interest in this, Frank?"

Nitti's smile was mostly a sneer. "Clifton's got a club 'cause he's got a silent partner."

"You mean . . . *you,* Frank? I thought the Outfit kept out of the Florida rackets. . . ."

It was understood that Nitti, Capone and other Chicago mobsters with homes in Miami Beach would not infringe on the hometown gambling syndicate. This was said to be part of the agreement with local politicos to allow the Chicago Outfit to make Miami Beach their home away from home.

"That's why I called you down here, Nate. I need somebody to talk to the kid who won't attract no attention. Who ain't directly connected to me. You're just an old friend of Clifton's from outa town."

"And what do you want me to do, exactly?"

"Tell him to clean up his fuckin' act."

So now I was in the audience, sipping my rum and Coke, the walls ringing with laughter, as Pete Clifton made such deft witticisms as the following: "Hear about the doll who found a tramp under her bed? She got so upset, her stomach was on the bum all night."

Finally, to much applause, Clifton turned the entertainment over to the orchestra, and couples filled the dance floor to the strains of "Nice Work If You Can Get It." Soon the comic had filtered his way through the admiring crowd to join me at my table.

"You look good, you rat bastard," Clifton said, flashing his boyish smile, extending his hand, which I took and shook. "Getting any since I left Chicago?"

"I wet the wick on occasion," I said, sitting as he settled in across from me. All around us patrons were sneaking peeks at the star performer who had deigned to come down among them.

"I didn't figure you'd ever get laid again once I moved on," he said, straightening his black tie. "How long you down here for?"

"Couple days."

He snapped his fingers, pointed at me and winked. "Tell you what, you're goin' boating with me tomorrow afternoon. These two cute skirts down the street from where I live, they're both hot for me—you can take one of 'em offa my hands."

Smiling, shaking my head, I said, "I thought maybe you'd have found a new hobby by now, Pete."

"Not me." He fired up a Lucky Strike, sucked in smoke, exhaled it like dragon breath from his nostrils. "I never found a sweeter pastime than doin' the dirty deed."

"Doing dames ain't the only dirty deed you been doing lately, Pete."

"Whaddya mean?"

"Your act." I gestured with my rum and Coke. "I've seen cleaner material on outhouse walls."

He grinned toothily. "You offended? Getting prudish in your old age, Heller? Yeah, I've upped the ante some. Look at this crowd, week night, off-season. They love it. See, it's my magic formula: everybody loves sex, and everybody loves a good dirty joke."

"Not everybody."

The grin eased off and his forehead tightened. "Wait a minute. . . . This isn't a social call, is it?"

"No. It's nice seeing you again, Pete . . . but no. You think you know who sent me—and you're right. And he wants you to back off the smut."

"You kidding?" Clifton smirked and waved dismissively. "I found a way to mint money here. And it's making me a star."

"You think you can do that material on the radio, or in the movies? Get serious."

"Hey, everybody needs an angle, a trademark, and I found mine."

"Pete, I'm not here to discuss it. Just to pass the

word along. You can ignore it if you like." I sipped my drink, shrugged. "Take your dick out and conduct the orchestra with it, far as I'm concerned."

Clifton leaned across the table. "Nate, you heard those laughs. You see the way every dame in this audience is lookin' at me? There isn't a quiff in this room that wouldn't get on her back for me, or down on her damn knees."

"Like I said, ignore it if you like. But my guess is, if you do keep working blue—and the Chez Clifton gets shut down—your silent partner'll get noisy."

The comic thought about that, drawing nervously on the Lucky. In his tux, he looked like he fell off a wedding cake. Then he said, "What would you do, Nate?"

"Get some new material. Keep some of the risqué stuff, sure—but don't be so Johnny One-note."

Some of the cockiness had drained out of him; frustration colored his voice, even self-pity. "It's what I do, Nate. Why not tell Joe E. Lewis not to do drunk jokes? Why not tell Eddie Cantor not to pop his eyes out?"

" 'Cause somebody'll pop *your* eyes out, Pete. I say this as a friend, and as somebody who knows how certain parties operate. Back off."

He sighed, sat back. I didn't say anything. The orchestra was playing "I'll Never Smile Again" now.

"Tell Nitti I'll . . . tone it down."

I saluted him with my nearly empty rum-and-Coke glass. "Good choice."

And that was it. I had delivered my message. He had another show to do, and I didn't see him again till the next afternoon, when—as promised—he took me out on his speedboat, a sleek mahogany nineteen-foot Gar Wood runabout whose tail was emblazoned SCREWBALL.

And, as promised, we were in the company of two "cute skirts," although that's not what they were wearing. Peggy Simmons, a slender, pretty pugnose blonde, and Janet Windom, a cow-eyed bosomy brunette, were in white shorts that showed off their nice, nicely tanned legs. Janet, whom Pete had claimed, wore a candy-striped top; Peggy, who had deposited herself next to me on the leather seat, wore a pink long-sleeve angora sweater.

"Aren't you warm in that?" I asked her, sipping a bottle of Pabst. I was in a short-sleeve sports shirt and chinos, my straw fedora at my feet, away from the wind.

"Not really. I get chilled in the spray." She had a high-pitched voice that seemed younger than her twenty-two years, though the lines around her sky-blue eyes made her seem older. Peggy laughed and smiled a lot, but those eyes were sad somehow.

I had been introduced to Peggy as a theatrical agent from Chicago. She was a model and dancer, and apparently Clifton figured this lie would help me get laid; this irritated me—being burdened with a fiction of someone else's creation, and the notion I needed help in that regard. But I hadn't corrected it.

Janet, it seemed, was also interested in show business; a former dentist's assistant, she was a couple years older than Peggy. They had roomed together in New York City and come down here a few months ago, seeking sun and fame and fortune.

The afternoon was pleasant enough. Clifton sat at the wheel with Janet cuddling next to him, and Peggy and I sat in the seat behind them. She was friendly, holding my hand, putting her head on my shoulder, though we barely knew each other. We drank in the sun-drenched, invigorating gulfstream air, as well as our bottled beers, and enjoyed the view—royal palms waving, white-capped breakers peaking, golden sands glistening with sunlight.

The runabout had been bounding along, which—with the engine noise—had limited conversation. But pretty soon Clifton charted us up and down Indian Creek, a tranquil, seawalled lagoon lined with palm-fringed shores and occasional well-manicured golf courses, as well as frequent private piers and landing docks studded with gleaming yachts and lavish houseboats.

"Have you found any work down here?" I asked the fresh-faced, sad-eyed girl.

She nodded. "Some cheesecake modeling Pete lined up. Swimsuits and, you know . . . art studies."

Nudes.

"What are you hoping for?"

"Well, I am a good dancer, and I sing a little, too. Pete says he's going to do a big elaborate show soon, with a chorus line and everything."

"And he's going to use both you and Janet?"

She nodded.

"Any thoughts beyond that, Peggy? You've got nice legs, but show business is a rough career."

Her chin crinkled as she smiled, but desperation tightened her eyes. "I'd be willing to take a Chicago booking."

Though we weren't gliding as quickly over the

water now, the engine noise was still enough to keep my conversation with Peggy private while Pete and Janet laughed and kissed and chugged their beers.

"I'm not a booking agent, Peggy."

She drew away just a little. "No?"

"Pete was . . . I don't know what he was doing."

She shrugged again, smirked. "Pete's a goddamn liar sometimes."

"I know some people who book acts in Chicago, and would be glad to put a word in . . . but don't be friendly with me on account of that."

She studied me and her eyes didn't seem as sad, or as old, suddenly. "What do you know? The vanishing American."

"What?"

"A nice guy."

And she cuddled next to me, put a hand on my leg.

Without looking at me, she asked, "Why do *you* think I came to Florida, Nate?"

"It's warm and sunny."

"Yes."

"And . . ." I nodded toward either side of us, where the waterway entrances of lavish estates, trellised with bougainvillea and allamanda, seemed to beckon. ". . . there's more money here than you can shake a stick at."

She laughed. "Yes."

By four o'clock we were at the girls' place, in a six-apartment building on Jefferson Street, a white-trimmed-pink geometric affair among many other such streamlined structures of sunny yellow, flamingo pink and sea green, with porthole windows and racing stripes and bas relief zigzags. The effect was at once elegant and insubstantial, like a movie set. Their one-bedroom apartment was on the second of two floors; the furnishings had an art moderne look, too, though of the low-cost Sears showroom variety.

Janet fixed us drinks, and we sat in the little pink and white living room area and made meaningless conversation for maybe five minutes. Then Clifton and Janet disappeared into that one bedroom, and Peggy and I necked on the couch. The lights were low when I got her sweater and bra off her, but I noticed the needle tracks on her arms just the same.

"What's wrong?" she asked.

"Nothing . . . What are you on? H?"

"What do you mean? . . . Not H."

"What?"

"M."

Morphine.

She folded her arms over her bare breasts, but it was her arms she was hiding.

"I was blue," she said defensively, shivering suddenly. "I needed something."

"Where'd you get it?"

"Pete has friends."

Pete had friends, all right. And I was one of them.

"Put your sweater on, baby."

"Why? Do I . . . do I make you sick?"

And she began to cry.

So I made love to her there on the couch, sweetly, tenderly, comforting her, telling her she was beautiful, which she was. She needed the attention, and I didn't mind giving it to her, though I was steaming at that louse Clifton.

Our clothes relatively straightened, Peggy having freshened in the bathroom, we were sitting, chatting, having Cokes on ice like kids on a date when Clifton—in the pale yellow sports shirt and powder-blue slacks he'd gone boating in—emerged from the bedroom, arm around Janet, who was in a terry-cloth robe.

"We better blow, Nate," he told me with a grin, and nuzzled the giggling Janet's neck. She seemed to be on something, too. "I got a nine o'clock show to do."

It was a little after seven.

We made our goodbyes and drove the couple of blocks in his white Lincoln Zephyr convertible.

"Do I take care of you," he asked with grin, as the shadows of the palms lining the streets rolled over us, "or do I take care of you?"

"You're a pal," I said.

We were slipping past more of those movie theater–like apartment houses, pastel chunks of concrete whose geometric harshness was softened by well-barbered shrubs. The three-story building on West Jefferson in front of which Clifton drew his Lincoln was set back a ways, a walk cutting through a golf green of a lawn to the pale yellow cube whose blue cantilevered sunshades were like eyebrows.

Clifton's apartment was on the third floor, a two-bedroom affair with pale yellow walls and a parquet floor flung with occasional Oriental carpets. The furnishings were in the art moderne manner, chrome and leather and well-varnished light woods none of it from Sears.

I sat in a pastel green easy chair whose lines were rounded; it was as comfortable as an old shoe but considerably more stylish.

"How do those unemployed showgirls afford a place like that?" I wondered aloud.

Clifton, who was making us a couple of rum and Cokes over at the wet bar, said, "Did you have a good time?"

"I like Peggy. If I lived around here, I'd try to straighten her out."

"Oh yeah! Saint Heller. I thought you did straighten her out—on that couch."

"Are you pimping for those girls?"

"No!" he came over with a drink in either hand. "They're not pros."

"But you fix them up with friends and other people you want to impress."

He shrugged, handing me the drink. "Yeah. So what? Party girls like that are a dime a dozen."

"Where are you getting the dope?"

That stopped him for a moment, but just a moment. "It makes 'em feel good; what's the harm?"

"You got 'em hooked and whoring for you, Pete. You're one classy guy."

Clifton smirked. "I didn't see you turning down the free lay."

"You banging 'em both?"

"Never at the same time. What, you think I'm a pervert?"

"No. I think you're a prick."

He just laughed at that. "Listen, I got to take

a shower. You coming down to the club tonight or not?"

"I'll come. But, Pete—where are you getting the dope you're giving those girls?"

"Why do you care?"

"Because I don't think Frank Nitti would like it. He doesn't do business with people in that racket. If he knew you were involved . . ."

Clifton frowned. "You going to tell him?"

"I didn't say that."

"Maybe I don't give a shit if you do. Maybe I got a possible new investor for my club, and Frank Nitti can kiss my ass."

"Would you like me to pass that along?"

A grimace drained all the boyishness from his face. "What's wrong with you, Heller? Since when did you get moral? These gangsters are like women—they exist to be used."

"Only the gangsters don't discard as easily."

"I ain't worried." He jerked a thumb at his chest. "See, Heller, I'm a public figure—they don't bump off public figures; it's bad publicity."

"Tell Mayor Cermak—he got hit in Florida."

He blew me a Bronx cheer. "I'm gonna take a shower. You want a free meal down at the club, stick around . . . but leave the sermons to Billy Sunday, okay?"

"Yeah. Sure."

I could hear him showering, singing in there, "All or Nothing at All." Had we really been friends once? I had a reputation as something of a randy son of a bitch myself, but did I treat women like Clifton did? The thought make me shudder.

On the oblong glass coffee table before me, a white phone began to ring. I answered it.

"Pete?" The voice was low-pitched but female—a distinctive, throaty sound.

"No, it's a friend. He's in the shower, getting ready for his show tonight."

"Tell him to meet me out front in five minutes."

"Well, let me check with him and see if that's possible. Who should I say is calling?"

There was a long pause.

Then the throaty purr returned: "Just tell him the wife of a friend."

"Sure," I said, and went into the bathroom and reported this, over the shower needles, through the glass door, to Clifton, who said, "Tell her I'll be right down."

Within five minutes, Clifton—his hair still wet—moved quickly through the living room; he had thrown on the boating clothes from this afternoon.

"This won't take long." He flashed the boyish grin. "These frails can't get enough of me."

"You want me to leave?"

"Naw. I'll set somethin' up with her for later. I don't think she has a friend, though—sorry, pal."

"That's okay. I try to limit myself to one doped-up doxie a day."

Clifton smirked and waved at me dismissively as he headed out, and I sat there for maybe a minute, then decided I'd had it. I plucked my straw fedora off the coffee table and trailed out after him, hoping to catch up with him and make my goodbyes.

The night sky was cobalt and alive with stars, a sickle slice of moon providing the appropriate deco touch. The sidewalk stretched out before me like a white ribbon, toward where palms mingled with streetlights. A Buick was along the curb, and Pete was leaning against the window, like a car hop taking an order.

That sultry, low female voice rumbled through the night like pretty thunder: *"For God's sake, Pete, don't do it! Please don't do it!"*

As Pete's response—laughter—filled my ears, I stopped in my tracks, not wanting to intrude. Then Pete, still chuckling, making a dismissive wave, turned toward me and walked. He was giving me a cocky smile when the first gunshot cracked the night.

I dove and rolled and wound up against a sculpted hedge that separated Clifton's apartment house from the hunk of geometry next door. Two more shots rang out, and I could see the orange muzzle flash as the woman shot through the open car window.

For a comic, Pete was doing a hell of a dance; the first shot had caught him over the right armpit, and another plowed through his neck in a spray of red, and he twisted around to face her to accommodate another slug.

Then the car roared off, and Pete staggered off the sidewalk and pitched forward onto the grass, like a diver who missed the pool.

I ran to his sprawled figure and turned him over. His eyes were wild with dying.

"Them fuckin' dames ain't . . . ain't so easy to discard, neither," he said, and laughed, a bloody froth of a laugh, to punctuate his last dirty joke.

People were rushing up, talking frantically, shouting about the need for the police to be called and such like. Me, I was noting where the woman had put her last shot.

She caught him right below the belt.

After a long wait in a receiving area, I was questioned by the cops in an interview room at the Dade County Courthouse in Miami. Actually, one of them, Earl Carstensen—chief of detectives of the Miami Beach Detective Bureau—was a cop; the other guy—Ray Miller—was chief investigator for the state attorney's office.

Carstensen was a craggy guy in his fifties, and Miller was a skinny balding guy with wire-rim glasses. The place was air-conditioned and they brought me an iced tea, so it wasn't exactly the third degree.

We were all seated at the small table in a sound-proofed cubicle. After they had established that I was a friend of the late Pete Clifton, visiting from Chicago, the line of questioning took an interesting turn.

Carstensen asked, "Are you aware that 'Peter Clifton' was not the deceased's real name?"

"I figured it was a stage name, but it's the only name I knew him by."

"He was born Peter Tessitorio," Miller said, "in New York. He had a criminal background—two burglary raps."

"I never knew that."

Carstensen asked, "You're a former police officer?"

"Yeah. I was a detective on the Chicago P.D. pickpocket detail till '32."

Miller asked, "You spent the afternoon with Clifton in the company of two girls?"

"Yeah."

"What are their names?"

"Peggy Simmons and Janet Windom. They live in an apartment house on Jefferson . . . I don't know the address, but I can point you if you want to talk to them."

The two men exchanged glances.

"We've already picked them up," Miller said. "They've been questioned, and they're alibiing each other. They say they don't know anybody who'd want to kill Clifton."

"They're just a couple of party girls," I said.

Carstensen said, "We found a hypo and bottle of morphine in their apartment. Would you know anything about that?"

I sighed. "I noticed the tracks on the Simmons' kid's arms. I gave Pete hell, and he admitted to me he was giving them the stuff. He also indicated he had connections with some dope racketeer."

"He didn't give you a name?" Miller asked.

"No."

"You've never heard of Leo Massey?"

"No."

"Friend of Clifton's. A known dope smuggler."

I sipped my iced tea. "Well, other than those two girls, I don't really know any of Clifton's associates here in Miami."

An eyebrow arched in Carstensen's craggy puss. "You'd have trouble meeting Massey—he's dead."

"Oh?"

"He was found in Card Sound last September. Bloated and smellin' to high heaven."

"What does that have to do with Pete Clifton?"

Miller said, "Few days before Massey's body turned up, that speedboat of his—the *Screwball*—got taken out for a spin."

I shrugged. "That's what a speedboat's for, taking it out for a spin."

"At midnight? And not returning till daybreak?"

"You've got a witness to that effect?"

Miller nodded.

"So Pete was a suspect in Massey's murder?"

"Not exactly," the state attorney's investigator said. "Clifton had an alibi—those two girls say he spent the night with 'em."

I frowned in confusion. "I thought you had a witness to Clifton takin' his boat out . . ."

Carstensen said, "We have a witness at the marina to the effect that the boat was taken out and brought back—but nobody saw who the captain was."

Now I was getting it. "And Pete said somebody must've borrowed his boat without his permission."

"That's right."

"So, what? You're making this as a gangland hit? But it was a woman who shot him."

Miller asked, "Did you see that, Mr. Heller?"

"I heard the woman's voice—I didn't actually see her shoot him. Didn't actually see her at all. But it seemed like she was agitated with Pete."

Other witnesses had heard the woman yelling at Pete, so the cops knew I hadn't made up this story.

"Could the woman have been a decoy?" Carstensen asked. "Drawn Clifton to that car for some man to shoot?"

"I suppose. But my instinct is, Pete's peter got

him bumped. If I were you, fellas, I'd go over that apartment of his and look for love letters and the like, see if you can find a little black book. My guess is—somebody he was banging banged him back."

They thanked me for my help, told me to stick around for the inquest on Tuesday, and turned me loose. I got in my rental Ford and drove to the Biltmore, went up to my room, ordered a room-service supper, and gave Frank Nitti a call.

"So my name didn't come up?" Nitti asked me over the phone.

"No. Obviously, I didn't tell 'em you hired me to come down here, but they didn't mention you, either. And the way they were giving out information, it would've come up. They got a funny way of interrogating you in Florida—they spill and you listen."

"Did they mention a guy named McGraw?"

"No, Frank. Just this Leo Massey."

"McGraw's a rival dope smuggler," Nitti said thoughtfully. "I understand he stepped in and took over Massey's trade after Massey turned up a floater."

"What's that got to do with Clifton?"

"Nothin' much—just that my people tell me McGraw's a regular at the Chez Clifton. Kinda chummy with our comical late friend."

"Maybe McGraw's the potential investor Clifton was talking about—to take your place, Frank."

Silence. Nitti was thinking.

Finally he returned with, "Got another job for you, Nate."

"I don't know, Frank—I probably oughta keep

my nose clean, do my bit at the inquest and scram outa this flamingo trap."

"Another three C's in it for you, kid—just to deliver another message. No rush—tomorrow morning'll be fine."

Did you hear the one about the comic who thought he told killer jokes? He died laughing.

"Anything you say, Frank."

Eddie McGraw lived at the Delano, on Collins Avenue, the middle of a trio of towering hotels rising above Miami Beach like Mayan temples got out of hand. McGraw had a penthouse on the eleventh floor, and I had to bribe the elevator attendant to take me there.

It was eleven a.m. I wasn't expecting trouble. My 9mm Browning was back in Chicago, in a desk drawer in my office. But I wasn't unarmed—I had the name *Frank Nitti* in my arsenal.

I knocked on the door.

The woman who answered was in her late twenties—a brunette with big brown eyes and rather exaggerated features, pretty in a cartoonish way. She had a voluptuous figure, wrapped up like a present in a pink chiffon dressing gown.

"Excuse me, ma'am. Is Mr. McGraw home?"

She nodded. The big brown eyes locked onto me coldly, though her voice was a warm contralto: "Who should I say is calling?"

"I'm a friend of Pete Clifton's."

"Would you mind waiting in the hall?"

"Not at all."

She shut the door, and a few seconds later, it flew back open, revealing a short but sturdy-looking guy in a red sports shirt and gray slacks. He was blond with wild thatches of overgrown eyebrow above sky-blue eyes; when you got past a bulbous nose, he kind of looked like James Cagney.

"I don't do business at my apartment," he said. His voice was high-pitched and raspy. He started to shut the door, and I stopped it with my hand.

He shoved me, and I went backward, but I latched onto his wrist and pushed his hand back and pulled him forward, out into the hall, until he was kneeling in front of me.

"Frank Nitti sent me," I said, and released the pressure on his wrist.

He stood, ran a hand through slicked-back blond hair that didn't need straightening, and said, "I don't do business with Nitti."

"I think maybe you should. You know about Pete's killing?"

"I saw the morning paper. I liked Pete. He was funny. He was an all right guy."

"Yeah, he was a card. Did he by any chance sell you an interest in the Chez Clifton?"

McGraw frowned at me; if he'd been a dog, he'd have growled. "I told you . . . what's your name, anyway?"

"Heller. Nate Heller."

"I don't do business at my apartment. My wife and me, we got a life separate from how I make my living. Got it?"

"Did Pete sell you an interest in the Chez Clifton?"

He straightened his collar, which also didn't need it. "As a matter of fact, he did."

"Then you were wrong about not doing business with Frank Nitti."

McGraw sneered. "What's that supposed to mean?"

"Mr. Nitti would like to discuss that with you himself." I handed him a slip of paper. "He's in town, at his estate on Di Lido Island. He'd like to invite you to join him there for lunch today."

"Why should I?"

I laughed once, a hollow thing. "Mr. McGraw, I don't care what you do as long as you don't put your hands on me again. I'm just delivering a message. But I will tell you this—I'm from Chicago, and when Frank Nitti invites you for lunch, you go."

McGraw thought about that. Then he nodded and said, "Sorry about the rough stuff."

"I apologize for bothering you at home. But you don't keep an office, and you're unlisted."

"Yeah, well, nature of my business."

"Understood."

I held out my hand. He studied it for a moment, then shook it.

"Why don't you give Mr. Nitti a call, at that number, and confirm your luncheon engagement?"

He nodded and disappeared inside the apartment.

Half an hour later, I knocked on the door again. Returning had cost me another fin to the elevator boy.

Mrs. McGraw, still in her pink chiffon robe, opened the door and said, "I'm afraid my husband has stepped out."

"I know he has," I said, brushing past her into

the apartment, beautifully appointed in the usual Miami-tropical manner.

"Leave at once!" she demanded, pointing past the open door into the hall.

"No," I said, and shut the door. "I recognized your voice, Mrs. McGraw. It's very distinctive. I like it."

"What are you talking about?" But her wide eyes and the tremor in her tone told me she was afraid she already knew.

I told her anyway. "I'm the guy who answered the phone last night at Pete's. That's when I first heard that throaty purr of yours. I also heard you warn him—right before he turned his back on you and you shot him."

She was clutching herself as if she was cold. "I don't know what you're talking about. Please leave!"

"I'm not going to stay long. Turn around."

"What?"

"Turn around and put your hands on that door."

"Why?"

"I'm gonna frisk you, lady. I don't figure you have a gun hidden away on you, but I'd like to make sure."

"No!"

So I took her by the wrist, sort of like I had her husband, and twisted her arm around her back and shoved her against the door. I frisked her all over. She was a little plump, but it was one of the nicer frisks I ever gave.

No gun—several concealed weapons, but no gun.

She stood facing me now, her back to the door, trembling. "Are you . . . are you a cop?"

"I'm just a friend of Pete's."

She raised a hand to her face, fingers curling there, like the petals of a wilting flower. "Are you here to turn me in?"

"We'll see."

Now she looked at me in a different way, something flaring in her dark eyes. "Oh. You're here to . . . deal."

"Maybe. Can we sit down over there?" I gestured to the living room—white walls, white carpet, glass tables, white chairs and couch, a white fireplace with a big mirror with flamingos etched in it.

I took an easy chair across from the couch, where she sat, arms folded, legs crossed—nice legs, muscular, supple, tan against the pink chiffon. She seemed to be studying me, trying to get a bead on me.

"I'd like to hear your side of it."

Her chin tilted. "You really think you can make a positive identification based just on my voice?"

"Ask Bruno Hauptmann. He went to the chair on less."

She laughed, but it wasn't very convincing. "You didn't see me."

"Do you have an alibi? Is your husband in on it?"

"No! Of course not."

"Your side of it. Let's have it."

She looked at the floor. "Your . . . friend . . . was a terrible man."

"I noticed."

That surprised her. Looking right at me, she asked, "You did?"

"Pete used women like playthings. They weren't people to him. Is that what he did to you?"

She nodded; her full mouth was quivering—if this was an act, it was a good one.

Almost embarrassed, she said, "I thought he was charming. He was good-looking, clever and . . . sexy, I guess."

"You'd been having an affair with him."

One nod.

Well, that didn't surprise me. Just because McGraw was his business partner, and a hood at that, wouldn't stop Pete Clifton from going after a good-looking doll like Mrs. McGraw.

"Can I smoke?" she asked. She indicated her purse on the coffee table. I checked inside it, found no gun, plucked out the pack of Luckies—Pete's brand—and tossed it to her. Also her lighter.

"Thanks," she said, firing up. "It was just . . . a fling. Stupid goddamn fling. Eddie was neglecting me, and . . . it's an old story. Anyway, I wanted to stop it, but . . . Pete wanted more. Not because . . . he loved me or anything. Just because . . . do you know what he said to me?"

"I can imagine."

He said, " 'Baby, you're one sweet piece of ass. You don't have to like me to satisfy me.' "

I frowned at her. "I don't know if I'm following this. If you wanted to break it off, how could he—"

"He blackmailed me."

"With what? He couldn't tell your husband about the affair without getting himself in a jam."

She heaved a sigh. "No . . . but Pete coulda turned my husband in for . . . for something he had on him."

And now I knew.

Clifton had loaned McGraw the *Screwball* for disposal of the body of Leo Massey, the rival dope smuggler, which put Clifton in a position to finger McGraw.

"Okay," I said, and stood.

She gazed up at me, astounded. "What do you mean . . . 'okay'?"

"Okay, I understand why you killed him."

I walked to the door, and she followed, the sound of her slippers whispering through the thick carpet.

She stopped me at the door, a hand on my arm; she was very close to me, and smelled good, like lilacs. Those brown eyes were big enough to dive into.

Her throaty purr tickled the air between us. "You're not going to turn me in?"

"Why should I? I just wanted to know if there were any ramifications for my client or me in this thing, and I don't see any."

"I thought Pete was your friend."

"Hell, he was your lover, and look what you thought of him."

Her eyes tightened. "What do you want from me?"

"Nothing. You had a good reason to do it. I heard you warn him."

"You're very kind. . . ." She squeezed my arm, moved closer, to where her breasts were pressed gently against me. "My husband won't be home for a while . . . we could go to my bedroom and—"

I drew away. "Jesus, lady! Isn't screwin' around what got you into trouble in the first place?"

And I got the hell out of there.

*   *   *

I said just enough at the inquest to get it over with quick, and was back in Chicago by Wednesday night.

I don't know whether Frank Nitti and Eddie McGraw wound up doing business together. I do know the Chez Clifton closed down and reopened under another name, the Beach Club. But Nitti put his Di Lido Island estate up for sale and sold it shortly after that. So maybe he just got out while the getting was good.

Mrs. McGraw—whose first name I never knew—was never charged with Pete Clifton's murder, which remains unsolved on the Miami Beach P.D.'s books. The investigation into the Clifton killing, however, did lead the state attorney's office to nailing McGraw on the Massey slaying; McGraw got ninety-nine years, which is a little much, considering all he did was kill another dope smuggler. The two party girls, Peggy and Janet, were charged with harboring narcotics, which was dropped in exchange for their cooperation in the McGraw/Massey inquiry.

Pete Clifton really was a prick, but I always thought of him, over the ensuing years, when so many dirty-mouthed comics—from Lenny Bruce to George Carlin—made it big.

Maybe Clifton got the last laugh, after all.

AUTHOR'S NOTE: This work of fiction is based on a real case, but certain liberties have been taken, and some names have been changed. My thanks to George Hagenauer, who uncovered this little-known incident in the life of Frank Nitti.

RELUCTANT WITNESS
A Nick Polo Story
by Jerry Kennealy

A private detective in real life, Jerry Kennealy weaves his experience into his work. One can even see him finding himself in the same situation as his Nick Polo when hunting for a "reluctant witness."

He has been nominated for the Shamus for Best P.I. Novel twice, and has served as vice president of PWA.

There are some obvious advantages to being born and raised in San Francisco—the people, the restaurants, and especially, the climate. The Pacific Ocean and Bay waters provide us with natural air conditioning. We natives just don't like heat. When the temperature plows through eighty degrees, we drop to our knees and pray for the blessed fog to come streaming back through the Golden Gate Bridge, all the while cursing the transplanted, harebrained, hair-sprayed TV forecasters who boast about the wonderful weather. If you want hot, muggy, steaming days and nights, stay in New York, St. Louis, or God forbid, Los Angeles.

The air conditioner in my car had decided to go on vacation while I was driving through Sacramento. Now I was some hundred miles north of the state capital, at the fringes of Shasta-Trinity

National Forest in the small town of French Creek, California, elevation five hundred and ten feet, population eight hundred and forty, summer temperatures as hot as those places in hell where I hope serial murderers, child molesters, and moderate politicians are feeling the tip of the devil's pitchfork.

The town's main street was called—what else? Main Street, a collection of old, shoulder-to-shoulder, two-story clapboard buildings. If one of them got weary of holding up its neighbor, the whole street would collapse.

I parked in front of Big Joe's General Store. The digital temperature gauge on the roof read 106. The sweating glass windows featured a display of fishing poles and creels, hiking shoes, straw hats, wicked-looking hunting knives, their tips embedded in a slice off a dry pine tree, canned foods, a baby stroller, a pyramid of paint cans, and a fading life-size cardboard silhouette of John Wayne in full cowboy regalia.

A cherry-red neon sign over the door advertised COLD BEER & FRESH PRODUCE.

I picked up an inexpensive Styrofoam cooler, loaded it with bags of ice and a six-pack of Pepsi.

Big Joe himself was at the cash register. He lived up to his name. He was at least as big as the cardboard replica of the Duke in the store's window.

"Hi, Mr. Fairley," I said as I pushed a twenty-dollar bill across the counter. "Nick Polo. I spoke to you on the phone a couple of times about the accident."

Fairley had a shaggy head of smoke-colored hair and a rough, red-skinned face dotted with murky gray spots that were moles or clusters of skin growths that had been burned off. He was wearing a plaid-flannel shirt, the sleeves rolled up to his biceps, showing off a pair of sinewy arms splashed with freckles. A toothpick dangled from his withered lips. He took his time ringing up my items then said, "Polo. You're the *in*surance man."

Big Joe stressed the "in" of insurance, his tone leaving no doubt of what he thought of people who made their living that way.

"I figure the only way I can get back some of the money they've screwed me out of over the years is to work for them, Mr. Fairly."

That got me a small grin along with a scoop of coins.

"Have you seen Al Lee lately?" I asked, pocketing my change.

"Nope." His eyes drifted toward the window. It was through that window that Fairley had witnessed the aftermath of a two-vehicle collision fourteen months ago. A Toyota pickup truck and a motorcycle had met almost head-on in the intersection. I was working for the pickup's insurance company. The driver had suffered severe injuries, but not as severe as those of the twenty-two-year-old man on the motorcycle. He was a quadriplegic. The medical and legal bills for both parties were enormous. Just which one of the insurance carriers ended up funding those costs depended on one thing. Which driver had run the red light. The only witness who supposedly had that information was a Mr. Al Lee.

Big Joe Fairly had run out of his store after hearing the tortured screech of brakes and the jarring bang of impact. Al Lee was standing on the side-walk. Fairly said that Lee had told him just one thing. "He ran the red."

My job was to find Lee and learn just who "he" was, the truck driver or the young man on the motorcycle.

"Wouldn't know where Lee might be working, huh?"

Fairly worked the toothpick from one side of his mouth to the other. "Like I told you on the phone, I don't know nothin' about Al Lee. Nothin' 'cept he used to do a lot more shoppin' here till you *in*surance people come lookin' for him."

I lugged my cooler out to the car, popped open a can of Pepsi, and got behind the wheel and decided it was time to call upon the reluctant Mr. Lee.

Did you ever feel that you just wanted to disappear? Make up a new identity and vanish? If so, a name like Al Lee would be a good start. Take the name Al. It could be Allen, Alen, Allan, Alan, Alynn, Aloysius—well, you get the idea. Most information databases key in on the first name, so think of how many hits you'd have if you just put in the name Al.

And Lee. Lee is now a more common name in California than Smith or Jones.

I had a tough time finding my Al Lee. He had left the scene before the police arrived at the accident. All Big Joe Fairley could, or would, tell the cops was that Lee "lived somewhere in the vicinity."

The police didn't make much of an effort to find him. I didn't really expect them to. I'd spent fifteen years in the San Francisco Police Department, and traffic accidents were at the bottom of the investigating pecking order. But the insurance carriers wanted Al Lee real bad. I was the fourth investigator working the case for my client.

"Find this guy!" senior adjuster Dean Bagley had told me. "Find him. I don't care what it costs!"

Ah, music to an investigator's ear. Big Joe Fairley had told the police that Lee was Caucasian, in his sixties and "short on height and short on hair."

I hadn't gotten much more out of Fairly, except that Al Lee had been a regular customer. The day of the accident, Lee had been in the store to pick up some groceries and fertilizer.

I ran checks on every A. Lee in Shasta County—coming up with a total of twenty-eight, including an Albert and an Alvin, neither of which was my man.

I then checked everyone with the last name Lee within a fifty-mile radius of French Creek, again coming up with a lot of Lee's, but not the right one.

I was beginning to think that Lee was either a figment of Big Joe's imagination, or that Al Lee wasn't the man's real name.

There could be a lot of reasons for that. Shasta County wasn't the prime marijuana-growing property that neighboring Trinity County was, but there was a lot of grass being grown in amongst the towering pines. French Creek had been a major gold-producing area at one time. Had Lee stumbled onto an old vein?

I was about ready to turn in a long, cleverly worded report to my client explaining how I had run up a bill of close to four thousand dollars and

still didn't have a clue where Al Lee was when I
decided to give Big Joe Fairley's phone bills a shot.

If Lee called in his orders, maybe Big Joe had
called him back to let him know when to come a-
calling for them.

Obtaining someone's phone records without benefit of subpoena is, of course, illegal. It also proved
profitable—for me. Most of the numbers Joe Fairley called were listed ones. There were four non-
published numbers, one that turned out to be billed
to an A. Lee, 1647 Lockhart Gulch Road, French
Creek.

I figured if I called Lee, he'd be long gone before
I ever got to his place, so it was knock-on-the-
door time.

A friendly tip. If you're ever looking for a small
road, in a small town, that doesn't show up on a
AAA map, call the local fire department for directions. The fire captain I spoke to gave me a make-
shift set of instructions: "You go out Compton
Road till you pass this old wooden bridge. Fifty or
so yards after the bridge, you turn right on a gravel
road. There's no road sign, so drive slow or you'll
miss it. Then you head east for a mile and come
to a fork in a road. Go left. That's Lockhart
Gulch Road."

I found the bridge, the gravel road and then the
fork in the road. A narrow dirt trail snaked up into
the dense forest of pines, oaks, madrones, and an
occasional redwood tree. I had all the windows
rolled down and drove slowly, following the fire
captain's directions. The road was so narrow that I
could have reached out and touched the trees.

A rural mailbox showed up every hundred yards

or so. I passed 1641, then drove nearly a half mile before spotting the next rusty mail box—numbered 1659. What the hell happened to 1647, Lee's box?

Maneuvering the car around involved a series of short, abrupt turns, then a quick shift into reverse, a curse when a fender grazed a tree, then more turns.

I spotted a small gouge in the road leading into a nest of head-high scrub brushes. There were faint impressions of tire tracks in the hard-packed dirt. I nosed the car up to a chain-link gate centered between two towering pine trees, switched off the engine and sat there for a moment listening to the pinging of the motor cooling off. I popped open another Pepsi and drained it, then got out of the car to check the gate.

It was constructed of thick, industrial-gauge steel, glazed with rust, and was unlocked. I yelled out Lee's name several times, then swung the gate open, got back into the car and drove forward. There were plenty more pine and madrone trees, but no sign of farm animals, or anything that could be harvested for a profit, including marijuana.

My car bucked and jolted up the trail for a couple of minutes before I came to a clearing. A good-sized log cabin sat in the middle of a neatly kept half acre or so of flowering rose bushes: reds, yellows, whites, pinks, and a staked vegetable garden.

The cabin's logs were heavily varnished; the roof shakes were dark as if they'd been oiled recently. A large TV satellite dish squatted on top of the roof, like a giant metal bird of prey.

I did what I always do when driving up to a

remote lodging, beeped the horn and prayed that there wasn't a big mean dog out there somewhere.

The cabin door opened wide and a short bald-headed man wearing jeans and a knit blue shirt walked out onto the porch. He was wiping an iron skillet with a towel. His face was weather-creased, his skin the color of nutmeg.

"Howdy," he called. "Can I help you?"

"I'm looking for Al Lee."

"Well, you found him, mister. Come on in. You look like you could use a cold drink."

I exited the car and took Al Lee up on his invitation.

"Sorry to bother you like this," I said when I was inside the cabin, "My name's Nick Polo. It's about that—"

A low, throaty growl cut me off in mid-sentence. That big, mean dog I'd been worried about was crouched at Lee's feet. A black rottweiler. Sitting on his haunches, his head came up past Lee's waist.

Lee had replaced the iron skillet with a long-barreled revolver, which was pointed right at my stomach.

"Drop your pants!" he ordered.

"Listen, Mr. Lee, all I want—"

"Drop 'em! The shoes first. Kick 'em over here, then toss me them pants or I'll have Sammy chew your balls off."

The rottweiler started barking at the sound of his name. At least I hoped that's what started him barking.

I kicked off my shoes, then slipped out of my pants, bundled them into a ball and gently tossed them toward Lee.

He let the pants fall to the polished wood floor, transferred his gun from his right to his left hand and snapped his fingers twice.

Sammy bounded toward me, skidding to a stop inches from my quivering legs.

"You so much as make a move and your balls are gone," Lee promised. He picked up my pants and carried them over to a dining table and quickly went through the pockets. He let out a grunt as he fingered the ID in my wallet.

"Nick Polo. San Francisco police inspector."

"That's an old card," I responded, trying to keep my voice calm, trying not to look at Sammy's drooling mouth. "I retired years ago. I'm working as an insurance investigator now, Mr. Lee. You can see my license in the—"

Lee threw the wallet at me, baseball style, an overhand fastball. "Lyin' bastard! You were going to try and snow me with the phony insurance line. How many are there?"

"How many what? Listen, you've got—"

The sound of the gun going off rocked me back on my heels. The bullet plowed into the flooring near my feet, away from the dog.

"How many cops," Lee demanded. "How many?"

His eyes were bulging and his face had reddened under his tan. The gun was pointed at my stomach again.

"At least twenty," I said, talking fast, not really sure what I was saying. "The sheriff, a few local cops and the FBI."

Lee took the false news stoically. He pulled a chair from the dining table and flopped into it.

"How'd you find me, Polo?"

"That accident you witnessed. We got your name and phone number from Big Joe Fairley."

He nodded his head as if that made sense to him. "You bastards never give up, do you?"

"Listen, Mr. Lee, why—"

He jumped to his feet and booted the chair across the room. "Don't give me that Lee shit!" He had the gun cradled in both hands, in a white-knuckled grip, waving it wildly around the room, as if the revolver had a life of its own and was trying to free itself.

I edged backward slowly, coming to an abrupt halt when Sammy started growling. Suddenly Lee let out a primal scream, wheeled the gun around, jammed the barrel in his mouth and pulled the trigger. Gray matter sprayed around the room, and Lee's body crashed into the table and spun around in a half circle on the floor, leaving a wavy smear of blood in its wake.

Sammy was on all fours, his head swiveling from me to his dead master. The dog finally lowered his head and slowly padded over to Lee's body.

I sprinted for the door, slamming it closed behind me, and hot-footed it over the scorched brown earth to my car, freeing the snub-nosed .38 from its hiding spot in the passenger seat back rest before digging a cell phone from the glove compartment.

I went through the rest of the Pepsi and a goodly amount of a pint of Jack Daniel's that I'd kept in the trunk for medicinal purposes before the sheriff showed up.

* * *

It took Sheriff Herb Rosen two days to come up with Al Lee's correct name. He called me at my flat in San Francisco and gave me the news. Lee was actually Daryl Springer, fifty-five years of age. Seventeen years ago Springer and his younger brother Jeb had burned down a Baptist church in Alabama. His brother had been trapped in the fire and burned to death. Daryl, a successful peanut farmer with a bad case of the hates, had disappeared.

"Was anyone really looking for him?" I asked Sheriff Rosen.

"Nope. Dumb bastard could have probably moved back home. The statute of limitations expired years ago."

I could hear a dog barking in the background. "What happened to Sammy, the rottweiler?"

"I got him. Nice dog, I'll find him a home. Think you might be interested, Mr. Polo? Make a hell of a watchdog, Sammy would."

I remembered standing in my shorts, quivering in fear, Sammy's big brown eyes fastened on my crotch. "No, thanks. And just make sure it's not you he's watching, Sheriff."

Senior insurance adjuster Dean Bagley flipped through the pages of my report. "So you didn't get a statement, huh, Nick?"

"Statement? Dean, I was lucky to get out of that cabin with my life, not to mention my testicles. The guy was crazy."

"Crazy, maybe," Bagley agreed, "but he was the only witness to our accident."

I leaned across Bagley's desk. "Al Lee's real

name was Daryl Springer. He'd been a peanut farmer in Alabama. He and his younger brother burned down a Baptist church. His brother died in the fire and Springer took off. It took the local sheriff two days to come up with his ID."

Bagley seemed to wince a bit when he looked at my billing page. "So, the cops have been looking for him all this time, huh?"

"No. Not really. The statute of limitations on the arson had expired years ago. The church people were covered by insurance, so they didn't care. Apparently Springer's brother Jeb was the real redneck in the family, and the community seemed to think that he got his just deserts by dying in the fire, so all Springer was running from was his own shadow."

Bagley raised his head and smiled at me. He was a handsome, narrow-faced man who looked at home behind a desk covered with files and forms. "Nick, I know you did a good job in running the guy down, but without a statement from him of some kind, I don't know how I'm going to authorize the company to pay your bill." He ruffled my bill between his fingers. "The whole bill anyway. Maybe I can get them to—"

"I should have brought Sammy along, Dean. He'd have convinced you."

Bagley's eyebrows rose toward his hairline. "Sammy? Who is Sammy?"

"Springer's rottweiler. He was planning to make a meal out of me when Springer shot himself."

Bagley pursed his lips for a moment, then stamped my bill with a big red TO BE PAID stamp.

"Next time, get the statement, then let the guy kill himself, okay, Nick?"

And you thought insurance companies had no compassion.

NOBODY'S RING
A Scott Elliott Story
by Terence Faherty

Terence Faherty won the Shamus for Best P.I. Novel in 1998 with *Come Back Dead*. The field that year was so deep that there were six books nominated instead of the traditional five. That's some indication of what a special book it was. I'm proud to present here the first Scott Elliott short story in which the Hollywood P.I. finds himself in possession of "nobody's ring."

ONE

I found the ring just as the small dinner party was breaking up. Moving on, I should say.

The four couples present, having disposed of baked chicken, potato wedges, and mushroom caps, were lingering over their coffees prior to adjourning to a movie house for part two of the evening's entertainment. It was a type of social gathering that was being duplicated—with minor menu variations—all over America on this Sunday in 1951. Except that our party was taking place in Beverly Hills, California, and the movie we were about to see starred one of the dinner guests and had been produced by another.

The star was Lillian Lacey, a Juno-esque actress who had made a career of appearing in her underwear in otherwise undistinguished English comedies. She'd recently come to America with her husband, a Greek émigré and hustler named Marcus Pioline, who had somehow persuaded Twentieth-Century Fox to build a picture around Lacey, *Professor Beware*. The title had been stolen from an old Harold Lloyd vehicle, but not the plot. As far as I'd been able to tell from the dinner conversation, the new story was based on the dubious premise that Lacey, who was built like Maureen O'Hara's healthier sister, was unattractive to men when she wore eyeglasses.

Our hosts were an old Hollywood couple, Carlos and Winnie Mannero. Mannero was a rare bird: a silent movie star who'd held on to his money. He'd been haunted by rumors of homosexuality back in his glory days, some involving his screen rival, Rudolph Valentino. It was said that his marriage to Winnie, a onetime contract player, had been forced on him by his studio, desperate to save his career in the first years of sound. The nasty rumors had persisted, but so had the marriage. Two decades into it, Carlos and Winnie were among the movie colony's most genuinely affectionate couples.

Less well-known locally were two of the Manneros' current guests, Sidney Shaw and his wife, Belle. Shaw was a producer for RKO, a jovial man who blamed his extensive hair loss on his long association with Howard Hughes. Belle, an attractive though quiet woman, was notable only for possessing genuinely blonde hair and having made no professional use of it, despite living in a town where it was practically legal tender. Unlike so many other wives of big shots, she was neither a former actress, mannequin, or showgirl. That put her at a disadvantage in the conversation department, but over coffee my wife, Ella, had drawn Belle out, her reward being a long description of Belle's recent visit to Spokane.

Ella had a weakness for oddballs and stray lambs, two groups that together made up the bulk of Hollywood's population, it often seemed to me. A publicist turned screenwriter, Ella considered out-of-step souls to be her stock in trade. They were also mine, though in a more practical way. I worked for a company called Hollywood Security, which specialized in trimming the briars into which little lambs strayed. Preferably those lambs under contract to well-heeled studios. We did our work discreetly, or tried to. It was a measure of our success that of those at the Mannero party, only Carlos and Ella knew what I did for a living. The others seemed to think I sponged off my wife, which was fine by me. It cut down on the need to chat.

I felt a more urgent need as Winnie supervised the clearing of the cups and saucers, a need born of all the coffee I'd drunk to get me through Belle Shaw's Spokane travelogue. Following my hostess's directions, I found the guest bathroom off the front hall. Winnie had called it a powder room, but it was big enough to be a powder magazine, with acoustics that made the departing java sound like Niagara in April.

The ring was on the edge of the powder room's sink, standing out against the sink's dark green marble like Constance Bennett against a chorus

line of coal miners. It was what is sometimes called
a cocktail ring: too much for all but the most un-
self-conscious brides, too much for everyday wear,
too much for daylight even. Its centerpiece was a
huge square-cut blue stone, the blue that of a pre-
dawn sky. It was surrounded by marquise diamonds, beautifully matched and wonderfully bright.
Between these diamond petals were chips of the
blue stone, almost submerged in the heavy gold of
the mounting.

I found Winnie Mannero in her kitchen and
showed her the ring. Flashed it at her, actually,
since it did things with the ceiling light that would
have made Edison proud.

"My goodness, Scotty! Where did you get that
horse choker?" And when I'd told her, "Mine?
Heavens, no. Carlos would have a stroke if I
bought something like that. If he tried to buy it for
me, he'd have two strokes. Odd, I don't remember
anyone wearing that tonight. And I would
remember."

She started to take the ring from me and took
my elbow instead, leading me into the living room,
the ring preceding us. And announcing us, since it
caught every eye as we entered.

The women were being helped into their wraps,
Ella by Mannero, the man I would have picked
for the job myself. She said, "Scotty, you shouldn't
have," but so sarcastically that I didn't feel a denial
was necessary.

"Scotty found it in the powder room," Winnie
said. "It's not the cook's and it's not mine, so who's
been careless?"

Lillian Lacey took the ring from me and gave it

a very professional examination. "What a sapphire!" she breathed, "and what stones!" her accent slipping from high Vivian Leigh to low Gracie
Fields in those six words. She tried the ring on and
didn't get it past her second knuckle. "Marcus, if
you're going to buy a girl a present, you should get
the right size."

"I've an excellent eye for size," Pioline replied,
patting her backside as he peered at the ring over
her shoulder. "It's not my doing."

"Mine either," Shaw said when we turned to
him. "Never saw it before." His wife proved it
wasn't hers by trying it on as Lacey had and not
doing any better.

The ring fit Ella's slender finger, but only just. It
was a less successful match for the blue of her always pale, currently hopeful eyes. "Finders keep-
ers?" she asked.

Everyone then talked at once, but we managed
to work out that Lacey had been the last one to
visit the guest bathroom before me. That didn't
advance the cause.

"I wouldn't have missed that sparkler, darlings,"
she assured us. "If I hadn't seen it, I would have
smelled it."

We didn't have time to probe further. Our showing of *Professor Beware* was a sneak preview being
held in Glendale, a drive and a half away. The eight
of us walked to our waiting cars, still joking about
the ring. Ella had surrendered it—reluctantly—to
Mannero. He stopped me by the edge of the drive
and handed it to me as the others looked on.

"Take it, Elliott, will you? There's something
about it makes my skin crawl."

TWO

"What's in it for us?"

The questioner was Paddy Maguire, the head of Hollywood Security, if not the brains behind the firm. That title belonged to his wife, Peggy, whom I could hear through the closed double doors of Paddy's office. She was discussing an unpaid bill with an accountant at MGM in a tone of voice Paddy had once described as "the original sound barrier." Her husband was leaning over his desk lamp, looking at the orphan ring through a jeweler's loop, a device I'd half expected Lillian Lacey to pull from her ample brassiere the evening before.

"Finder's fee," I said.

"Is that so? What do they pay in Beverly Hills for finding the bathroom? 'Cause the way you tell it, that's all the work you did."

Paddy had been around Hollywood since they put the name on the hill, first as an actor, then as a studio guard, and finally as a successful if not an especially reputable businessman. He'd given me a place to land when I'd gotten out of the service in '45, a fact that made me patient with him most days.

"I'm figuring to stop around some jewelry stores this afternoon," I said. "Can't be too many that handle that weight of hardware. If I ask real nice, maybe they'll tell me who they sold it to."

Paddy traded his spyglass for the cigar he'd been smoking when I'd come in. He kept the ring, enclosing it in a fist that was a little smaller in diameter than a Sunday paper.

"You're thinking it was some passerby who slipped in to use the convenience between Miss Lacey's visit and yours?"

"No," I said.

"No," Paddy agreed. "So the rightful owner is someone at the Mannero party. Someone who didn't care to acknowledge this beauty in public."

I lit a Lucky Strike, figuring I was there for a while.

"That being the case," Paddy continued, "there's no reason for you to wear out your tires. They all saw Mannero hand it to you. The interested party will be calling soon to claim it."

"Suppose more than one person calls. Wouldn't it be better if I had some documentary evidence?"

Paddy thought it over, unconsciously scratching his outermost chin with the ring's diamond collar. When he caught himself, he cleaned it on his sleeve and passed it over. "I'll play armchair detective for once," he said. "I'll tell you who's going to call and why.

"According to what I hear, this Marcus Pioline is something of a goat. Or, as his Greek forebears might have put it, a satyr. He had a couple of little flings at Twentieth while his wife was filming her picture, one of them with that pinup who made the little splash in *All About Eve*. Marilyn something."

"Monroe," I said.

"My guess is the ring was a gift for Monroe, or whoever followed her in the rotation. Somehow Lillian Lacey got her mitts on it. Maybe because the love interest was indiscreet enough to return it.

Lacey brought it to the party and left it in the necessary for someone else to find."

"Why?"

"To let her husband know, in a civilized English way, that the jig was up. Or to watch his reaction."

"She didn't watch," I said. "And he didn't react."

"Or you didn't catch it. Anyhow, I'm willing to back my judgment. My sawbuck against yours says that Pioline calls before you get back."

"Done," I said, ten bucks for a free afternoon being a trade I'd make anytime.

THREE

I'd told Paddy that there couldn't be many shops in greater Hollywood that carried a ring like mine, which showed how little I knew on the subject. At every place I visited, I received—in addition to the standard no—a suggestion or two on other potential stops. After a couple hours of stopping and starting again I made a mental note to apologize to Ella for all the rocks I hadn't bought her over the years. Then I received a tip that was worth something. A gossipy clerk on Wiltshire told me that another jeweler in Beverly Hills had recently put out a call for marquise diamonds of the size in question.

The jeweler's name was Ablewhite, and he had a shop in a little concourse of shops off the lobby of the Beverly Stratford, the hotel where I'd first met and danced with Ella. Ablewhite's was tucked between a gown mill that claimed to be a branch of a Paris operation and a luggage store with London in its name. They formed an interesting foil for the little jewelry store, giving it a glitter by association. Ablewhite's merchandise should have produced its own glitter, but not an earring was visible through the shop windows, which were painted black. The only variety was provided by the firm's name, done in gold leaf, and the claim beneath the name: "Established in 1927." In Californian that meant "here since the flood."

The inside of the shop was more forthcoming in that there were three lighted display cases. But the jewelry within the cases was spread so thinly that the place looked more like a museum than a salesroom. No price tags were in evidence, but the size and weight of the pieces matched the ring that was dragging down my pocket. Matched it and then some.

A buzzer had sounded when I'd entered, but no one emerged from the back of the shop until I'd had time to pass my nose over all three cases. Then a little man in a faded green jacket slipped through a black curtain. He wore black silk sleeve protectors, though it was his jacket's shoulders and collar that really needed the protecting. They were covered in dandruff. The accumulation was remarkable, given how sparse the man's white hair was. I could clearly see veins standing out all over his skull, so many that it seemed he'd put his scalp on inside out that morning.

The eyes examining *my* scalp were very sharp, despite the heavy glasses through which they were forced to work. The right lens of those glasses had something I'd never seen before, a circular magnifier ground into its lower half.

By the time I'd reached Ablewhite's, I'd had my fill of halfhearted greetings from sales help who didn't like the cut of my gabardine. So I placed the ring on a velvet pad on the center display case before I said hello.

I needn't have bothered speaking. Ablewhite—I was convinced I was dealing with the man himself and not some proxy hired for his looks—had eyes only for the ring. "Where did you get this?" he demanded, his voice as gentle on the ears as a calliope.

"You wouldn't believe me. Your work?"

"Yes. A special order. A *rush* special order. I don't understand this. It was only just delivered."

"To whom?"

Ablewhite turned his magnifier on me and reached a decision regarding my color and clarity. An unfavorable decision. "I'm not satisfied with your explanation," he said. "I think I should call the authorities."

"I haven't given you an explanation," I reminded him. "And if by authorities you mean the cops, we're old friends." I placed a business card on the case. While he was distracted by it, I plucked the ring from his hand.

"I beg your pardon," I said. "But I'd like to return this little item personally. If you tell me who it belongs to, I can do that and get home in time for *Kukla, Fran, and Ollie*."

The jeweler looked from the ring to me, figured he wasn't going to wrestle it back, and said, "The customer's name is Shaw. Mr. Sidney Shaw."

So much for Paddy's armchair work. "Mr. Shaw picked this out himself?"

"No one picked it out. I told you, it was a special order. A rush special order, phoned in two weeks ago, for a cocktail ring to match a bracelet Mr. Shaw purchased here last spring. We completed the ring and delivered it on time."

"Delivered it where?" I'd never been to Shaw's house. Of course, if Paddy was half right, the addressee wouldn't have been Mrs. Shaw. It would have been Miss Tootsie-on-the-side. But her address would have been useful too.

Ablewhite brought the count against my boss to oh-and-two by saying, "The ring was delivered to the Shaw residence."

Then he gave me an address in Pasadena. He added very specific directions for the first part of the trip, which is to say, he told me how to find the door out of his shop.

FOUR

I used one of the Stratford lobby's plush phone booths to call Hollywood Security. I wanted to take Paddy down a notch or two, but the great man was out. Peggy, who answered his line, had taken a phone message for me. From Sidney Shaw. Paddy had been right about that much. I needn't have left my desk.

"You're to call him at RKO," Peggy said. "He stressed that. At his office, not his home. I respect a man who protects his home life."

"Me too," I said.

I dialed the number Peggy had passed me, wondering how many nickels I'd have to spend before they tracked Shaw down. I'd forgotten I held the magic ring. His very stiff and very proper secretary had Shaw on the line before I'd bitten off the last T of my name.

"I guess you're wondering why I called," Shaw began, laughing nervously.

"Guess again," I said.

His laugh became a titter. "Right. I couldn't believe it when I phoned your home today and Ella told me where you worked. Hollywood Security. I never connected you with that outfit. For some reason I thought you had a position at the Santa Anita racecourse."

First in line at the betting window, I decided he meant. "About this ring."

"Right. Talk about embarrassing. My wife, Belle, is the one who left it in the Manneros' john."

"It didn't fit your wife."

"That's because it wasn't made for her. It was delivered to her by mistake."

"By whom?" I asked. I'd stacked some nickels on the ledge beneath the phone. I poked the stack now. It shifted but stood.

"A jeweler you wouldn't know. Someone from out of town. Out of state."

I poked the stack of coins again, and it tumbled over. "You order it in person?"

"No," Shaw said and hesitated for a beat. "By mail. That's how the foul-up happened. Anyway, Belle got hold of it and brought it to the party to embarrass me."

"How'd she happen to know it wasn't hers? Maybe you'd forgotten her size."

Another laugh. "No chance to try that story. The thing is, the ring matched a bracelet I'd given a certain party last spring. Belle found out about that, and there was a row. When she saw the ring, she knew. Or thought she did. But Belle's not what you'd call aggressive. So she decided to test me."

"For my money, you passed," I said, remembering his lawyerly response to the ring: "Never saw it before." I asked, "Have you talked to your wife about it?"

"Hell, no. What she only suspects won't hurt me. But I need to get that ring back before it causes any more trouble."

I offered to stop by RKO, but that was too public for Shaw. So were our offices. He read off the address of "a friend's" and asked me to meet him there sometime after six, the earliest he could possibly get away.

My car—my shiny new car—was still parked in a space down the street from the hotel. It was a Hudson Hornet, a coupe in a body style the maker called a "Hollywood hardtop." That was an innocent enough nickname, but it had caused Ella to snort with laughter on the showroom floor. The top in question was a deep blue, and the rest of the car a pearly bluish gray. Offsetting those conservative tones were the Hornet's chrome badges, which depicted an H being pierced by a runaway rocket ship. From what I'd read, this artwork wasn't making an idle boast. A fearless race driver had taken a Hornet with the stock six-cylinder all the way up to a hundred and twenty miles an hour.

I got only halfway to that speed record on my drive to the little hillside house Ella and I had recently bought, a twenties vintage fixer-upper that had, according to our war-vet real estate agent, "charm enough to piss away." I squeezed the Hornet into the hydrangea-narrowed drive and slipped in through the back door.

Ella was in the little bedroom she used as a study. She was dressed in sweatshirt and dungarees, her almost blonde hair pinned up and her bare feet on her ex-kitchen-table desk. In her lap were pages of the script she was struggling with, whose latest title was *Private Hopes*.

"The Hollywood hardtop himself," she said, her pencil still in her mouth. "To what do I owe the honor?"

"Just passing through," I said. "Where's Billy?"

"Taking his nap. Why?"

"I was thinking about that project you mentioned this morning. I thought we might make a start."

Ella's project was a second child, our son having reached the grand old age of one. "We've a problem there," she said. "Billy's sleeping in our room. He likes a change of scene."

I was partial to one myself. I gave the desk a test nudge. "This seems solid enough. Let's try it. Maybe it'll make the next guy literary."

"I'd like the next guy to be a girl," Ella said, standing. She wiggled out of the sweatshirt. Beneath it she was wearing only a rosy glow. "Think female."

"I'm on it," I said.

FIVE

The address Shaw had given me belonged to what the locals called a bungalow court, one of a collection of single-story apartments grouped around a modest courtyard. In the movies these courtyards were invariably graced by would-be starlets struggling to perfect their tans. The real-life garden belonging to 5 Charlotte Court and its neighbors was sans bathing beauties, which was understandable, the sun being knee-deep in the Pacific. Not that I would have paid much attention to any had they been present. Not after the workout Ella had given me.

She'd been so thorough that it was twenty past six when I rang number 15's electric bell. No one answered. I got an identical response on the 624 and 625 attempts.

I lit a Lucky and turned back to the courtyard. This time I did see a female, albeit a fully clothed and none too young one. She was watching me through a gap in the chintz curtains of the apartment across the way. When I caught her eye, she pulled the curtains together. I took the rejection in stride.

By then I was figuring that Shaw had been held up at the studio. So I had to decide whether to wait him out or go home, safe in the knowledge that he'd call me sooner or later. It occurred to me that, given Shaw's uncertainty about his arrival time, he might have arranged with his "friend" for me to wait inside, where I might find a comfortable chair and maybe even something wet. I rang the bell again for form's sake and then tried the knob. Sure enough, the door was unlocked.

I forgot all about my drink and my comfortable chair as soon as I stepped into the bungalow's front room. Someone had fired a gun in that room so recently that the stench of burnt powder trumped my Lucky. I tossed the cigarette over my shoulder and reached for my trusty .45 automatic. Then I remembered that I'd left it in the office so as not to spook any sensitive jewelers.

The front room's venetian blinds were closed and no lamps were burning, so the still open door behind me was providing what light there was. That meant that I was silhouetted for anyone crouching in the shadows. I stepped to my left and did a little crouching myself. No one took offense.

When my eyes adjusted to the gloom, I saw that the parlor was empty. Empty of people. In the furniture department, it was overstocked, the pieces modern and expensive-looking. The abstract paintings on the walls were also elbowing each other for space. Even the items of bric-a-brac on the built-in shelves that lined the far end of the room were less arranged than shoehorned in.

I registered all that in a glance and then moved again, still in a crouch. To my left was a small dining room that doubled as the hallway to the kitchen. I took a step that way, but my nose told me not to bother. The powder scent was fainter there.

I returned to the front room and wove my way to an open door near the crowded shelves. I could see only the top half of this opening, the bottom being shielded by an armless sofa that had nowhere better to be. I slipped around the sofa and almost tripped over two feet.

They were well-shod male feet. The male they belonged to was lying on his back, his legs in the living room with me, the rest of him in the black room beyond. I leaned over him and felt around for a wall switch. The little room I lit was a bedroom. A woman's bedroom. The man blocking its doorway was Sidney Shaw.

I noted his dull open eyes and the blood that was staining his shirt. Then a voice behind me said, "Police. Don't move."

SIX

I landed in the office of Detective Sergeant Grove, an old acquaintance of mine. And of Paddy's, on whose secret payoff Grove had once been. 'Long about his last promotion, Grove had shaken free of Hollywood Security, a trick I'd admired at the time. On this particular evening I regretted it.

"The eye-hound across the court called the police," Grove was telling me. "A little before you got there. In fact, she thought you were a cop answering her call. When you started smoking and rocking on your heels, she was let down. She's phoned me since to complain about your performance. I told her that was your wife's department. I told her that the only training you got from that crook Maguire was on shortchanging your sorry customers."

"Are you saying one of your pay packets was

light?" I asked that because we were alone and because there didn't seem to be any chance of getting on Grove's good side. From a camera's point of view, he didn't have one, his face having lost an extended bout with acne. Maybe even smallpox. He changed the oil in his wavy hair less often than I did the Hornet's and wore suits that were on the far side of sharp. "Why did this neighbor call anybody?"

Grove was still chewing on my first question. He swallowed, hard. "She heard a shot, or something that might have been a shot. None of the other near neighbors was home. Then the busybody, Miss Armine, saw someone leave number fifteen in a godawful hurry. Following which you stumbled in, just in time to tell me all about this."

He produced the ring, which the patrolmen who'd frisked me had found. The cop had kept it, maybe because it hadn't matched my ensemble, maybe on the not outlandish assumption that I'd lifted it from the jewel case in the murder room. Grove cleared me of that charge now, but in a way that told me he had his pick of others.

"The tenant of the murder apartment, a Miss Dawn Davee, has turned up. She says this ring isn't hers. But she also says it matches a certain bracelet she keeps in a safe deposit box. A present from the corpse. That raises the possibility that this ring was also a present, that you found it on Shaw and pocketed it."

Grove had me in a nice little corner. I could free myself easily, but only by telling him exactly what he wanted to know: the complete history of the ring. It was only force of habit that was keeping me from telling him, since I had no client or fee to protect. I shrugged inwardly, found my pack, and shook Grove out a cigarette that was also a white flag. I lit another for myself before carrying him, rhetorically, to the Mannero bathroom.

I ended with my appointment with Shaw. Grove said, "That fits nicely. Miss Davee tells us that Shaw asked her to catch an early movie this evening."

"Did she describe her relationship with Shaw?"

"She danced us a little dance on the subject. Comes down to, Shaw was her sugar daddy. He paid the rent on the apartment, for instance. And picked up her singing lessons. Guess he threw in the odd sparkler too." He dropped the ring on the blotter. "Glad I don't have to pay for sex."

I thought of asking him how long he'd been using self-service. Instead I inquired about the person the nosy Miss Armine had seen leaving the bungalow.

"Woman," Grove said, "bundled in a raincoat and wearing sunglasses. But definitely a blonde. That struck Armine particularly because the woman she's used to spying on, Davee, is a brunette. We're having trouble reaching the widow, Mrs. Shaw. You happen to know her?"

"We've met."

"She blonde, by any chance?"

"Blonder than Goebbels' pinups."

SEVEN

I didn't get to the office until late the next morning, as I was anticipating a lecture from Paddy on the evils of cases without retainers. I might not have gone in at all, except that I was tired of hearing from Ella about poor Belle Shaw and how I'd handed her to the police on the proverbial platter.

I was surprised to find my boss as bright and cheerful as his yellow suspenders. "How'd it go with the law?" he asked from his reclining desk chair. "They put a new spring in your step?"

"Not so you'd notice," I said.

"Sorry I wasn't home when your call came in. That Ann Sothern business heated up unexpectedly."

"Uh-huh." I was still puzzled at Paddy's good humor but too sour myself to ask about it. I hadn't taken my usual seat. I stayed standing through my report on finding Ablewhite and stumbling across Shaw. Then I made a move to leave but didn't get far.

The question Paddy stopped me with was "What are the chances of getting Mrs. Shaw off?"

"Last I heard, the cops hadn't even talked to her."

"They have since. More than talked to her. They're holding her on suspicion. So I'm wondering what we might do to help."

In my confusion, I fell back on his question of the previous morning. "What's in it for us?"

"A blank check signed by Mr. Howard Hughes, head of RKO. I just got off the phone with him. Called him on the off chance he'd take an interest in his employee's murder." Paddy laid a large finger aside his even larger nose. "Call it business sense."

"Uh-huh," I said again.

"Turns out Sidney Shaw was no favorite of Howard's. But he does have a soft spot for a damsel in distress. So I'm asking, what are the chances?"

I shrugged. "What's her alibi like? Weak, I take it."

"It would need a transfusion to get to weak. She was out driving. By herself. Seems it's a hobby of hers."

Hers and a million or so other people in greater Los Angeles. "There is something I wanted to check on, a discrepancy between Ablewhite's story and Shaw's."

"That's my boy," Paddy said. "I knew your altruism and our bottom line would come together one of these days. Go do your checking. I'll set up a meeting for you with the grieving widow as soon as Hughes's lawyers bail her out. And don't forget to record your mileage."

EIGHT

It was seven point six miles to the Stratford Hotel and Ablewhite Fine Jewels. As soon as I entered the shop, the title character emerged through the black curtains, generating dandruff at a furious rate. The cause was the morning paper he carried, which was open to the story on Shaw's murder.

"Where is it?" he demanded before the front door's buzzer had called it quits.

"It?" I asked, just to raise his soothing voice an octave.

His veiny skull fairly pulsed beneath the fringe

of hair. "The ring! It's not mentioned here. Do you still have it?"

"Sorry," I said. "It's Exhibit A." That one skipped over his glove, so I added, "The police have it."

He crushed the paper between his hands, the force surprising me.

"What's the problem?"

"Problem? That ring was purchased on account. Mr. Shaw has had an account with us for years. It currently has a large balance."

And the account holder was currently in a refrigerator. "Sorry again," I said.

"You're in the recovery business, aren't you?" Ablewhite dropped his paper and searched his pockets for my card. "You recover that ring for me, and I'll pay you a handsome fee."

Paddy would have been overjoyed. We suddenly had clients coming out of the woodwork. One was plenty for me, though. "Today I'm working for Mrs. Shaw. She's in a bigger jam than you are. If you answer a few questions for me, I know she'll be grateful. She'll do her best to settle her husband's account." Belle or her rich Uncle Howard.

"Mrs. Shaw?" Ablewhite looked accusingly at the newspaper that had let him down again.

"She'll be in this afternoon's edition. Do we have a deal?"

"What do you want to know?"

"You said Shaw ordered the ring by phone. Are you sure it wasn't by mail?" That was the discrepancy between Ablewhite's story and Shaw's. A slender thread if ever there was one.

The jeweler's old hauteur returned momentarily. "Mr. Shaw didn't order the ring by phone or by mail."

"But you said—"

"I said I took the order by telephone. But it wasn't placed by Mr. Shaw. It was done by his secretary."

Whose phone personality I'd briefly met yesterday. "The one who sounds like Margaret Dumont?"

"What?"

"Stuffy and proper."

"No," Ablewhite said. "Anything but. I believe she was chewing gum when she talked to me."

There was something wrong there, but I passed over it. I didn't want the old man to have his breakdown before I was through with him. "The bracelet that the ring matched, the one Shaw bought last spring, that was also a phone order?"

"No. Mr. Shaw picked that out in person." The jeweler tapped the display case between us.

"He have it delivered or did he take it with him?"

"The latter. He took all his purchases with him."

"Except his last one. Is that how the mistake was made? Did you send the ring to his house when you were supposed to hold it for him?"

Ablewhite was shaking his head so hard, the snow on his shoulders was threatening to drift. "I followed his instructions to the letter. His secretary's instructions. She told me exactly where to deliver that ring."

NINE

I expected Howard Hughes's lawyers to occupy the top floor of the top building in town, but they were jammed into a utilitarian suite in an old brick earthquake-survivor near the county courthouse. The room they provided for my interview with Belle Shaw was small and decorated with linoleum and a naked radiator.

It had good light, though. I was able to satisfy myself at first glance that Belle, though tired, was holding up. The pale skin of his face was sagging a little and her eyes were teary and red, but she managed a smile at the sight of me.

"Never thought I'd be seeing you again so soon," she said, as though that was the big news of the day. "How's Ella?"

"Worried about you. The legals will get you home soon. I just need to ask a few questions first. Did they explain why I'm here?"

She nodded. "Never guessed you were a guardian angel, Scotty."

"We work both sides of that street." I offered her a stick of gum from a pack I'd purchased expressly for that purpose. She declined with a weary smile. I tried a cigarette next, which she just declined. "What do you know about Dawn Davee?"

"I know she was a friend of Sidney's."

I took her hand. "The cops aren't listening in, Belle."

"Sorry. Dawn Davee was my husband's mistress.

I've known about her for a year. Suspected for a year."

"What did Shaw say about it?"

"The usual things. She didn't mean anything to him. It was just a weakness, a fling. He meant to end it. He promised me he would. I believed him. Then that awful ring came."

"Came how?"

"By messenger. To the house."

"When?"

"Early last week. Monday. The name on the package—Ablewhite—didn't mean anything to me, but I recognized their work."

"How?"

"Last summer Sidney and I were at Ciro's. Dancing. A woman on the dance floor kept staring at us. Poor Sidney was white. I realized it must be the woman my friends had been whispering to me about. Dawn Davee. She was smirking away and flashing a bracelet at me, a beautiful sapphire bracelet with diamond edging."

"What did you do?"

"Nothing. I knew that creature was trying to break up my marriage. I made up my mind then and there to save it. I thought I had. Then that awful ring came.

"Of course I knew who the ring was for and that it had come to me only by mistake. I didn't know how to ask Sidney about it. I flew up to my mother's in Spokane for a couple of days to think it out. I decided to bring it to the Mannero party. To confront Sidney in front of witnesses. But I lost my nerve. I slipped it into the powder room when I was supposed to be helping Winnie serve the coffee. Just to see how Sidney would react."

"You didn't call me to get the ring back," I observed.

"I never wanted to see it again."

We talked about her alibi next. It turned out she always went driving when Shaw called to say he'd be late. She couldn't stand to be cooped up at home, she told me, not when she suspected that her husband was with Davee. She could remember last night's route only vaguely. She hadn't stopped for gas, hadn't spoken to anyone who might remember her.

I asked if her husband knew about these drives of hers.

"Yes. I told him all about them. I wanted him to feel guilty. Guess I should have taken up drinking instead."

"What can you tell me about the shooting?"

"Nothing. Except that I didn't do it. I wouldn't even know how to find Dawn Davee's apartment."

TEN

I knew how to find that apartment, but I had no reason to go back there. Its resident had temporarily relocated to a motel nearer the edge of town. Halfway to Burbank, in fact. I'd picked that tidbit up by keeping my ears open during my time in Detective Sergeant Grove's office. I found my way to the motel now, after advising Belle Shaw to get some sleep.

The motel was called the Los Encantos, though

there was nothing particularly Spanish about it. It
wasn't old, but it had a worn quality. I wondered
if it was a hideaway GIs had used during the war,
those lucky enough to have found sentimental
women. That kind of traffic used up a place in a
hurry. Then I wondered if Davee had picked the
motel because she had fond memories from those
days, which was too much wondering altogether.

Davee answered my knock in a genuine hurry.
As advertised, she was a petite brunette, petite everywhere but in the eyes, which were brown with
golden flecks and lashes as long as a first mortgage.
The eyes weren't unfriendly, not yet. I identified
myself as the man who had found Sidney Shaw.

"You're the guy with the ring," Davee said.

"And you're the lady without it."

"Without more than that, big boy. What do
you want?"

There was no need for me to repeat the offer of
gum I'd made to Belle. Davee was chewing her
own, with a practiced motion. It was gin-flavored,
to judge from her breath.

"I could stand a drink."

"Haven't got any. So what's it about? We're letting the flies in."

"I came to ask you why you had that ring delivered to Mrs. Shaw." That stopped the chewing
cold. "Now can I have my drink?"

Davee turned her back on me and reentered her
combination bedroom and parlor. I followed, shut-
ting the door on any flies who hadn't already gotten
in. My hostess walked to the dresser and retrieved
a full glass, saying, "Help yourself."

She was stalling with that offer, playing for time

in which to organize an answer. But that was okay by me. I'd fired off my one and only big gun, so I needed a little regrouping time too.

My guess about Davee and the ring had been suggested by several things, Shaw's hesitation on the phone over how the ring had been ordered and the bad guess he'd come up with being two of them. Shaw hadn't known a thing about his very generous gift until he'd seen it at the Manneros'. His "secretary" had come up with the whole idea herself, right down to the delivery instructions. Belle and I had both assumed the ring had found its way to her by mistake, but it hadn't. Ablewhite had given me that piece. He'd also slipped me a clue or two on the true identity of the person who'd placed the order.

A bottle of Booth's stood next to a bucket of melting ice on the dresser. I looked around for vermouth and onions without much hope before pouring a little of the gin into the guest tumbler.

Davee, seated on the bed, hadn't used the intermission as productively. The comeback she fired off when I turned to her was "I don't know what you're talking about."

"Give it up, Dawn. Ablewhite will identify you as the woman who phoned him. He's so anxious to have somebody pay for that ring, he'd finger Margaret Truman. You don't even have to tell me why you sent it to Belle, not if you don't want to. She told me herself. You were trying to break up her marriage."

"What marriage?" Davee asked. "That hadn't been a marriage for years. She hadn't been a wife to Sid for years."

"Then why didn't he leave her?"

"Because he was a man. All she had to do was sniff and a month's hard work by me was out the window. He was going to leave her, though. He promised me. And I take a promise like that very seriously. All he needed was a little push.

"That's why I sent the ring. I figured she'd blow up and that would be that."

"Instead of which, what happened?"

"You're asking me? I guess I pushed too hard. So she shot him. Now we're both out a husband."

"I meant, what happened before Shaw got shot?" She lifted her now empty glass and didn't answer. "He must have known right away who'd sent that ring and why. Was he sore? Did he threaten to end it with you?"

"Drink up and get out," Davee said. "On second thought, just get out."

ELEVEN

I phoned in my report to Hollywood Security, figuring Howard Hughes might be antsy for an update. Time was crucial, as it turned out, but for another reason.

"Good work," Paddy said when I'd told him about the ring's real origin. "I'll pass that on to Grove right away."

"Wait a minute. I'm not ready to go to the police yet. There's a lot to work out."

"We've no time, Scotty. I've heard from a bosom chum downtown that the police are close to clearing Belle Shaw all by themselves. We've got to get our oar wet, or Mr. Hughes may decide he didn't need us after all."

I went home unsatisfied with the state of the world and stayed that way all night. The next day we learned that the police were questioning Dawn Davee, but no one, not even Paddy's well-paid "bosom chum," could tell us whether our information or some other break was behind it.

I was home that evening, playing with Billy on the living room rug, when the front bell rang. Ella called out "doorbell" from the kitchen, either so Billy would make the connection or I'd get moving.

The caller was Detective Sergeant Grove, though I had to look twice to be sure, as there was something different about him. He'd left his cocky attitude at the office, I decided.

He looked at Billy, wiggling on the floor, like he'd never seen a baby before. "Yours?" he asked.

"I hope that wasn't a crack," I said. And then, "Relax, I was making a joke. Come in."

He did and even sat down, but he kept his hat on. "Thought you might want to hear about our big break," he said. "The one that got the Shaw woman off."

I poured a little bourbon in a glass and passed it over. "I would at that."

"We found the murder weapon. That is, a helpful citizen found it and turned it in. Restaurant owner whose joint is a couple blocks from Davee's apartment. It was in one of his garbage cans. A thirty-eight, older than this house of yours."

"How'd he happen to find it?"

"A customer called about a lost purse. Some busboy was sent out to check the garbage and turned up the gun."

"Traced it?"

"Not yet," Grove said in a tone that told me he wasn't holding his breath. I wouldn't have either.

"So why was finding that good news for Belle?"

"It was what the gun was wrapped in. Namely a blonde wig. That's bothered me from the start. I mean, why does a dame go to the trouble of bundling up in a raincoat and wearing sunglasses but leave her hundred-watt hair hanging out in the breeze? The wig's the answer. She wanted that yellow hair to be seen."

"She who?"

"Thanks to your legwork, we're figuring Dawn Davee. She tried her stunt with the ring, it cost her her future with Shaw, so she killed him. And she did it in a way that would point to the woman she hated, the one who'd beaten her. If what Maguire told us—you told us—is right, Davee could have learned about Mrs. Shaw's habit of going driving from Shaw's pillow talk. If so, she knew framing the wife would be easy."

"What about Davee's own alibi? Wasn't she at the movies?"

"Yeah. Cary Grant movie, *People Will Talk*. None of the theater staff remember her, but they wouldn't, even if she actually put in an appearance. The show she claims to have gone to was packed."

"She admit any of this?"

"The ring business. Not the killing. I'd really like to trace that wig. It had a maker's label in it once, but someone tore it out. I've had men making calls on shops all day. Nothing so far."

"This is Hollywood. The studios have more wigs than the House of Lords."

"The house of whose? This wasn't what you'd call studio quality, but we've started inquiries in that direction too."

Ella entered then and asked Grove if he'd stay for dinner. He reacted as though she'd asked if he'd ever considered adoption, gulping down his drink and bolting for the door.

On the front step I asked, "Did the busboy find the missing purse?"

"No," Grove said. "Lady called back to say she'd found it herself."

I was still thinking of that a few hours later as Ella and I lay in bed. As she lay in bed and I tossed on it.

"Scotty," she finally said.

"Am I keeping you up?"

"Are you kidding? You're keeping the whole neighborhood up."

I padded into the living room, smoked a Lucky, and then dialed Paddy's home number. If he'd been asleep, he shook it off quickly.

"What's the matter, Scotty?"

"Know anyone in Spokane?"

"I did in my vaudeville days. A theater owner who didn't heat his dressing rooms."

"I mean someone in our line of work."

"What's this concerning?"

"The Shaw murder. A new development."

"We haven't received Mr. Hughes's check yet. Is this development likely to please him?"

"Depends on how he feels about brunettes."

Paddy's sigh woke the neighborhood again.

TWELVE

Late the following afternoon the Hornet and I drove out to Pasadena, to an address I'd been given by Ablewhite way back at the beginning of the business. The front door of the residence I found, a big late model colonial, was opened by a maid. She showed me into a room where Belle Shaw was seated at a desk, writing. Answering condolence notes from friends, I thought. Maybe even one from Ella.

Belle was dressed in black, a color I'd never liked on a blonde. I liked it even less on her.

"Scotty! What brings you here? News?"

"Yes," I said. "Bad news. We found the shop in Spokane where you bought the wig. Not all that many to check up there. Shopkeeper remembered a woman who bought one to match her own hair. She told him she was going to have hers cut off for an operation. Broke his heart."

Belle was every bit as collected as she'd been in the lawyers' offices. More so, as her eyes were dry and clear. She was thinking of that office visit too. "I shouldn't have mentioned Spokane to you downtown. But I was afraid you'd remember me telling Ella about it at the party."

"I would have," I consoled her. "Sooner or later."

"What are the odds of the man who found the ring being a detective? Sidney told me you were some kind of lounge lizard. You don't look like one to me."

"Thanks," I said. "Speaking of the party, you didn't bring the ring there to confront your husband. You wanted it seen publicly. Handed over to the police even. So it would always be at the center of the mystery, a clue that would eventually point to Dawn Davee."

Belle nodded. "I saw her hand in that from the start. It was her all over: all brass and no brains. I thought I could make her gamble work for me, but I wasn't sure how. I went to Spokane to think, like I told you."

And came back with a wig and a gun and a plan. I restated what she'd told me so I'd be sure I understood it: "The ring business didn't drive you to shoot your husband. It only gave you an opportunity. A way to kill Shaw and send Davee up for it."

"I didn't need driving," Belle said. "I was sick to death of his lies and empty promises. You saw that woman's apartment. She was furnishing a house. His house. It was only a matter of time until she got it. I saw to it that she never would."

"Afterward you dumped the wig and the gun at the restaurant. Later, when you were out on bail, you called the place about a missing purse."

"I had to make sure someone found them. Otherwise, I was only setting myself up."

From where I stood, it looked a lot like she had anyway.

Belle was still anxious for comments, just as Lillian Lacey had been after her movie's preview. "The purse business was too much, wasn't it? I should have gambled that the ring and the gun would be found without it."

"Stashing them together was bad all by itself," I

said. "Only someone who wanted the murder to look like a frame would do that."

The front bell rang, the sound reaching us as an echo's echo. "Sergeant Grove?" Belle asked.

"Yes."

"To think, I called you a guardian angel."

And I'd warned her that I worked both sides of that street. I didn't feel up to reprising the line now.

Belle stood up. "I'll get my hat."

THIRTEEN

The next day I got a call from Old Man Ablewhite. He was in his usual snit.

"You told me this Mrs. Shaw would pay me for the ring. Mrs. Shaw, who's been arrested again. Who's going to pay me now?"

Paddy had been asking me the same question all morning. In the jeweler's case, I was able to make a practical suggestion. "Call the district attorney. Maybe you'll get the ring back by and by."

"I'd rather have my money," Ablewhite said, by which he meant his markup. "Who'll want that ring now?"

Who indeed. Who had ever wanted it, really? But that was getting us too close to philosophy.

"I'd try fishermen," I said. "Seems it's surefire bait."

He thanked me politely and hung up.

THE LITIGANTS
AN ALO NUDGER STORY
by John Lutz

John Lutz is a past president of PWA. He has two series
P.I.'s, the St. Louis–based Nudger series and the Florida-
based Carver series. His Nudger story "What You Don't
Know Can't Hurt You" won the Shamus for Best P.I. Short
Story in 1983, the year of that award's inception. Later, his
Carver novel *Kiss* won the award for Best Novel in 1989. He
has been nominated for Best Short Story three other times.

"The Litigants" is a Nudger story which John wrote with
tongue firmly in cheek.

Nudger thought there was no good reason why
Lawrence Fleck should be alive. The pugna-
cious little attorney in the cheap chalk-stripe black
suit, the cockeyed toupee, and the surrounding
aroma of cut-rate, cloying cologne stood with his
fists on his hips in front of Nudger's desk and
glared down at him.

When Nudger merely stared back, Fleck picked
up his coat from where he'd tossed it on a chair,
brushed it off, then folded it and laid it over the
chair's arm, where it might stay cleaner. It was
made of some kind of mottled, curly fur Nudger
had never seen before. Fleck glanced around and
scrunched up his bulldog face as if he'd just inhaled

a bug. "You got an office looks like a rat hole, Nudger."

"Now that you walked in."

Fleck snorted contemptuously in his best courtroom manner—his only courtroom manner. "We got business to discuss. I'm here to hire you."

"I don't work for ambulance chasers."

"You're listening but you're not hearing, Nudger. Just like always. I said the word hire. That means the word money. Exactly what losers like you need."

Hmm. Nudger knew Fleck was right about that last part. Nudger's former wife, Eileen, had joined a militant feminist group called WOO—Women on the Offensive—whose pro bono lawyer was planning on dragging Nudger back into court to attach damages onto his alimony payments. Eileen and her attorney were claiming that Nudger was responsible for the marriage's failure, which deprived Eileen of children in her prime fertile years, for which deprivation Nudger should pay compensation. Sort of nonchild-support payments. The attorney, a truly frightening woman named Shirley Knott, was attempting to make history with this test case by establishing legal precedent. Important new ground might be broken. She'd chosen Nudger for her plow.

"Money up front?" Nudger asked.

"A little way back," Fleck said with a shrug. "There's a big settlement waiting to happen in this case, and when I get my money you'll get yours."

"I can't eat pie in the sky," Nudger said. "But maybe we can barter. Trade services."

Fleck looked suspicious, dishonest, tempted.

"We wouldn't have to claim income on our tax returns . . ." he said thoughtfully.

"It'd be a wash anyway," Nudger pointed out, "but it would still be fun not to claim it. Tell me why you want to hire me, then I'll tell you about someone named Shirley Knott. I think you two should meet."

"Here's the deal," Fleck said, pacing with short, lurching strides and flailing his arms for emphasis as he talked. "Client named Arty Mason comes to me, says a woman ran into his old Chevy. She's driving a Mercedes, barely gets scratched. Just about totals Arty's car, he says."

"What do you mean, 'he says'? Have you seen the car, the estimates for repairs?"

"All that stuff," Fleck said with a backhanded wave of dismissal. "There are some questions from the insurance company as to how old a lot of the damages are, but that's insignificant. In fact, the whole accident might be insignificant, because Arty tells me the collider came to him and offered to pay fifteen hundred dollars straight to him, leave the insurance companies and any sort of police accident report out of it."

"Collider?"

"Legal term, Nudger. *She* ran into *him.* Collider's this bit of eye candy named Nora Bosca."

" 'Eye Candy' is a legal term, too, I guess. Nora Bosca was driving the other car?"

"What I said. You were listening but not hearing again, Nudger. I advised my client not to accept the collider's offer. Know why?"

"Sure. She was a wealthy woman who might have

something to hide. So you and this Arty might be able to extort money from her."

Fleck backed away as if slapped and glared down at Nudger with nostrils flared. "That's an insult to me and my profession, and coming from a cheap keyhole peeper."

"Did it work?"

"Yes. She came across with five thousand. Arty said no to that, too, so she gave him ten thousand. Plenty angry about it, though. I don't think we could have gotten any more."

"Seems like the end of the case," Nudger said.

"It was, until Arty's back started acting up because of the accident. A week ago we filed against Nora Bosca for medical expenses."

"I'm not surprised. You got greedy and figured out a way to go back for seconds."

"Don't be so judgmental, Nudger. I'm sworn to get all I can for my client. And you oughta see poor Arty. He can barely get around. Wears a brace."

When someone's looking, Nudger thought.

"But you're right," Fleck said. "I figured the rich babe'd come around with more money, ask us to drop the charges. But she hasn't, and we haven't heard from her attorney." Fleck scratched his head, moving his bargain toupee another half inch toward his right ear. "What I got is guys watching me, I think. Following me."

"You think?"

"It's just an inkling, I admit. But Arty called me yesterday. He's got the same inkling. I—we figured it'd be smart to hire somebody to look into this, see what's happening."

"See if that somebody gets beaten to a pulp or

killed," Nudger said, "so you'd know for sure something serious is going on."

"It could occur like that," Fleck admitted. "Are those pigeons over there on that ledge?" He was staring out the window at the building across the street.

Fleck knew he hated pigeons and was trying to divert the conversation away from personal injury at the hands of thugs unknown. "I'd rather not be hurt or killed," Nudger said.

"Goes without saying. How come they don't fly south in the winter like other birds? You'd think something smart as a pigeon would know to do that."

Nudger considered calling off the deal. Then he thought about Eileen. About Shirley Knott. He shuddered. Both women were natural colliders.

"I'm supposed to give a deposition tomorrow," he said to Fleck. "You're coming with me."

At three the next afternoon, Nudger and Fleck sat side by side at a large mahogany table in a legal office across the street from the county courthouse. On the walls were framed photographs of Old West scenes. Some of them were shots of public hangings.

"They rent these rooms for depositions," Fleck whispered knowledgeably to Nudger.

A court stenographer was seated at the end of the table. The door opened and the despicable Henry Mercado, Eileen's divorce lawyer and live-in lover, entered with Shirley Knott. Mercado nodded at Nudger and smiled. Even Nudger knew he was there not just as a witness but to share Nudger's confidence.

Shirley Knott was a small, erect woman in a severely tailored purple suit. She was wearing a white blouse with a man's tie that had on it what to Nudger looked like a design of tiny swastikas. Her black hair was combed in a high arc above a wide forehead and piercing dark eyes. Her features were harsh and symmetrical, with bloodless, thin lips set in a straight, thin line. Had those lips ever kissed or smiled?

She sat down across from Fleck and said, "You bastard! Is that real fur?"

Fleck looked down at his cheap, mottled coat draped over the chair near him. "Of course not. I'd only wear synthetic fur. I'm a recovering hunter."

Pretty nifty, Nudger thought. Fleck did have a survivor's quick instincts.

Formality took over. All present gave names and addresses to the court stenographer, and the deposition began.

"Remember you're under oath," Shirley Knott told Nudger. "Any of your lies will come back to haunt you."

Nudger looked over at Fleck.

"She's right," Fleck said.

"You were the one in the marriage who didn't want children, Mr. Nudger?"

"It was a joint decision. I was a cop and I—"

"So that's why you alone decided?"

"No! We agreed to wait."

"And there was a period of . . . dysfunction on your part?"

Nudger glanced at the court stenographer, a prim

woman in her sixties. She was staring silently over the rims of her glasses at him. "Temporary. Only temporary. I was distressed because of a shooting incident. I've hated guns ever since."

"Sometimes a gun isn't a gun, Mr. Nudger. Don't you agree?"

Nudger looked at Fleck. "What does she mean?"

"Technically anything with grooves inside the barrel isn't a gun. Legal terminology, splitting hairs. I object to the question. It's irrelevant."

"*You* are irrelevant," Shirley Knott told Nudger's attorney.

The deposition went downhill from there.

Still trembling with anger and humiliation, from both the deposition and his argument with Fleck afterward in the parking lot, Nudger drove across town to talk with the aggrieved and litigious Arty Mason.

Mason opened the door to his low-rent apartment and ushered Nudger in. He was a wizened little guy about fifty, wearing wrinkled blue pajamas. On his feet were gray fuzzy slippers that were supposed to look like rabbits, only the head was missing from the one on his right foot. He was moving with difficulty because of some kind of aluminum brace attached to his back. Nudger was suspicious of the brace. It was held together with adhesive tape and looked like something made from parts of a disassembled walker. It was, in fact, the only back brace Nudger had ever seen that had a wheel.

"How's the back?" Nudger asked, watching Mason lower himself sideways into a chair.

"Pure agony," he said, wincing with pain. "I gotta lie flat or wear this thing." Nudger could see beyond him into the bedroom. The bed was made and unruffled.

Mason answered all Nudger's questions politely and through a grimace, pretty much substantiating what Fleck had said about the accident.

"What makes you think you and Fleck are being watched?" Nudger asked, folding the sheet of paper he was taking notes on and slipping it into his pocket.

Mason looked undeniably afraid. "Listen, Nudger, I used to work for a guy who ran a gambling joint, before the state horned in on the business. I know when I got the orange mark on me."

"Orange mark?"

"Like on a tree when it's scheduled to be chopped down."

Nudger swallowed. He'd never heard that one. "You think somebody's going to try to kill you?"

Mason nodded. "I know the signs. Somebody's tailing me, watching, sizing up the best place and time to act. Believe me, I know exactly how it's done."

Nudger stared at him. "Do you know about this because you've done the same thing yourself?"

"I done lots of things in my misguided youth," Mason said noncommittally.

Good Lord! Nudger thought. *What has Fleck got me into?*

He couldn't help checking his rearview mirror every few seconds as he drove away from his meeting with Mason.

On Grand Avenue he stopped at White Castle

and bought some of their little square hamburgers in a takeout sack, then went to Claudia's South Side apartment. Over an aromatic lunch of hamburgers, French fries, and an old bottle of refrigerated wine Nudger had uncapped, he discussed the case with Claudia. She loved him. She would understand and perhaps offer some advice.

When he was finished talking, she said, "There might be something to this nonchild-support idea."

"I was thinking, is somebody going to try to kill me over this?" Nudger said.

Claudia slowly tore a corner of bun off her last hamburger, then poked it in her mouth and chewed thoughtfully. "The ticking biological clock . . ."

"Just because lots of divorced women say they wasted the best years of their lives on their ex-husbands doesn't mean they're owed money," Nudger said.

"And 'What do I have to show for it?' "

"Huh?"

"That's the rest of what women say about those wasted years, the question they ask. Especially if they don't even have children. Maybe they *should* be compensated for all that lost time, have something to show for it. I don't see why the ability to bear children couldn't be viewed legally as a diminishing asset."

Nudger was getting frustrated. There was a disconnect here. "Right now I'm thinking I could have the orange mark on me. I might have to defend myself at some point. I'm wondering if I should go to the safety deposit box and get my gun."

"They wouldn't necessarily need to have been married," Claudia said.

My God! Nudger thought.

He took a swig of wine. Years ago he'd saved Claudia from suicide. She was emotionally delicate and might go to see her psychiatrist, Dr. Oliver. As far as Nudger was concerned, Dr. Oliver caused more problems than he solved. From time to time he advised Claudia to see men other than Nudger in order to achieve self-actualization. Nudger wasn't sure what self-actualization was. He thought Claudia was actual. He should never have told her about Shirley Knott and WOO. Fleck should never have told him about Arty Mason and the collider. But Nudger had. Fleck had. Nudger was knee-deep in it.

Maybe sinking.

The next morning Nudger decided to follow Nora Bosca.

He sat parked in his old Ford Granada where he could watch the luxury condo on Hanley Road that matched the address Fleck had given him. His assumption was that eventually the Mercedes would exit the underground garage.

A woman emerged from the building and strode to a nearby parking lot. She was eye candy even if she wasn't Nora Bosca, tall, mink-coated and blond, with a model's way of walking that drew stares.

And she was Nora Bosca. A few minutes after she'd disappeared, a late-model black Mercedes with her license number turned north from the lot onto Hanley. The big car's right front fender was dented, but not badly. It hadn't taken much to total Mason's old Chevy.

Nudger started the Granada and chugged along behind the gliding Mercedes in heavy traffic.

Nora Bosca didn't drive far, only to the Flam Building on Meramec Avenue, which Nudger knew housed a million lawyers, all of them more expensive and effective than Lawrence Fleck.

He trailed along behind her when she entered the building; then he rode the elevator with her and three other women to the fifth floor. Nudger stepped out of the elevator when Nora Bosca did. He walked fifteen paces, pretended to have forgotten something, and turned around just in time to see her enter the offices of Gird and Gird, Attorneys at Law.

Nudger went back to his car and waited. It had become colder and the sky was spitting a combination of snow and sleet. The Granada's heater was keeping the interior warm, but the windshield kept fogging up on the inside where the wipers couldn't help.

If Nora Bosca came out of the Flam Building within the next two hours, Nudger missed seeing her. The gas gauge was almost on empty now, and he was getting drowsy. Exhaust leaks were a worry in the old car. He decided to give up on tailing Nora Bosca, at least for today, and drove to his office.

Before going upstairs, he ducked into Danny's Donuts, which was located directly below his office, and asked his ersatz receptionist Danny if anybody had been by to see him.

Danny, who was wearing a greasy white apron and his usual basset hound expression, was alone in the shop, standing behind the stainless steel counter and reading a newspaper. The place smelled cloyingly of baked sugar, as did Nudger's office, as did Nudger. Sometimes women thought he was wearing cologne and were repelled.

"Big guy looked something like a horse," Danny said, "wearing an expensive suit. 'Bout an hour ago. Didn't leave his name. Didn't have to."

"Why's that? You recognize him?"

"Recognized him as trouble, Nudge. You best be careful."

"Did he leave a message?"

"Said he'd be back, is all."

"Anything else about him?"

"Breathed through his mouth instead of his nose. That kinda guy. That kinda nose." Danny's gaze slid to the fresh-baked lineup of Dunker Delites laying like feces on white butcher paper in the display case. "You had lunch?"

"Sure did," Nudger said, moving toward the door. "Thanks anyway."

"You best be careful, Nudge," Danny repeated, and went back to reading the sports pages spread out on the counter before him.

Nudger chewed an antacid tablet as he entered through the street door next to the doughnut shop and climbed the creaking wood stairs to his office. The higher he climbed the warmer he got, until he entered the office, which was cold. The radiator was malfunctioning again.

He kicked the old iron radiator, then swiveled its valve handle. It hissed angrily at him. Leaving his coat on, he sat at his desk, slid the phone over to him, and called Police Lieutenant Jack Hammersmith at the Third District station house. Hammersmith had been Nudger's partner years ago when they were uniformed officers in the St. Louis Police Department. That was before Nudger's nervous stomach and fear of guns had proved to be career obstacles and led to his present occupation.

"I need a favor, Jack," Nudger said when finally he was put through to Hammersmith.

"Couple of hundred," Hammersmith said.

"I don't need money, Jack."

"I didn't mean money. I meant that when you ask for a favor, you always wind up asking for a couple of hundred more of them."

"I want to give you a woman's name. Also her car's license number. I'd like to know more about her. She was involved in a simple fender bender and offered to settle out of court with Lawrence Fleck's client rather than draw any attention from the police or courts."

"Fleck the lawyer? Why do you keep getting mixed up with that little ferret?"

"So I don't have to borrow money from you, Jack."

"Hmm. Give me details."

Nudger did.

"I can tell you a lot without even checking," Hammersmith said when Nudger was finished. "Gird and Gird is a mob-connected law firm. And Nora Bosca is the widow of Manny Boscanarro."

Nudger gripped the receiver harder and sat back in his desk chair. The old radiator was hissing and clanking loudly now as if laughing uproariously at him, hurling heat into the room. He unbuttoned his coat. "Manny Boscanarro the drug czar?"

"The same, Nudge."

Six months ago Boscanarro's body had been found stuffed in a trash can, minus arms and legs. It took a while to identify him. Plastic surgery had been attempted and botched. He still looked enough like his old self for a rival drug cartel to recognize him and kill him. And for narcotics detectives and his wife, Nora, to identify him. The killer or killers were still at large.

"The widow didn't seem too broke up over his death," Hammersmith said. "Just enough sentimentality to ask for the expensive gold chain and engraved heart the corpse was wearing as a necklace."

"That could explain the guy who looked like a horse . . ."

"Don't know who he'd be," Hammersmith said, "but I'd bet he's dangerous."

"Speaking of dangerous," Nudger said, "you ever heard of WOO?"

"Who?"

"WOO."

"Haven't a clue. He a Chinese gangster or something?"

"Never mind," Nudger said.

"I do know Fleck might not be dealing straight with you. If you're mixed up with Nora Bosca and Fleck, be extra careful."

Nudger swallowed an antacid tablet almost whole. "I always am."

"Sometimes to the point of paralysis," Hammersmith said, and hung up the phone.

Nudger kept the receiver to his ear, depressed the phone's cradle button, then called Fleck and filled him in on the day's activities.

"Don't believe everything Hammersmith tells you," Fleck said. "He's a cop. They got their own agenda."

"There's something in your voice. You sound scared."

"I am. So should you be, Nudger. It's unhealthy to be involved with drug criminals or their widows. But it could explain why Arty and I are being watched. Somebody probably wonders why the grieving widow's seeing a lawyer. I'm gonna call Arty and tell him we better drop the case."

"Count me out, too."

"Hah! You can't quit. You owe me, my friend. Remember, we're bartering here. I need to know for sure. I want you to find out exactly who's on my tail. Just like we agreed. Don't you recall me representing you during that deposition?"

"I recall you were in the room," Nudger said.

"Well, I got some other info for you. Listen *and* hear, Nudger. I met with Shirley Knott and found out Eileen's been examined by a doctor who's willing to testify she's forty percent fertile."

"Forty percent what? I don't understand."

"She's medically certified to be sixty percent less capable of achieving pregnancy than when she was married to you. The other side's got itself an expert witness."

"What's all that mean?" Nudger asked, befuddled.

"Means a whole lot of nonchild support, my friend."

Nudger sank lower into his chair. He was sweating, full of woe, cursing WOO. "I already pay alimony," he said numbly. "Why should I have to pay for children? We never even had any children."

"That's precisely the point. Didn't you *hear,* Nudger?"

Nudger wanted to kill Fleck.

"We still bartering, Nudger?"

"Still are," Nudger said wearily. "Have you noticed a guy hanging around who looks something like a horse?"

"What kind of horse?"

"Dammit! What difference does it make?"

"Well, a thoroughbred would be a tall, lean guy. A quarter horse or Shetland pony—"

"A big, mean horse!" Nudger said.

"No," Fleck said thoughtfully. "I noticed a guy you might say looked a lot like an ox."

"Are you insane?"

"No, and I'm a better lawyer than you think, Nudger. You'll see. I'm going to help you. But you've gotta keep working hard for me or—"

Nudger slammed down the receiver.

He fled from the sweatbox office and drove down Manchester to Citizen's Bank, where he reluctantly withdrew his old service revolver from his safety deposit box.

After a late breakfast the next day he decided to drive to Fleck's office and look the Napoleonic little lawyer in the eye when they talked about Arty Mason's suit against Nora Bosca, and about Eileen's claim for nonchild support.

Fleck's office was in a small strip shopping center. It was sandwiched between a dollar store and a place called Hot Plants, which sold indoor and outdoor decorative plastic foliage.

Nudger had parked and was about to get out of the Granada when he saw Fleck and Shirley Knott emerge from Fleck's office. Fleck was wearing an obviously vinyl jacket today. Shirley was bundled in blue denim with studs all over it. Nudger watched them walk together to a restaurant at the far end of the shopping strip. Fleck politely held the door open for Shirley Knott. They were probably going to have their idea of a power breakfast. Probably going to talk about Nudger. The prospect nauseated him so that he climbed back into his car. He sat for a while, sucking but not chewing an antacid tablet until the sizable chalky disk was completely dissolved. It brought some relief, though not much.

The notion of joining two of the most contemptible people he'd ever met was out of the question.

Who Nudger wanted to see was Claudia. Maybe he could meet her somewhere for coffee and they could talk. Maybe they could go to her apartment afterward.

When he called from a public phone just inside the entrance of a supermarket, she was cool to his invitation.

"Is something wrong?" Nudger asked.

"*Very* wrong. I don't think we should see each other for a while, Nudger."

His stomach seemed to be devouring his other organs. This was pain. "Have you gone back to Dr. Oliver?"

"Far from it. I've begun to realize he's the one who's caused most of my problems. His advice to see other men so I might attain self-actualization, the sedatives that dulled my senses, the long sessions that went nowhere productive . . ."

Nudger was heartened.

"I sought other advice and I've decided to sue Dr. Oliver," Claudia said firmly.

Nudger was shocked. "He's an established medical professional, Claudia. He has malpractice insurance, squads of lawyers. You can't afford to sue Oliver."

"I have help, Nudger. I've joined WOO."

"We need to talk."

"We shouldn't, under the circumstances. It would be legally unwise for both of us."

"Claudia—"

"I'm sorry, Nudger, but I have to learn who I am to be who I am. I'm confident I'll find I'm a better person, one who I know I can be."

"What on earth does that mean? I know who you are. You're the woman who likes—"

She hung up.

He stood traumatized. He turned right. He turned left. He didn't know where to turn next. Finally he decided to seek solace in his work. He'd stake out the condo and follow Nora Bosca again. He would be doing his job, holding up his end of his agreement with Fleck. This was what it had come down to. This was all he had. Driven by obligation and dismay, he got his legs moving so he was lurching toward the automatic doors, dodging grocery carts and cursing his stars.

*　　*　　*

The big Mercedes with the dented fender nosed like a prowling shark out of the underground garage this time. Nudger thought Nora Bosca was going to take the same route today and visit her attorney. Instead she turned left on Delmar, then took the Inner Belt north. Nudger swiped at the Granada's windshield with one of his old undershirts that he used as a rag, aiding the defrosters as he stayed behind the Mercedes in heavy traffic.

The sleek black car exited on Natural Bridge, then turned down a side street and pulled into the parking lot of a small motel near the airport. Nudger parked near the entrance and watched the Mercedes drive to the far end of the lot and stop almost out of sight next to a large dented green Dumpster. He felt like the cheap peeper Fleck had called him, aware that his metabolism had picked up. Something was happening here, all right. And some part of him was enjoying it.

Large snowflakes started to fall, obscuring his vision. Also Nora Bosca's. Nudger got out of his car and unobtrusively walked parallel to the front of the motel, staying away from the office. Then he moved along a row of parked cars until he was out of sight of the Mercedes. He crouched behind a red pickup truck.

Nora Bosca had gotten out of her car. She strode into Nudger's line of sight, kicking out with her long legs and fur-topped boots, glancing around furtively. Nudger ducked low and watched over the truck's hood. The door opened as she arrived. She didn't even have to break stride before she was inside the room and out of sight.

But Nudger had seen enough.

He drove to a phone and called Hammersmith, then returned to the motel through the driving snow.

There were so many red lights blinking there it looked like the place was on fire.

The county police wouldn't let him get close until Hammersmith arrived, sirens screaming, in the first of two major case squad units. He nodded to Nudger and they walked toward the motel room Nora Bosca had entered. Its door was wide open and people were packed into the room. Thick uniform coats made everyone look bulky and immovable. When Nudger and Hammersmith were five feet from the door, they were stopped by a big man in a blue parka who flashed a badge and said he was Captain Farmington of the county police and he was in charge. The corpulent Hammersmith, bulkiest of the bulky in his tentlike camel-hair coat, puffed up even larger and said this was a major case squad investigation and he was the officer in charge. Two deadpan guys in identical tan trench coats arrived and said they were FBI and they were in charge. There was a lot of arguing and shoving, and it seemed somebody from all three units took part in hustling Manny Boscanarro and his wife, Nora, to a waiting unmarked Pontiac with tinted windows and a stubby antenna on its trunk. They were the only ones without coats.

*   *   *

"But Boscanarro was found dead!" Fleck said incredulously.

They were in Nudger's office. The radiator was working okay for a change, and the winter sun was brilliant through the half-melted sheet of ice on the window. "You're listening but you're not hearing," Nudger told Fleck. "The plastic surgery job on the dead man in the trash barrel wasn't actually botched. It was made to seem that way, done on some poor guy who resembled Manny Boscanarro enough that he'd pass for him with a botched face-lift. Since the victim's arms had been cut off, there were no fingerprints. And Boscanarro had no dental records in this country. Six people identified the body, even his wife. And she claimed a gold necklace with their names engraved on it."

Fleck started to pace, grinning and flailing his pudgy little arms. "Well, I'll be flamboozled!"

"Wouldn't be the first time," Nudger said.

"Our barter deal worked out just fine!" he said.

"For you," Nudger told him.

"You too, my friend!" Fleck said triumphantly. "Shirley has advised Eileen to drop the nonchild-support case."

Nudger was astounded. "*Shirley Knott* did that?"

Fleck actually looked embarrassed. "I persuaded her. Or we persuaded each other. We've uh, become close. Neither of us planned on it, but it happened."

There truly is someone for everyone, Nudger thought. Wolf and gray wolf.

"What about WOO?" he asked. "What about making legal history?"

"Shirley and I are preparing to press another historic case, this time in the field of animal rights."

"What animals?"

"Primates, specifically."

"Primates don't have legal rights."

"*You* are a primate, Nudger."

That gave Nudger pause.

"The Constitution refers to men only," Fleck continued, "but obviously women are also meant to enjoy its rights and protections. Who's to say that women are the only primates excluded by the literal language? It's the kind of legal technicality that might change the world."

"Which particular primates are your clients?"

"The ones in the Primate House at the zoo. Shirley—and I—think three of the chimpanzees have occupied the premises long enough to claim squatter's rights by law."

Nudger was momentarily dizzy. "You can't claim the chimpanzees own the building!"

"Possession is nine points of the—"

"Get out!' Nudger screamed. "Get out!" Then, calmer: "No, wait."

Fleck paused at the door and cocked his head in the opposite direction that his cheap toupee was tilted. He was looking at Nudger with an uncharacteristic injured expression on his puggy little features. "What?"

"Thanks."

"You, too," Fleck said. "I'll send my bill." And he was out the door and gone.

Nudger sat with his face cupped in his hands, trying to fathom it all. He heard the door open and close and knew Fleck had returned.

But when he peeked through his fingers he saw that it wasn't Fleck.

It was an enormous man in a neat brown suit. He was breathing through his mouth and had a long, narrow face with a bent nose and wide-set eyes that made him look like a horse.

"You're Nudger," he said, and proffered a giant hand.

Instinctively Nudger shook it, and his own hand was mashed painfully before it was released.

The horselike man sat down. Nudger wondered which breed Fleck would choose to categorize him. Clydesdale, maybe. He stared at Nudger in a way that was unnerving. Nudger unobtrusively opened his top desk drawer and slid his throbbing hand inside, toward the gun that rested there.

"My name's Clyde Davis, Mr. Nudger. Can you guess why I'm here?"

Nudger's heart was hammering, his stomach writhing. "Because of Manny Boscanarro?"

Clyde Davis looked puzzled, crossed his legs, and smiled in a way somehow more bovine than equine. "I don't know anyone by that name. I'm here because you've been harassed. We've learned that an accusation against you was recently withdrawn, but not until after you suffered monetary loss and great emotional stress in a frivolous lawsuit that made mockery and misuse of the courts. You deserve compensation, Mr. Nudger."

Nudger stayed his hand over the gun. "*We've* learned? You're from a law firm?"

"No, Mr. Nudger, but I'm here to help guide you through future litigation as you press your case. I'm from MOO."

Nudger began to withdraw his hand from the drawer but found that he couldn't.

He just couldn't.

He sat staring at the man from MOO.

His hand hovered over the gun.

THE MISSING HEIR
A STANLEY HASTINGS STORY

by Parnell Hall

Parnell Hall has been nominated for Best First Novel and Best Novel. He has also served as a president of PWA. "Missing Heir" is the first Hastings short story.

The man who invaded my office the first thing on a Monday morning was not at all who I wanted to see. His suit was shiny, his mustache was trim, his eyes were small and hard. His nails were manicured, and he smelled like a barbershop.

He looked like a process server.

You must understand, I don't get served often in my business. I'm a private investigator, but the work I do is not the kind to lay me open to lawsuits. I don't follow people's wives to motels, hide in closets to take incriminating pictures, or do any of that stuff that's apt to get one sued, if not punched in the nose. I work for a negligence lawyer investigating accident claims. I sign injured people to retainers, photograph their broken arms and legs, and set the machinery of their suit in motion. Occasionally, that will involve serving a summons on the defendant in that action.

So I guess that was why the man grated on me so much.

I *am* a process server.

Anyway, I sized him up and decided to take my medicine. We were standing outside a door that said STANLEY HASTINGS DETECTIVE AGENCY. If he was there to serve Stanley Hastings, detective, I was going to have a hard time denying being him once I'd stuck my key in the door. I suppose I might have deflected the man by explaining how the sign had been given to me by friends as a joke, and if he knew anything about New York state law, the only detectives in New York City were police detectives, so while I might claim to be a private *investigator,* any sign implying I was a private *detective* was bogus at best.

Instead I said, "Hi, I'm Stanley Hastings, what can I do for you?"

He said, "I want to hire a private detective."

Under the circumstances, I did not go through the rigmarole of explaining there was no such thing. The word *hire* in my business is one I have come to recognize. It implies money. Money I could earn. As a failed actor/writer who regarded the private eye business as a stopgap between what I considered to be my real work, it had taken me longer than you can imagine to learn this.

"Fine," I said. "Come on in."

I unlocked the door and led him into my one-room office, which wasn't much, but on West Forty-seventh Street would have run me a pretty penny if I'd been paying for it. It actually had once been the office of my father-in-law's plastic bag company, before he'd moved the headquarters of his operation to his manufacturing plant in the Bronx. He still carried it on the company books, and allowed me to use it as my office, which came in handy whenever I wanted to impress a client, perhaps con them into offering me money in the belief that I was something I really wasn't.

"Sit down," I said, indicating a chair. I went and sat at my desk, tried to look professional. "Now then, what can I do for you?"

He sat in a chair, sized me up. His mustache twitched. "It's about money," he said.

I liked that. If there was a job to do, it would be good if money was involved.

"Go on," I said. "But make it fast. I gotta go out on a case."

He frowned. "You already have a case?"

"I do three or four cases a day."

"How is that possible?"

"It's not like in the movies. I do negligence work. A case for me involves signing someone to a retainer, and photographing the crack in the sidewalk that tripped them. I have no trouble doing that three or four times a day."

He looked at me sideways, as if wondering if I really was the person he wanted to hire. I know that look.

I put up my hands. "But that doesn't mean I can't take other work if more important work comes along. So, why don't you tell me your trouble and we'll see if there's anything I can do about it?"

"I'm not sure you can."

"Neither am I. If you wanna tell me your troubles, fine. Otherwise, go find someone else who's willing to listen. Like I say, I got work."

"Okay," he said. "Let me run this by you. See what you think. My name's Philip Cushman. I'm an investment broker, live in Manhattan, married four years, no children. My wife, Denise, left me six months ago, went back to using her maiden name, which is Milford. She started to file divorce proceedings, never followed through with it. So we're still legally married."

"You're looking for a divorce?"

"I'm looking for my wife."

"I beg your pardon?"

"I don't know where she is. I live on East Eighty-eighth Street. She did too, up till six months ago. Then she packs up, moves into some dive in the West Village." He shrugged. "I say dive, that's just prejudice on my part. She got a room on Charles Street for more rent than I pay for the whole apartment. She moved in there, set up shop, started hitting me up to pay for it."

"Did you?"

"What, are you nuts? She runs out on me and wants me to foot the bill? I wouldn't give her a dime. That's when she filed suit for divorce."

"I thought you said she dropped it."

"In a manner of speaking. Actually, she skipped out."

"I beg your pardon?"

"Packed up and left town. Without telling anyone. Without leaving a forwarding address. I tried to find her, had no luck."

"Why'd you try to find her?"

He smiled. "There you go. Now you put your finger on it. Why indeed?"

Philip Cushman popped open his briefcase, took out a manila file. He reached into the file, selected a paper, pulled it out.

"Here you are," he said. He looked at the paper, passed it across the desk to me.

I put on my reading glasses. Wondered if they would be one more blow to Philip Cushman's idea of a P.I.

The piece of paper proved to be a letter written on the rather ornate letterhead of the law firm of Farber and Guest, with offices in Cincinnati, Ohio. The letter was addressed to Mrs. Denise Milford Cushman at the apartment on East Eighty-eighth Street. It read:

Dear Mrs. Cushman,

We regret to inform you of the death of your uncle, Maxwell Milford, last month at the age of sixty-three. However, Mr. Milford had been battling cancer for some time, and this was not unexpected.

As Mr. Milford had no close heirs, he has seen fit to leave the bulk of his estate to you. Mr. Milford had a house, a car, and disposable assets in excess of five hundred thousand dollars.

Please contact our office at your earliest convenience to see about claiming your inheritance.

I looked up from the letter. "Five hundred thousand dollars?"

"In excess of."

"That's a nice excess," I said. "Correct me, but there's one thing I don't understand."

"What's that?"

"If this letter's to your wife, how come it's in your possession?"

"You see the address? It was sent to me."

"Actually, it was sent to her."

"Yes, but she no longer lives there. Or anywhere

else, for that matter. I suppose, technically, I shouldn't have opened it. But seeing as how I had no way to pass it along, I had to know what it was."

"And now that you do?"

"I have to find her, of course."

"Why?"

He frowned. "What?"

"Why do you have to find her? The money's coming to her, not you."

He put up his hands. "Technically, yes. But, technically, we're still married. The divorce never went through. Which is a wonderful thing, because when it does, the terms will be different. She'll be the one with the money who wants out. I'll be the aggrieved party being left. It's a wonderful thing about equality and women's rights. They got the right to lose their shirts in a divorce just like us."

"Uh-huh," I said. "So that's it in a nutshell. Your wife's got some money coming to her, so you want me to find her?"

"That's right."

"You got any leads to go on?"

"I can give you her last known address."

"I can assume you tried there yourself?"

"Yes, but I'm not a private eye. Also, her friend's didn't like me much." He looked at me dubiously. "So, will you take the case?"

"Well," I said, "I can't dump the work I've already got. But I can put a hold on accepting more. If you want, I'll look into it, but there's no guarantees."

"I understand," he said. "What are your rates?"

I hesitated. I was going to say two hundred bucks a day, but since I couldn't give full days at first, that wouldn't be fair. I decided to see if a steep hourly rate would scare him off.

"Okay," I said. "Fifty bucks an hour, plus expenses."

He nodded. "Fine."

I pulled up at the Charles Street address at two in the afternoon. Before that I'd interviewed a man in Queens who'd tripped on his front steps, and a boy in Brooklyn who'd fallen off a playground swing. Both were a piece of cake. Easy assignments, and no trouble finding a place to park.

Not so on Charles Street. As I cruised around the Village, looking for a place to leave my car, I wondered if it was fair to bill Philip Cushman fifty bucks an hour for looking for a parking space. A Ford minivan solved my problem by pulling out from the curb. I parked my Toyota, set the code alarm, and walked up Charles Street to the address.

Denise Cushman's room turned out to be a third-floor walkup over a tattoo parlor. The downstairs door was locked. There were names on the bells of every apartment but hers. Evidently, her room hadn't been rented yet.

There was no bell for a super, which would have been my first choice. A neighbor was my second. Denise Cushman lived in 3C. 3B said THOMPSON. I buzzed it.

Moments later a voice said, "Yeah?"

"Mr. Thompson?"

"Yeah?"

"I'm looking for Denise Cushman."

"She's gone."

"I know. I'd like to talk to you about it."

"I got nothing to say."

"I was hoping you could help me locate her."

"Well, I can't."

"Too bad. She's come into money."

It took me a second to realize the noise I heard was the door being buzzed open.

Frank Thompson looked like an aging hippie. Of course, sometimes I think *I* look like an aging hippie. But trust me, there's no comparison. And it wasn't just the fact he lived in Greenwich Village. His hair, what was left of it, hung to his shoulders. His beard, though gray, was full. He wore a sleeveless string shirt. His arms were an art gallery. He looked as if he'd single-handedly kept the tattoo parlor downstairs open all these years.

"What's this about money?" he said as he opened the door.

"Denise has come into some money. As soon as I find her, it's hers."

"You don't have her address?"

"Her last known address is here."

"That's strange. She should have contacted someone."

"You knew she was going?"

"Actually, no. It was a surprise to me. That no-account husband of hers came around, next thing I know she moved out."

"Yeah, he's a piece of work," I said.

Thompson liked the sound of that. He sized me up, said, "Why don't you come in?"

I entered, found myself in a crash pad from the sixties. The bed was a mattress on the floor. The bookcases were boards and cinder blocks. One chair had been upholstered with an American flag. There were psychedelic drawings on the walls.

"Sit down," he said, motioning me toward Old Glory. He flopped down on the mattress, which seemed to double as a couch. On the coffee table in front on him was a huge ceramic ashtray filled with cigarette butts. He grabbed a pack of Camels, pulled one out, lit it up. As an afterthought, he offered the pack to me.

"No, thanks," I said. "But knock yourself out. What can you tell me about Denise Cushman?"

"Nice lady," he said. "A little too straitlaced. A little too repressed. She was just finding herself."

"You knew her well?"

"Not well enough. If that's what you mean. She wasn't here that long. She was just getting acclimated. Which she was, by the way. She got a job at a coffee shop on Bleecker. Waitress work, just part-time, but she was making good tips. Then she up and moves out. Damn shame."

"Where'd she go?"

He shrugged his shoulders. "I have no idea. One day she's here, the next she's gone. It's not like she said goodbye. Heck, I don't even know how long she was gone before we knew it."

"How'd you find out?"

"Mail piled up in her box downstairs. Postman complained to the super."

"How'd he find him?"

"Huh?"

"There's no super listed on the bell."

"Oh, he's apartment 1A. Vinnie don't like to be bothered, don't list his name. But the postman knows."

"That's nice," I said. "So the super opened the apartment?"

"That's right."

"And she was gone?"

"Lock, stock, and barrel. Cleaned out her stuff and left. Didn't tell anyone. Not that she'd been here long enough to know anyone. Except for me. But I was her neighbor. She could have knocked on my door."

Maybe. As I watched the human tattoo suck on his cigarette, it occurred to me *I* might not have knocked on his door.

"Uh-huh," I said. "And in the days before she left, she didn't say anything that would have given you a hint that she was going to go?"

He shook his head. "No, not at all. I thought she was happy here. Particularly with getting a job. She seemed real pleased when she got the job."

"And where was that again?"

"Coffee shop on Bleecker. The Cozy Cup." He shrugged. "Okay place, but a little pricy."

"What isn't these days?"

The coffee shop where Denise Cushman had worked had a bright yellow storefront with the words COZY CUP painted on it in royal blue. Inside, it featured tiny wooden tables and wood and metal chairs. In one end was a coffee bar with stools. In the other was a small platform about a foot high where poetry could be read or a guitar could be played. From all appearances, the Cozy Cup could have been a coffee house from the sixties.

Except for the prices. Here was one place where Mr. Thompson and I had a meeting of the minds.

One glance at the menu, and I wasn't about to order. Even at fifty bucks an hour. Even on Mr. Cushman's expense account. Coffee's coffee, and I'm old enough for the phrase, Got a dime for a cup of coffee? to echo in my head.

Anyway, ignoring the tables, which were being serviced by a young waitress in a leotard and short skirt, I bellied up to the bar, if that's what it was, figuring the man behind it could probably help me out. As usual, I was dead wrong. The middle-aged man at the coffee bar was the employee, the lackey, the stooge, and the young woman flitting from table to table owned the place. Luckily, business was slow—understandable at their prices—and I was able to catch her eye.

The young waitress/owner had curly blonde hair and a sunny smile that diminished only slightly when she found out I wasn't about to order a double decaf latté whatever. "Denise Cushman?" She frowned and shook her head. "I'm sorry, that doesn't ring a bell."

"She might have been using her maiden name. Milford."

Her eyes widened at that. "Oh, of course. Denny Milford. So that was her real name." She lowered her voice, leaned in confidentially. "I knew she'd had a bad marriage, but I didn't want to pry."

"She talked about her marriage?"

"Well, not in specific terms. Just that her husband was an absolute rat. A snake in the grass. She hated him, she was afraid of him, she wanted nothing to do with him. She was closing the book on that part of her life, and the sooner she was rid of him, the better."

"She was divorcing him?"

"And how. She filed the papers and everything."

"She had a lawyer?"

"Yes, she did, and lucky to get him."

"How so?"

"She had no money to pay him. When she started here, she was stone broke. But she asked around, found a lawyer who would take it on a contingency basis. You know, the lawyer could get paid out of the settlement. Her husband's got some money, see. The creep."

"Uh-huh," I said. The thought I was earning fifty dollars an hour of the creep's money to be talking to this woman did not please me. "So why'd she leave?"

The woman shrugged her shoulders. "Hey, you got me. She was happy here. A little old to be starting as a waitress, but she took to it. Did well with the customers, from what I saw. I never would have thought she'd leave."

"So why did she? You have any idea?"

"It was him."

"Huh?"

"Her husband, that's what I think. He was around, bothering her. After she filed for divorce. The creep, intimidating her, trying to get her to back off. If she left town it was because of him."

"You think she left town?"

"I know she did. If she was here, she'd be working. The creep frightened her away."

"Where? Where did she go?"

She frowned, cocked her head, looked at me. "Why do you want to know?"

"She's come into some money. Her uncle died.

She's his principal heir. There's a considerable amount involved.''

That's all I said. I felt bad saying it, but it was my job. Still, I didn't lie to her. Everything I told her was absolutely true. I just didn't mention I was working for the creep husband.

A sin of omission.

Her face brightened. "Well, is that right?" she said. "Denny's got money coming? Well, how about that. Sometimes things work out."

"And sometimes they don't," I said. "The problem is, they can't give her the money if they can't find her."

"I wish I could help you. I just don't know where she is."

"She gave no indication she was going to leave?"

"None at all. It makes no sense. She was so happy here. After years of living with a creepy husband. She finally gets out on her own. Gets a job. Hey, it's just waiting tables, but she was so happy to have it. Because she was on her own, you know. That's why it had to be the creep frightened her away. Otherwise, she never would have left. But, no, she never gave a hint she was going."

"Uh-huh. And how long ago was this?"

"I don't know. Must be two, three months."

"And you haven't heard from her since?"

"Not a word. Unless . . ."

"Unless what?"

"Well, a postcard came the other day. It was kind of strange. I think we still have it. Sam," she called to the man at the bar. "We still got that card?"

"What card?"

"Postcard came in the mail. The miss-you postcard."

"Oh, that. Yeah, I think it's here." He rustled around next to the cash register, pulled out a postcard, held it up. "Here you go."

The waitress took the postcard, handed it to me. On the back was a cartoon drawing of a cat, a happy cat with long whiskers and a big smile. The postcard was addressed to no one in particular, just the Cozy Cup on Bleecker Street. There was no salutation or signature. The postcard simply read:

Miss you guys!

I looked at the waitress.

"See," she said. "This *sounded* like her. But why she would send us a postcard like this is beyond me. She could at least have signed her name."

"Yeah," I said. "Unless she was very, very frightened, and didn't want anyone to know where she was."

I felt bad when I said that.

The postcard was postmarked Islip.

Sergeant MacAullif produced a ritual groan when I walked in the door.

I put up my hand. "Oh, please," I said. "Stop pretending you're not glad to see me. I happen to know you just sit here waiting for me to interrupt you from your normal, boring police routine. My cases are the only ray of light in your drab existence. If it weren't for me, you would have been in analysis for manic depression years ago."

"Are you having fun?" MacAullif said.

"Fun? I never have fun. It's work for me, fun for you. My life-and-death cases are your sport. As I recall, in the past you've managed to joke even when I was arraigned for homicide."

"You had to admit, that was pretty funny."

"It depends on where you sat. Have *you* ever been arraigned for homicide?"

"I always try to stay on the right side of the law."

"You think I don't?"

"Your record speaks for itself."

"A dismissal does not go on your record."

"My point exactly."

"Why are we arguing?"

"Who's arguing? You came in here spewing some wacky theory about how I live for your visits."

"Because you groaned."

"What?"

"You groaned when I walked in. I was pointing out why that was manifestly unfair."

"It's fair in this case," MacAullif said. "You're in here spreading garbage, and I have no idea why. Let me give you a hint. I happen to have my hands full this afternoon, so start making sense or you're out on your ear."

I gave MacAullif a rundown of the Denise Cushman situation. He didn't seem impressed.

"You got a postcard?"

"That's right."

"An anonymous postcard?"

"Uh-huh."

"A woman takes off without telling anybody, and weeks later she sends a postcard saying, Miss you guys?"

"What's wrong with that?"

"Nothing's wrong with that. I just don't see why you bring it to me."

"I was hoping for a little help."

MacAullif threw up his hands. "You were hoping for a little help. And you wonder why I groan when you walk in the door. Here's a simple, ordinary case, the type any P.I. would be proud to call his own. Here's a nice, straightforward case, and how much, might I ask, are you making on this?"

"Fifty bucks an hour."

"Not bad. Not as much as you'll have to pay the shrink that deals with your resultant psyche, but still, could be worse. So, fifty bucks an hour is what you get paid for the work you do. Tell me, how many hours of work did you hope to save by asking for my help?"

"It's not like that."

"No? You're looking for this woman's address. With limited leads, you could probably putter around a few days, rack up a cool grand. But you'd like me to spend an hour of my time, for which I am not getting paid, to do you out of several hours of yours. What a fascinating thought process. I can't wait to hear what you have in mind."

"When you do, perhaps you'll be less sarcastic."

"Oh, and why is that?"

"Because I want something I can't do for myself. It would take a police officer making a special request."

"Gee," MacAullif said. "If this is as well thought out as I'm sure it is, how could I possibly refuse? So, whaddya want?"

"It occurred to me, if this postcard is from Denise Cushman, and it actually *is* from Islip, then there's a good chance that's where she's actually living. If she's renting a house or apartment there, it might be in her own name."

MacAullif scowled. "You want me calling real estate agents?"

"Not at all. But if she rented an apartment, she'd have to have electricity. There may be a lot of real estate brokers, but there's only one ConEd. I know they wouldn't give me the time of day, but if you were to make a phone call, see if a Denise Cushman had paid for a hookup in Islip."

MacAullif considered. "I must admit, that might work. However, it occurs to me there's another installation you could check out might be a little easier."

"Oh? And what is that?"

"The telephone."

Denise Cushman lived over a convenience store on the main drag in Islip. I was happy enough about finding her not even to mind the look on MacAullif's face when the information operator told me yes, they had a new listing for a Denise Milford. Even his ribbing at how many hours I'd cost myself could not dampen my spirits. Because, even though, as I said, there were no guarantees, still I like to give service. I'd been skeptical about my ability to do the job in the first place, so succeeding was a considerable relief.

The town of Islip, Long Island, was about a two-hour drive from Manhattan and, from what I could see, consisted of the New York Institute of Technology, a weather station, a strip of bedraggled shops and restaurants, and not much else. I parked my car in front of the convenience store, got out, and looked at the bell.

Her name was right on it. Denise Milford.

I hoped she was home. I hadn't tried calling when I got the number, not knowing what I wanted to say, and not wanting to tip her off.

I pushed the bell. After a while, a woman's voice said, "Yes?"

"Denise Milford?"

"Who is it?"

"It's about your uncle Maxwell."

"What about him?"

"He's dead. He left you some money."

"Come on up."

The door buzzed open. I pushed through, went up a flight of stairs.

She met me at the door. She was younger than I had expected, a thin woman with curly red hair, freckles, and green eyes. She opened the door on a safety chain, said, "Who are you?"

I showed her my ID. "I'm a private investigator. I've been tracking you down because of your inheritance."

"Okay," she said. "Come in."

She let me in, and I saw at once why she could use the money. She had obviously left her husband with little more than a suitcase. The apartment she had rented was barely furnished. In fact, it was a stark one-room affair, boasting a convertible couch, a dresser, and a floor lamp. There were no cooking facilities, no mini-refrigerator, no hot plate, no microwave. The only luxuries at all were a VCR and a portable TV, which Denise evidently could not do without, as Blockbuster rental tapes were stacked up on the floor.

I shuddered to think this was the existence her husband had driven her to. Reminded myself for the hundredth time I don't take sides, it's just my job.

"Well, what's this all about?" she said. "You say Uncle Maxwell died?"

"That's right," I said. I moved to the couch, set my briefcase on the coffee table, unsnapped it, and took out the letter. "I have here a letter addressed to a Mrs. Denise Milford Cushman. If you can give me some assurance that you are that woman, I'd be happy to give it to you."

She narrowed her eyes. "I beg your pardon?"

"Can you prove you're Denise Cushman?"

She looked at me as if I were an idiot. "This is my apartment."

"Actually, the name on the bell is Denise Milford."

"Yes, I've gone back to using my maiden name. Which is Milford. But you know that." She pointed at the paper. "Isn't Uncle Maxwell's name Milford?"

"Yes, it is. But try to understand. This is your money. How would you like it if I turned it over to the first person who asked for it?"

"You have the money?"

"No, of course not. I was speaking figuratively. Yes, this is Denise Milford's apartment. How do I know you're not some neighbor who stopped by to water the plants?"

"Plants?"

"Another bad example. But you get the point.

Before I turn over the letter, I'd like to see some form of identification."

"Oh, yes, of course."

Her purse was lying next to the coffee table. She scooped it up, rummaged through it, came out with a wallet. She reached in and sorted through her cards.

"Here's my Social Security card. Here's my Blue Cross/Blue Shield medical insurance. Here's my Mastercard, Visa, and American Express—all worthless, Philip cancelled them, of course. Here's my Blockbuster card, which he didn't think to cancel."

"How about a driver's license?"

"I don't drive."

"You live way out on the island and you don't drive?"

"You think I could afford a car?"

"How did you get out here?"

She frowned. "What difference does it make?"

"No difference. I was just wondering."

"A friend drove me."

"And what are you doing out here?"

"Watching TV."

"You got a job?"

"Not so you could notice."

"What are you doing for money?"

"I got some saved up from my last job."

"What will you do when it's gone?"

"I don't know. Why do you ask?

"Just wondering."

"Well, it's none of your business. I'm here, and, yes, it's inconvenient, and if I've got some money coming, I'd like to know it."

"You've got some money coming," I said, and handed the letter over.

She took the letter. As she read it, her eyes widened. She looked at me. "Five hundred thousand dollars?"

"That's right."

"I had no idea."

"I'm sure you didn't."

She frowned, probably taking the remark as a comment on her living conditions. "So what do I have to do to collect the money?" she said.

I indicated the letter. "Simply contact the lawyers."

"I don't have to go through you?"

"No, you don't."

She frowned again. "Then why are you here?"

"I had to find you."

"Yes, but if you had the address, why didn't you just send the letter?"

"I didn't have the address. Like I said, I'm a private investigator. I tracked you down."

"The lawyers hired a private investigator?"

"Not directly."

"What does that mean?"

I said nothing.

She looked at me. Her eyes widened. "You're working for *him*, aren't you? *He* hired you."

"Mrs. Cushman—"

"Miss Milford. I'm using Milford now."

"I understand."

"I don't want to see him, I don't want to have anything to do with him."

"Yes, I know."

"Does this money have strings attached? If it's my money, why are you working for him?"

"The letter came to him. He had to find you."

"He hired you?"

"That's right."

"Then I didn't inherit money?"

"Yes, you did. The letter is genuine. You can contact these lawyers and you'll get paid."

"I don't have to go with you?"

"No."

"I don't have to go anywhere, I don't have to do anything?"

"Not at all. Look, here's the law office, there's their number, call 'em on the phone."

"What about you?"

"Huh?"

"What will you do?"

"I'll report back to your husband, who'll report to them that he hired an investigator to find you. I wouldn't be surprised if he billed them for my time."

"Yeah, that's Philip," she said. "Tell me, how'd you find me?"

"From the postcard."

She nodded. "Yeah. I guess I shouldn't have sent it."

"Or maybe you shouldn't have left."

"What do you mean?"

"It took a while to find you. I went by your old apartment. Your neighbor was nothing to speak of, but the coffee shop was something else. I got the feeling you were happy there. And I got a feeling you're not happy here. I'm thinking maybe you shouldn't have run away."

"That's none of your business."

"I know it isn't. It's just, I got a job to do, and I don't always like it. If you ran away so your husband couldn't find you, I understand that. In this case I'm kind of the good-news/bad-news guy. The good news is you've got a lot of money, and the bad news is your husband found you."

"I don't have to see him, though."

"No, you don't. I do have to report finding you."

"I understand."

"You going to run away again?"

She frowned, looked at the letter. "I don't know what I'm going to do."

I didn't like it.

Richard Rosenberg didn't like it, either. He leaned back in his desk chair, cocked his head at me, and said, "What's in Islip?"

"Not much."

"That's not exactly helpful. What's in Islip?"

"I'm not sure what you're getting at. Do you mean, what's in Islip that would attract a woman like that?"

"Not exactly."

I shifted in my chair, tried to think of what to say next. Richard Rosenberg could be annoying when he wanted to be. I could hardly complain, since I'd called on him for help; still, it was exasperating. A little man with a seemingly inexhaustible source of nervous energy, Richard Rosenberg was the negligence lawyer I worked for, and while he loved arguing in court, at times he liked nothing better than to just sit back and pontificate. I had a feeling this was one of those times.

"All right, Richard," I said. "I seem to be missing the point. What is it you're trying to say?"

That was the right approach. Richard actually smiled. "Let's see if the Socratic method can draw it out of you. All right, what is it about the current situation that makes it so important?"

"You mean, why did I bring it to you?"

Richard raised his finger. "No. Interesting point, but separate. I know why you brought it to me. Because you're a bleeding-heart wuss who can't bear to turn this woman over to her husband."

"Can you blame me?"

"Not at all, if that was what was important."

"You don't think it's important?"

"I know it's important to you. But it's not important to the situation. I ask again, what's in Islip?"

"And I don't know what you're getting at. The New York Institute of Technology's there. There's a weather station. There's a few stores—" I broke off as Richard waved his hands.

"No, no, no. You're way off track. Let me go over what you just told me. This woman was working in a coffee shop in the Village?"

"That's right."

"She was happy there?"

"Yes."

"Then why'd she leave?"

"Because her husband found her."

"And when was that?"

"About three months ago."

"What did she do then?"

"She packed up and left."

"And where did she go?"

"To Islip."

Richard raised his finger. "Ah. Three months ago to Islip. And what's in Islip? You don't know. But what does she do in Islip? She spends the next three months holed up over a convenience store in an unfurnished room with nothing for company but a TV and a VCR until you arrive out of the blue to tell her she just came into half a million dollars." He laced his fingers together. "Is that an accurate assessment of the facts?"

"Close enough," I said. I shouldn't have.

"Well, could you point out where it's wrong?"

"No, I take it back, it's accurate."

"Fine," Richard said. "Then, I ask you again, what's in Islip?"

"I don't know."

"Well, you could find out. Instead of talking to me, you could do a little work on your own. Make some phone calls. To the woman's landlady perhaps, whoever she rented the apartment from. I don't know how you ever expect to solve anything without the facts."

I squinted my eyes, looked at him. "Richard, are you telling me *you* know what's in Islip?"

Richard looked surprised. "Yes, of course."

I called Philip Cushman, told him I'd found his wife. I refused to answer any of his questions, told him I'd report to him in my office. While that didn't please him any, he got the point. I expected to be paid for my services, and he couldn't write a check on the phone. If he wanted to know what I'd found out, he could come on up.

Philip must have wanted to know, because he was there in a half hour. I opened the door and let him into my office. He drew back slightly at the sight of the two men seated in chairs just inside the door.

"Come in, Mr. Cushman," I said. "I have the report on your wife. She's not here, of course, she refuses to see you, but I have the proper documentation, which these two men are here to supply. So there's no reason why we can't complete this transaction."

"You found my wife?"

"Yes, I did. In Islip, Long Island. However, she indicated she might not stay there long once you knew that she was there."

His face darkened. "You weren't supposed to tell her."

I put up my hand. "Now, Mr. Cushman, I don't believe that was ever specified. But it is somewhat of a side issue. Come in, sit down, let me tell you what I learned."

He came in somewhat grudgingly, sat at the chair in front of my desk. I went around behind the desk, picked up a piece of paper, passed it over.

"What's this?" he said.

"A bill for my services. One thousand, two hundred fifty dollars. Plus expenses, which were negligible, twenty-seven fifty, largely gas and tolls. That comes to twelve hundred, seventy-seven fifty, less your two-hundred-dollar retainer. So if you'd care to write me a check for one thousand, seventy-seven fifty, I am ready to proceed."

"You want me to pay you now?"

"It's why I did the work."

Philip Cushman looked at me for a moment, then popped open his briefcase, drew out a checkbook, and wrote a check. I took it, folded it, stuck it in my pocket.

"Thank you," I said. "Now then, let me tell you what I found. As you know, when she left you, your wife got a room in the West Village, began to work in a coffee shop. You found her there, intimidated her, shortly after which she left."

"Hey," Philip Cushman said. "Whose side are you on?"

"It's not a question of sides," I said. "These are the facts. How you feel about them doesn't alter the situation. Anyway, after that she disappeared, poof, was never seen again, and next turns up in a room over a convenience store in Islip, Long Island."

"How did you find her there?"

"Shrewd detective work," I said. "Actually, she wrote a postcard to the coffee shop. Not a good move if she didn't want to be found. She didn't sign it, but it had a postmark. Which told me the town. She also made the mistake of listing a phone in her maiden name. At any rate, I found her in Islip." I gestured toward the chairs by the door. "Which is where this gentleman comes in. Allow me to present Richard Rosenberg, of the law firm of Rosenberg and Stone. Mr. Rosenberg, when confronted with the problem of your wife having moved to Islip, immediately asked the question, What's in Islip?" I looked at Philip Cushman and smiled. "Do you have any idea?"

"No, I don't. And I don't care, as long as you found my wife."

"Excellent point," I said. "That is, of course, all that matters from your point of view. But from mine, and from Richard's, and, if I may say so, from the attorneys of the late Maxwell Milford's estate, there are other considerations just as important. And the one that's been intriguing us all is, what's in Islip? Are you *sure* you have no idea?"

The frustration on his face was almost comical. "Yes, I have no idea. I have no idea what you're *talking* about. Who *cares* what's in Islip?"

"Well," I said, "obviously your wife did. To move there from the West Village and stay there for three months. It would appear that there was something in Islip that attracted her very much. I am going to ask you again, what's in Islip?"

"I don't *know*!" he said.

I nodded. "That's understandable. I didn't know, either, when Richard Rosenberg asked me. He asked me again and again, in an annoying manner, just as I'm asking you. And I couldn't tell him, either. It was a shock when he finally told me. Let me ask you again, what's in Islip?"

Philip Cushman looked fit to be tied.

I chuckled.

"What's so funny?" he snarled.

"I feel like Laurence Olivier in *Marathon Man* asking Dustin Hoffman, Is it safe? It's a rather unique form of torture. So, have you figured out what's in Islip?"

"No," he said sarcastically. "I give up. What's in Islip?"

"She is."

He blinked. "What?"

"*She's* in Islip. That's what's in Islip. She is. She's the *only* thing in Islip. She's the only thing *important* in Islip. And why is she in Islip? She's in Islip so I can *find* her in Islip. So she can send a postcard from Islip that will *lead* me to Islip. You see what I mean?"

"No. You're making no sense at all."

"Then let me fill you in. Your wife leaves you, moves out, starts a life of her own. After a while she files for divorce. You're vulnerable to such an action. She has no money, you got a bunch, plus another woman on the side. Knowing you will not do well in a divorce action, you try to intimidate your wife into dropping the suit. Immediately thereafter she disappears, and the story goes out she's left town."

I nodded approvingly. "Which is a very good story. Many a man has killed his wife and disposed of the body. But to dispose of her possessions, too? Well, the circumstances would have to be just right. Take a woman who's run out and is traveling light. Just a suitcase or two. In the dead of night, given a couple of hours, you could pack all her belongings, make it look like she'd left town. The divorce action would disappear, and all your problems would be solved."

I shook my head. "Only, what should happen, irony of ironies, a couple of months later a letter comes in the mail indicating your wife has just inherited a half a million bucks. Sort of a kick in the face, kind of hard to let the money go. Except someone who'd stooped to murder would hardly draw the line at fraud. So your wife is dead, big deal. The law firm is in Cincinnati, your wife and her uncle weren't particularly close, the lawyers won't know what your wife's supposed to look like, all you need is the proper buildup for her to resur-

face again. Only it's gotta be somewhere where she
won't run into anyone who would blow the game.
So, you have your current sweetheart rent a room
in Islip, send an anonymous postcard to the coffee
shop your wife worked in, and then hire a credu-
lous P.I. to go find her.

"Which answers the original question. What's in
Islip? She's in Islip. And why is she in Islip? She's
in Islip so I'll find her in Islip. Which I did."

I shook my head. "Only problem is, instead of
reporting this to you and the attorneys for the estate of Maxwell Milford, I took it to Richard Rosenberg, who pointed me in the right direction."

I moved my gesture from Richard to the man
sitting next to him. "And to Sergeant MacAullif
of the Homicide Department of the NYPD. Who
interrogated the young lady in question, a Miss Ro-
salyn Parks, whom I believe you know. Miss Parks,
as I'm sure you will understand, had trouble explaining having rented the apartment in Islip in the
name of Denise Milford just last week. At any rate,
the long and the short of it is as a result of that
interrogation Sergeant MacAullif has a warrant on
him for your arrest for the murder of your wife."

I shrugged my shoulders, cocked my head. "I'm
sure there are some gaps in the story, so if there's
anything you'd like me to fill in, please feel free
to ask."

Philip Cushman couldn't think of a thing, and
within minutes he was on his way downtown.

I, for one, was glad to see him go.

I was also glad he'd written me a check. It was
not lost on me that, busy as the NYPD was likely

to keep Mr. Cushman in the next few days, he might not get around to stopping payment on it.

I suppose I did feel a little bit guilty. Because Philip Cushman had hired me to find his wife, and, technically, I hadn't really done it. And, as I say, while I'm not the best private investigator in the world, I do like to give service.

It's just not always possible.

THE BIG BITE
A NAMELESS STORY
by Bill Pronzini

Bill Pronzini has worn many hats in the P.I. genre. Novelist, anthologist, short story writer, first president of PWA, the winner of the very first Best Novel Shamus, and the youngest PWA Life Achievement Award winner. He has been nominated for Best P.I. Novel three times and won twice with *Hoodwink* in 1982 and with *Boobytrap* in 1999, a testament to the timeless appeal of both writer and detective. He has also been nominated for Best Short Story three times, winning with "Cat's Paw" in 1984. As of this writing Nameless is the longest-running current P.I. series. *The Snatch* was the first in 1971 and *Crazybone* (Carrol & Graf, 2000) is the twenty-sixth.

I am proud to present the first Nameless short story in five years, "The Big Bite."

I laid a red queen on a black king, glanced up at Jay Cohalan through the open door of his office. He was pacing again, back and forth in front of his desk, his hands in constant restless motion at his sides. The office was carpeted; his footfalls made no sound. There was no discernible sound anywhere except for the faint snap and slap when I turned over a card and put it down. An office building at night is one of the quietest places there is.

Eerily so, if you spend enough time listening to the silence.

Trey. Nine of diamonds. Deuce. Jack of spades. I was marrying the jack to the red queen when Cohalan quit pacing and came over to stand in the doorway. He watched me for a time, his hands still doing scoop-shovel maneuvers—a big man in his late thirties, handsome except for a weak chin, a little sweaty and disheveled now.

"How can you just sit there playing cards?" he said.

There were several answers to that. Years of stakeouts and dull routine. We'd been waiting only about two hours. The money, fifty thousand in fifties and hundreds, didn't belong to me. I wasn't worried, upset, or afraid that something might go wrong. I passed on all of those and settled instead for a neutral response: "Solitaire's good for waiting. Keeps your mind off the clock."

"It's after seven. Why the hell doesn't he call?"

"You know the answer to that. He wants you to sweat."

"Sadistic bastard."

"Blackmail's that kind of game," I said. "Torture the victim, bend his will to yours."

"Game. My God." Cohalan came out into the anteroom and began to pace in front of his secretary's desk, where I was sitting. "It's driving me crazy, trying to figure out who he is, how he found out about my past. Not a hint, any of the times I talked to him. But he knows everything, every damn detail."

"You'll have the answers before long."

"Yeah." he stopped abruptly, leaned toward me.

"Listen, this has to be the end of it. You've *got* to stay with him, see to it he's arrested. I can't take any more."

"I'll do my job, Mr. Cohalan, don't worry."

"Fifty thousand dollars. I almost had a heart attack when he told me that was how much he wanted this time. The last payment, he said. What a crock. He'll come back for more someday. I know it, Carolyn knows it, you know it." Pacing again. "Poor Carolyn. High-strung, emotional . . . it's been even harder on her. She wanted me to go to the police this time, did I tell you that?"

"You told me."

"I should have, I guess. Now I've got to pay a middleman for what I could've had for nothing . . . no offense."

"None taken."

"I just couldn't bring myself to do it, walk into the Hall of Justice and confess everything to a cop. It was hard enough letting Carolyn talk me into hiring a private detective. That trouble when I was a kid . . . it's a criminal offense, I could still be prosecuted for it. And it's liable to cost me my job if it comes out. I went through hell telling Carolyn in the beginning, and I didn't go into all the sordid details. With you, either. The police . . . no. I know that bastard will probably spill the whole story when he's arrested, try to drag me down with him, but still . . . I keep hoping he won't. You understand?"

"I understand," I said.

"I shouldn't've paid him when he crawled out of the woodwork eight months ago. I know that now. But back then it seemed like the only way to keep from ruining my life. Carolyn thought so, too. If I hadn't started paying him, half of her inheritance wouldn't already be gone. . . ." He let the rest of it trail off, paced in bitter silence for a time, and started up again. "I hated taking money from her— *hated* it, no matter how much she insisted it belongs to both of us. And I hate myself for doing it, almost as much as I hate him. Blackmail's the worst goddamn crime there is short of murder."

"Not the worst," I said, "but bad enough."

"This *has* to be the end of it. The fifty thousand in there . . . it's the last of her inheritance, our savings. If that son of a bitch gets away with it, we'll be wiped out. You can't let that happen."

I didn't say anything. We'd been through all this before, more than once.

Cohalan let the silence resettle. Then, as I shuffled the cards for a new hand, "This job of mine, you'd think it pays pretty well, wouldn't you? My own office, secretary, executive title, expense account . . . looks good and sounds good, but it's a frigging dead end. Junior account executive stuck in corporate middle management—that's all I am or ever will be. Sixty thousand a year gross. And Carolyn makes twenty-five teaching. Eighty-five thousand for two people, no kids, that seems like plenty but it's not, not these days. Taxes, high cost of living, you have to scrimp to put anything away. And then some stupid mistake you made when you were a kid comes back to haunt you, drains your future along with your bank account, preys on your mind so you can't sleep, can barely do your work . . . you see what I mean? But I didn't think I had a choice at first, I was afraid of losing this crappy job, going to prison. Caught between a rock and a hard place. I still feel that way, but now I don't care, I just want that scum to get what's coming to him. . . ."

Repetitious babbling caused by his anxiety. His mouth had a wet look and his eyes kept jumping from me to other points in the room.

I said, "Why don't you sit down?"

"I can't sit. My nerves are shot."

"Take a few deep breaths before you start to hyperventilate."

"Listen, don't tell me what—"

The telephone on his desk went off.

The sudden clamor jerked him half around, as if with an electric shock. In the quiet that followed the first ring I could hear the harsh rasp of his breathing. He looked back at me as the bell sounded again. I was on my feet, too, by then.

I said, "Go ahead, answer it. Keep your head."

He went into his office, picked up just after the third ring. I timed the lifting of the extension to coincide so there wouldn't be a second click on the open line.

"Yes," he said, "Cohalan."

"You know who this is." The voice was harsh, muffled, indistinctively male. "You got the fifty thousand?"

"I told you I would. The last payment, you promised me . . ."

"Yeah, the last one."

"Where this time?"

"Golden Gate Park. Kennedy Drive, in front of the buffalo pen. Put it in the trash barrel beside the bench there."

Cohalan was watching me through the open doorway. I shook my head at him. He said into the phone, "Can't we make it someplace else? There might be people around. . . ."

"Not at nine p.m."

"Nine? But it's only a little after seven now—"

"Nine sharp. Be there with the cash."

The line went dead.

I cradled the extension. Cohalan was still standing alongside his desk, hanging onto the receiver the way a drowning man might hang onto a lifeline, when I went into his office. I said, "Put it down, Mr. Cohalan."

"What? Oh, yes . . ." He lowered the receiver. "Christ," he said then.

"You all right?"

His head bobbed up and down a couple of times. He ran a hand over his face and then swung away to where his briefcase lay. The fifty thousand was in there; he'd shown it to me when I first arrived. He picked the case up, set it down again. Rubbed his face another time.

"Maybe I *shouldn't* risk the money," he said.

He wasn't talking to me so I didn't answer.

"I could leave it right here where it'll be safe. Put a phone book or something in for weight." He sank into his desk chair, popped up again like a jack-in-the-box. He was wired so tight I could almost hear him humming. "No, what's the matter with me? That won't work. I'm not thinking straight. He might open the case in the park. There's no telling what he'd do if the money's not there. And he's got to have it in his possession when the police come."

"That's why I insisted we mark some of the bills."

"Yes, right, I remember. Proof of extortion. All right, but for God's sake don't let him get away with it."

"He won't get away with it."

Another jerky nod. "When're you leaving?"

"Right now. You stay put until at least eight-thirty. It won't take you more than twenty minutes to get out to the park."

"I'm not sure I can get through another hour of waiting around here."

"Keep telling yourself it'll be over soon. Calm down. The state you're in now, you shouldn't even be behind the wheel."

"I'll be okay."

"Come straight back here after you make the drop. You'll hear from me as soon as I have anything to report."

"Just don't make me wait too long," Cohalan said. And then, again and to himself, "I'll be okay."

Cohalan's office building was on Kearney, not far from where Kerry works at the Bates and Carpenter ad agency on lower Geary. She was on my mind as I drove down to Geary and turned west toward the park; my thoughts prompted me to lift the car phone and call the condo. No answer. Like me, she puts in a lot of overtime night work. A wonder we manage to spend as much time together as we do.

I tried her private number at B & C and got her voice mail. In transit probably, the same as I was. Headlights crossing the dark city. Urban night rid-ers. Except that she was going home and I was on my way to nail a shakedown artist for a paying client.

That started me thinking about the kind of work I do. One of the downsides of urban night riding is that it gives vent to sometimes broody self-analysis. Skip traces, insurance claims investigations, employee background checks—they're the meat of my business. There used to be some challenge to jobs like that, some creative maneuvering required, but nowadays it's little more than routine legwork (mine) and a lot of computer time (Tamara Corbin, my techno-whiz assistant). I don't get to use my head as much as I once did. My problem, in Tamara's Generation X opinion, was that I was a "retro dick" pining away for the old days and old ways. True enough; I never have adapted well to change. The detective racket just isn't as satisfying or stimulating after thirty-plus years and with a new set of rules.

Every now and then, though, a case comes along that stirs the juices—one with some spark and sizzle and a much higher satisfaction level than the run-of-the-mill stuff. I live for cases like that; they're what keep me from packing it in, taking an early retirement. They usually involve a felony of some sort, and sometimes a whisper if not a shout of danger, and allow me to use my full complement of functional brain cells. This Cohalan case, for instance. This one I liked, because shakedown artists are high on my list of worthless lowlives and I enjoy hell out of taking one down.

Yeah, this one I liked a whole lot.

*   *   *

Golden Gate Park has plenty of daytime attractions—museums, tiny lakes, rolling lawns, windmills, an arboretum—but on a foggy November night it's a mostly empty green place to pass through on your way to somewhere else. Mostly empty because it does have its night denizens: homeless squatters, not all of whom are harmless or drug-free, and predators on the prowl in its sprawling acres of shadows and nightshapes. On a night like this it also has an atmosphere of lonely isolation, the fog hiding the city lights and turning street lamps and passing headlights into surreal blurs.

The buffalo enclosure is at the westward end, less than a mile from the ocean—the least-traveled section of the park at night. There were no cars in the vicinity, moving or parked, when I came down Kennedy Drive. My lights picked out the fence on the north side, the rolling pastureland beyond; the trash barrel and bench were about halfway along, at the edge of the bicycle path that parallels the road. I drove past there, looking for a place to park and wait. I didn't want to sit on Kennedy; a lone car close to the drop point would be too conspicuous. I had to do this right. If anything did not seem kosher, the whole thing might fail to go off the way it was supposed to.

The perfect spot came up fifty yards or so from the trash barrel, opposite the buffaloes' feeding corral—a narrow road that leads to Anglers Lodge, where the city maintains casting pools for fly fishermen to practice on. Nobody was likely to go up there at night, and trees and shrubbery bordered one side, the shadows in close to them thick and clotted. Kennedy Drive was still empty in both directions; I cut in past the Anglers Lodge sign and drove up the road until I found a place where I could turn around. Then I shut off my lights, made the U-turn, and coasted back down into the heavy shadows. From there I could see the drop point clearly enough, even with the low-riding fog. I shut off the engine, slumped down on the seat with my back against the door.

No detective, public or private, likes stakeouts. Dull, boring, dead time that can be a literal pain in the ass if it goes on long enough. This one wasn't too bad because it was short, only about an hour, but time lagged and crawled just the same. Now and then a car drifted by, its lights reflecting off rather than boring through the wall of mist. The ones heading west might have been able to see my car briefly in dark silhouette as they passed, but none of them happened to be a police patrol and nobody else was curious enough or venal enough to stop and investigate.

The luminous dial on my watch showed five minutes to nine when Cohalan arrived. Predictably early because he was so anxious to get it over with. He came down Kennedy too fast for the conditions; I heard the squeal of brakes as he swung over and rocked to a stop near the trash barrel. I watched the shape of him get out and run across the path to make the drop and then run back. Ten seconds later his car hissed past where I was hidden, again going too fast, and was gone.

Nine o'clock.

Nine oh five.

Nine oh eight.

Headlights probed past, this set heading east, the

car lowslung and smallish. It rolled along slowly
until it was opposite the barrel, then veered sharply
across the road and slid to a crooked stop with its
brake lights flashing blood red. I sat up straighter,
put my hand on the ignition key. The door opened
without a light coming on inside, and the driver
jumped out in a hurry, bulky and indistinct in a
heavy coat and some kind of head covering; ran to
the barrel, scooped out the briefcase, raced back
and hurled it inside; hopped in after it and took
off. Fast, even faster than Cohalan had been driving, the car's rear end fishtailing a little as the tires
fought for traction on the slick pavement.

I was out on Kennedy and in pursuit within seconds. No way I could drive in the fog-laden dark-
ness without putting on my lights, and in the far
reach of the beams I could see the other car a
hundred yards or so ahead. But even when I accel-
erated I couldn't get close enough to read the license plate.

Where the drive forks on the east end of the
buffalo enclosure, the sports job made a tight-angle
left turn, brake lights flashing again, headlights
yawing as the driver fought for control. Looping
around Spreckels Lake to quit the park on 36th
Avenue. I took the turn at about half the speed,
but I still had it in sight when it made a sliding right
through a red light on Fulton, narrowly missing an
oncoming car, and disappeared to the east. I wasn't
even trying to keep up any longer. If I continued
pursuit, somebody—an innocent party—was liable
to get hurt or killed. That was the last thing I
wanted to happen. High-speed car chases are for
damn fools and the makers of trite Hollywood films.

I pulled over near the Fulton intersection, still inside the park, and used the car phone to call my client.

Cohalan threw a fit when I told him what had happened. He called me all kinds of names, the least offensive of which was "incompetent idiot." I just let him rant. There were no excuses to be made and no point in wasting my own breath.

He ran out of abuse finally and segued into lament. "What am I going to do now? What am I going to tell Carolyn? All our savings gone and I still don't have any idea who that blackmailing bastard is. What if he comes back for more? We couldn't even sell the house, there's hardly any equity. . . ."

Pretty soon he ran down there, too. I waited through about five seconds of dead air. Then, "All right," followed by a heavy sigh. "But don't expect me to pay your bill. You can damn well sue me and you can't get blood out of a turnip." And he banged the receiver in my ear.

Some Cohalan. Some piece of work.

The apartment building was on Locust Street a half block off California, close to the Presidio. Built in the twenties, judging by its ornate facade, once somebody's modestly affluent private home, long ago cut up into three floors of studios and one-bedroom apartments. It had no garage, forcing its tenants—like most of those in the neighborhood buildings—into street parking. There wasn't a legal space to be had on that block, or in the next, or anywhere in the vicinity. Back on California, I slot-ted my car into a bus zone. If I got a ticket I got a ticket.

Not much chance I'd need a weapon for the rest of it, but sometimes trouble comes when you least expect it. So I unclipped the .38 Colt Bodyguard from under the dash, slipped it into my coat pocket before I got out for the walk down Locust.

The building had a tiny foyer with the usual bank of mailboxes. I found the button for 2-C, leaned on it. This was the ticklish part; I was banking on the fact that one voice sounds pretty much like another over an intercom. Turned out not to be an issue at all: the squawk box stayed silent and the door release buzzed instead, almost immediately. Confident. Arrogant. Or just plain stupid.

I pushed inside, smiling a little, cynically, and climbed the stairs to the second floor. The first apartment on the right was 2-C. The door opened just as I got to it, and Annette Byers put her head out and said with excitement in her voice, "You made really good—"

The rest of it snapped off when she got a look at me; the excitement gave way to confusion, froze her in the half-open doorway. I had time to move up on her, wedge my shoulder against the door before she could decide to jump back and slam it in my face. She let out a little bleat and tried to kick me as I crowded her inside. I caught her arms, gave her a shove to get clear of her. Then I nudged the door closed with my heel.

"I'll start screaming," she said, Shaky bravado, the kind without anything to back it up. Her eyes were frightened now. "These walls are paper thin, and I've got a neighbor who's a cop."

That last part was a lie. I said, "Go ahead. Be my guest."

"Who the hell do you think you are—"

"We both know who I am, Ms. Byers. And why I'm here. The reason's on the table over there."

In spite of herself she glanced to her left. The apartment was a studio, and the kitchenette and dining area were over that way. The briefcase sat on the dinette table, its lid raised. I couldn't see inside from where I was, but then I didn't need to.

"I don't know what you're talking about," she said.

She hadn't been back long; she still wore the heavy coat and the head covering, a wool stocking cap that completely hid her blond hair. Her cheeks were flushed—the cold night, money lust, now fear. She was attractive enough in a too-ripe way, intelligent enough to hold down a job with a downtown travel service, and immoral enough to have been in trouble with the San Francisco police before this. She was twenty-three, divorced, and evidently a crankhead: she'd been arrested once for possession and once for trying to sell a small quantity of methamphetamine to an undercover cop.

"Counting the cash, right?" I said.

". . . What?"

"What you were doing when I rang the bell. Fifty thousand in fifties and hundreds. It's all there, according to plan."

"I don't know what you're talking about."

"You said that already."

I moved a little to get a better scan of the studio. Her phone was on a breakfast bar that separated the kitchenette from the living room, one of those cordless types with a built-in answering machine. The gadget beside it was clearly a portable cassette player. She hadn't bothered to put it away before she went out; there'd been no reason to, or so she'd have thought then. The tape would still be inside.

I looked at her again. "I've got to admit, you're a pretty good driver. Reckless as hell, though, the way you went flying out of the park on a red light. You came close to a collision with another car."

"I don't know what—" She broke off and backed away a couple of paces, her hand rubbing the side of her face, her tongue making little flicks between her lips. It was sinking in now, how it had all gone wrong, how much trouble she was in. "You couldn't have followed me. I *know* you didn't."

"That's right, I couldn't and I didn't."

"Then how—?"

"Think about it. You'll figure it out."

A little silence. And, "Oh God, you knew about me all along."

"About you, the plan, everything."

"How? How could you? I don't—"

The downstairs bell made a sudden racket.

Her gaze jerked past me toward the intercom unit next to the door. She sucked in her lower lip, began to gnaw on it.

"You know who it is," I said. "Don't use the intercom, just the door release."

She did what I told her, moving slowly. I went the other way, first to the breakfast bar, where I popped the tape out of the cassette player and slipped it into my pocket, then to the dinette table. I lowered the lid on the briefcase, snapped the catches. I had the case in my hand when she turned to face me again.

She said, "What are you going to do with the money?"

"Give it back to its rightful owner."

"Jay. It belongs to him."

I didn't say anything to that.

"You better not try to keep it for yourself," she said. "You don't have any right to that money. . . ."

"You dumb kid," I said disgustedly, "neither do you."

She quit looking at me. When she started to open the door I told her no, wait for his knock. She stood with her back to me, shoulders hunched. She was no longer afraid; dull resignation had taken over. For her, I thought, the money was the only thing that had ever mattered.

Knuckles rapped on the door. She opened it without any hesitation, and he blew in, talking fast the way he did when he was keyed up. "Oh, baby, baby, we did it, we pulled it off," and he grabbed her and started to pull her against him. That was when he saw me.

"Hello, Cohalan," I said.

He went rigid for three or four seconds, his eyes popped wide, then disentangled himself from the woman and stood gawping at me. His mouth worked but nothing came out. Manic as hell in his office, all nerves and talking a blue streak, but now he was speechless. Lies were easy for him; the truth would have to be dragged out.

I told him to close the door. He did it, automatically, and turned snarling on Annette Byers. "You let him follow you home!"

"I didn't," she said. "He already knew about me. He knows everything."

"No, you're lying . . ."

"You were so goddamn smart, you had it all figured out. You didn't fool him for a minute."

"Shut up." His eyes shifted to me. "Don't listen to her. She's the one who's been blackmailing me—"

"Knock it off, Cohalan," I said. "Nobody's been blackmailing you. You're the shakedown artist here, you and Annette—a fancy little scheme to get your wife's money. You couldn't just grab the whole bundle from her, and you couldn't get any of it by divorcing her because a spouse's inheritance isn't community property in this state. So you cooked up the phony blackmail scam. What were the two of you planning to do with the full hundred thousand? Run off somewhere together? Buy a load of crank for resale, try for an even bigger score?"

"You see?" Annette Byers said bitterly. "You see, smart guy? He knows everything."

Cohalan shook his head. He'd gotten over his initial shock; now he looked stricken, and his nerves were acting up again. His hands had begun repeating that scoop-shovel trick at his sides. "You believed me, I know you did."

"Wrong," I said. "I didn't believe you. I'm a better actor than you, is all. Your story didn't sound right from the first. Too elaborate, full of improbabilities. Fifty thousand is too big a blackmail bite for any crime short of homicide, and you swore to me—your wife, too—you weren't guilty of a major felony. Blackmailers seldom work in big bites anyway. They bleed their victims slow and steady, in small bites, to keep them from throwing the hook. We just didn't believe it, either of us."

"We? Jesus, you mean . . . you and Carolyn . . . ?"

"That's right. Your wife's my client, Cohalan, not you—that's why I never asked you for a retainer. She showed up at my office right after you did the first time; if she hadn't, I'd probably have gone to her. She'd been suspicious all along, but she gave you the benefit of the doubt until you hit her with the fifty-thousand-dollar sum. She figured you might be having an affair, too, and it didn't take me long to find out about Annette. You never had any idea you were being followed, did you? Once I knew about her, it was easy enough to put the rest of it together, including the funny business with the money drop tonight. And here we are."

"Damn you," he said, but there was no heat in the words. "You and that frigid bitch both."

He wasn't talking about Annette Byers, but she took the opportunity to dig into him again. "Smart guy. Big genius. I told you to just take the money and we'd run with it, didn't I?"

"Shut up."

"Don't tell me to shut up, you son of—"

"Don't say it. I'll slap you silly if you say it."

"You won't slap anybody," I said. "Not as long as I'm around."

He wiped his mouth on the sleeve of his jacket. "What're you going to do?"

"What do you think I'm going to do?"

"You can't go to the police. You don't have any proof, it's your word against ours."

"Wrong again." I showed him the voice-activated recorder I'd had hidden in my pocket all evening. High-tech, state-of-the-art equipment, courtesy of George Agonistes, fellow P.I. and electronics expert. "Everything that was said in your office and in this room tonight is on here. I've also got the cassette tape Annette played when she called earlier. Voice prints will prove the muffled voice on it is yours, that you were talking to yourself on the phone, giving yourself orders and directions. If your wife wants to press charges, she'll have more than enough evidence to put the two of you away."

"She won't press charges," he said. "Not Carolyn."

"Maybe not, if you return the rest of her money. What you and baby here haven't already blown."

He sleeved his mouth again. "I suppose you intend to take the briefcase straight to her."

"You suppose right.

"I could stop you," he said, as if he were trying to convince himself. "I'm as big as you, younger—I could take it away from you."

I repocketed the recorder. I could have showed him the .38, but I grinned at him instead. "Go ahead and try. Or else move away from the door. You've got five seconds to make up your mind."

He moved in three, as I started toward him. Sideways, clear of both me and the door. Annette Byers let out a sharp, scornful laugh, and he whirled on her—somebody his own size to face off against. "Shut your stupid mouth!" he yelled at her.

"Shut yours, big man. You and your brilliant ideas."

"Goddamn you . . ."

I went out and closed the door against their vicious, whining voices.

Outside, the fog had thickened to a near drizzle, slicking the pavement and turning the lines of parked cars along both curbs into two-dimensional black shapes. Parking was at such a premium in this neighborhood, there was now a car, dark and silent, double-parked across the street. I walked quickly to California. Nobody, police included, had bothered my wheels in the bus zone. I locked the briefcase in the trunk, let myself inside. A quick call to Carolyn Cohalan to let her know I was coming, a short ride out to her house by the zoo to deliver the fifty thousand, and I'd finished for the night.

Only she didn't answer her phone.

Funny. When I'd called her earlier from the park, she'd said she would wait for my next call. No reason for her to leave the house in the interim. Unless—

Christ!

I heaved out of the car and ran back down Locust Street. The darkened vehicle was still double-parked across from Annette Byers' building. I swung into the foyer, jammed my finger against the bell button for 2-C and left it there. No response. I rattled the door—latched tight—and then began jabbing buttons on all the other mailboxes. The intercom crackled; somebody's voice said, "Who the hell is that?" I said, "Police emergency, buzz me in." Nothing, nothing, and then finally the door release sounded; I hit the door hard and lunged into the lobby.

I was at the foot of the stairs when the first shot

echoed from above. Two more in swift succession, a fourth as I was pounding up to the second-floor landing.

Querulous voices, the sound of a door banging open somewhere, and I was at 2-C. The door there was shut but not latched; I kicked it open, hanging back with the .38 in my hand for self-protection. But there was no need. It was over by then. Too late and all over.

All three of them were on the floor. Cohalan on his back next to the couch, blood obscuring his face, not moving. Annette Byers sprawled bloody and moaning by the dinette table. And Carolyn Cohalan sitting with her back against a wall, a long-barreled .22 on the carpet nearby, weeping in deep, broken sobs.

I leaned hard on the doorjamb, the stink of cordite in my nostrils, my throat full of bile. Telling myself it was not my fault, there was no way I could have known it wasn't the money but paying them back that mattered to her—the big payoff, the biggest bite there is. Telling myself I could've done nothing to prevent this, and remembering what I'd been thinking in the car earlier about how I lived for cases like this, how I liked this one a whole lot . . .

WHAT'S IN A NAME?
A JOHN FRANCIS CUDDY STORY
by Jeremiah Healy

Jeremiah Healy has been nominated for Best First Novel with *Blunt Darts* in 1985, and has been nominated five times for Best Novel, winning in 1987 with *The Staked Goat*. He's also been nominated five times for Best Short Story. His most recent Cuddy novel is *Spiral* (Pocket Books, 1999). He is a past, and possibly the most vocal and active, president of PWA.

ONE

Harry Mullen said, "John Francis Cuddy. You want to sit behind your old desk?"

I looked past Mullen to the high-backed swivel chair he'd inherited from me at Empire Insurance after my wife, Beth, had died and I'd gone private. "The one in front of the desk is fine, Harry."

I sat down as he waddled around our shared piece of furniture. It was mid-October, and Mullen had put on even more weight since the last time I'd seen him. Also, the smell of stale cigarette smoke in the office seemed stronger than it should have been from just wafting off his clothes.

"You still hooked on the nicotine, Harry?"

Sinking into the high-backed chair, he sniffed, then frowned. "That bad in here?"

"Like you'd hosted a poker game last night."

"Jeez." Mullen waved his hand ineffectually in front of him. "Did I tell you last time, they catch me using my smoke catcher in here, I'm canned?"

I pictured his little black appliance with the grill and humming motor. "You told me, Harry. Why not just go outside like everybody else in Boston?"

His waving hand made a pass over the desktop, cluttered with manila file folders. "Who's got the time?"

I nodded toward the file closest to him. "That the one you want me on?"

"Yeah." Mullen opened it, leafed through the first few pages. "Life policy. Insured was one Mah-*goo,* Brian D."

I took out a pad and pen. "Spelling?"

"Capital M, small c, capital G-e-o-u-g-h. And B-r-y-a-n, not I." Mullen looked up at me, smiling with teeth as yellow as the keys on an old piano. "But what's in a name, huh?"

"This countryman of ours fresh off the boat?"

"Uh-unh. Born here, along with his brother, Matthew. Looks like their mother came over from Dublin, though."

"How do you know that?"

"She's the one took out the policies on them."

So the mother's place of birth would be in the file, too. "Where's she now?"

"Dead three years, but her will provided for future premiums to be paid ten years after."

I remembered a few arrangements like that from

my time at Empire. "Meaning Mom wasn't too sure of her boys' futures?"

"And with reason. Bryan, our decedent, was kind of a ne'er-do-well, used his small inheritance from the old lady to buy this ramshackle cottage up in Beacon Harbor."

I'd had a few cases there. "Old lobsterman's place?"

"According to the investigating officer."

"Who is?"

"Patrizzi, sergeant on the municipal force."

"I know him. He's good."

"Then maybe he won't have a problem with your looking into things."

I shifted in my chair. "Looking into exactly what, Harry?"

Mullen riffled more papers in the file. "Seems Mom was primary beneficiary, the boys reciprocal alternates."

"So, Bryan dies, Matthew gets the proceeds."

"Or the other way around, which now ain't real likely."

"And you think Matthew might have hastened his beloved brother's departure?"

"Could be,'" said Mullen. "The face amount's only twenty-five thousand, but people have been popped for less."

"Bryan was shot?"

"Uh-unh. 'Bludgeoned' to death with a piece of firewood, apparently during a botched burglary."

"And something makes you think the brother."

Mullen smiled, the yellow teeth absorbing any light that tried to glint off them. "Matthew spent a hard three in Walpole for burglary."

Our state prison, now called "Cedar Junction" by the commonwealth's more euphemistic correctional officials. "Three years for simple B&E?"

"Talk to Patrizzi about it. But all Empire cares is whether brother did brother."

"In which case, you get to keep the twenty-five."

A hurt look from Harry Mullen. "Not me, John. The company."

TWO

Two brothers, John?

"And Irish, too." Kneeling on the close-cropped cemetery grass, I arranged the tulips so the heads pointed toward her gravestone. ELIZABETH MARY DEVLIN CUDDY. The name on the granite's growing fainter, but not the memories of the wife who lies beneath it.

You shouldn't stay on your knees like that this time of year. The dampness seeps up into clothes and bones both.

I got to my feet. "Yes, Mom."

I could feel Beth smile as a freighter lugged through the choppy water below her hillside in South Boston.

John, you were always enough of the little boy that you needed a woman who was both spouse and mother to you.

Something caught in my throat as I said, "I know I needed you, Beth."

And now you're muddling through without me. As you'll continue to do.

"But not forever."

You've only the one life to live, John. Make it count for something more than visiting a grave.

I nodded, though without completely agreeing with her.

Beacon Harbor's a twenty-mile drive north of Boston, but the fall foliage muted the traffic, and besides, Empire Insurance was paying portal-to-portal for my time. I found the police station again, nestled near the wharves before the town ever knew such sites would be worth top-dollar to developers someday.

As I got out of my old Prelude, I saw from the back a man walking toward the water. Narrow head, thin shoulders, plaid shirt over khaki slacks.

With a sandwich bag in his hand.

"Patrizzi?"

The man turned and smiled, then raised the bag to chest level. "Hey, Cuddy, you eat yet?"

"I figure, the taxpayers in their infinite wisdom don't grant us a raise in four years, may as well enjoy the view, right?"

I said, "Right," around the bite of sandwich in my mouth.

After I'd told Patrizzi why I was there, he'd steered me to his favorite deli in the quaint, cobble-stoned old town before settling on a public bench. Just out of the sea breeze, we overlooked some of the cabin-forward wooden boats bobbing at white, poker-chip moorings.

Patrizzi took a sip of iced tea from a bottle shaped like a split of red Bordeaux. "Pretty soon these lobstermen aren't gonna be able to operate out of here." A gesture toward the finger of land with a lighthouse topping it. "They're building condos there on the point, and the real smells of a working harbor won't be what the high rollers'll want coming over their cedar decks at cocktail hour."

"I understand this Bryan McGeough lived in a lobsterman's shack?"

"Yeah. Remember the one I showed you, the time you were up here on that dead artist guy?"

"I do."

"Well, the artist's place was a fucking castle next to the shithole McGeough lived in."

"The brothers local boys?"

"Unfortunately. Bryan was the older, the kind of loser gets more belligerent the more booze he puts away. But Matthew's been in and out of trouble, too, since he was old enough to throw a stone through window glass."

"My contact at Empire thinks Matthew might have graduated from stones to firewood."

Patrizzi chuckled with his mouth full. "Yeah, that hunk of birch was real convenient. Goes great with the botched-burglary story."

"Especially since Matthew did serious time for a . . . prior transgression."

"The stupid shit. Hits a house in the daytime, doesn't check to see a ten-year-old's sleeping in a back bedroom."

The light dawned. "Which kicked a simple B and E up to Home Invasion."

"And got Matthew his stretch in state instead of county."

I chewed a while. "You wouldn't think he'd make the same mistake twice."

Patrizzi gave me a sideways glance, then went back to watching the boats. "Glass in the rear door was broken, outside in. Television, boombox, crappy little camera taken."

"What wasn't?"

"Stash of cash Bryan kept under one of the many loose floorboards in his bedroom."

I thought about it. "And Matthew claims he knew the cash was there."

"Right. Which, despite his proven specialty in the field, makes him not likely to be the burglar this time."

"He says."

"You're right. Cash counted out to two hundred nine. Not much of a call bet to rake in a pot of twenty-five large on Bryan's policy."

"Matthew the only heir?"

Patrizzi nodded. "So he'd eventually get even the two-oh-nine back from his brother's estate."

"Unless Matthew was convicted on a murder charge."

Patrizzi gave me another look, then decided he wasn't that interested in the harbor after all. "I'll tell you, Cuddy. I got motive, I got means, I got opportunity. Only I talk with this Matthew, and it don't feel right, you know what I mean?"

I remembered Patrizzi as a good cop, but he was maybe better than I remembered. "What does the state police investigator think?"

Another chuckle as the last of his sandwich disappeared. "She's a wizard on the computer, but this is her first assignment that comes close to the street. All she sees is the circumstantial shit, not the people."

"Meaning there's more than just Matthew on the scene?"

"Last month our Bryan filed a criminal assault complaint."

"Against who?"

"His brother's boss."

"Matthew's boss?"

"That's right," said Patrizzi. "Contractor named Ish Torenstein."

"Spelled I-s-h?"

"You got it. Short for Isaac. Ish goes about six feet, two-twenty. He somehow felt that Bryan was hitting on his wife."

"And so Torenstein starts hitting on Bryan."

"At the company barbecue, no less."

"Wait a minute," I said. "How come Bryan's at an employee thing thrown by his *brother's* boss?"

"Ask Ish. Or Matthew. Or better yet, both."

I watched Patrizzi for a minute. "You really have a bad feeling about this, don't you?"

He crumpled his wax paper and dropped it back into the bag. "Our Bryan autopsied out with a blood-alcohol content of point two-oh."

"Staggering drunk."

"Probably, though he hit it hard enough generally that maybe he was still somewhat functional."

"Like at the picnic?"

"Talk to Bryan's neighbor, too. She's the one found the body. Or her dog did."

"Her dog?"

"Yeah. Neighbor's name is Greene, Renée, both with three e's. She's new in town, subbing at the elementary school. Kind of horsey for my taste, but supposedly she's magic with the kids, so the board's gonna offer her a full-time slot come January."

"Can you take me out there?"

"Don't need to. We've released Bryan's house as a crime scene, and with that back door busted, you won't have any trouble getting in."

"How about Ish Torenstein?"

An odd smile from Patrizzi this time. "His company office is out on Route One. They can probably tell you where he's working today."

Patrizzi rose from the bench and hook-shot his paper bag into a trash can. "Cuddy, whoever did Bryan McGeough oughta get a medal instead of a cell. But you shake anything loose, let me know, okay?"

I watched him walk back up the cobblestones toward the station, whistling a happy tune.

THREE

Bryan McGeough's house was a little closer than Ish Torenstein's office, so I drove first to the murder scene. Both sides of the street were lined with small cottages on postage-stamp lots. Some of the buildings had been added to and fixed up, appearing now to be year-round homes. The address I'd gotten from Harry Mullen fell more in the "before" than "after" category.

Patrizzi never told me which abutting shack belonged to the neighbor who'd found McGeough's body, so I started with the one on the right. A Boston whaler lay cradled in its trailer off the driveway, but there was no answer at the door, and nothing in the mailbox. The house on the left had a small Japanese compact occupying its drive, but nobody answered my knock there, either. Its mailbox held four pieces of mail, however. Two catalogs were addressed to "R. Greene," one local utility bill to "Renée Greene," and an envelope with a veterinarian's return address—forwarded from Yelverton, Iowa—to "Pooky Greene."

Gruff barking began behind me a breath before a smoky voice yelled, "Can I help you?"

I turned and saw a tall woman coming toward the cottage, a German shepherd with some hound in its family tree lunging on a stout leash. Detective Patrizzi's "horsey" might have been unkind, but, on first impression, it was descriptive. A big-boned blonde in her thirties, Greene had striking features that once would have been called handsome. Dressed in a heavy sweatshirt and jeans, she strode purposefully up the little flagstone path until her dog was growling, and straining two feet away from me.

"Renée Greene?"

A cock of the head. "And you'd be just who?"

"John Cuddy." I handed Greene her mail and took out my license holder, opening it for her to read. "I've been asked by an insurance company to look into the death of Bryan McGeough."

Greene stared at my ID, curling her lower lip so that she looked peculiarly like her dog. "Pooky, that's enough."

The words, plus a forceful yank on the leash, resulted in the dog sitting back on its haunches, whining faintly.

Greene said, "What kind of insurance?"

"A life policy on your former neighbor." I put the holder back in my pocket. "Matthew McGeough's the beneficiary."

"That's Bryan's brother, right?"

"Right."

Greene blew out a breath that lifted the bangs off her forehead. "I was the one who found Bryan."

"Detective Patrizzi told me."

"Which is why you're here?"

"Yes."

"Okay." Another breath. "I guess I can go through it one more time."

Greene tucked the mail under her free arm, then led an unconvinced Pooky in a safe circle around me. She unlocked the door and waved a come-in with her key case.

The interior of the cottage was neat but spare, as though Greene had cleaned the place out but hadn't quite moved in herself.

I said, "Have you lived here long?"

"Arrived just over a month ago."

"From Iowa?"

Greene looked at me sharply as she shooed Pooky into a—probably *the*—small bathroom and closed the door. "How did you know that?"

"A piece of your mail. Or your dog's."

"My . . . ?" She took the envelopes from under her arm and flipped through them. "Oh, the vet's notice. They do that in Iowa. Call pets by their owner's last name, I mean."

"Nice touch."

Greene grinned, but not in a friendly way. "You buttering me up for something?"

"I'd just like to hear your version of what happened."

"Well," said Greene, moving to a love seat that substituted for a couch in the miniature living room, "I don't really know 'what happened,' but I can tell you what I saw."

I took the old rocker opposite her. "That'll do fine."

Greene folded her arms into the folds of sweatshirt under her breasts, maybe something she'd learned to hide biggish hands. "It was like today."

"How do you mean?"

"I'd gotten home from school—I'm subbing?"

"Detective Patrizzi told me that, too."

A nod. "It was about two-thirty, and I changed clothes. The police asked me if I noticed anything odd about Bryan's house then, but I didn't. I just came in my front door there and put on jeans like today and took Pooky for a run along the beach." Greene tried a tentative smile. "She loves that, and we don't have too many beaches in Iowa."

"That why you moved here?"

Greene seemed to hesitate. "To the area, anyway. My mother was French-Canadian, but grew up in Massachusetts on the ocean. After both my parents died back home, I decided to make a fresh start near the water."

"Fresh start?"

Greene frowned. "You ever live in Iowa?"

Point taken. "So that day, you went walking with Pooky."

"Running, actually. She gets kind of antsy

cooped up in this place all day. But it was all I could afford in Beacon Harbor, and I still owe a lot of sweat equity before winter."

I looked at the walls. Not yet insulated.

Greene said, "Well, when we got back from the beach, Pooky started growling and straining at her leash, like with you before. She wanted to go over to Bryan's in the worst way."

"Was that unusual?"

"Pooky and Bryan didn't get along real well."

"Any reason?"

"I think Pooky could sense he wasn't a man of honorable intentions."

A quaint way to put it. "Did Mr. McGeough ever make . . ." I searched for a matching phrase, ". . . unwanted advances?"

"Just once." Greene screwed up her features so they looked even more mannish. " 'Renée, I've never had a girl your size before. Oughta be a real challenge.' "

"His words?"

"Every one of them. That was the last time Bryan ever set foot in this house."

"He was here?"

"I tried to do the neighborly thing, like we do in the Midwest? Invited him in for a drink. He'd downed the first one before I turned around."

"Mr. McGeough liked the stuff?"

"I'd hear him once in a while, coming home late next door. Banging into things, you know. Some nights, I was amazed he didn't wrap his pickup around a tree."

"If we could go back to the day you—"

"Right, sorry." Greene blinked a few times.

"Well, like I said, Pooky was hellbent to get over there, so I went along. I thought maybe she was playing Lassie, you know?"

"That Mr. McGeough might have been hurt . . ."

". . . and Pooky wanted to rescue him." Greene closed her eyes. "But it was a little too late for that."

"How do you mean?"

"As soon as I was around the back of his house, I could see the glass in the door was broken. When I looked through where the pane'd been, I could see the smashed pieces—what do you call them?"

"Shards?"

"Yes, yes, the shards were all over the floor on the inside. And, because of where Bryan . . . where the body was, I could see his hand and arm, so I tried the door, and it opened."

Greene hesitated again. "When I got to him and could see his head . . ." One of the large hands went to her mouth, and she closed her eyes. "It was all bashed in, and there was this bloody piece of firewood next to the body. Well, I knew anybody looking like that just had to be dead, so I got out of there real quick and called the police from here."

"You ever meet Matthew McGeough?"

"Only just. I was leaving the house for work one morning, and Bryan yelled over to me from his driveway. 'Hey, big girl, this is my brother, Matt.' " I never did talk with the man, but I got the impression from Bryan that he'd been in some kind of trouble."

"Matt had been."

"Right, but that Bryan had gotten Matt into some other kind of trouble, too."

"And what kind was that?"

Renée Greene rolled her lower lip under again. "I think it had to do with somebody's wife?"

FOUR

After leaving Greene to liberate Pooky from the bathroom, I did a walk-through of Bryan Mc-Geough's cottage. "Shack" really was more like it, the inside maintained pretty much as you'd expect a drunken bachelor to keep house. There were still some blood and police-tape marks that were consistent with what Greene had told me about finding her neighbor's body.

I went back outside to the Prelude and looked for an access road to Route 1.

Torenstein Construction had a sandwich-board marquee at the far end of a strip mall that looked to be dying of starvation. The company's office was a free-standing concrete bunker with a front door like a tavern might need in a bad section of town: black metal except for a double-glazed, diamond-shaped window reinforced with chicken wire.

The door was unlocked, though, so I just pulled on the handle to get inside.

The first thing I heard was a woman's voice saying, "Well, why the fuck aren't they there?"

As I cleared the doorway, I could see a counter to my right. A woman with big chestnut hair was turning toward me, a portable telephone squeezed by her jawbone against her collarbone. She wore a gold lamé blouse that showed some cleavage over tight green slacks. Her hands were going through the yellow copies of multipart forms, the fingernails longer than a gull's beak.

I sparked a smile, though, as she said into the phone, "Look, asshole, the purchase order says we put it through your guy on the twenty-seventh, which is three weeks ago. . . . I don't care he was on vacation then, you gotta have somebody back-stopping your . . . When? . . . No, no good. Ish needs them on site by tomorrow noon. . . . Well, then maybe he comes by and helps you 'break them loose.' You want that? . . . I didn't think so. . . . Yeah, call before. . . . Oh, love you, too, Donna."

The woman pushed a button on the phone. "Suppliers." She looked me up and down, then leaned over the counter, stressing the lamé some. "Why do I get the feeling you aren't in construction?"

"John Cuddy, Ms. . . . ?"

"It's Torenstein, but I like first names. Mine's Layla."

I guessed her to be late twenties. "After the Eric Clapton song?"

"Yeah," said Torenstein, her eyelashes actually fluttering. "But I'm more the heavy metal than the unplugged version, if you know what I mean?"

I let my ID holder fill the gap in the conversation. Torenstein looked from the laminate back up to me, even though there's no photo on it.

"Private eye?" she said. "We haven't had an on-site accident in two years."

"I'm not here about an accident. I've been asked

by an insurance company to look into Bryan McGeough's death."

The only color left on Torenstein's cheeks came from her rouge. "Bry?"

"Yes. I understand you knew him?"

"Kind of." Torenstein went back to her yellow multiparts. "His brother, Matt, works for us."

"Was the company picnic the first time you met?"

Her face came up sharply. "Who told you about that?"

"Police records of an assault complaint."

"Oh, that wasn't anything." Torenstein gave me a smile. "Ish thought Bry was moving on me."

"Was he?"

"Yeah," she said, a little coyness in the lilt of her head. "Bry thought he was irresistible."

"Was he?" I repeated.

Torenstein leaned back across the counter. "He was cute in that Irish way you guys have."

"But your husband didn't quite agree."

She frowned. "Look, Bry has a few beers, he starts putting his hands here and there." Torenstein demonstrated on me as best she could, given the two feet of Formica between us. "Ish spots it, comes over and belts him one across the mouth. Bry's a real man, he laughs it off. Instead, the weasel goes formal with the complaint thing."

"And what happened at the courthouse?"

Torenstein got coy again. "Thought you told me you knew all this?"

"Just that the complaint was made."

"Well," another lilt, "some legal clerk talked Bry out of pushing it, so everybody made nice-nice.

Hell, Matt's still working for us, that oughta tell you something."

"Can you tell me where he's working?"

"Matt? The big condo site we're doing out by the lighthouse on the point."

What Patrizzi had been smiling about during our lunch at the harbor. "Thanks."

As I turned, Torenstein said behind me, "You know, John, I seem to have this weakness for the whole Irish gene pool."

I looked back at her.

Layla Torenstein's tongue came out to wet her lips. "You got any more . . . questions?"

"No," I said, and reached for the door handle.

"Cuddy, can I put you on hold there?"

"Carla, I'm calling from a pay phone."

"What, you don't have a cellular yet?"

"It's on order with my fax machine."

"Look, don't get me started on you and the twentieth century, all right?"

"Just come back to me quickly?"

I heard a click, then mercifully no Muzak. Carla operated a computer information service for nebbishes like me who couldn't work one ourselves, but she was no-frills when it came to the amenities.

I'd waited two minutes, twenty-three seconds when I heard another click and "Okay, Cuddy, where's the fire?"

"I have some names I'd like you to run."

"What're you looking for?"

"Anything interesting. It's an insurance-death case."

"Let's have them."

I gave her all the people I'd seen that morning except Harry Mullen and Patrizzi, having to spell most of them.

Carla sighed. "Christ on a crutch, Cuddy. Ish, Renée, Layla. This Matthew's the only one sounds normal."

"Can't always tell a can by its label."

"Me, I try to look on the bright side that way."

"Which is?"

"Screwy names like these, it'll make the search go faster."

FIVE

Speaking of which, Torenstein's could have been Jonah instead of Isaac, because his construction site looked like the skeleton of a huge whale.

Most of the posts, beams and joists were erected and tied in, like a rib cage with forty-five-degree bends in its cartilage. I pictured a realtor's brochure: "The waterfront units, perched over a smashing surf, enjoy cathedral ceilings and wraparound windows from which views of both the lighthouse and ocean abound."

I asked a Latino guy working at a table saw for Matt McGeough. He pointed past two African Americans carrying an eight-by-eight on their shoulders toward a guy in his twenties banging away with a nail gun. I walked over, waiting until the blacks and left before I said anything above the firecracker noises.

"Matthew McGeough?"

The man stopped and turned. "Boss sees you without a hard hat, he's gonna go ballistic."

"I hear it wouldn't be the first time."

"Huh?"

"That Ish Torenstein went ballistic." I got to within three feet of McGeough and stopped. "John Cuddy. I'm investigating your brother's death."

McGeough squeezed his eyes shut for just a second, and I felt a little tug in my gut as he said, "Cop?"

"Private."

"Then I don't got to talk with you."

"Learn that at Walpole?"

A barely noticeable nod. "They like us to call it Cedar Junction now. Soothes the visitors."

"Your brother come by often?"

Another flinch from McGeough's eyes, and another little tug behind my belt buckle. "Yeah, he did. Bry stood by me the whole time, man. 'That's what family's for,' he'd say."

"I heard Bryan didn't respect some other families quite as much."

"Look," the eyes hardening, the nail gun shifting in his hands, "you're not getting anything out of me about Ish. He hired an ex-con when a lot of other people wouldn't. So the guy shows some temper. Bry had it coming at the picnic, behaving like that when I got him invited in the first place."

"Maybe Mr. Torenstein didn't think the lesson took."

"I don't know what anybody else thinks but me."

"Then what do you think about the insurance policy on your brother's life?"

"That's why you're here?" A bitter laugh. "Look,

I forgot Ma even took those things out. And I never thought they were for us."

"Even after she died?"

That same flinching blink, and I was leaning toward Detective Patrizzi's view of McGeough as a suspect.

"Let me tell you something, man. I'm not getting rich working construction, but I'm working. I did my time on the home-invasion thing, and I'm doing my time with Ish. Maybe people wanted to hand Bry money, but I work for what I get."

"Hand him money?"

McGeough didn't laugh this time. "The night before . . . before Bry dies, we're over at his place drinking beers, and he's talking about coming into some easy cash. 'Like that Dire Straits song, Matt,' he says to me. 'Get your money for nothing, and your chicks for free.' Then Bry laughs like crazy."

"About what?"

"Who knows? Like I said, we were drinking, and he was probably just pissing in the wind."

"But it seemed to you like the cash was going to be—"

"The fuck you doing on my site without a hard hat?"

A voice like rolling thunder, and I turned to meet the boss.

Ish Torenstein was in his forties and, at the six feet and two-twenty that Patrizzi had pegged, a little shorter and heavier than I am. It felt like his right forearm alone made up the difference in weight as he led me by the elbow out from under anything that could fall from the framing.

"Mr. Torenstein—"

"I gotta pay workers' comp and liability insurance, I gotta deal with OSHA inspectors, I gotta listen to a town hall guy don't know a carpet tack from a railroad spike. And then a suit like you thinks he can just stroll onto my site and not get bounced for it?"

"Mr. Tor—"

He used his strong grip to spin me by the elbow. "I got a good mind to kick your ass all the way back to that little car's gotta be yours over there."

I glanced toward the Prelude fifty yards away. "That would take some doing."

Torenstein flared. "What, you think I can't?"

Very casually, I reached over to his free elbow, finding the nerve bundle inside the bone notch and pressing the pad of my index finger against it.

Torenstein coughed, then sagged a little at the knees.

I said, "I've no desire to show you up in front of your crew here, so why don't we both let go and just talk this out, okay?"

A ratcheting nod from his head as he breathed raggedly and released my elbow just a fraction before I released his.

Hoarsely, Torenstein said, "What the fuck do you want?"

I explained about the policy on Bryan McGeough's life.

Torenstein flared again, but without getting physical. "And you think I had something to do with that? The guy was an asshole around my wife, so I squared it right there."

"And your message got through?"

"Hey, I married a young broad, you know? Layla's spirited."

"I meant your message as applied to Bryan McGeough."

Torenstein ran his good hand down his face in a now slow burn. "Look—Cutty, is it?"

Cuddy, with two d's."

"Cuddy, this Bry was an asshole, but his brother's a good carpenter. Use your eyes on my crew. I got a regular rainbow coalition working for me, but not because I'm some kind of liberal. Uh-unh, it's that guys from different backgrounds see things different, can make suggestions on the job that the fancy-schmancy architect never even thought about. Improvements that make the owner happy, and the building better, something you can bring your family out to show them, say, 'I built this fucking place, and it's better than it would've been with anybody else on it.' "

"Great speech, but I lost track of your message to Bryan McGeough."

Torenstein still simmered. "Let me tell you, then. If I caught Matt's brother moving on my Layla again, would I have rapped him another good one? You bet, maybe two or three, knock a coupla teeth out of his shit-eating grin, make the point. But I'm sure as hell not gonna brain him with a piece of firewood when I got something like Matt's nail gun over there. I'd riddle the guy like he was a pin cushion and get myself some real pleasure from it."

One decisive nod this time. "Now, why don't you walk back to your little car and drive the fuck off my site so we can get some work done here?"

Without waiting for an answer, Ish Torenstein

turned away and lumbered back into the empty bowels of his ascendant whale.

SIX

Arriving at my office in Boston, I checked with the answering service. Seven messages in all, three on the McGeough case.

I returned Carla's first and got a busy signal.

Detective Patrizzi's number was next. Out on the street for a while.

Then Carla again. Still busy.

Harry Mullen's message was the third, and he picked up after three rings.

"Hey, John, how're we doing?"

I could hear a little whirring sound in the background. "Shouldn't smoke on the phone, Harry."

"Jeez, how could you tell?"

"That black box has a motor, and your phone is—"

"Christ, thanks." I heard a scraping noise from his end. "That better?"

"I don't hear the whirring anymore."

"Maybe I shouldn't worry about the cigarettes so much," said Harry. "Just go up to the head of Boston office, blow a few smoke rings in her face, and quit before she can fire me."

"Not until you hear what I have to say."

"I'm hearing you, John, but so far you ain't telling me anything I want to know."

I reviewed my stops in Beacon Harbor and shared my evaluation of Matt McGeough as a suspect.

Mullen said, "Same thing that detective up there thinks huh?"

"Patrizzi and I seem to agree that the circumstantial stuff points in the wrong direction; only we don't have any other likely candidate."

"Don't matter to Empire. If the beneficiary's legit, we cut the check."

"Well, I'm still waiting to hear on some computer data searches. Give it two days, and if the searches don't turn anything, I'll submit a report advising that you can give brother Matt his money."

"Sounds good, John. And thanks for hopping on this one so quick."

"Thanks for thinking of me, Harry."

I did paperwork on other cases the rest of the day, trying Carla twice more with busy signals both times. About nine-thirty the next morning, my phone rang.

"Cuddy, I got something for you."

"What you should get is call-waiting."

"Don't bullshit me this time, okay?"

Her voice seemed odd. "Carla, you all right?"

"It's just that sometimes . . . Well, you're the one deals in the real world with this shit, and I just pull it off a screen, but that don't mean I don't feel something, too."

"What are you—"

"Okay, okay. You got a pen?"

"Yes."

"It's about your 'Greene, Renée.' Took me a while to access things out in Iowa, had two modems cooking all yesterday afternoon."

"So what's the story?"

"You gotta drop the third e," said Carla in a tone I now recognized as subdued.

My pen hovered over the last letter in "Greene" before I spoke. "I think you're wrong there. I've seen four pieces of correspondence with her name on them, all from different places. Each showed her as 'Green' with an 'e' at the end."

"Cuddy," in the subdued voice again, "I'm talking about the other third e."

SEVEN

It was pushing eleven by the time I arrived at the little clumping of shacks on Greene's street. Her car was in the driveway, but again no answer came to my knock, so I began walking in the direction she and her dog had appeared from the prior day.

After three blocks the road petered out to gravel and then just packed sand, some trash cans nearly filled by people still staunch enough to brave the almost-winter wind but conscientious enough to deposit their litter. The beach in front of me was more gradual and sandy than the promontory where Torenstein and his crew were erecting condos. Here driftwood angled along the tide line in pieces as large as telephone poles or as small as the stick Pooky carried between her teeth as she pranced along.

I spotted Renée Greene a little farther on, half standing and half sitting on the stump of a uprooted tree. As I approached, she saw me, then called out to her dog.

Reaching Greene half a beat before the growling Pooky, I said, "No school today?"

She looked up at me. "Didn't need a sub, anyway."

"But, come January . . ."

Greene looked harder for a moment before wrestling the branch from Pooky's mouth and bringing it behind her head like a tomahawk.

I said, "Should I be worried about what you can do with wood?"

A grunt, then she let fly with the stick, sending it a ways and causing Pooky to tear off after same, paws spewing roostertails of sand.

Greene said, "I thought it'd be easier to have her running back and forth like this, so she doesn't pick up on your tone of voice."

"Like she did with Bryan McGeough?"

Greene sighed this time, then rested her rump back on the driftwood stump. "Just what are you thinking?"

"I'm thinking that you were known in Yelverton, Iowa, as a big sports fan, great host at tailgate parties."

Greene's head snapped up. "How did you . . . ?"

"Computer search. It picked up a local newspaper article on a football game."

Greene shook her head, and I had the feeling she was shaking off the pose as well. "Overcompensation."

"What?"

"Overcompensation," she said. "We do that, you know."

"I didn't, but I also found out that back home, your first name was spelled R-e-n-é."

"We do that, too." Another sigh, more resigned this time. "Easier to fudge things if you can keep a name people often misspell."

"Ms. Greene, what's the term I should be using?"

"My, aren't we polite." Then a sniffle. "Sorry, you *are* trying to be polite." The large hands wrestled each other in her lap. "Okay, term for the condition: 'gender dysphoria,' a deep and abiding sense that you're a woman in a man's body. Or vice versa. Term for the person involved: lots of them to choose from, but I prefer transsexual."

Pooky came back with her prize. Greene hurled it out a little farther this time.

I said, "Have you had the . . . operation yet?"

"No. I've been through months of daily estrogen therapy, though. And weekly electrolysis, too— I'm lucky, with blond hair the beard doesn't show as much, but of course it isn't only the five o'clock shadow we worry about, appearance-wise."

"You mentioned taking estrogen?"

"It gives me these breasts." Greene looked down her front. "B-cups, and quite attractive. The drug also shrivels the genitalia." She shuddered. "But not quite enough."

"That how Bryan McGeough caught on?"

"He chatted me up the first few times we saw each other. Bry was a pretty cute guy, and I was . . . flattered, to be honest. That what I'd dreamed about in Iowa for almost thirty years seemed to be coming to pass here."

"So you had him over for that drink."

"And before I knew it, he had Pooky closed up in the bathroom, and Bry was all over me." Greene looked up just as her dog arrived back with the branch. "As a guy all my life, I just didn't have the . . . instinct to sense what was happening until he had a hand up between my legs."

I kept quiet.

Pooky woofed twice, and Greene sailed the stick, but only half the distance of the last toss. "Bry started to laugh, the bastard. He knew I'd been subbing at the elementary and was approved to be hired on full-time next semester." Greene glanced up. "That was going to be how I'd afford my operation and the time off to recover. Earn the money January through June, have the surgery in early July, and be back in the classroom by Labor Day with no one any the wiser."

"Except for Bryan McGeough."

A pained smile. "I begged him not to say anything. After the way I had to . . . 'live' in Iowa, I wanted a fresh start here, like I told you before. A fresh start in leading the new, real life I was always meant to live."

I thought about Matthew's comment at the job site. "Bryan asked you for money."

"A hundred dollars a week, two hundred once I got on full-time at the school. I tried to explain to him I needed that money for my surgery, for the convalescence. But Bry just laughed. 'Hey, big *girl,* how do you think the parents'll like their little kids' teacher waving a dick under her dress?' And . . . and he went on from there."

Pooky came back, woofing again as she dropped the branch at Greene's feet.

I said, "What did you do?"

"Walked over to Bry's house the next day, after I thought he'd maybe calmed down. I knocked on the back door, but got no answer, so I went in. Bry was passed out on the couch, probably drinking from the time he'd left my place. I must have surprised him, though, because he came at me, violent-attack mode. I tried to fight back, but Bry had my arm and was bending it—real pain—and so I picked up the log and swung it. Unfortunately, he was stepping that way—into the log, I mean—and he . . . he just went down."

Pooky woofed some more. I reached toward the sand and tossed the stick end over end maybe forty yards away. The dog got the hint and tore after it.

"Thanks," said Greene, then closed her eyes. "I looked down at the pool of Bry's . . . blood seeping out from under his hair, and . . . and I got out of there before any stained my shoes. I went back to my house, settled my nerves, then waited till the next day to walk Pooky over there and kick in the glass. I took his television and a few other things to make it look right before I called the police."

I watched Greene sniffle again, then wring the big hands in her lap. "It just doesn't seem fair. All I want to be is what I feel I am, a woman who loves teaching the children who love her." A hesitation. "But now that's all wrecked."

"Not necessarily," I said.

Greene's face jerked up. "What?"

"I was hired to find out whether brother killed brother. I'd become pretty sure of the answer before learning about you. My report to the insurance company doesn't need the extra boost."

Greene blinked rapidly. "I . . . I don't understand what you're saying."

I let my eyes rove down the beach, Pooky loping back with her prize. "The proceeds from the policy on Bryan's life can be paid in all good conscience since Matthew had nothing to do with his brother's death."

"But what . . . ?" Greene blinked some more. "Where does that leave me?"

I thought about my talk with Beth at her grave. "Make your fresh start count for something beyond fixating on somebody who's already dead. Be good to the kids you teach, Ms. Greene, and put all this behind you."

"You're just going to let me . . . go?"

"No. I'm going to let you stay."

Walking away from the water, I could hear Pooky woofing louder and louder. It almost covered up the other sound, the crying one, but even that faded into the October wind whipping around the place where Renée Greene liked to run her dog.

IT COULD GET WORSE
An Al Darlan Story
by Edward D. Hoch

Edward D. Hoch is the most prolific mystery short story
writer of all time, hands down. He has appeared in every
issue of *Ellery Queen's Mystery Magazine* for over thirty
years. He was president of The Mystery Writers of America
the year PWA was formed, and welcomed us into the fold
with open arms. The first Darlan story appeared in 1957,
when he was known as Al Diamond. After one more appearance under that name an editor suggested a change
because Richard Diamond was then on T.V., and Diamond became Darlan. Possibly Ed's least-known character, he is my
personal favorite of the many series characters Ed has created.

I had an Al Darlan story in my very first PWA anthology
sixteen years ago, and am proud to have one here.

These were quiet days at Darlan & Trapper Investigations, and I hoped they stayed that way
even if it was bad for my bank account. My young
partner, Mike Trapper, was off on vacation with
his new wife, Marla, and I was getting too old to
handle any rough stuff alone. The last thing I
needed was for Fritz Munday to walk through my
office door and peel five hundred-dollar bills off
his roll.

"I want to hire you, Darlan," he said without
preamble.

"Why? Are all your regular goons locked up?" Munday was a brisk businesslike man who looked like a retired banker. He ran a string of illegal poker clubs around town, noted for their high-stakes games that sometimes ran for days. Players who welshed on their debts had been known to wind up in the hospital with a broken arm or leg. A lot of people, including the police, had tried to tell him he was living in the past, that his sort of strong-arm tactics belonged to another era. But Fritz Munday belonged to another era too, and maybe that's why he wanted to hire me.

"I don't want you for rough stuff," he said.

"That's good."

"I need a detective. I've had some trouble."

"What sort?"

"Have you heard about the Cutter? That's what my table girls call him."

"I don't get around as much as I used to."

"He's been showing up at my places. You know how the tables are. I have my girls at each one to make sure the house gets its five percent cut out of all the pots. The guy waits until there's a break in the action with no one looking and he cuts them. He cuts my girls."

"What do you mean?" I asked.

"He cuts them with something. A razor, I don't know what. He cuts their hands, and one time he cut a girl's face. Then he's gone before the other players can grab him."

I pulled over my yellow legal pad and started taking notes. "How many attacks have there been?"

"Six over the past month."

"Always the same man?"

"Young, under thirty. Well dressed with a suit and tie. Hair cut short. One girl said he reminded her of these religious people who come around to your door on weekends."

"What's his motive?"

Fritz Munday shook his head. "Beats me. I keep expecting to get a shakedown letter. You know, an extortion thing. But I haven't heard a word."

"Does he have a favorite place he's hit more than once?"

"Twice upstairs at the Caribbean Club, the other four at different places of mine."

"The girl whose face was slashed?"

Munday nodded. "At the Caribbean. She thought she recognized him and asked him about the earlier cutting. That's when he slashed her."

"I'll want to talk to her."

He wrote an address and phone number. "She's out of the hospital, but she may need some face work if the scar doesn't heal right."

"Have you reported it to the police?"

"My games are not sanctioned by law. You must understand that." He pointed to the hundred-dollar bills still on the desk between us. "That's for the rest of this week, plus expenses. I'll pay you a thousand a week for the rest of this month, with a bonus if you find him."

"I'll do what I can," I promised.

We were operating without a secretary at the present time, so the following morning I turned on the answering machine and went off to interview Miss Forrest LeClair. With that name I figured her for an exotic dancer between engagements, so I was surprised to find her sharing an apartment with another girl a block from the City College campus. Both were students there.

"Forrest LeClair?" I asked the short blond girl who answered the door.

"That's my roommate," she answered, bellowing over her shoulder, "Forrest! There's a guy here to see you!"

Forrest LeClair was tall and slender as a boy, more attractive than her roommate, with dark hair and pale skin marred now by an adhesive bandage that covered most of her right cheek. "Are you from the police?" she asked, eyeing me uncertainly.

I showed her my license. "Private. Your boss, Mr. Munday, hired me."

She led me into the cramped sitting room of their apartment, and when the blond girl continued to hover, she dismissed her with "It's all right, Grace." Then she turned to me, her smile puckered at one end by the bandage. "You're investigating the attack on me?"

I nodded. "Munday said you got a good look at the cutter. Could you tell me exactly what happened?"

She took a deep breath. "It was Sunday evening around ten, four nights ago. Usually Sundays are slow with weekend games winding down. There were maybe ten players in the place, at just two tables. I usually work weekends because of my classes, and I was due to get off at midnight. The room boss, Charlie, had sent the other girls home, and I was covering both tables, collecting the house's five percent of every pot. I wasn't paying that much attention to the players, but there was this one thin guy in a dark suit. He stood out from the others and looked vaguely familiar. I remembered when one of the girls was slashed on the hand about four weeks ago, and I was pretty sure that guy had been in the place then too. When I saw him cashing in his chips, getting up to leave, I asked him about it. Asked him if I hadn't seen him there that night. He—I don't know, he had nothing in his hands except a deck of cards, but suddenly his hand moved like a blur, faster than my eyes could follow. I felt nothing at first. I thought he'd tried to hit me and missed. Then someone said my face was bleeding."

"Was he still there facing you?"

"He turned away, and the other players came running up to me. Charlie came out of the office to see what had happened. By that time the cutter was gone. Charlie drove me to the hospital to get stitches. I almost fainted when I saw my face in the mirror."

"Would you recognize the man again?"

"I certainly would. I can still see his face when I close my eyes."

"Try to think. Was there anything unusual about him? Any scars or blemishes?"

"No, his skin was very smooth. His eyes—they seemed a bit slanted, like Oriental, but I couldn't be sure. All the time his expression was blank. It never changed."

"What's Charlie's last name?"

"Charlie Baxter. He's worked for Mr. Munday a long time."

"How about you? Have you worked Baxter's room long?"

"Just a few months. I was at Grayson's, another of the poker rooms, before that. But the Caribbean Club is closer to campus, so I got a transfer."

"No trouble at the other place?"

"Not while I was there. I heard talk this same guy slashed one of their girls a few weeks ago, though."

"You know these poker clubs are illegal, don't you?"

"I guess so. But the cops never bother us. It's easy work, and I need the money for school. I'm just finishing my junior year."

I thanked her and stood up to leave. "You've been a big help, Miss LeClair."

"Will you find him before he cuts someone else?"

"I certainly hope so."

Baxter was a bulky man with the look of a retired wrestler. I found him in the poker room over the Caribbean Club, straightening things up before the evening games began. "It looks bad for me when he cuts two of my girls," he told me. "I should have spotted him myself."

"What about the first girl?"

"Ten stitches across the palm of her hand. She quit the job and moved back to Omaha. Can't say I blame her."

"When was this?"

"About a month ago. It was the first of the attacks. There were four more just like it at Fritz's other clubs. Then he came back here."

"Why do you think he went for Miss LeClair's face?"

A shrug. "She recognized him from before."

That got me thinking. "This was the sixth attack, and he started repeating the poker clubs he was targeting. Does Munday just have five places in town?"

"That's all right now. He keeps a low profile so the neighbors don't raise an uproar."

"Do you always employ attractive young women to collect the house take?"

"The guys like it, you know. They dress nice, tuxedoes and ruffled shirts, and it's easy work. Usually we get college girls."

"Do they ever date the players after the games?"

"Fritz has got a rule against it. He doesn't want any trouble with the vice squad."

"Aren't the games themselves trouble?"

"He's a friend of Lieutenant Schwinn. The cops don't worry much about illegal poker games."

"What about this Cutter? You think it's a shakedown?"

Another shrug. "Don't know what to think. Fritz says he hasn't gotten any messages asking for money."

I took out the list of locations Munday had given me. "Which was the second place he hit?"

The stocky man studied the list. "Grayson's on the West Side. It's a cigar store with a back room. They used to take bets on horse races there before the state legalized off-track betting."

"Is Cage Grayson still around?" I knew him slightly from the old neighborhood, but I hadn't thought about him in years.

"Still around, over sixty, but at the store every day."

If the cutter was starting down his list again, he might be calling on Cage's place next. That was the only lead I had.

I stopped back at the office to check the day's mail and caught a call from my partner, Mike Trapper. He was phoning from Aruba and insisting I should be there with them. "There's nothing like it, Al. It's all sun and sand, plus some fancy shops to separate Marla from her money. How's the weather up there?"

"Not bad for April. We've got one new case."

"Need me?"

"I think I can handle it. Enjoy the beach."

I couldn't really complain about how Mike spent his money. He'd bailed me out with his dad's dough when my original agency was on the verge of bankruptcy. I hung up and looked out the dirty window. It was getting dark. I locked up the office and went back to my car.

Grayson's cigar store, which also sold newspapers and paperbound books, had a metal sign out front proclaiming HEADQUARTERS FOR YOUR READING AND TOBACCO NEEDS. From two blocks away I could see the red flashers of the police cars reflecting off the sign. I pulled into a parking space and walked the rest of the way. The first familiar face I saw was Lieutenant Schwinn from Homicide.

"That you, Darlan?" he asked, peering through the neon-lit twilight. With his flat-headed brush cut and narrow eyes, he looked like a cat waiting to pounce on you for any wrong answer.

"It's me. What's going on here?"

"Cage Grayson got himself killed. Throat cut at one of his own poker tables."

"Sorry to hear that. I was dropping by to see him."

"What about?"

"A business matter."

He motioned me into the shadows next to the building, out of sight of the other detectives. "There have been rumors around town that someone is trying to shake down Fritz Munday by attacking the employees of his poker clubs. You wouldn't know anything about that, would you?"

"First I've heard of it."

"Some regular customers have been staying away. Grayson was alone back there with his killer."

"Anyone see who did it?"

"A fairly tall guy in a leather jacket and baseball cap. He was wearing a mask, one of those creepy things that looks like a human face but doesn't change expression. The clerk at the counter didn't notice it was a mask going in, but when the guy came out of the back room, walking fast, he went in to check and found Grayson dead." He eyed me suspiciously and added, "If you know anything about this, Darlan, now's the time to tell me."

"I don't know a thing," I answered honestly. In fact, I was beginning to think I knew less than most everyone else.

In the morning the story made page one of the paper, below the fold. It said that Grayson's throat had been cut from behind, probably by a thief. No description of the man was given. I waited till nine o'clock and then phoned Fritz Munday. "I'm glad you called, Darlan," he said. "Did you read the morning paper?"

"I didn't have to. I was there."

"You were what?"

"I went to see Cage Grayson last night, about your problem. He was dead and the police were already on the scene."

"Too bad you didn't get there a bit earlier. Cage was a friend of mine from way back. He didn't deserve an end like this."

"I think we have to expect a further escalation in this matter."

"It's already happened. I received a special-delivery letter just a few minutes ago. It reads: *It could get worse. Prepare $250,000 in used fifty-dollar bills* and await instructions."

"Is it signed?"

"The Cutter."

I sighed. This thing was moving too fast for me. "I'll be right over."

The message was as he'd described, printed out on a computer with perfect, untraceable letters. It had been mailed from the main post office at nine the previous evening, about an hour after Grayson's killing. "What are you going to do?" I asked.

"I'm not going to pay the bastard, that's for sure! You find him for me, and I'll do a job on his throat myself."

"We need to prepare a package in any event," I told him. "Let's see—he wants fifty packets of a hundred bills each. Cut up some newspapers and top each bundle with a real fifty, then put them in a suitcase. You know the routine."

"Anything else?"

"Close your clubs tonight. Tell the regulars it's out of respect for Cage. No point in giving this guy another chance to kill someone."

"All right," he agreed readily.

"One other thing. Someone told me Lieutenant Schwinn is a friend of yours. Are you paying him to ignore your clubs?"

"He's not on the take, if that's what you're asking. Sometimes we do favors for each other. What are you thinking?"

"I'm just wondering if those girls were attacked to focus police attention on your operation. When the first cuttings didn't work, he slashed the LeClair girl's cheek. And when the police still weren't called, he killed Cage Grayson. Maybe he just wants to force you out of business, one way or another."

"He may succeed," Munday answered grimly.

"Do you have any rivals who'd like to see you ruined?"

"None that I'm aware of."

The next question was difficult, but it had to be asked. "Just how big a blow would a quarter-million be to you?"

"Close to a year's profits. Not enough to ruin me, but it would hurt. Worse than that, if the word got around, someone else might try the same thing. Or something worse."

I remembered the words from the extortion note. *It could get worse.*

*   *   *

We both knew that the next letter, if there was to be one, would come the following morning. I arranged to be at Munday's office precisely at nine o'clock. Meanwhile I wanted to speak with Lieutenant Schwinn again, and I found him at Headquarters. He looked up as I entered the squad room and said, "Well, Darlan, what brings you up here? You want to confess to the Grayson killing?"

"Hardly, but I want to learn more about his death."

"Buy a newspaper," he said dismissively.

"Come on, Lieutenant. We can help each other on this one."

"OK, you first."

I decided I had to lay some cards on the table. "My client is Fritz Munday. He hired me because of a series of attacks on the girls at his poker clubs."

"Illegal poker clubs," the detective amended. "We may go easy on them, but we don't condone them."

"They're legal in some states," I pointed out.

"Not here. What sort of attacks are you talking about?"

"Five girls have had their hands cut, by a razor or something. The latest one, last Sunday, had her cheek slashed. And now Cage Grayson gets his throat cut."

Schwinn grunted, making some notes while I talked. "The girls must have seen their attacker."

"Tall, thin, probably under thirty, well dressed in a dark suit and tie. He has smooth skin and a sort of oriental look to his eyes."

"The man who killed Grayson was wearing some

sort of mask. That implies he went there with murder in mind. He didn't want anyone seeing his face
this time."

"Maybe. What can you tell me about the wound,
Lieutenant? Did you recover the weapon?"

"It was a knife with a serrated edge. He must
have taken it with him. The medical examiner says
there's evidence the killer got behind Grayson,
pulled his head back by the hair, and cut his throat
with a single slice, left to right."

"Right-handed."

Schwinn shrugged. "Most people are. That doesn't
tell us anything."

"Did Grayson have any special enemies?"

"We were working on the theory that some big
loser might have killed him, though that seems un-
likely. It's not as if he dealt the cards or anything.
You tell me about these girls being cut, but it's the
same thing. Why would a loser have a grudge
against them? They just collected the house cut of
the pots."

"Someone might be trying to shake down Munday," I suggested innocently. "The violence seems
to be escalating."

"If you hear anything, let me know," he said as
I got up to leave.

I was seated in Munday's office at nine the next
morning when the special-delivery letter arrived. It
was Saturday and the building was deserted except
for the custodian mopping the hallway. Munday
took the envelope from the postman and ripped it
open, not even considering the possibility of a letter
bomb. The message was brief and to the point: *Put*

$250,000 in suitcase. Leave in Dumpster behind your building at eight tonight. No cops or the attacks will continue. It could get worse. The Cutter.

"What do you think?" Munday asked me.

"You'd better do it. What's the setup out back? Is there a place where we could watch from, maybe catch him in the act?"

"Not in this building. The Dumpster is up against a blank wall."

"Let's take a look."

The green rubbish container, showing the scars and dents of age, was at the end of a short alley that ran between the wall of Munday's building and a dry cleaner next door. I studied the place and decided, "That's where I need to be, behind that side window in the dry cleaner's place. Can you arrange it?"

"Sure. They know me."

It was dark by eight o'clock when I took up my position inside the dry cleaner's shop. I'd brought my flashlight and snub-nosed .38 revolver along for company, even though Mike Trapper kidded me about carrying such an old-fashioned weapon. Just at eight, Fritz Munday appeared at the mouth of the alley carrying the suitcase. I hoped he'd prepared the bundles as I'd instructed. He lifted the lid of the Dumpster and placed the suitcase on top of a pile of plastic rubbish bags. Then he retreated back to the street.

I was settling down for a long night's wait, figuring it might be hours before the extortionist showed himself, when I heard a sound from the next room. Someone had entered the dry cleaner's through the back door, the same door that I'd used. "Don't shoot," a familiar voice cautioned. "It's just me."

"Munday! What are you doing back here?"

"It's my money, Darlan. I'm keeping an eye on it along with you. I've got a gun too—a nine-millimeter Glock with three times the firepower of that antique you're carrying."

"Put that away and sit down here. We'll probably have a long wait."

We did. The hours dragged on as we kept our eyes focused on the alley and the rubbish container. Somewhere around midnight I asked him about Charlie Baxter, the manager of the card room over the Caribbean Club. "Baxter's a good man, I guess. He's only worked for me a year or so. Not like Cage, who'd been with me from the beginning."

"How'd he get that name? Was he locked up for a while?"

Fritz Munday chuckled. "That's what everyone thought, and he did have a juvenile record. But in the neighborhood we called him Caz. It was a slang term for an easily accomplished fraud or robbery. Specifically in Grayson's case the seduction and occasional rape of young women and deflowering of virgins, something he was still notorious for in his sixties. Caz became Cage and the name stuck. He wasn't a bad sort, though. I could always trust Cage, which is more than I could say for some of the others."

"Do you think one of your room managers could be directing the cutter, hoping to put you out of business?"

"Hell, anything's possible. It's a great business so long as you know who your real friends are."

There was a sudden clatter from the alley, and we saw a cat run from a cluster of empty bottles. It was the most exciting thing that happened all night. Around four o'clock I suggested we give up and go home. "Maybe he knows we're watching," I suggested.

"How could he know?"

"Maybe there'll be another message in the morning."

We waited until the first streaks of dawn appeared in the eastern sky. Then I went out the back door of the dry cleaner's shop and walked over to the Dumpster. I had a crazy notion that the suitcase would be gone, vanished without a trace while we watched all night. But it was still there, and the doctored bundles of money were still inside.

There was no message on Sunday morning, and Munday phoned me in the afternoon to say he'd still heard nothing from the Cutter. I'd managed to get a few hours' sleep and was feeling a bit more human. "What are you going to do about opening your card rooms?" I asked.

"Well, I don't have a new room manager for Grayson's place, so I can't open them all. I'm going to try opening just one tonight. Sundays are slow anyway unless a game runs over from Saturday. We'll see how it goes."

"Which one are you opening?"

"I think the Mazda on the west side. It's an upscale restaurant with a party room downstairs that we use when it's not booked. We'll open there at nine tonight."

"How can you notify your players in time?"

Munday grinned. "Hell, we've got a web page on the Internet. People check in every day."

Maybe I was wrong about his living in the past. I suppose it shouldn't have surprised me, coming from someone who carried a 9mm Glock.

Later that afternoon I phoned Forrest LeClair's apartment. "If you're free tonight," I said, "there's a chance we might be able to catch the man who slashed you."

She hesitated. "What do I have to do?"

"Sit in a car with me across from the Mazda restaurant and watch who goes in."

"I can do that."

"Will you recognize him?"

"I'll never forget that face."

"Be ready in an hour. I'll pick you up."

It was growing dark by the time we found a suitable parking place across from the restaurant. If the Cutter came at all, it wouldn't be until after the games got going at nine. We had more than an hour to wait. "How's your face?" I asked.

"It doesn't hurt much, but they told me it'll be red for six months and there'll be a scar. I'll probably have to get plastic surgery. But at least I'm alive. What makes you think he'll show up here tonight?"

"He's trying to shake down Munday by escalating the attacks. I don't think he'll let a night go by now without trying something."

She lit a cigarette and settled back to wait with me. Shortly before nine we saw people starting to arrive. There were a couple of attractive young women first, whom Forrest identified as table girls, followed by a middle-aged man and then a pair of younger men. "The players," she said. "I recognize the guy on the left. He's a regular at the clubs."

"But no sign of the man who slashed you?"

"Not yet."

Just after nine two more men went in, separately. Then there was nothing for fifteen minutes. I was beginning to doubt my theory. "How about that one?" I asked as another man approached on foot from the corner.

"No. He's too fat. The man who cut me was—" Suddenly she grabbed my sleeve. "That's him, over there!"

I followed her pointing finger and saw a slender young man in a dark suit just entering the side door of the restaurant. "You're sure?"

"I'm sure."

"Come up with me."

"No. As soon as he sees me he'll know why I'm there."

She was probably right. "Stay here, I'll be back."

I followed the young man through the same door into the restaurant. This late on a Sunday evening the place was all but deserted. "Can I help you, sir?" the hostess asked.

"Poker," I said quietly. She motioned toward a narrow staircase to the lower party rooms. At the bottom I found myself in a large, empty party room. Hearing low voices, I walked across to a door in one of the sliding partitions on the opposite side. A smaller section of the room had been set aside for the poker games, and two of the four tables were in use. The slender man was playing at one of them with two older men. The table girl, in her ruffled shirt and tuxedo jacket, sat watching. I joined them, buying fifty dollars' worth of chips from the girl and anteing up on the next hand. One of the older men was dealing and he nodded, acknowledging my arrival.

I sat in for twenty minutes and won two fair-sized pots. When it was his turn, the slender man opposite me, his face the smooth mask with slightly slanted eyes that Forrest LeClair had described, dealt cards with the precision of a robot. He was an unskilled bettor, though, and won only a single small pot when the others dropped out. The girls took a break every hour, rotating around the tables. By this time there were three games going on, and another table girl had joined the new group. Our girl left to go to the ladies' room. The man across the table put down his cards. "Deal me out," he said, leaving his dwindling pile of chips where they were. I got up and followed him.

There was a small bar at one end of the room, and he ordered a beer, then left it sitting there as the girl came back from the ladies' room. "I'll show you a trick," he said, holding out a deck of cards he'd taken from his pocket.

"What?" the girl asked uncertainly.

"Just pick a card."

She was reaching for it when I grabbed her wrist and yanked it away. "Let me do it," I said.

The slim man's pale face twisted with anger. He pulled the cards back and fingered one from the deck with his left hand, sweeping it at me with a sudden arc. I stepped aside easily and drew my .38. "Try that again and you're a dead man!"

He tried it again and I shot him in the hand.

It was all confusion after that, and suddenly Lieutenant Schwinn was removing the revolver from my grasp. "We can handle it now," he told me.

"Where did you come from?"

"You think you're the only one who figured he'd come here tonight?"

I bent and carefully picked up the fallen card, holding it by the edges. It was the jack of spades and it had his blood on it. The pasteboard had been carefully slit along one edge and a razor blade inserted into it. I handed it to Schwinn. "You'll need that for evidence."

"Where are you going?"

"Someone's waiting for me outside."

She'd gotten out of the car and crossed the street to the Mazda. "I saw the police running in. Did you get him?"

"We got him."

"Did he confess?"

"He will."

She touched the bandage on her cheek. "Who is he, anyway?"

I shrugged. "Probably he's someone who hates women."

"If that's true, why did he kill Cage Grayson?"

"He didn't. I can give you four good reasons why he didn't. It was you who did that job, Forrest, and you'd better start praying for a sympathetic jury."

Later, at the squad room, Schwinn sighed and told me, "We finally identified him. He's a former mental patient named Thomas Cahin. Been out of the hospital about two months and stopped taking his medication. It happens too much these days."

"What about Forrest LeClair?"

"She's in the next room waiting to be questioned. We found the serrated knife between the seat cushions in your car. You'd better tell me the rest of it."

"All right. You see, the killing of Grayson was supposed to be an escalation of the Cutter attacks, but the crimes differed in at least four ways." I counted them off on my fingers. "The earlier victims were all women. They were cut with a sharp blade like a razor, not a serrated knife. The Cutter wasn't afraid to show his face, while Grayson's killer left the place wearing a mask. Most important of all, we established that Grayson's killer was right-handed, while the Cutter used his left hand. I was pretty sure when Forrest told me she was facing him when he slashed her right cheek, and I verified it tonight when he swung at me with his razor blade."

"So the Cutter didn't kill Cage Grayson. But how does that make it the LeClair woman?"

"The table girls referred to their assailant as the Cutter, and that was the name on the extortion notes Munday received. But their assailant never called himself that, and probably didn't even know about the name. I suspected the notes weren't from the real Cutter, and this wasn't about extortion. When Munday's suitcase full of money was never picked up, I was sure of it. Grayson's killer wanted to connect the crimes, to piggyback on the Cutter's outrages. Signing the notes with *The Cutter* made me suspect one of the table girls or perhaps a room manager who knew about the name. Forrest had worked at Grayson's poker room for a time, and Munday told me had a reputation of seducing and sometimes raping young women. Perhaps Forrest had a motive for killing him."

"More. I need more, Darlan."

"How about this? The killer, wearing a mask, enters the back room at Grayson's cigar store and cuts his throat. How? By getting behind him, yanking back his hair, and using the knife. Don't you see what's wrong with that picture? Grayson would hardly let a masked man, or woman, get behind him even if he didn't see the knife. The killer had to remove the mask once inside that back room, and Grayson had to recognize and trust the face that he saw. Perhaps he thought it was a little love play when she got behind him. It had to be one of the table girls, probably one he'd seduced. Which one? Well, Forrest is tall and slender as a boy. She could probably pass for one, but why bother with the mask? It was noticed as the killer left, and the body was discovered at once. Why not simply wear a wig or hat, disguise yourself in some less noticeable way? What was there about the killer's face that had to be covered by a mask?"

"The bandage," Schwinn answered.

"Exactly! Forrest LeClair would have been noticed and identified at once by anyone who saw her face. I suppose it was after she was cut that she got the idea. Grayson had seduced her, maybe even raped her. Even though she moved to another poker room, she didn't forget it. She killed him and sent those notes so the whole thing would look like an extortion attempt."

Lieutenant Schwinn got to his feet. "It might be enough to get a confession out of her."

It was.

When Mike Trapper came back a few days later he asked what was new. "Nothing much," I told him. "There was a case involving a serial slasher, beautiful women, seduction and rape, a masked killer, extortion and a shooting. But I handled it."

THE SLEEPING DETECTIVE
AN IVAN MONK STORY
by Gary Phillips

When I asked Gary to do an Ivan Monk story, he said he
had an idea for a takeoff on the British mini-series of several
years ago, *The Singing Detective*. I told him to go for it.
"The Sleeping Detective" is the result, a clever pastiche of
not only that mini-series, but some other famous detective
series, as well. *Only the Wicked* (Write Way, 2000) will be
the next Monk novel.

Monk wasn't quite himself. His arms swung
loose at his sides as the heels of his brown
wing tips echoed in the long hallway. The corridor
stretched underneath Los Angeles International
Airport. It was the last old part of the sprawling
facility, constructed in 1961 and still connecting the
TWA terminal with the outside. Wait, he asked
himself, what year is this anyway?

His heels clacked a rhythmic pattern as Monk—
no, it was McGill, yeah, his name was McGill, and
it was 1967—strode confidently along the tiled passageway. The walls were also covered in tile, done
in multicolored linear designs.

McGill cared nothing of style or theories of ar-
chitecture. He cared nothing that he'd been double-
crossed and left for dead in a windblown shack in

263

the Tehatchapis. He projected little about what willful fate had spared him the grave after being shot twice, point-blank. No, the only thing McGill cared about was getting back the $67,000 owed to him. And if he had to do it over the bodies of his best friend Veese and his wife, Jill, so be it.

McGill's tie herked and jerked as his tall, fluid frame pounded toward the end of the corridor. His face was as empty of emotion as the hallway was devoid of other passengers. His close-cropped, prematurely gray hair complemented his crisp Brooks Brothers suit. The muscles in his legs flawlessly propelled him toward the end of the passageway, and closer to his goal.

S'funny, but he didn't ache from the wounds, the holes his dear darling lovingly put in him. This while her boyfriend, Veese, the guy he'd saved once on a job gone wrong, looked on, licking his lips. If McGill was the chatty sort, and he wasn't, he'd be vague on the details of how he got out of that below-freezing cabin at night and got himself healed up.

Suddenly he was no longer in the airport. The echo of his shoes blended in with the sounds of midday traffic. The sun was bright and glinted off the windshield of the new Biscayne he'd stolen as he parked on the rise. He removed the hand shading his eyes. Up there past that wall and shrubs was the door to their love nest. If he could still remember how to smile, he would have.

Now he was moving across the threshold, the .357 Magnum in his right hand. His left hand was in Jill's face, pushing her back and out of his way. She'd been so shocked upon seeing him, all she could do was whisper his name over and over. Not that it mattered to him if she called out Veese's name. He wanted him to step into the cross hairs.

Everything—his motion, her falling, the door banging back—happened in slow motion, defying logic and the laws of gravity. He kicked in the door to the bedroom, aiming and firing in the same heartbeat that thudded in his throat. The recoil of the pistol made his arm twitch. It wasn't his .45, and absently he wondered why he'd traded that for this bruiser. He emptied the gun's six bullets into the unmade, and unattended, bed. He whirled as real time jumped back on track.

"A ghost, an avenging specter." Jill had a hand to her forehead as if she were fevered. "McGill, I—" She couldn't finish, didn't dare to offer an excuse.

He stood there, spent, close on her, and despite himself that familiar feeling flooded over him, if only momentarily. He pointed the gun barrel at the bed. "Where?"

"Gone."

"How long?"

"Months. He stops by every so often. Sends money by courier each month."

"When?"

"Today, later."

He glanced back at the bed. Behind the headboard was a floor-to-ceiling mirror so Veese could watch himself as they made love. On the nightstand was a box. It was open, and on its side read CONTINENTAL DONUTS.

He turned back to her as they sat on the couch. For some reason his eyes were closed and he couldn't get the lids to lift. . . .

"Ivan," she said, kissing his ear. "Ivan, when did you get in, baby?"

He yawned, his arms encircling the pillow. "Ummm," he drooled, "after five." He lay half awake, the details of the dream fleeing his conscious mind.

Jill Kodama got off the bed, rubbing the back of his head. "I didn't hear you get in. You must have driven straight from New Mexico after I talked to you yesterday."

"Wanted to get home, sleep."

She leaned over and kissed his cheek. She smelled like flowers. "Aren't you a bit perfumed up for a judge?"

"You want me to smell like cigars and Old Spice like you do?" She slapped his butt under the blanket. "I'll call you later, see if you want to come downtown for dinner. Let's try Ciudad. The Veese case I'm trying is about wrapped up."

"Is he guilty?"

"That's for a jury to decide, citizen Monk."

He opened an eye, a kraken awakening from the depths. "Is he guilty?"

She was at the door to their bedroom. "I'd say he has blood on his hands. Call you." She left, and he tried to get back to sleep. After some effort, as his body wound down again, the phone rang, and rang, and rang.

"Boss, somebody's been puttin' the nab on our doughnuts."

It was Elrod, the manager of Continental Donuts, the small business he owned in the Crenshaw District. Elrod's bass was an indication of the size of a man who'd give Jesse Ventura palpitations.

"You mean, some cat broke in and took our doughnuts but not cash?" he breathed into the handset. Why wouldn't they let him sleep?

"No," the manager boomed, irritated. "For the last week, glazes, fancy twists, maple and chocolate crullers and jelly-filled have been gettin' filched while the shop's been open. Sixty-seven, I counted. Sixty-seven doughnuts have been taken."

Monk was going to question just how the big man could be so exact in his count, but he didn't want to encourage a long discussion. He coughed, clearing his throat and rolling onto his back. "You have suspects?" He scratched himself.

"Well," Elrod rumbled on the other end, "I hate to say it, but it has to be one of the staff. The inventory has been gettin' filched off the racks as the goods cool in the back."

"You mean the new guy, Moises, right?"

"Aw, see, I don't want to say that for sure." Elrod, like Monk, had been born and raised in the 'hood. Unlike Monk, he was also an ex-con, and was sensitive to the notion he should disparage someone trying to be responsible.

The new guy was a young man from the area where the shop was located. For the last two months since he'd begun, there had been no suggestion of problems with him. If anything, Monk had noticed the young man had looked more harried and thinner the last week or so as he'd been diligently working with Elrod in learning how to perfect his doughnut making.

"It ain't mutant rats, is it?"

Elrod didn't deign to answer such a ridiculous remark.

"Okay, how about you see if you can correlate the times you've noticed doughnuts missing with Moises' shifts. If the times are the same, then I'll have a talk with him. You haven't said anything to him yet, have you?"

"No, you're the private detective. I was kinda figuring you'd want to take over this investigation."

"Carry on, my swarthy cohort."

"I'll let you know."

Monk hung up and lay on his stomach. Of course, now the missing doughnuts intrigued him, and he had to concentrate to stop himself from thinking about them. He put on the radio, the volume low. If nothing else, he'd get filled in on a few current events, and hopefully the drone of voices would be an electronic lullaby to put him back to slumber land.

He switched from FM and National Public Radio to AM and KNX, the all-news station. He settled under the covers once more, tamping down deep whatever angst he might be developing about missing doughnuts. There was a report about a tie-up on the 101 in both directions. Monk smiled inwardly, feeling superior that he didn't have to be out there with those poor bastards today.

Tom Hatten, the entertainment reporter, came on after a commercial. "I'm saddened to report today the passing of Jack Denning, one-time fifties and sixties leading man of such neoclassic tough-guy films as *Prison Cell 99* and *Desperation Alley*. Younger listeners attuned to TV Land reruns will no doubt remember Mr. Denning in later years as the mysterious reclusive millionaire Raxton Gault in the cult seventies TV show *The Midas Memorandum*."

Monk began to drift off, an image of Denning in snap brim hat and trench coat punching out some crook slipping past his eyelids. Hatten went on, his voice seeming to come to him as if though thick glass. "And, of course, the older crowd out there, like yours truly, have fond memories of Jack Denning as half of that sleuthing man-and-wife team the Easterlys, a late fifties, early sixties TV show that . . ."

Alex Easterly was walking Sergei, the silver-tan Afghan hound, through the park. The grass in the park was awfully green, more like carpet than real blades, it occurred to him. There were places where the grass bulged, and it was as if it wasn't somehow lying flat upon the earth. And the park bench where the man waited for him, what of those bushes behind him? Wasn't that glint a jiggling wire leading from the greenery, shaking the limbs as if there was a slight wind?

"Mr. Easterly?" The man looked off, past Easterly's shoulder. He stood and they shook hands.

"Yes, he said, sitting next to him. Sergei rested on his haunches, his head regally erect. What kind of dog didn't pant? "You said over the phone there was a matter you could only talk to me in person about, Mr. Jones. Or should I say, Mr. Masters." He took out a cigarette case inlaid with whitish jade tinged with green. When the hell had he started smoking those? "Care for one?" he said, snapping the case open as if he'd done it a thousand times before.

Nolan Masters declined, showing the flat of his hand. "I guess you're as sharp as they say you are."

"You're not exactly unknown, Mr. Masters." He lit the cigarette and placed it in his mouth. In doing so, his fingers brushed against his chin—where was his goatee? But damned if that cigarette wasn't smooth as he didn't know what. "I peruse a number of publications, Mr. Masters, including *Business Today*."

"Yes, well," the other man began, uncrossing his legs. "It's my business that I need help with, unfortunately. Someone has been stealing some of our, well, let's call them plans, shall we? This is hush-hush stuff we've been keeping under wraps until the right moment to introduce them on the market, you see."

He was about to reply but turned his head at a sound. Was that someone watching them over there, beyond the ring of light from the street lamp next to the bench? "You know I'm retired now, Mr. Masters?" The damned dog hadn't looked their way once. He just stared off in the direction he heard the sound coming from. "Any of this have to do with the space race, Mr. Masters?"

Flustered, he blurted, "How—why did you ask that? My company makes tubes and transistors for radios and TVs."

"As I said"—he dropped the cigarette—"I read various publications." He ground out the butt, a black area appearing in the supposed grass beneath his toe. "Our new President Kennedy in his last speech made it clear we need to be doing more to reach the stars for the U.S.A. This Sputnik satellite

the Russians put up caught a lot of us sleeping."
He winked at the man, but he wasn't sure why.

"And your company has done work for the State
Department before." Finally the dog looked at him,
panting. There was the snap of a finger and the
dog stopped, then resumed his previous rigid
stance.

Masters leaned forward as if a great weight were
upon him. He stared at the ground, his hands
pressed together. "As per your reputation, Mr.
Easterly, I knew you to be the man for the job."

He then stared intently at Easterly. Oddly, he
seemed to be suppressing a smile as he did so. "An
experienced sleuth, and someone from outside who
could easily go undercover in my company to ferret
out what may be spies in my organization. Because
of the press to get our work done, I've made several new hires. And Mr. Easterly, in under three
days—sixty-seven hours, to be precise—I need to
deliver a top-secret device to the government. I
must know if I've been compromised or not. Of
course, you can name your price."

"This is for my country, sir." Yeah, but didn't
he have a mortgage he had to help pay? "How will
you introduce me?"

"As the new accountant."

"What happened to the previous one?"

"He was murdered."

Kettle drums suddenly boomed, and a guitar and
horn joined in. Easterly frowned as the camera
came in tight on his face. Things went black, and
when the lights came up again, he was dancing with
his wife, Jill Easterly, in their posh living room.
Now a swinging jazz number played on the stereo

unit: a lot of vibes and strings. Ice melted in two tumblers amid amber liquid on the wet bar.

She murmured in his ear. "I thought you said walking Sergei was excitement enough, Alex?"

"I'm just helping out an old friend, dear. Nolan and I were in the army together. And he's asked me to look into how to better the security at his company, that's all." He spun her around. She was a gorgeous woman.

"Uh-huh, how come you've never mentioned him before?" She came back into his arms. She smelled like flowers.

"I don't talk about everybody from my past." They danced real slow, his face near hers. He turned to kiss her.

Her lips were on his. "This wouldn't have anything to do with the fact Masters Electronics is rumored to be aiding our space effort, does it, darling?"

Alex Easterly frowned, pulling his face back from hers. "Yes, well, that's so, only—"

She put her arms around his neck. "Do you think I while away my days reading Jane Austen and getting my hair done? Not that you noticed my new hairstyle." She lightly touched the ends of her coiffured locks.

Alex Easterly suddenly didn't feel like romancing his wife. As if someone were reading his mind, the music abruptly ceased too. But he was so flustered, he didn't notice that it had happened. "It's not that, dear, really. It's simply I didn't want you to be concerned, that's all."

She walked to the bar and shook a cigarette loose from his pack of Lucky Strikes lying there.

She shook two loose and lit one, inserting the thing in his mouth. "Don't you think I might want to know if my husband is facing danger, going up against what may be a spy ring?" She'd lit the other cigarette for herself, talking over it as it dangled from her lipsticked mouth.

Jill Easterly then sipped from her drink. "Did you think I'd sit home and weep and be hysterical?"

"No, I know you're an independent woman." He felt as if he was in the dock and she was cross-examining him. This must come from reading that new magazine *Cosmopolitan* and what not.

"And didn't you think I might be of some help in this matter, considering some of my investments have been made in Masters Electronics?"

"I didn't know that," he reluctantly admitted.

"Of course you didn't, honey." She blew smoke at the ceiling and belted down more alcohol. "You seem to believe that because I inherited money, I just trot down to the bank now and then and draw out some and not think about where it comes from."

She sat down and crossed her legs, her foot bobbing up and down. "I admit, when Daddy died, I was befuddled as to the whys and wherefores of his steel and shipping empire. Of course, his law firm was very solicitous, helping the little woman figure out all those complex contracts and business relationships." She fluttered her eyes dramatically.

Alex Easterly sagged against the bar, his hand blindly seeking his own drink. "It's as if I'm seeing you for the first time," he muttered. He drank deeply.

"Sweetie," she said, "I haven't been hiding anything from you. But you work so hard solving cases—the gaunt woman matter as a good example—and trying to keep me from helping you, you haven't noticed that I've focused my inquisitiveness on other things too."

Easterly came over to his wife. "And how was it that Masters came to call on me?"

Jill Easterly inclined her head and puckered her lips. "A word to a friend of a friend. That's how business is done, you know that."

He had to smile. He sank to one knee beside her chair. "I may be getting long in the tooth, but maybe I can learn a few new tricks, huh, partner?"

Her fingers played with the nape of his neck. "Yes, that is so, Mr. Easterly." She kissed him tenderly. Then, "I think your going undercover is a good idea. While that takes place, I'll use my entré from the financial end to investigate some of the board members."

"Any particular suspects?"

"Oh, not exactly the fellow travelers you and Nolan might be thinking about, my love. There's this Shockman on the board who is brilliant in electronics but dreary in human understanding. In fact, during the war years he was a youth member of the German-American Volksbund. And I have it on solid background he's maintained his crypto-fascist ties. The East may be red, but there are plenty of those with brown shirts still in their closets."

"You're full of surprises, Mrs. Easterly."

"Ain't I, though?"

He rose to fill their drinks. In doing so, he happened to catch their reflections in the mirror on the wall. Absently, he noted the gray in his temples that seemed to have increased since breakfast. At the bar he had to look around again, a troubling notion gnawing at him.

"What is it dear?"

"Ah, ruminating on our next steps." In the mirror he blinked at the middle-aged Negro, or was it colored now? He was dressed impeccably: monogrammed sleeves and creased pants. This fellow's arm lifted when Easterly lifted his arm. By George, he was this fellow, and he was mixing drinks for himself and the woman in the chair. And damned if he hadn't paid attention before, but she was Oriental. That was his wife, right?

"Alex, are you okay? You look distracted."

"The case, the enormity of it, I guess." As if he were an automaton, he brought her the drink.

"Umm," she said, taking her glass. She put it on the floor beside the chair and stood. The mellow jazz score started again.

Hearing the signal, Easterly put his drink down too and began dancing with her again. "He said we had sixty-seven hours," he whispered in her ear.

"As I said, love," she began, "the answer might not be what you think. The missing doughnuts may be missing because the thief is looking for something else."

He looked hard at her as a knock sounded at their door. The knock persisted as the fire alarm also went off. Easterly seemed to be moving through hot tar to reach the door. The bell's ringing drowned out all other sound. . . .

"Elrod," Monk slurred into the receiver.

"Oh, you're still sleeping," he asked innocently.

"I called over to the office, and Delilah said you'd probably be taking the day off. I guess she said why, but I guess I wasn't listening. This doughnut thing's got me worked up."

"The times that Moises has been at work don't jibe with the times you've counted doughnuts missing, do they?"

Elrod was quiet on the other end for several moments. "Damn, that was pretty good, chief."

"Then it doesn't look like he's our man," Monk amplified. "He doesn't have a key, right?"

"No, and he couldn't have had a duplicate made either."

"Then when the probable has been eliminated, my dear colleague, all we have left is the improbable. Or words to that effect."

"Meaning what?"

"Has to be one of the regulars." He yawned.

"Yeah, I was afraid of that."

Through the walls Monk could hear a power motor starting up. He was doomed. "Who's been around?"

"Let's see," the big man rumbled, "Abe Carson, Peter Worthman, and Karen Osage." He snapped his fingers. "And Willie, Willie Brant stopped by too."

Oh was a defense attorney whom Monk had done some work for. "She's not a regular," he pointed out.

"No, but I remember her 'cause she asked about you. This was yesterday and you were still out of town." He got quiet again. "You just drove back this morning, didn't you?"

"Don't sweat it, El D. You've got me curious about the missing doughnuts too."

"Aw, man, I'm sorry, I should have realized," he apologized.

"The game is afoot. Okay, from your list the one that doesn't fit is Karen, but she only showed up yesterday. Yet the doughnuts were gone before she showed up."

"That's right," the big man said on the other end of the line. "She didn't tell me what she wanted, but said she'd try to get a hold of you today."

"That leaves us with the—hey, what the hell did Willie want? He hardly ever comes by the dough-nut shop. I always see him at Kelvin's." Monk was referring to the Abyssinia Barber Shop and Shine Parlor on Broadway in South Central Los Angeles he and Willie, a retired postman, frequented.

Elrod said, "You know, now that we're talking about it, I'm not sure, but I think Willie was here more than once in the last couple of days."

"Just to hang out?" Monk wondered aloud.

"The first time he came in after Abe showed up. They just seemed to be shootin' the shit and all. Willie broke down with his cheap ass and bought a small coffee and then complained about having to pay for a second refill. And," he added omi-nously, "that was the night I first noticed some chocolate twists had been taken."

Another power motor joined the first—must be gardener day in Silverlake, he glumly concluded. "Why would Willie steal our goodies, Elrod? He can't be selling them on the side."

"He might. Should I question him on the sly, like?"

He didn't have to activate much of his imagination to see how that might go. "Hold off, all right? How could he be sneaking the doughnuts out? If you're not there, Josette or Donnie or Moises is around, right?"

"Unless one of them is in on it with him." Elrod sounded like Jack Webb drawing in his dragnet.

"I tell you what, before you start hauling everybody in and putting them under the hot lights, let's sleep on this, dig? Let me catch a few hours of Z's, then I'll come over and we can formulate a plan."

"A plan is good," the other man concurred.

Monk, despite his interest in the doughnut caper, could feel the lead weights pulling his eyelids down. "We'll figure it out, Elrod, you'll see."

"Okay. Get some rest."

The line went fuzzy, and Monk stretched and scratched himself like a domesticated bear. The mowers were still going, but their engines were like a motorized melody to his overtired body. He lay still, curled up under the covers again. The world went about its business outside the bedroom, and no doubt bad actors were out there doing bad, bad things. And apparently one of them was a reprobate scarfing down his ill-gotten doughnuts. And he was probably washing down Monk's meager profit margins from the shop with cups of exquisite coffee.

The answers, he reminded himself, would have to wait until he joined the waking again. Although, he advised himself, a cup of coffee would be just the right nectar of nourishment right now. And for him, he could drink the stuff day or night and go right to sleep. He got up and traipsed into the kitchen. Kodama had left the coffeemaker on, and he poured a cup. He walked back to the bedroom carrying the morning *L.A. Times*.

Propped against the headboard, he leafed through the paper. In the Calendar section he saw a piece about a new film version being made from Ferguson Cooper's last book, *Platinum Jade*. This novel was the final in the series of sardonic and surreal tales Cooper had written about two South Side Chicago cops called Tombstone Graves and Hammerhead Smith. Cooper, a black writer who would later reinvent himself with "mainstream" novels about race and class in the seventies and early eighties, would subsequently disavow the hard-boiled books as merely ways to meet the rent while living in Kenya and Cuba.

But toward the end of his life, Cooper admitted he'd had a lot of fun writing about Graves and Smith, and thus published *Platinum Jade* in 1983. The book was both running commentary on the co-opting of the civil rights movement, women's lib and the Reagan-led backlash against social safety nets, as well as a pretty solid mystery. Monk sipped some coffee and put the paper and cup aside. He stretched and soon his head sagged against the headboard, blissfully sleepy.

"Carson is a carpenter. Honest Abe they call him. Ain't that sweet?" Hammerhead Smith snickered in his basso profundo voice and tossed aside the bio and photo of the man printed on card stock. He pushed the aged bowler back on his large head, crossing his size-seventeen Stacy Adams on the desk where he'd propped them up. His hand, as large as a car engine's fan, held up the next Criminal Investigations Division print off the desk.

"Peter Worthman, longtime labor organizer and general rabble-rouser," Smith's partner, Tombstone Graves, illuminated upon eyeballing the photo. "He's operated in some interesting circles over the years: backroom deal making with pols, getting thousands of workers to strike and stay united on the picket line, and been married to more brainy, good-looking women than I can shake your dick at."

"You the one the chicks go for, man," Smith said, not without a touch of jealousy. "Here I am, all six feet eight big dark burnished inches of me, and with thumbs that are, shall we say, longish." He winked, chomping on the smoldering cigar in his mouth. "But no, you with your Savile Row and St. Laurent suits, alligator and ostrich skin ankle boots . . ."

The dig was coming, but Graves didn't mind, so much now anyway. It was his gruff partner's way of saying he liked him. "But to top it all off"— Smith flapped the file card in the air—"that bullet-scarred mug of yours seems to actually turn the ladies on. They love to feel your scars, Je-sus."

"Back to the case," Graves said, hiding his ego boost. "Worthman can be ruthless, so we can't rule him out."

Smith unlimbered his brogans from the table and straightened in his chair. "He's no pie-card union fat cat sitting on his can collecting his worker's cut from their dues check-offs,"

"Spoken like the son of a city hall clerk that

you are," Graves said, adjusting his gold chain-mail cuff link.

"My point, fashion plate, is why in the hell would Worthman—hell, any of these supposed suspects—be involved in the theft of sixty-seven assorted doughnuts? In fact, why the hell did the Captain assign this goofball penny-ante misdemeanor to us anyway?"

"Because there's more to it than what's apparent, Sergeant." The new voice belonged to Captain Mitchum. Phones rang, perps and cops bustled and argued, yet there was a quality to his baritone that cut through the institutional din. He was standing near their desks, his lidded eyes at once giving nothing away yet taking in everything. He shoved his hands in the box-style coat he always favored. His barrel chest strained against the coat's buttons.

"Word just hit the streets that the shop owner where those doughnuts were swiped is offering sixty-seven grand for their return."

"A thousand dollars a doughnut?" Graves asked rhetorically, gazing at his partner.

"It would seem," Mitchum confirmed. "Could be there's more missing than icing and jelly."

"Like something hidden in the doughnuts." Smith shoved the bowler even farther back on his broad forehead.

"And, ah"—Mitchum moved the file cards around on the desk—"don't forget that our good counselor Osage also legally goes by the name Kodama." He tapped the woman's card for emphasis.

Smith was staring at the photos, then suddenly clapped his mammoth hands together. "And she defended Willie Brant."

"How do you know that?" Graves asked.

"I was down at the courthouse last week on that Veese matter. So I'm strolling down the hall, and who do I see all huddled up on the bench outside one of the courtrooms but Osage and Brant? Me and her nod at each other and I keep going. But I recognize Brant from his picture here."

"We got to get out and circulate," Graves said.

"Keep me posted." In that particular gait of his, Mitchum stepped back into his office, whistling a tune.

The next thing Graves knew, he and Smith were tooling along Quincy in their big, beat-to-hell-looking Ford. Underneath the hood, the gas-guzzling 425-cubic-inch V8 performed like a champ. It was nighttime, but Graves couldn't remember what he'd done after the conversation in the squad room. Presumably, he reasoned, he and his partner had been busy working the case.

Smith guided the car along several rain-slick streets. Lit neon announcing everything from cocktail lounges to twenty-four-hour shoe repair was reflected in the shallow puddles. Odd too, Graves reflected, he didn't recall any rain storm either. Must be working too hard. The car pulled to a halt across the street from an office building that must have been constructed during the Warren G. Harding administration. From the upper floor the chiseled eyes of stone gargoyles looked down from their perches.

"She's in," Smith stated, glaring up at a lit window on a particular floor. He blew white cigar smoke into the ebon sky.

As he extricated himself from the passenger seat,

Graves said, "Let's see what our beautiful defense attorney has to say about missing doughnuts."

The two men made for an imposing pair as they crossed the narrow thoroughfare, cars of various eras cruising by. The hem of each man's rumpled top coat came to mid-shin, and flailed behind him like dusters worn on the plains a century ago. Smith towered over most civilians, but people tended to forget that Graves, too, was large, six feet two and built like an aging linebacker. Together, the duo reached the vestibule of the building.

"How long we been doing this, partner?" Smith flicked the butt of his cigar into the street. As it bounced, it gave off orange and yellow sparks.

"You thinking of retiring?" Graves replied. He didn't know how long they'd been chasing criminals. It seemed to him this occupation of theirs, if that was the right term, had been a forever job.

"Just making small talk," Smith deflected. His pale grin gave away his true feelings, but he didn't pursue the matter further as the night watchman let them in. Their flat cop feet slapped against the marble floor of the lobby, the sound bouncing everywhere in the cavernous area.

In the elevator, Smith said, "I was wondering, that's all, Tombstone. I've been trying to figure out what it all means, ya know?" He adjusted his bowler, shading his deep-set eyes.

Tombstone Graves said, slumped against the far wall, "Our lives of absurdity, you mean?"

The elevator stopped, and the doors opened on an opulently appointed reception area. "Exactly, my man, exactly."

"Gentlemen," Karen Osage, a.k.a. Jill Kodama,

greeted them from a doorway to their right. She was a handsome woman of average height and a build belying her fortysomething years. Her hair was of a moderate length with auburn highlights. She wore a dark blue power suit and a magenta blouse underneath. Her look told them she was formulating several moves ahead of their questions even before they spoke.

"Come on in." She made a gesture with a sheaf of papers she held toward her inner office. They hung their top coats up.

"About these missing doughnuts," she said after everyone was settled. She grinned and lit a thin cigar after offering the two of them one from her humidor. "I can be unequivocal in that my client, Mr. Brant, had nothing whatsoever to do with these items being eaten."

"How do you know they were eaten?" Smith jabbed. His bowler rested on the mound of his knee.

"Why else would a hungry person take food?" She looked from the big man to his partner. Her eyes stayed on him for more than a beat.

"We think there may have been something hidden in one or more of the doughnuts," Graves put in. "We know that the doughnut shop owner has been involved in some questionable activities in the past."

"Allegations, not convictions," she averred.

"And we find it interesting that your other client happened to come to the doughnut shop at or around the time the doughnuts went bye-bye." Smith worked his tongue on the gristle stuck between his teeth from the pastrami sandwiches they'd scarfed down for dinner.

"What's your point, Detective?" Again, she did a sideways glance at Graves. As she did so, she repeatedly touched a ring on her finger. A particular kind of ring Graves had seen before.

"Of course," Tombstone Graves suddenly blurted out.

"What?" Smith glared at him.

"Of course," his partner repeated, snapping his fingers. Kodama, too, was standing, and he felt an irresistible urge to kiss her. So he did. And to his pleasure, she kissed him back. "You're terrific," he told her.

"So are you, big boy. I knew you could do it."

"You two mind telling me what the hell's going on?" Smith was now dressed in a chef's apron with streaks of flour on it. He adjusted his chef's hat as he sank doughnut dough into the industrial deep fryer.

The oil crackled and popped to a beat that hummed in Graves's head. He and the attorney slow-danced to Nat King Cole singing "It's Only a Paper Moon." The fish in her aquarium sang the melody. As the great crooner went on, the sound of the doughnuts frying replaced his voice, and Monk woke with a start.

He rubbed a hand over his face and looked at the time: a few minutes past eleven in the morning. Scratching his side, he dialed Elrod. Idly, he considered mentioning to the big man how he looked in a bowler in his dream.

"I know why the doughnuts have been missing,"

he announced after pleasantries. "And why Moises did it."

"You talked to him?"

"Nope." He didn't explain further. "I'll be there around three, Elrod. See you then." With that he hung up and finally slept soundly.

Moises had been destroying doughnuts because the one material thing in his life, his high school ring, had disappeared. He was sure it had somehow been sucked off his thin finger by the sticky doughnut dough. He was also replacing the doughnuts as he learned how to make them by working with Elrod. His accomplices in this deed were the other employees Josette and Lonnie, whom he'd enlisted, swearing them to silence. He didn't want to seem like a flake to Elrod, his immediate boss.

Moises had figured once he knew how to make the various styles of doughnuts, he could sneak in and replace all of them.

As it turned out, the ring had been left on the shelf above the washbasin in the back. The young man had taken it off one time cleaning up and had forgotten it was there. Subsequently, a can of cleanser had been placed in front of the ring, and it was therefore out of sight.

Monk had recalled on a subconscious level the last time he'd seen Moises, the ring had been absent from his finger. While days before that, he'd observed the kid was very keen on keeping the ring clean. The private eye had seen him use a cloth to rub it after he'd laid down the chocolate on a rack of french crullers.

Karen Osage finally caught up with Monk. She wanted him to look into a matter for a client of hers. It seems this Nolan Masters was plagued by industrial thefts from his high-tech electronics firm.

And Monk soon tired of the regulars at his doughnut shop calling him the sleeping detective.

TICKET TO MIDLAND
A TRES NAVARRE STORY
by Rick Riordan

Both of Rick Riordan's Tres Navarre novels have been nominated for Shamus Awards. *The Big Red Tequila* won for Best First P.I. Novel in 1998. *The Widower's Two-Step* was nominated for Best Paperback the following year. I have the feeling there are many more Shamus nominations—and wins—to come. The new book is called *The Last King of Texas* (Bantam, 2000.)

It's not a good sign when your Friday night begins like the first line of a joke.

A private eye, a lawyer, a policeman, and a prostitute go out to dinner.

It's even worse when you have the least reputable profession in the foursome. I was the private eye. My date had the second least reputable profession. She was the lawyer.

Carranza's Restaurant sat on an acre of dandelion-whiskered asphalt just east of downtown, between the KATY railroad tracks and the elevated ramps of I-35. When Maia and I arrived, on a December evening colder than *chupacabra's* blood, the place wasn't exactly crowded.

The winter sun was just setting. Orange light streamed in the back windows, scoring the hardwood floors. The ceiling fans were still, the tables deserted. The building felt like a limestone shell—an exoskeleton shed by the 1800s, left to dry and crack apart. In the room to the left, three octogenarian customers lounged at the butchery counter. I could smell smoked sausage and venison tamales.

I told Maia Lee that the meat market was the last vestige of the original grocery store started by Mr. Carranza, a former riding companion of Pancho Villa.

Upstairs in the dining area, I pointed out the secret trapdoor next to our table. I told Maia that it led to a stairwell customers had once used to escape to their horses when the sheriff came knocking, back in the 1920s, when these upper rooms had been a bordello.

Maia didn't stop looking anxious, or irritated.

She had fourteen hours left in Texas. We had a lot to discuss—history more recent than Pancho Villa.

"I don't understand why you agreed to this—" she started to say, but stopped when our dinner companions appeared at the top of the stairs.

Officer Pedro "Pete" Madrigal looked like a balloon creature in his blue polyester uniform—huge chest, legs, and arms bulging like separate twisted-off sections. His coppery head was nearly bald except for a stubble of black around the crown. His jaw, his neck, his hands were brutally thick. You couldn't tell he was just a kid—twenty-six, three years on the force—unless you caught the occasional nervous tremble in his lips.

He escorted Evelia Ruiz by her upper arm. Evelia had that smile on her face—that look of painful euphoria that speaks of drug addiction. She'd lost weight, which wasn't good. Her color was pale. She wore a red wool sweater and skin-tight jeans and seventies platform clogs. Her hair was permed into a black thatched hut.

She and Pete sat down across from Maia and me.

"Guys," I said, "this had better be good."

Pete Madrigal gave me a pained look, then tilted his head sideways toward Evelia.

Evelia Ruiz said, "I need you to find my baby."

I tried to look past her smile—the amused, taunting expression she's worn so long to attract customers that it carried no more emotional weight than a neon cantina sign. Evelia was seventeen, four years on the street. Covering her feelings had become as instinctive as covering her age or her forearm tracks.

Her eyes told me the request was serious.

"You've got my attention," I said.

Evelia looked at Maia Lee.

"It's okay," I promised. "This is Maia."

"Your old girlfriend," Maia corrected. "Not old. What happened to your baby, Ms. Ruiz?"

The waitress interrupted. We ordered a pitcher of beer and four barbecue platters.

Evelia stared past me, out the east windows of the restaurant.

Pete Madrigal shifted in his seat. "Tres—tell Evie this is a bad idea, putting this on you. Tell her if the baby's missing, she needs to report it."

"They'll take him," Evie murmured. "If the police find my baby, they'll take him away from me. I did a stupid thing, Tres. Joey convinced me."

Joey Ruiz was her husband. An older man, about

nineteen—a dope dealer, heroin user, occasionally Evelia's pimp. An all-around charming kid who owed a lot of bad people money. My stomach began to turn cold.

"The black market?" I asked.

Evelia's eyes widened. "*Chingate,* no! Nothing like that. I just—loaned him. We did it twice and nothing went wrong. This third time—"

"Wait a minute," Maia interrupted. "When you say loaned . . ."

Nobody responded.

Maia looked at me. "INS?"

I said, "Yeah."

"Jesus Christ."

If there are fashion trends in human smuggling, the hottest "in" thing for illegal immigrants that season was posing as a family to get across the Texas-Mexico border. A man and a woman with a baby, if caught, would not be detained because the Border Patrol lacked facilities for family detention. Despite the horror stories, INS was a generally humane organization. They felt compelled to let family units go, even though they knew the illegals would simply continue their northern journey. If you didn't happen to have a baby to help you get across, babies could be found.

"How much, Evie?" I asked.

She shrugged. "The first time it was for a cousin of Joey's. We were just helping out. Two hundred dollars. Joey Jr. looked great when we got him back. The second time we rented him for four hundred. This third time—it was to pay back Joey's friend, Andres Carillo. Andres brings people and *chiva* across, cuts Joey good prices on black tar.

Joey said he had to have the money, Tres. He told me this was the easiest way to get it."

Maia said, "You gave your baby to a smuggler so he could rent to illegal aliens. So your husband could pay off his heroin debts."

Maia is a defense attorney, one of San Francisco's best. She has defended some of the sickest and wealthiest sociopaths in Northern California, and has always shown professional dispassion. Looking at Evelia Ruiz, however, Maia's eyes were cold.

Pete Madrigal looked at Evie the way he always did—with a mixture of love, worry, and desolation. Pete and Evelia were second cousins. Since he'd joined the force, Pete had taken on the role of Evelia's protector because no one else in the family would. He knew he was failing at his crusade. He didn't like it.

"The baby was due back a week ago," Pete said. "Then Joey's supplier, this guy Andres, demanded a ransom, an extra ten grand he said Joey owed him. Otherwise the baby would not be coming home. Joey told Evie not to worry. Said Andres was just playing hard-ass and he'd take care of things. Then Joey turned up missing—hasn't been home in two days. According to what Joey told Evie, the deadline for Andres getting his money was midnight tonight."

"And you've known about this since when?" I asked.

Pete stared at Evie accusingly. "About ten minutes before I phoned you, Navarre. Evelia made me swear not to call it in—not unless you agreed it was the thing to do. So I'm asking you to agree."

"Andres wouldn't hurt my baby," Evie said.

Pete grunted. "For revenge on a ten grand debt, Andres Carillo would slit his mother's throat."

Evie reached for my hand across the table. Her fingers were dry and cool. "If you can find my baby, Tres, it's got to be tonight. Joey must be in trouble or something. He wouldn't forget about this. Me and him were talking about getting away—like West Texas or something. Going straight, you know?"

Pete snorted.

Evelia's hand tightened on mine. "It's true," she insisted. "If I have to come clean with the police, I'll never see my baby again. They'll give him to Child Services, foster care."

"Maybe that would be best," Maia said.

Evelia let go of my hand. She sat back, tried to stare down Maia Lee. "I want my baby back. I'm his mother."

Maia's retort would not have been kind, but she was interrupted by the waitress bringing our food and beer. We sat and looked at the plates so morosely the waitress asked if something was wrong. I told her no. She left, still looking troubled.

"The odds are bad, Evie," I said. "Very bad. But I'll try."

Maia stared at me.

Pete curled his meaty fingers. "You know that's not the way to go, Tres."

"I'll see what I can turn up tonight," I said. "If I don't find your baby, and I probably won't—then you go with Pete to SAPD first thing in the morning. Deal?"

Evelia's shoulders relaxed. She nodded.

Pete produced a business card from his pocket,

handed it across the table. "My ex-partner from patrol is in Narcotics now, Ben Kalmus. He can maybe give you a line on Andres Carillo."

"And you just happen to have his card handy."

"Sure." Pete's voice turned bitter. "I get used to people ignoring my advice."

Evelia patted his hand reassuringly, then started listing for me all the places where her wayward husband might hang out. She gave me a photo of the baby, Joey Jr. He was eleven months old. "A really, really good kid," Evelia told me.

Joey Jr.'s hair was black chick fuzz, his cheeks like chestnuts, his eyes wide and brown and full of amazement. He was wearing a fuzzy blue sweater that looked hand-knit from the uneven collar line.

The rest of our dinner was quick and joyless. I tasted nothing but pepper.

After Pete and Evelia left, Maia snatched the baby photo out of my hand. She examined it angrily. "Goddamn you, Tres."

"I owe Evelia a favor."

"Then let's find her kid and give it to Child Protective Services. Evelia doesn't seem to want it."

I looked at Maia in her winter clothes—black wool slacks, black cowl-neck sweater that made the skin of her throat and face glow like amber. The lines of her nose, her eyes, her mouth—all so familiar.

"Evie probably means it," I said. "About wanting to go straight."

Maia cursed me in Mandarin.

"I must not have trained you well enough," she said. "You still have a shred of optimism."

"I asked you down, didn't I?"

That silenced her.

She stared resentfully at Joey Ruiz, Jr., then shoved the photo back under my barbecue plate.

"You'll help?" I asked.

Then she gave me the really cold stare. "My plane leaves at nine in the morning. We had nothing else to do tonight, did we?"

Narcotics detective Benjamin Kalmus was the sweetest-looking Sherman tank I'd ever met.

He had long eyelashes, doe eyes, a cherubic smile. His voice was rich and deep and gentle, and he must've weighed three hundred pounds even before the Kevlar assault armor.

"Waste of time, Mr. Navarre," he apologized. "I'd help Pete Madrigal any way I can, but you can't go in there. Even if you could, we've been sitting on the house the last forty-eight hours. Your man Joey hasn't come in or out."

Kalmus stared out the tinted van windows. He picked at the POLICE sign on his vest pocket. Apparently he did a lot. The sign had peeled away until it read LIC.

The building across the street was a dilapidated quadplex—chipped green shingle walls, boarded windows, red metal front door with a peephole slat just big enough to get shot through. It was one of a dozen condemned two-story boxes lining the ridge above Fort Sam Houston, opposite the San Antonio Botanical Center. Wind came off the parade grounds and swept up the hill with such force that it shook the van, made a few pathetic strands of red and gold Christmas garland dance on the telephone wires.

"Andres Carillo?" Maia asked.

Kalmus smiled. "He's in there. Just came back from Laredo this afternoon. The thing is, ma'am, my name's on this arrest warrant, so it's my butt on the line. You two don't get any closer than this."

In the back of the van, Kalmus's five-member team waited impatiently. One was a patrol officer. The other four were narcotics detectives geared for the raid—black Kevlar, standard-issue Glocks in tactical thigh holsters, vest pockets stuffed with extra clips and plastic flex cuffs. They had a schematic of Andres Carillo's stash house taped up on the back door.

Probably days of work had gone into this. Maia and I walked in just as they were staging up. We excel at bad timing.

"Five minutes with Andres," I said. "Nothing that will interfere with your arrest."

"I'm bending the rules just talking to you, Mr. Navarre. Sorry."

Maia Lee nodded. "Okay, Detective."

She opened the shotgun door and slid out. The night wind ripped through the van.

Kalmus lost his smile. "Lady, what the hell are you doing?"

"Knocking on Carillo's door myself," Maia said. "We went with you, we'd follow your rules. But I guess you gentlemen must be used to changing your plans. We'll try not to tip your hand too much."

Kalmus stared at Maia like she was thirty unexpected kilos of coke he'd just run into face first.

He looked back at his team. He looked at me. "This woman is visiting you for the holidays?"

"Yeah. Sort of like my Christmas present."

"I hate the holidays."

Then he told his men to move out.

The raid itself took all of ninety seconds. Maia and I stayed back as directed. Kalmus, being the largest, went up the steps first with the ram—a three-foot metal cylinder with a square head, decorated all down the sides with KXTJ TEJANO HITS! bumper stickers. Placement advertising. Probably the radio station's share of the junkie listening market had gone up considerably. The other detectives lined up shortest to tallest behind Kalmus. He bashed the door open and they made the entry— peeling off into different rooms of the house, shouting orders in Spanish and English.

Kalmus went last.

No gunfire.

After a ten-count, he reappeared in the doorway and waved us in. "Ladies and gentlemen."

The first thing that hit me was the smell—rotting ground beef, or dead squirrels in the attic, maybe. The living room was done in yellow wallpaper and green shag carpet, with a television and a sofa that resembled a boiled yam. The only light was from a twenty-watt bulb on the ceiling. Three Latino men knelt on the floor, their hands cuffed behind their backs with plastic flex cord. Two of them Kalmus ignored. He walked up to the third, put his knees a few inches from the man's nose, and said, "How you doing, Andres?"

Andres Carillo smiled up a him sleepily. He was in his early twenties, lean as a wolf, with chopped black hair and a three-day beard. His stained army fatigue shirt was untucked over black jeans. The bulletproof glaze in his eyes told me he'd been shooting up some Yuletide cheer.

"Hey, fucker," he said to Kalmus. "You told me you weren't a cop. You were a fucking undercover cop."

"Yeah. Sorry about that, Andres."

Andres giggled like he was delighted. "I'll kill you, man."

Ben Kalmus read the warrant, then slapped a copy on top of the TV. He read the three handcuffed men their Miranda rights in Spanish and English, asked if they understood. Then he squatted in front of Carillo and said, "You want to tell us where it is? Make things easy?"

"Where what is, man?"

Kalmus nodded to his team. They dispersed. Within seconds the house was filled with the happy sounds of tromping combat boots and smashing furniture. Before Kalmus left to join the fun, he looked at Maia and me. "You said five minutes. That's what you've got."

I knelt next to Andres. Maia stood over us.

"Where's the baby?" I asked him.

Andres Carillo tried to focus on me. When he smiled, he displayed one chipped gray incisor completely out of alignment with the rest of his teeth. "Baby?"

"Joey Ruiz's baby."

A dim twinkle of recognition. "Hey, man—I gave that kid back."

"And when was this?"

"What day is *Dos Mujeres* on, dude—Wednesdays? Joey came here Wednesday. I gave him the kid. Then I skipped town for a few days. Haven't seen him since."

"Joey's been missing since Wednesday, Andres," I said. "The mother hasn't seen the child."

He laughed. "Shit, man. That's rough."

Maia reached behind Andres and grabbed his wrists by the flex cuff. She yanked his arms up at the wrong angle. Andres yelped, "Hey!" and tried to get up, but he had no leverage. He crumpled back to his knees, Maia still lifting, forcing Andres to bend over until his forehead pressed against the carpet like a Moslem at prayer.

Her face stayed completely calm as she pushed Andres' arms to eleven o'clock, about half an inch shy of being twisted out of their sockets. The other two cuffed men just watched.

"Mr. Carillo," Maia said, "our time is short. You gave Joey a deadline of tonight to bring you ten grand for the child. I want to know where the child is. I want to know that he's safe."

"I told you." Andres' voice was even tighter than his arm joints. "Joey came here Wednesday. Ease up, okay?"

Maia did not ease up.

Andres tried to catch his breath. He was drooling very attractively on the carpet. "Look. Joey came in here all pissed off—drew a piece on me. He had a suitcase with him. He told me him and his old lady were leaving town, and he'd fucking kill me I didn't give him the kid. I told him, 'Okay, okay. Don't go ape shit.' I showed him where the kid was. Joey ran *me* out of here—out of my own house. That was Wednesday. I left town for a few days, got back today. Joey's long gone. So shit,

man—good riddance. Wherever Joey Ruiz went, he
can stay there."

Ben Kalmus and another detective stood stone-
faced in the interior doorway.

Kalmus said, "That's your statement, Andres?"

"You find my stash?"

"Oh yeah," Kalmus said. "Three big old cubes
of it, labeled FRAGILE: STEREO PARTS. Nice touch,
that."

"Good," Andres groaned. "Get me to jail—away
from this bitch."

Maia gave his arms one more little love twist,
then released.

Kalmus said, "We've got a problem upstairs, Andres. You want to tell me what's in the back bedroom closet, unit on the top left?"

Andres tried to sit up. "I don't even use that
apartment, man."

Kalmus nodded at us to follow him. The other
detective dragged Andres Carillo to his feet.

At the top of the stairs, the rotting smell intensi-
fied. By the time we got to the bedroom, I had a
good idea what we were going to see.

On the floor of the bedroom closet, Evelia's husband, Joey Ruiz, was curled into fetal position, very
dead, his arms crossed over the gunshot wound in
his chest as if he were shy about it. Someone had
dumped talcum powder all over his body in an unsuccessful attempt to reduce the smell. It just made
Joey look like he'd been shot during a snowstorm.
His shirt, the carpet, the hair on his arms—everything was crusted with blood, speckled white and
pink from the powder. A roach had gotten stuck
in the dried puddle next to his elbow. Joey's eye-

brows and hair were dusted with talcum, his face pale except for his lower cheek, which was sunburn red.

Nearby on the bedroom floor, a large blue suitcase lay open and empty. There was nothing else in the room—no furniture, no clothing, no visible stains or marks on the carpet.

Detective Kalmus made a tsk-tsk-tsk sound.

"God forbid I should be a homicide dick and have to wear a tie all day." He gave Andres his sweetest smile. "But if I was reading this—lividity in the cheek, blood spill on the floor—I'd say Mr. Ruiz was killed right there. Forced to lie down in the closet and then shot through the heart. That the way it happened, Andres?"

Andres's eyes widened. He seemed to be sobering up nicely. "I told you. Joey ran me out of here three days ago. Ain't seen him—I didn't *do* this, man!"

Maia said, "Where's the baby, Andres?"

"Don't touch me, lady!"

Maia's hands curled into fists.

I touched her arm. "Let's go."

Reluctantly, she followed me downstairs. Andres Carillo's protests of innocence got louder and louder behind us. Kalmus was talking over him, telling his people to contact Night CID and Homicide.

Maia and I stepped out onto the tiny front porch. The wind tore at our overcoats—clean, mercilessly cold, smelling of wood fires.

"You get a look at the chest wound?" Maia asked me.

"I wasn't trying to."

"Forty caliber," she guessed. "Probably a Glock. Close range but not point-blank."

I nodded. I've known M.E.'s who have a worse eye for entrance wounds than Maia. "What are you thinking?"

She paused. "I'm thinking we'd better find this child."

Kalmus joined us on the porch. He gave us the doe eyes for a few seconds. Then with an uncomfortable grunt, he pulled the heavy metal shock plate from the center of his raid vest.

"What were you saying about a baby?" he asked.

Maia shook her head. "My mistake. Client privilege."

Kalmus chuckled. "Goddamn private investigators. You want the red carpet but won't roll it out for anybody else, will you?"

"Funny," I said. "I've often thought the same thing about cops."

Kalmus tapped his knuckle on the shock plate. "All right. For Pete Madrigal's sake—only because he sent you. The guy who tipped us to this stash house called me Wednesday night. He made one comment I couldn't quite figure."

"A regular narc C.I.?" Maia asked.

"Naw. Run-of-the-mill scumbag named Pato. I busted him last year when I was still on patrol. He called out of the blue, offered me a lead on Andres Carillo. Wanted a hundred bucks. I told him Narcotics was a poor family; I could maybe swing forty. He ended up taking the money, but last thing he said was, 'Shit, Detective, I make more money baby-sitting.'"

The porch got quiet except for the wind and Kalmus's knuckle pinging against metal.

The scumbag named Pato proved exceptionally helpful after only a few minutes with Maia Lee.

By one a.m., he'd directed us to a house on the far South Side where he said he'd been paid a hundred bucks to drop off two items—one in the dumpster and one at the front door. Pato insisted to the point of tears that he'd been paid by a guy he'd never seen before.

If Pato had used a garbage can, we would've been out of luck, but dumpsters are emptied much less frequently. The brown paper grocery bag was still there, stapled shut.

We let Pato go before we opened it, which I soon realized was a good thing. Pato would've slit his own wrists had he seen what he'd inadvertently thrown away.

"About fifteen thousand in twenties," Maia estimated. "Two airline tickets for this Sunday's flight—Midland-Odessa International. Midland has an airport?"

I shone my pencil flashlight on the tickets. They were made out to James and Evelia Ruiz. There was also a six-month lease agreement for an apartment in Midland, a receipt for the deposit paid in full, in cash.

"Who would pitch this much money?" Maia asked.

We looked at each other, starting to form the same conclusion, I thought. Then our eye contact turned into something different—the change as subtle as an engine shifting from idle to drive. For a couple of heartbeats Maia and I looked at each other with the old familiar hunger, across a two-year chasm of mutual exile.

Maia cleared her throat. "You want to watch the house for a while?"

"I didn't mean our visit to go like this."

"Tres . . . there's no sense pushing on it."

"I know." I was surprised my voice came out at all. "Three days we haven't pushed on it. Let's watch the house."

I took the paper bag and moved away from the dumpster.

We stood at the back of the property, at the intersection of a nameless dirt road and the access ramp for Loop 410. This far south, in the most rural part of San Antonio, the highway was dark and silent.

We couldn't see much of the house—a ramshackle collect of clapboard rooms, a backyard dominated by bare pecan trees and an old-fashioned ten-foot satellite dish. Someone had put a big plastic nativity scene in the radar dish so it could be seen from the highway. By the looks of it, the nativity had been set up years ago and left there ever since, but even a broken baby Jesus is right once a year.

After ten minutes of freezing and staring into the dark, I grabbed a pebble and chucked it toward the house. Nothing. On my second try, the pebble clattered against a wall. On my third, I hit glass with a loud *plink*. A child's cry lifted into the night like an air raid siren.

Lights came on—a curtainless window illuminated yellow. Inside, a heavy-set Latina woman in a turquoise bathrobe lifted a child from a crib and draped him over her shoulder. The boy was about one year old, with fat brown cheeks and fuzzy black hair and a bunny-white jumper with little sewn-on booties, Joey Jr.—looking cranky and sleepy but otherwise perfectly fine. I recognized the lady, too. I'd seen her at a family barbecue I'd been invited to about a year ago. I couldn't swear to her name, but she was a cousin of Evelia Ruiz.

Six in the morning and it was still dark. Maia and I sat in her hotel room at La Mansion del Norte, a portable crib between us, Little Joey Jr. lying peacefully on his back as he chewed Maia's key chain. Maia had thoughtfully removed the pepper spray and other deadly objects before giving it to him.

The queen-size bed was made. One packed suitcase was set on the luggage stand. Maia was dressed to travel—gray flannel skirt and jacket, white blouse. With the crib and the happily cooing child at her feet, she looked completely out of place—like a Hong Kong supermodel in a *Cosmo* shoot. *Fashion industry moms—how do they do it?*

I tried not to dwell on the fact that she was leaving in three hours, or that our last date together would be a conference with Evelia Ruiz. The portable crib had been the easiest thing to arrange. The other phone calls had been more difficult.

"It's sad," I said. "The relationship might have worked out."

Maia ran her fingers along the edge of the playpen. "Joey Ruiz is dead. All you can do now is bring justice, and that's never enough."

She met my eyes, then seemed to realize we weren't talking about the same thing. She looked away just as our guests knocked at the door.

I let them in. Pete Madrigal gave me a crushing handshake. Evelia rushed to the crib. She lifted Joey Jr. and kissed him fervently. The kid had a good grip. Maia's keys kept jangling in his little fist. After a few seconds the baby got uncomfortable with his mom's affections and started kicking, making "eh, eh, eh" sounds to get down.

Evelia put him back in the crib, smoothed his hair. Then she turned to hug me and planted a sticky kiss on the cheek. "Oh, Tres."

She was trembling.

Pete and I guided her to the bed, where she sat, curling forward until her head was in her hands.

Pete Madrigal sank next to her, put his arm around her shoulders.

"It's okay now," Pete told her. "It's going to be okay."

The gentleness in his voice made my throat burn.

I said, "It's not quite okay, Evelia."

Evelia looked up, brushed a tear off her cheek. "Wh—what? He's not okay?"

"The baby's fine," I said. "It's about your husband's murder—some details I didn't tell you on the phone."

Evelia's eyes went vacant, her expression reduced to that meaningless addict smile. "How can there be more?"

"I told you," Pete interrupted. "Leave Andres Carillo to me. We *will* nail his ass. I promise you that."

"Evelia," I said, "a stranger dropped off your

son two nights ago at your cousin Lupe's house out on South Loop 410—no explanations, just told her to keep Joey Jr. safe for a few days. Lupe had a hard time explaining why she didn't call you up immediately."

"That *puta* hates me," Evelia murmured. "Pete knows that. His cousin, too."

"Which is maybe why she was willing to go along," Maia said.

Pete Madrigal scowled. "What?"

Maia shook her head, disappointed. "Come on, Officer Madrigal. You can do a better job looking mystified. You killed Joey Ruiz."

Hesitation. Then he forced a laugh. "I only wish."

Peter smiled apologetically at Evelia, then at me, looking for commiseration. I didn't give him any.

"You tailed Joey to Carillo's place," Maia continued. "When Joey ran Carillo off, you went in—forced Joey Ruiz into the closet, shot him with your sidearm, a Glock. You called up Pato, a cooperative scumbag you knew from patrol. Pato took Joey's belongings to the dumpster and the baby to your cousin's for safekeeping. Then Pato called your old partner, Ben Kalmus, and gave him the tip on the stash house. It wasn't a hard guess that Kalmus would collar Andres Carillo for you, solve Joey's murder. You figured you'd wait a couple of days, the baby would miraculously turn up at a cousin's house, and you'd explain it away as some softer-hearted colleague of Carillo's, trying to make good. Everybody would be happy, you'd be a hero to Evelia, and Joey Sr. would be remembered as

the guy who was killed in a drug deal after aban-
doning his wife and kid."

Evelia stared at her cousin. "Pete?"

Madrigal's face was a mask, his eyes focused on
Maia Lee. "I assume you can prove all this."

"We can't prove any of it," Maia admitted. "So
far Pato is refusing to sell you out. I'd be surprised
if he wasn't already on a bus out of town. Your
cousin can testify she never saw you with the baby.
Police probably won't place you at the murder
scene, and there's an excellent circumstantial case
against Andres Carillo. If you were my client, I'd
say you were home free."

"Pete?" Evelia demanded.

"Evie . . ." He moistened his lips. "What I
did—"

He tried to take her hand, but she stood
abruptly, stumbling into the crib as she backed
away.

"You *killed* him?" she screamed.

The baby didn't seem the least bit alarmed by
the change in his mother's voice. He held up Maia's
keys and gurgled a question. Maia Lee rose from
her chair and took Evelia by the shoulders.

Peter Madrigal said, "You deserved better,
Evie."

He rested his hand on the spot where she'd been
sitting. His voice was slow and calm—the way you'd
address a little girl. "I love you. I couldn't watch
him hurt you and the baby anymore. I didn't
plan . . ."

He faltered, looked at me. "Come on, Tres.
You're a good man. Tell Evie. Tell her Joey

would have killed her eventually, one way or another."

Evelia's crying was a dry, choking sound. She turned toward Maia.

Maia brushed a strand of hair out of the younger woman's eyes. "Joey was trying," she said gently. "He'd scraped together several thousand dollars. He'd bought airplane tickets and paid for an apartment in Midland. The documentation was with him when he went to Andres Carillo's to get the baby back. Probably he ran Andres out of that house because he wanted to search for a little more spending cash, but he never got the chance. Peter Madrigal came in and killed him, then went to great pains to dump the contents of the suitcase away from the scene so you wouldn't know what Joey was really up to. Joey was about to come back to you, Evie. He was trying to make a life for you and the baby."

"No." Pete's voice grew louder, more dangerous. "Joey Ruiz never did anything right by her. He never could."

Evelia kept crying, as if all her seventeen years of bottled-up horror were just now coming loose.

"You didn't shoot Joey Ruiz because he was hurting Evie," I told Pete. "You shot him because he was trying to do the right thing. He would've taken Evelia away from you. For that you killed a man in front of his own child."

I almost wished he would attack me. On some crazy, suicidal level, I would've understood that, preferred to draw blood with Pete Madrigal to get my own rage out. But I knew Pete too well.

His chin fell. He brought his hands together

at the fingertips. I could almost see his anger imploding.

"I never meant to hurt you, Evie," he whispered. "I love you."

The door to the adjoining suite opened.

Benjamin Kalmus came in, followed by my friend Sergeant Gene Schaeffer from Homicide and a guy from the surveillance unit who'd been taping it all.

Peter looked up at them with hollow eyes. I don't think Evelia even noticed. Her head stayed buried in Maia's gray flannel coat.

Kalmus pinched his nose awkwardly. "Pete—go with the sergeant, buddy. Okay?"

Pete rose like an automaton. He accepted a pat on the back from Kalmus, then left the room with Schaeffer and the surveillance tech. The door clicked shut behind them.

Ben Kalmus' eyes might even have been more bloodshot than my own. They were certainly less friendly. He pulled a battered flight ticket from his pocket and handed it to me. American Airlines. Evelia Ruiz. Midland, Texas—Sunday morning.

"Make her use it," Kalmus said.

"Giving away evidentiary material," I said. "Isn't that illegal?"

"Very," Maia confirmed. "She'll be on the flight, Detective. Thank you."

He shook his head. "Don't thank me, Counselor. I want her gone. Pete Madrigal was worth twenty of her and her kid. He threw himself away trying to help a whore."

He looked back at me. I tried to remember why I'd ever thought of his face as gentle.

"And you," Kalmus said. "You used me to bring

him down, Navarre. Your girlfriend may be going, but you and I are staying in town. You just made an enemy you don't want."

He left the room.

Evelia Ruiz cried. She held fast to Maia, and I stood in the middle of the room, feeling empty—nothing behind me but a sleepless night, nothing to look forward to but a weekend of departures. I wanted to be the one holding Maia Lee.

Evelia's baby finally sensed that something was wrong. He dropped the keys and stood up in the crib, looking concerned, holding his little chubby hands up, grabbing air. "Eh, eh, eh."

"Hard to be the one left out," I agreed.

His mother kept crying. Maia Lee stared past me toward the hotel room door, her eyes seeing patterns I couldn't even guess at.

Somebody had to. I went to pick up the child.

THE GATHERING OF THE KLAN
A Milan Jacovich Story
by Les Roberts

When Les Roberts wrote his first short story, "Pig Man," for my anthology *Deadly Allies II*, he drew from personal experience. Now he's done the same thing with this Milan Jacovich story about a Ku Klux Klan gathering in Cleveland, Ohio. Before he wrote the story, however, he had to wait for the outcome of the actual event to see if the city of Cleveland burned down. "It's all true," he wrote me, "but the murder."

Les's background in this business has been well documented. Winner of the first PWA/St. Martin's Press Best First P.I. Novel contest fourteen years ago, author of two P.I. series, past president of PWA. This story can only add to the luster that is Les.

Just about the biggest controversy to hit Cleveland since the old Browns released Bernie Kozar in mid-season back in the early nineties was the announcement that our African American mayor had granted a permit for a rally outside the Cleveland Convention Center on a Sunday afternoon in August to an out-of-town contingent of the Ku Klux Klan.

Probably no one was as surprised as the klunks, klowns and kleagles themselves; their usual M.O. was to apply for a permit in some northern city and then sue for the right to free speech when the permit was denied. They had accumulated quite a comfortable little nest egg from collecting such judgments in towns in Michigan, Pennsylvania and Minnesota over the last several years, and they were probably planning on collecting big from liberal and heavily black-populated Cleveland.

Everyone was mad at the mayor. The police department's union, the black community, the city council and the county commissioners, all of his many political enemies and rivals, and most of the media had taken the opportunity to try to shoot him down. Everyone was terrified that Cleveland would once again become a national laughingstock, to say nothing of the genuine fear that one hastily hurled racial slur or one thrown beer can could set off a riot that would see the city go up in flames.

The mayor pleaded that his hands were tied and talked a lot about the First Amendment, and begged the citizenry to behave itself and not give the national media any sound bites with which to tarnish the image that Cleveland had taken such pains to rebuild and polish over the past twenty years.

I try to stay out of politics; as the sole owner of a small business—Milan Security, which I christened after my own first name, Milan, since my surname is almost impossible for many people to pronounce—supplying industrial security and private investigations, I have enough to do just trying to keep solvent. My natural dislike and loathing for anyone promoting racial hatred made me follow the story closely in the newspapers, but I had no intention of getting involved in it one way or the other.

Until Earl Roy Ruttenberg, the regional president and exalted Grand Dragon of a southern Ohio branch of the Klan, walked into my office five days before the rally, wanting to hire me as his personal bodyguard for the weekend of the rally.

He was close to fifty, some forty pounds overweight, slightly balding, and had a complexion like four-day-old cottage cheese. He came in flanked by two over-muscled young men who were twenty years younger; both had bad hair and Elvis sideburns and UP WITH WHITE PEOPLE T-shirts, and looked as though they were totally ignorant of even the whereabouts of the nearest dentist. One of them had a girlish, soulful look like Paul McCartney. Ruttenberg sat in one of my client's chairs, but his two trained orangutans positioned themselves on either side of the door.

I listened to his offer of a two-day job as his bodyguard and turned him down flat.

"I'm truly sorry to hear that, Mr. Jacovich," he said, his accent that blend of Southern and Midwestern that you hear down near the Kentucky–Ohio border and which is referred to as "briar," after the somewhat disdainful sobriquet "briarhopper."

"Sorry," I said.

"I've asked around, believe me, gotten lots of recommendations, and you're definitely my first choice."

"I can't imagine why," I said. "First of all, I'm Catholic, and secondly, I despise everything you stand for and I have nothing but contempt for the line of shit you're trying to sell."

Ruttenberg smiled easily. "A lot of people feel that way."

"Maybe you should go find a bodyguard that doesn't."

"You're not saying that you'd like to see me dead, are you?"

"I don't want to see anybody dead, Mr. Ruttenberg. But if the whole world was on the *Titanic* and I was in charge of the lifeboats, I don't think you'd get one of the first seats."

He laughed; he had a *yuk-yuk-yuk* kind of laugh that grated on my nerves almost as much as his racial attitudes. The T-shirt muscle boys guffawed, too, but I don't believe they got the humor; they were programmed to laugh when the Grand Dragon did.

"You seem as if you're pretty well protected already," I said.

"Oh, Ozzie and Jay are great for the everyday stuff. But I know that our being here on Sunday has caused a lot of controversy, and I was hoping to find someone who really was plugged in to Cleveland, who knew the crazies to look out for."

"From where I stand, it seems to me that the crazy we have to look out for is *you*."

"Ah-ha-ha," he said, but it wasn't a laugh this time. "I'm a crazy who's prepared to pay you very well, though."

"If I tried to spend your kind of money, Mr. Ruttenberg, I'm afraid I'd disappear in a puff of sulfurous smoke."

"You'd druther see some wild-eyed funky nigger with a razor cut my throat?"

I glanced out my office window at the Cuyahoga

River, which ran past the building. As a big guy who used to play defensive tackle on the Kent State football team, I figured that with a good enough throw I could probably toss Ruttenberg into it with ease. "Say that word again in here, Mr. Ruttenberg, and you're going to have to swim home." The muscle guys stirred uneasily at the threat. "And the same goes for Ozzie and Harriet over there, too. Try me if you think I'm kidding." I fantasized the scenario for a few seconds and added, "Please try me." Hope springs eternal.

"I am truly sorry I offended you, Mr. Jacovich," Ruttenberg said. "It's just a word, after all."

"It's an ugly, hate-filled word that I never allow in my presence. I can't fault you for being stupid, because you probably can't help it. I can, however, blame you for being rude. Remember that. Or don't bother, you're leaving anyway."

"I think you owe me the courtesy of a hearing, at least."

"I don't owe bigots the sweat off my ass."

"Looky here," he said. "We're entitled to our b'liefs just like anyone else. And I can assure you that my people are completely under control and will cause no trouble at all unless they are physically provoked. *Physically* provoked, you understand. We've been called names by the best of them; that doesn't bother us."

"Then you won't have any trouble and you won't need me. Besides, this city is going to great expense to make sure nobody offs your sorry ass when you put on your clown costumes and wave the flag."

"They are at that, and I appreciate it." He said the next-to-last word like Andy Griffith used to, without the first syllable. "It's the time leading up to the rally that has me worried.

"We don't want any riots. That'd run counter to our purposes. But d'you have any idea what might transpire here if anything happens to me? Or to *anyone*? Chaos," he intoned, pronouncing both the *C* and the *H* like he would if he were saying "chicken." He leaned back in the chair and crossed his legs. "People will get hurt, maybe innocent people, maybe some of your tippytoe-dancing liberal and black friends. You see the truth in that?"

I did, but I didn't tell him so.

"You want that happening here in your city? I don't b'lieve you do, do ya?"

Once again, I wouldn't give him the satisfaction of answering a question that was, after all, rhetorical.

"So here's the deal. The city of Cleveland is providing security at the rally, but before that we're on our own. Now, we're gonna check into our hotel on Sattidy afternoon. We want you there just to make sure there isn't any trouble. We eat dinner, you join us—dinner is on me, of course—and at nine o'clock we turn in. We're country people, we go to bed early. Sunday morning you meet us at the hotel, you escort us to the rally, and then the Cleveland po-lice take over and pertect us from those people who don't like what we have to say and wanna deny us our right to free speech under the First Amendment of the Constitution of the United States. You're free to leave then. You don't even have to stay and listen to the speeches." He gave me what he thought was a winning smile.

"Although you really oughta, you might learn somethin'."

"I could learn the same things from the wall of a truck stop men's room."

His mean little eyes got even smaller; he didn't like that. He didn't like *me*. I could live with it.

He was a gamer, though, I had to grant him that. He didn't give up. "So you gonna he'p us out here? Or are you willin' to jus' sit back and maybe watch your hometown burn?"

Now, I am not possessed of sufficient hubris to think that the safety of Cleveland's citizenry depended on me. But the son of a bitch did have a point. American cities today are as volatile as gasoline fumes, and it wouldn't take much of a spark at a public breast-beating where one group disses another in the ugliest of racial terms to set off a conflagration for which Cleveland would have to apologize for the next thirty years.

Maybe I could make a very small contribution toward keeping a spark from striking.

"All right, Mr. Ruttenberg, I'll do it. As long as we completely understand each other."

"What's there to understand?" Ruttenberg asked, taking a checkbook out of the breast pocket of his discount-store suit.

"That I despise everything about you," I said.

My pal at *The Plain Dealer,* Ed Stahl, whose column used to grace page two every morning but, due to the paper's new format, was now buried deep inside where nobody could find it, was frankly appalled. Over the past three weeks since the rally was announced, he had filed several scathing col-

umns excoriating the Klan and the mayor for grant-
ing them access to public space, along with the
mayor's political enemies who protested that he
was coddling bigots and racists who were using the
opportunity to savage him for their own aggran-
dizement, and just about everyone else in town,
too. Ed had received several ugly and even threatening voice mails for his pains, most of them from
gravel-voiced men who sounded, he said, like refu-
gees from *Deliverance.*

"I think you're making a mistake, Milan," he
told me over pasta at a table by the window in the
front room of Piccolo Mondo on West Sixth Street.
"Those people are pigs. You know what happens
when you lie down with pigs."

"I do," I said. "But it seems preferable to a riot."

"That Earl Ruttenberg is bad paper."

"He's a fat clown, Ed. And the only people who
will listen to his crap are the morons who think
like he does in the first place. He's preaching to
the choir."

"If that's true, Milan, you win. So why are you
worried about rioting?"

"Because there's a hell of a lot of people in this
town, of all colors, who think Ruttenberg and his
people should be used as garden fertilizer. If rocks
and bottles and bullets start flying, there won't *be*
any winners."

He gulped down a slug of his favorite poison,
Jim Beam on the rocks, and grimaced. Ed has an
ulcer, and has no business drinking anything
stronger than buttermilk.

"Is the money enough that you can live with
yourself afterward?"

"I'll let you know Monday morning," I said.

He glanced up at the door and his shoulders grew rigid. "Oh my," he said. "Oh my fucking stars . . ."

I followed his gaze. Entering the restaurant was one of the most familiar faces—and loudest voices—on the local scene. After a long tenure as de facto leader of Cleveland's African American community, Clifford Andrews had been elected to a lively and volatile mayorship for four years that were characterized by violent temper tantrums and black-power rhetoric, before losing City Hall in a close election seven years ago to the current two-term incumbent, a setback for which he had never forgiven his former friend, and had been not-so-subtly trying to undermine his successor ever since. Now forced into the private practice of law on Cleveland's largely black east side, Andrews had made enough political hay out of the issuance of the KKK permit to last the farmers of Kansas several lifetimes.

He bore down on us, eyes lasering into Ed Stahl, his cocoa-brown face glistening with perspiration, flanked by two very large black men one might be forgiven for mistaking as Cleveland Browns offensive linemen, and stopped at our table.

"Hello, Clifford," Ed said.

"Stahl, don't you 'hello-Clifford' me, you race-baiting son of a bitch." Andrews was enough of a presence that most people look up when he enters a room, but the volume of his voice made sure that anyone who had missed his grand entrance at first corrected their oversight.

Ed just smiled up at him with the innocence of a Christmas-card cherub. "I'm glad to know you're still reading my column, Clifford. Although only you would call it race baiting."

"You say I'm trying to start a riot in this city just to make myself look good? I ought to crack you across the face."

I shifted uneasily in my chair. Clifford Andrews was sixty-three-years-old and suffered from arthritis, but was not beyond the bar-fight stage, not by a long shot. During his administration he had been known to throw ashtrays, crockery, and on one occasion, a folding chair at people who angered or disagreed with him. He also outweighed Ed Stahl by about eighty pounds.

"Clifford," Ed said, remarkably calm under the circumstances, "if I only wrote my column so that no one ever got their feelings hurt, I'd wind up selling ties at Dillard's. I think you acted irresponsibly, and whether you like it or not, it's my job to say so. Nothing personal."

"We'll see about that," Andrews said. Then he looked at me and his eyes blazed even more. "You're Jacovich, right?"

"Close enough, Mr. Andrews," I said. He had incorrectly pronounced the *J;* the correct way is YOCK-o-vitch. But I sensed Clifford Andrews didn't care one way or the other.

"I hear that you're the son of a bitch who's actually gonna protect those scum."

"Word gets around."

"How can you even look in the mirror?" He sneered. It was almost funny coming from him, the man who'd fanned media fever and street anger over the triple-K hate hoedown from a warm coal to a white-hot ember.

Almost.

"I guess from time to time we all have trouble looking in mirrors, Mr. Andrews," I said.

His dark skin grew even darker as the blood rushed to his face. Then his lips tightened into a smile that could best be described as satanic. "You'll get what's coming to you, too. You and your honky racist employer, too. I'll see to it," he promised, and stalked off into the inner dining room. His two companions gave me a lingering look before they followed him.

Everybody else in Piccolo Mondo was giving *us* the looks. I just ignored them, but Ed boldly stared them down until they went back to their pizza and pasta.

"Move over, Ed. I guess I've just joined you on Clifford Andrews's shit list."

Ed laughed. "Welcome to the club. His shit list is longer than the one that tells who's naughty and nice." He took a carbon-crusted briar pipe out of his pocket and stuck the well-chewed stem between his teeth. No smoking was allowed in the dining room, but there was no law against pretending to. "I have to say that as mad as Clifford has ever been at me, he's never threatened me before, Milan."

"That bothered me, too," I said. "Well, look on the bright side—he didn't throw any furniture."

But Andrews did hurl a good bit of invective my way when he spoke to the Channel 12 news anchor, Vivian Truscott, on the six o'clock news that evening, calling me an even worse racist than Earl Ruttenberg, who, in Andrews' words, "at least has the guts to be up-front about it." I've been called dirtier names, I suppose, although rarely with less justification, but I still had to hope that my two sons didn't hear it.

Those particular three of my allotted fifteen minutes of fame on the news show did prompt two unexpected office visits the next morning, one from a longtime business associate and the other from someone I had heard about but never met.

The business associate was Willard Dante, who ran the largest manufacturing company of residential and security devices in Ohio, in the not-too-close exurb of Twinsburg. He garnered national recognition a few years ago with his development of a stun belt that had civil libertarians picketing outside his factory, but my relationship with him was based more on the alarm systems, surveillance cameras and security paraphernalia which I purchased from him on occasion for my more paranoid industrial clients. He was the kind of church-tithing, flag-waving super patriot I didn't have anything to do with socially, but our business dealings had always been cordial.

"I was on one of my rare trips downtown anyway today, Milan," he said heartily after I'd poured him a cup of coffee, "so I thought I'd pop in and tell you in person that I thought what Cliff Andrews said about you on TV last night really stinks the big stink. You deserve better."

I shook his outstretched hand. "Thanks, Will, I appreciate it. But I can't say it really bothered me. Andrews rants and raves all the time. Not that many people listen to him anyway."

"Well, I think you're doing the right thing. Somebody somewhere is going to blow Ruttenberg away for his sins one of these days, but I'd just as soon it didn't happen here. I'm glad you're on board to see it doesn't happen."

"The police are going to baby-sit him in public on Sunday," I said. "There's more security planned than if the pope was going to show up."

"I know," he said. "The mayor is breaking out the tear gas, and I heard a rumor there would be snipers up on the rooftops. Snipers, for God's sake, In *Ohio*! So what does Ruttenberg want *you* to do for him?"

"Make sure he and his Keystone Klunks check into their hotel with no problem, for one thing. And then I have to eat dinner with them. The next morning I drive him downtown to his slimefest, and then I'm through."

"I'd think that they would be staying at a downtown hotel, for the sake of convenience," Dante said.

"They're too cheap for that, Will. They've booked twenty-five rooms at a dinky little motel out by the airport."

"My stars," he said. He was the only person I'd ever met who said "my stars" as an exclamation and didn't sound like somebody's grandmother. "That's tacky. Where are you going to eat with them? McDonald's?"

"No, they picked this little low-end steak house close to their motel, a place called Red's, for God's sake. I think I'm going to eat before I go."

He laughed. "Anything I can do to help out? Want to rent some security cams?"

"I don't think we'll need them, Will."

He nodded, looking a little disappointed. "Well, listen, pal, I just wanted to let you know that I'm with you a hundred and ten percent on this one, and that what old windbag Andrews said about you last night is not going to affect our business relationship in the slightest."

"I appreciate the support, Will."

"What are friends for?" he said.

Well, it was nice to get an attaboy when the rest of the world seemed ready to hang me on the wall. A few of my friends had called me at home the previous evening to complain about Andrews' vilification of me on television, but no one had dropped in except Willard Dante. I had visited his Twinsburg plant several times, but I don't think he'd ever been in my office before.

About five minutes after he left, my second visitor arrived, and I wondered if they had crossed paths in the parking lot. I'd seen him on television, seen his photo in the newspaper countless times, and had even heard him speak once when he made an unsuccessful run for the office of county commissioner a few years earlier. The Reverend Alvin Quest of the Mount Gilead Baptist Church on Cleveland's east side was a moral and spiritual leader in the black community who had also made a brief and spectacularly unsuccessful run for a U.S. Senate nomination a few years earlier. He was a consistent voice of reason and, when the occasion called for it, of fire.

In my office, however, he spoke with warmth and courtesy in a soft and well-modulated voice, his dark eyes sparkling behind his small, thick-lensed spectacles.

"It's a pleasure meeting you, Reverend Quest," I said. "I've been an admirer of yours."

He smiled. "Thank you," he said. "That's good to hear."

"So I hope you haven't come up here to give me a spanking about this Klan thing."

"Just the opposite," he assured me. "To be sure, Clifford Andrews and I share the same goals, but we usually differ sharply in how we want to accomplish them. I apologize for his rashness on the news last night."

"No harm, no foul."

"Actually I came here to offer you any help I can."

That one brought me up short. "Help?"

He nodded. "It would be very destructive to what our people have tried to accomplish in Cleveland if anything untoward were to happen to Mr. Ruttenberg or any of his minions. To say nothing of tarnishing the name of a city that has come so far in the last twenty years. So it is vitally important to me that Earl Ruttenberg stay safe as long as he is in our city. I'm more than happy to dispatch some of our people to help you with your security."

"You think that's such a good idea, Reverend? Letting the world see black men actually protecting the head of the KKK?"

"Oh, we'll be there having our say as well. The city of Cleveland has set aside a special area for protesters, just like they have for the Klan supporters. I'm sure you read that in the papers."

I nodded.

"But it will be a peaceful, quiet, dignified protest. I want to let everyone know that there are other avenues besides violence, that we defy those sad, silly, misguided fools in their sheets and hoods. That there is sanctity in human life, and that under the skin, people are all the same. Isn't that what Martin Luther King preached?"

"Martin Luther King," I said, "never met Earl Roy Ruttenberg."

Not knowing, of course, that soon Dr. King was to have his chance.

It was Saturday afternoon and I was sitting in the so-called lobby of the Pine Rest Motel on Brookpark Road near the Cleveland Airport. I don't know why they had named it that; there wasn't a pine tree within ten miles, and if the lobby furniture was of the same quality as the beds in the rooms, it wasn't very restful, either. It wasn't the kind of hot-pillow joint where hookers plied their trade in cubicle rooms and pushers passed dime bags down by the ice machine, but it wasn't exactly the Ritz Carlton, either.

I was wearing a .357 Magnum in a shoulder harness under my sports jacket, but nobody seemed to notice that. Maybe sitting in the lobby heeled was the Pine Rest's dress code.

For the past hour there had been a trickle of rough-looking white males with one piece of luggage apiece checking in at the desk; a few of them gave me suspicious glances bordering on hostile, but I suppose when your main source of recreation is running around wearing sheets and hoods and foaming at the mouth about blacks and Jews and Catholics, suspicion and hostility are your daily portion.

Finallly, at a few minutes after four, a vintage Cadillac pulled up in front of the motel office. Earl Roy Ruttenberg got out of the backseat, and Ozzie and Jay exited from the front. I walked out of the lobby into the heat of August.

"I see you got here all right," I said to Ruttenberg. I made no effort to shake hands, nor was he expecting me to do so.

"So far, so good. Kind of a boring trip up from Medina, with all that highway construction. All quiet around here? Any suspicious-looking characters?"

"A bunch of them," I said, "but they're all with your group."

"Heh-heh," he said. "No, I was thinking of those folks of the Negro persuasion."

I assured him that no "folks of the Negro persuasion" were in evidence except the room maids, walked him in to the front desk, followed by Ozzie and Jay, who today were sporting mirrored sunglasses in a pathetic attempt at looking cool, macho and bad-ass. I watched while they checked in. It had been prearranged that the boys of bummer would share a room next to Ruttenberg's, which turned out to be a suite, a sitting room with a bedroom attached.

I sat on the sofa and watched him unpack. He had brought a brown suit, white shirt and an ugly tie, which he put in the closet, extra socks and underwear and a pair of brown shoes that went in the dresser drawer, and a sports jacket, gray slacks and a bilious green polo shirt, which he laid out on the bed. Then I watched in amazement as he lovingly unpacked and hung up his white robe and hood. It was almost funny.

Almost.

"Tell me," I said, "do you have those sheets laundered commercially, or does your wife wash and iron them for you?"

"Go ahead and have your fun, Mr. Jacovich," he said good-naturedly. This time he pronounced it correctly.

"Where did you learn the correct pronunciation of my name?"

"Oh, I heard some loud-mouthed boogie talking about you on television the other night."

I started to get up from the sofa, but he raised a hand like a traffic cop stopping a line of cars. "Take it easy, now. You just told me I couldn't use the N-word; you didn't say nothing about boogie."

I just sighed. When he's right, he's right.

From his briefcase he took several stacks of flyers and brochures of racial filth and put them on the table near the window. I avoided them the way I would pile of rancid garbage.

He pulled a silver hip flask from his pocket and unscrewed the top. "Join me?"

"No thanks."

He laughed. "Fussy who you drink with, huh?"

"Something like that."

"Don't be that way. No reason we can't be friends, is there?"

"There are a thousand reasons. I'm here to see no one takes a shot at you or sticks a knife in your eye, and I'll do that to the best of my ability. If you were looking to hire a friend, you dialed the wrong number."

"Your loss," he said. He unscrewed the top of the flask and took a long pull at it. "Aaaaahhh," he breathed in satisfaction. The smell that wafted across the room told me it was not very good bourbon.

"What do you get out of this, Mr. Ruttenberg?" I said, partly to make conversation and partly because I really wanted to know. "You have to be aware that here at the beginning of the twenty-first century, the vast majority of the people are either hating your guts or just laughing at you."

"Some folks do," he admitted. "Like you. But I think you'd be s'prised at how many folks are starting to think my way. *Our* way."

"That's why you travel with two bone breakers and hired me as extra security, huh? Because everyone loves you."

"Of course not. Not the kikes or the spics or the pope lickers. And certainly not the mud people."

"Damn," I said.

"What?"

"We're going to have to amend our little agreement, Mr. Ruttenberg, and put a moratorium on all the racial and ethnic slurs, or I'm not going to be able to keep from pounding the piss out of you."

"Just trying to get your goat, Jacovich. And I seem to have done a good job of it. Well, okay, I'll be good. But I can't guarantee what kind of words my friends might say at dinner tonight. You gonna pound the piss out of all of them?"

I didn't respond.

"But let me answer your question. What do I get out of it? The, um, *minorities* in this country are

going to take over if we're not careful. The Jews
have all the money and they control all the newspapers and television, the blacks have all the jobs,
and the Catholics keep on grinding out new little
Catholics like sausages to suck up our tax money
in welfare. This country was founded by white men.
What I get out of it is reminding the white people
of this country of that fact so they don't let the
U.S. of A. slip out from between their fingers. And
to remind the *others* that there's a whole bunch of
folks who just aren't about to let them take our
birthright from us."

"I see," I said, feeling as if an elephant had just
stepped on my chest. I'd heard this kind of foamy-
mouthed crap before; all of us have. But I never
looked at it across the same room before, and it
was causing me difficulty in breathing.

"So what I get out of it," he went on, "is a U.S.
of A. that I'll be proud to leave to my children and
grandchildren."

I suppressed a shudder. The thought of Earl Roy
Ruttenberg actually breeding and reproducing was
an unsettling one.

I had brought a paperback along with me, figuring I'd rather read than have to talk to him, so I
sat by the window, occasionally glancing up from
the page and out into the parking lot to make sure
no one was out there with a bazooka, while Ruttenberg went into the bedroom to make some
phone calls. He emerged at a quarter to seven in
the sports jacket and snot-green shirt, his jowly face
glistening from a very recent shave.

"Let's eat!" he said, and actually rubbed his
hands together.

* * *

Red's Steak House is for people who have arteries like firehoses. Gnarly steaks, french fries, meat loaf, roast duck, pork loin, and anything else one might cook with grease were featured prominently on the menu. For those who don't eat red meat, there was fried perch. Other than the desserts, there was not much else. There is a lounge attached to the dining room, the kind of bar where ordering a frozen daiquiri is indicative of either seriously impaired judgement or a death wish.

The Klan had been relegated to what Red's laughingly called their banquet room, a private dining room with two long tables—each table was actually five tables pushed together—that seated sixteen people each. Ruttenberg ensconced himself at the head of one of them and indicated that I should sit next to him. But frankly, I didn't think I could eat a thing, despite Ruttenberg's generous offer to pay for my dinner. It was less the prospect of a heart attack on a plate that engendered a loss of appetite, frankly, than the company. I opted instead to stand at the door, just in case I had to earn my money, and unbuttoned my jacket in the event I had to draw my weapon quickly. Ruttenberg actually seemed a little hurt, but Ozzie and Jay flanked him and made him feel safe, so he didn't need me.

Most of the flint-eyed, slack-jawed men I'd seen checking into the Pine Rest had showed up, some of them tackily and gaudily dressed for the occasion. I guess they operated on the theory that you can't spew misanthropic hatred at the dinner table if you aren't gussied up for the part.

After everyone had enjoyed a pre-dinner cocktail or four, the first course was brought out. As befitting his exalted station in life, Ruttenberg was served first. It was soup, chicken noodle from the look of it, and for a while the only sound in the room was sucking and slurping, like standing next to a sewer grating after a heavy rain. Then, when the soup plates had been cleared away, Earl Roy Ruttenberg tapped on his water glass with a fork, waited until his followers had quieted down, and rose.

"My fellow patriots," he said when he had everyone's attention. "First off, I wanna thank y'all for being here. The camaraderie of white men is something special—warm and loving and strong in its devotion to a righteous cause. And I am reveling in that camaraderie right now."

Applause, heartfelt and enthusiastic. Nothing like a warm-and-fuzzy to fire up a lynch mob.

"Naturally, we're hoping for a big turnout tomorrow," Ruttenberg went on. "But that really isn't important anymore. Because just by *being* here, we've won the game. The Negro politicians who run this town are at one another's throats already, and we couldn't have asked for more help from the liberal news media than if we'd paid for it!"

"Hear! Hear!" somebody said.

"But I wanted to give each and every one of you my personal and sincere thanks. We are the last line of defense in the United States, and I am just damn proud of all of you for—"

He stopped, got a strange look on his face, and burped.

" 'Scuse me," he said. "I am proud of each and every . . ."

And then his face got very flushed, his eyes grew wide, and he bent over almost double from the waist and vomited down the front of his green shirt.

If you've ever given serious thought to putting rat poison in your basement, you would probably rethink it if you'd watched Earl Roy Ruttenberg die. It took him about seven minutes, and from his roars of agony, his writhing on the floor, his vomiting black bile, and the horrible contractions that sent his body into spasms every few seconds, it was not an easy seven minutes. Someone called the paramedics, but they arrived far too late.

The Klansmen were bumping into each other in panicked disarray, but they were muttering darkly about revenge and payback as well. It's apparently true that when you cut off the head of a snake, the rest of the body lives on.

Lieutenant Florence McHargue of the Cleveland P.D.'s Homicide Division arrived a few minutes after the paramedics. She was cranky because such a high-profile victim had dragged her away from her Saturday night, and even crankier because she was a black woman whose duty had thrown her among a rattled mob of Ku Kluxers. She temporarily ordered them all out into the main dining room of Red's Steak House, where they milled around bumping shoulders like nervous steers in a slaughterhouse pen.

She wasn't exactly overjoyed to find me there, either. Lieutenant McHargue doesn't like me very much, but as far as I've been able to tell she isn't really fond of anyone.

"I heard on TV that you were going to hold Ruttenberg's hand," she said. "This serves you right." She looked down at the body, which had been hastily covered with a couple of tablecloths until the coroner's technicians could arrive. "Serves him right, too."

"And there are only about three hundred thousand people in greater Cleveland with a motive, too. This should be a slam-dunk for you, Lieutenant."

"Let's start with slam-dunking *you*," she said. "Talk to me."

"I can start with Clifford Andrews. I suppose you know about him hanging me out to dry on television the other night. Did you also hear that he threatened both me and Ruttenberg publicly in Piccolo Mondo the other day?"

"Oh, yes," she said. "That got back to me in a hurry."

"I'd think, then, that you'd start with slam-dunking *him*."

"I will, believe me. But the fact is that while in public Andrews is a fire-breathing race baiter, privately he is a very logical, reasonable, and even charming man. Most of the time, anyway."

"When he's not throwing furniture."

"At his age, he's lucky he can still lift it, much less throw it."

"Nobody had a better motive," I reminded her. "It kills two birds with one stone. He rids the world of Earl Roy Ruttenberg, and he makes the mayor look like a doofus."

"The mayor does that himself without anyone's help," she observed dryly; the mayor and the police rank and file regarded each other the way the Albanians do the Serbians. "What else?"

"Not much," I said. "Ruttenberg was a little obsessed about his safety, but obviously just because he was paranoid, it didn't mean someone wasn't after him. Hate has a way of blowing up in your hand."

"We're questioning all the kitchen help and the wait staff. Who knew the Ruttenberg crowd would be eating here?"

"I have no way of knowing who they told. I know I didn't tell anybody." Then the skin prickled on the back of my neck. "Except Willard Dante."

"The stun-gun guy?"

"That's the one. I happened to mention to him that the Kluxers were going to be having dinner here. But he's a Pat Buchanan conservative; why would he want to kill Ruttenberg?"

"Why indeed " she said, and jotted his name down in her notebook. "This town catches fire this afternoon and his phone will be ringing off the hook with people wanting security cameras and alarm systems and even stun guns to protect themselves from rioters. What made you tell him and no one else?"

I had to think about that for a while. "Because he asked."

"Uh-huh," McHargue said.

Willard Dante's house was in the elegant little village of Gates Mills. Apparently the stun-gun business was a lucrative one. He seemed surprised to see me on his doorstep, because I hadn't called first. From what I could see over his shoulder into the formal dining room, he and his wife were apparently hosting a dinner party for two other couples, a casual one because he was wearing white sailcloth slacks and a fuschia polo shirt.

He looked shocked when I told him about Ruttenberg.

"But why come all the way out here to tell me?" he wanted to know. "I had nothing to do with him."

"Is there someplace we can talk?"

He looked nervously back at his guests. "Sure, in the garden room."

Which turned out to be a quaint little utility room that had been done up with white wicker furniture and trellises against the walls. It was a peaceful room, the kind of room one sits in when the pressures of business are great and the batteries need a little peaceful recharging.

"Will," I said after we were both sitting down, "why did you come to my office the other day?"

"I told you. I was in the neighborhood, and I thought what a lousy deal you'd gotten from Clifford Andrews's talking about you on TV like that, and I wanted to drop by and show you some support."

"Support because I needed it, or support because you thought Earl Ruttenberg was a patriot?"

His face flushed. "That's a shitty thing to say, Milan. Sure, I'm a right-wing conservative, and sure, I've lived in Cleveland all my life and my favorite color isn't black, but I'm no Kluxer. I thought Ruttenberg was pig shit, to tell you the truth."

"Enough to slip rat poison into his chicken soup?"

"You aren't serious!"

"You made a point of asking me where Ruttenberg was staying and where they were going to eat. Why would you want to know that?"

Out in the dining room, everyone laughed. They were having a lot better time than their host. "I told you I dropped by for support and friendship," Dante said, "and that's true. But I also came to see if I could do a little business. Remember I asked you if you wanted hidden cams put up?"

"I remember," I said.

"So trying to turn a buck or two makes me a bad guy?"

"Not necessarily."

"It sure doesn't make me a murderer."

"Who else did you tell about Red's Steak House and the Pine Rest motel?"

"Nobody," he said. "Who the hell would I tell?" Then his eyes got big and round. "Oh, wait," he said. "In the parking lot outside your office. I just happened to mention it in passing. Reverend Quest. Was he coming to see you, Milan?"

Lieutenant McHargue wasn't glad to see me the next morning; she never is. And she was overwhelmed with work, trying to coordinate the police presence at the Klan rally for that afternoon. But I had, after all, cracked her case for her, and she couldn't be downright rude and toss me out of her office.

"Go figure," she grumped. "A man like Alvin Quest. God!"

"He made a full confession?"

She nodded. "He sent one of his people in to Red's Steak House and got him a job as a busboy—using a phony name, of course; that's how the rat poison got in the chicken soup. The kid is long gone from the city and Reverend Quest will go to the execution chamber before he'll tell us his name. Quest's lawyer will probably plead temporary insanity. He may have something at that. Find me twelve jurors in this town who are going to send Alvin Quest to death row." She took a deep breath. "Frankly, I'm more pissed off at him for trying to incite a riot in my city than for ridding the world of garbage like Ruttenberg."

"It's the same scenario as Clifford Andrews," I said, "only Quest's was more dignified and with a little come-to-Jesus thrown in. Certainly Quest had every reason in the world to hate Earl Roy Ruttenberg and want him dead. And if things blow up this afternoon, the mayor is going to have a whole Western omelet on his face. And that would give Quest the wedge he needed to run for mayor himself."

"Well, the joke's on him, Jacovich, and you, too. Because there isn't going to be any blowup. We've got every cop who can drag his or her ass out of bed with riot gear and tear gas, ready to uphold the Constitution and protect the rights of a bunch of mouth breathers with pillow cases over their heads. Or we will have," she said pointedly, "if you get the hell out of my office and let me do my job."

"Good luck this afternoon."

"Are we going to see you at the rally?"

"And listen to that kind of filth? No, thanks. I

have better things to do with a summer Sunday afternoon."

"Like what?" she said.

"I was thinking about straightening out my sock drawer."

I didn't go near my sock drawer, after all, but I did stay home and watch the Indians play the Oakland A's on television. Jim Thome didn't hit a dinger, but the Tribe won anyway.

I stayed around for the six o'clock news, though, and was delighted to hear that the Klan rally passed without incident that afternoon. Less than a hundred Klan supporters showed up, probably because the keynote speaker was in cold storage with a tag on his toe. About twice that many anti-Klan protesters linked arms and sang "We Shall Overcome." The biggest contingent of all was the press, and they had precious little to write about when it was all over. No incidents whatsoever, no sound bites for the networks to use to castigate poor old Cleveland, and when it was all done, the mayor came out smelling like the Rose of Tralee.

I was damned proud of my city that day. Cleveland can be a tough town, but it's always, always fair.

CHARACTER FLAW
A ROBBIE STANTON STORY
by Christine Matthews

"Christine Matthews" is a pseudonym for a poet/playwright and horror writer who, eight years ago, turned her word processor toward mystery writing.

Robbie Stanton has appeared prior to this story in the anthologies *Deadly Allies II* and *Vengeance Is Hers,* and is very much herself a work in progress. Christine Matthews's first novel, *Murder Is the Deal of the Day,* written in collaboration with Robert J. Randisi, was published in 1999. She is currently at work on her next story and her next novel, while serving as membership chair of PWA. She was the driving force behind *Eyecon '99.*

If it hadn't been for the blood matted in her hair, I would have noticed Skye Cahill's turquoise eyes first.

"Miss Stanton?" she asked in such a calm voice. "Are you *the* Roberta Stanton? The one from TV?"

"Yes."

"I just killed someone—well, not just someone . . . I'm pretty sure he was my father."

I stood back from the door. "Get out of the hall." I let her into my apartment so easily. I wasn't the least bit frightened. Not even after noticing the gun in her right hand.

I guess I was at that raw patch in my life. There didn't seem to be a clean spot left on my body or psyche that hadn't been hurt. It felt like I'd been frightened for years. Then one day I just got pissed off. But the terror returned. In tidal waves. Then suddenly . . . it passed. All of it—the good and the bad. Nothing mattered. And it was at that point in my life I let a frightened stranger enter my apartment.

She stood in the middle of the kitchen, unsure where to turn. Like a dog circling until he finally plops down for a nap.

I pointed to a dining room chair. "Why don't you sit there?"

"Yeah. Okay . . . I'll do that . . . I'll . . ."

"How about if I take this?" I reached for the gun hanging from her limp hand.

"Okay." No struggle. She let me take it and then eased herself onto the stiff chair. "Could I have some coffee? A Coke? I need caffeine. All the way over here I felt so tired, like I was going to fall asleep. Isn't that crazy?" She looked at me, realizing how her last word stung and quickly added, "Sorry."

I laid the gun on the counter, in plain sight, but closer to me just in case I needed to go for it. Then I poured last night's coffee into a clean mug and set it in the microwave. "Well, I did spend time in a mental hospital."

She took the coffee from me and shrugged. "So you hired a hit man, big deal. If I had the money, I wouldn't have had to kill my father myself."

"But I was messed up back then . . ."

"That's why I came to you. I remembered reading all about your trouble growing up, how they took your license away, and how you finally got out last year. I knew you—of all people—would understand how I feel."

I sat down across from her, folding my hands on top of the table. "Understand what?"

"That it was *his* fault, not mine."

Before we got any deeper into our new relationship, I thought it best to tell her, "I have to call the police, you know. If what you're saying is true and you killed a man?"

She looked at me like I was an idiot. "Of course. But I came to hire you first."

I picked up my cordless, curious to see her reaction. "I make the call first and *then* we talk while we wait."

"Fine." She gulped the hot coffee down; I wondered how she managed without burning her throat. "Call."

"I figure we've got at least ten minutes—tops," I told her after hanging up.

"It won't even take that long," she said, reaching for her purse.

I jumped for the gun then, and she grinned like I'd fallen for the punch line of a tired old joke. While I held it on her, she groped around in her tote bag.

"I made this on the way over here." She handed me a cassette tape.

I took it with my free hand. Turning it over, I asked, "What is it?"

"Details. I thought it was important you have my side of the story before you go investigate."

"So you're hiring me to establish the fact that you killed your father? I don't get it." I put the gun back on the table, feeling foolish pointing the thing at her that way.

"No, I want you to check out the man. You'll find his body at the address I wrote on the tape. I can stall the police for a while. You go there, look around . . . to make sure."

"He's dead, right?"

She nodded.

"Then I still don't get it."

Suddenly she was a little girl. "I need you to tell me that there is no doubt—whatsoever—he was my father."

Before I could ask any more questions, the police were knocking at my front door.

Reaching in her pocket, Skye pulled out two hundred-dollar bills. "Here"—she thrust them at me—"for gas, your time, whatever. Please."

I lied . . . so sue me. I managed to convince the police that Skye Cahill and I had been friends for years, explaining we were practically sisters. I handed over the gun, and they took her in for questioning. Then I promised to come down after I could arrange bail. Another lie? It all depended on what I found at the address she'd written on the tape.

Elkhorn is a small town about twenty minutes outside of Omaha. The only thing I had ever heard about the place concerned its strip clubs. Since time was definitely not on my side, I decided the quickest and straightest shot would be Maple Road, which I steered toward while listening to Skye's voice coming out of my cheap car speakers.

My name is Skye Louise Cahill, I'm twenty-five years old. I'm a filmmaker and I live in Los Angeles—in the Valley. The only way I know how to do this effectively is to pretend this recorder is a camera. Maybe if I distance myself, you can understand better.

Her voice took on a tone that was both detached and informative. I felt as though I was listening to a documentary.

The trailer sits by itself in a vacant lot. There are no trees for shade, not one blade of grass for color. It's gray now, but she assumed it used to be silver.

I was taken by surprise when she referred to herself in the third person but soon got used to it. . . .

A small window on the side that faced her had a box pushed against it, blocking anyone from looking inside. The only thing adhering to the structure was dirt. No antennas, no paint, not even an address.

She stood a few feet from the door, kicking a large dirt clump, watching it crumble into the air. Trying unsuccessfully to walk a few feet without stepping into a hole, she made her way to the side, to an entrance. It took her a few more minutes before she knocked.

"Yeah? What do you want?" a man yelled.

"I'm looking for Edward Blevins. Is this number three-twenty-nine?"

She could feel him on the other side of the door, could hear him shift his weight. If he thought making her wait would discourage her, he was very wrong. She sat down on the wooden box which served as a stair.

He couldn't leave without her seeing him. She'd circled the lot several times and knew for a fact there was only one door. He couldn't even move around inside without jostling the trailer. The late afternoon sun was at her back, and she could feel her blouse sticking to her damp neck.

"Is this three-twenty-nine Oak or isn't it?"

"Who wants to know?"

The immediate response startled her enough to make her stand. Facing the door, she shouted, "I do!"

Only silence filtered from inside the trailer. She hoped he was spying on her, searching to make sure she was alone, or harmless—worth the effort to answer. She had turned to sit down again when the door suddenly opened.

"Get your ass off my property. I don't know who the hell you are, what you're selling, or what church you're collectin' for, and I don't give a damn—"

"I'm not collecting or selling anything! I just came to talk to Edward Blevins. Is that you or not? Just tell me so we can both stop yelling!"

The heavy-set man stepped out onto his wooden step and slammed the door behind him. Easing onto the ground, he forced her back a few steps. "So what if I am?"

"I'd look you straight in the eye and tell you I'm your daughter."

"Helena's kid?"

"Yes."

"How the hell is she?" he asked without smiling or softening his face in any way.

"I wouldn't know. We've never met."

"What the hell you talkin' about, girl?"

"She put me up for adoption."

"Then how do I know you're Helena's . . . and mine? What the shit you trying to pull here?"

She shoved the birth certificate in his face. "Here. It says you're my father."

"Look, it's too goddamn hot to stand around. I guess it would be all right if you came inside. Just till I get a good look at that."

It was roomier than she expected. Dark, except for one lamp in the corner, by the kitchen area. A bit of sunlight managed to filter through the skylight between dirty streaks and bird shit.

He pointed her toward a folding chair teetering against a wall while he threw himself onto a stained sofa. "Says here you was born in May of seventy-four."

"In Ardmore, Oklahoma."

"I can read," he snapped. "Suppose I am this Edward Blevins. What do you want? It sure don't look like you suffered none. I bet you had real nice folks an' a pretty little room all to yourself. Your mama done the right thing, givin' you away."

"How long did you know her?"

"A few months was all. But that don't mean shit. Lots of guys knew Helena." He laughed.

"And you got her pregnant?"

"Hell, sweetheart, I got six kids in town that I know of, if you get my meanin'?" He laughed again, and she thought she'd be sick. "Helena got herself knocked up if you so much as shook her hand. She already had four kids when I knew her. Workin' the hell outta welfare; she was really somethin'."

They stared at each other for a while before she asked, "Haven't you ever wondered about me? Even for one minute?"

"It might surprise you, girlie, sittin' there with your pink frills an' shiny shoes, but I got a lot more important things on my mind. Things ain't been all that easy for me."

She pulled her chair closer to him.

"What now?" he complained. "Lookin' for your

roots ain't gonna make things easier for any of us. You came to see me—you seen me. Guess we're finished."

"Do you ever think about my mother?"

"Jesus H. Christ, give me a fuckin' break here." His voice rose as his face grew red. He lifted himself off the couch and took a few steps toward the small refrigerator. Pulling it open with the toe of his shoe, he groaned as he reached down for a beer. Returning to his seat, he twisted off the cap, tossed it onto the floor and took a swig.

She watched him.

"Is that all you think I got to do with my time? sit and wonder about some whore I slept with once or twice? Shit, I got better things to do. Not like you."

"You can't begin to understand me."

He grunted. "Look, I'm just tryin' to survive out here. Takin' any job I can to keep the electricity on. Sure, I had some good times with your old lady. So what? I earned 'em. An' I had me a good job down at the lumber yard. Even a car. Then that load of two-by-fours fell on top of me. Now it's beggin' each month for comp checks those lousy bastards owe me. In case you ain't heard, baby, life ain't stinkin' fair."

She watched him drink half his beer down in one long gulp and was glad he hadn't offered her one. Any act of kindness would have thrown her concentration off.

While I marveled at the dramatic flair Skye had for telling a story, the tape stopped. I waited for the cassette player to click to the other side. A semi came speeding past the passenger's side, splashing my car. That's when I realized what didn't feel right about the recording. Right before it started up again.

"I've had my problems, too."

He threw the bottle, and the remaining beer spattered across the wall behind her as well as on her clothes. But she never took her eyes off him. She could tell her defiance startled him.

"Now, just what kind of troubles do you have, Skye Blue? Just what the hell is it you have to worry about?"

Her eyes fogged over with rage, and she could hear it pulsing in her ears. "Why, just last year I was worrying about where I could go to get an abortion. I think it was just after my husband skipped town. And before that I was a little concerned about a vacation I was planning. Just a few weeks to myself to get away from the beatings, some time to let the bruises heal. I worry about a lot of things, Mr. Blevins. I try to imagine what kind of a tramp my mother was and could my father possibly be the asshole I imagine? I can feel you inside me, and I wonder if I just sit here quietly and listen to you, will this anger go away? Ever?"

He sneered. "Well, lookin's free. But I ain't never said if I is or I ain't your daddy. Even though I do see my likeness a little around your mouth. Whooo boy, what your mama could do with her mouth."

"I've wondered about you on Father's Day, birthdays and at Christmas. Especially while I was cleaning up the broken glass from all those happy family gatherings. And while I was pushing slop down the disposal, I wondered what kind of scum could spawn a piece of garbage like me. Because, dear father, I enjoyed it. I actually enjoyed pushing everyone around me. It didn't matter how much they said they loved me or how kind they were. I pushed until they had no choice but to fight."

"Good God, I do believe you are my daughter." He smiled. "Now get outta here." He worked his way up to a standing position.

She slid the small revolver out of the pocket of her jacket and into his gut. "For years and years, more years than I can remember, I've thought about this. I've thought that if you were dead, maybe . . ."

He grabbed her hand, squeezed it inside his large meaty paw and pushed the gun deeper into his belly. "Do it, then."

There wasn't a struggle, it was more of a stand-off. He glaring down at her, she glaring back.

"Are you deaf *and* stupid? I said do it!"

There was a slight hesitation. Then her voice changed.

I pulled the trigger. His stomach exploded. The small room echoed, God, it was loud. Then I pulled the trigger over and over. It felt wonderful.

"I guess that's all of it, Miss Stanton. There's no question I killed someone. I just need to know if he was really my father. I'd hate to have gone through all this for the wrong person. I'm sure you know how I feel, after what you did to your own father—framing him for a murder you arranged, setting him up like that. But somehow I don't think it was a fair trade-off considering you got put away and he just had to suffer a little bad press. They never get what they deserve, do they?"

I waited for more, but the rest of the tape was blank.

I knew Elkhorn wasn't large enough for me to get lost too badly. But just to save time, I pulled into a gas station. I was directed toward West Papillion Creek where it intersected with the Old Lincoln Highway. After that it was just a few turns before I found myself on Oak.

I checked the address again. Three-twenty-nine was a blue split-level colonial house on a freshly mowed lot. It sat on the edge of a cul-de-sac, and as I stood there rechecking my directions and the address on the tape, I can't really say I was surprised. Puzzled would have been a more accurate way to describe my feelings.

"Beep! Comin' through!" a little boy warned as he peddled close to my toes on his Big Wheel.

"Do you know who lives in this house?" I asked before realizing he shouldn't be talking to a stranger.

"My girlfriend, Tiffany Thompson." And he was off, beeping a man mowing his lawn.

I started back to my car but hesitated. How many times had I stopped for directions only to find out the thing I was seeking had been right in front of me? I turned back toward the blue house and walked up the flagstone path to the front door.

A teenage boy answered the bell. "Yeah?"

I flashed my suspended license. "My name is Roberta Stanton, I'm a private investigator."

"Look, the cops already been here. My dad told them all he knows. Which ain't much."

"Can I speak to your father, then?"

"He's watching a game now, and if I interrupt him, he'll get pissed. Why don't you just go ask the cops about that crazy lady?"

The word "crazy" flew out of his mouth and

slapped me in my ego. For two years I had been trying to get on with my life, all the while being labeled crazy by the press. And at that moment I knew why I was standing in front of that door in a small town asking a snotty kid for help. Skye Cahill and I had this very tiny character flaw in common. Maybe I had felt sympathy for her from the start. But I knew one thing for sure. I wasn't crazy. Now I had to find out about her.

"Is Tiffany your little sister?" I tried a different angle.

He rolled his eyes. "No. She's my mother."

"Can I talk to her?" I tried returning his sarcastic tone. "Or is she watching a game, too?"

"Wait here," he said, and slammed the door.

Not even a full minute passed before Tiffany Thompson came to the door. She was petite and very pretty with auburn hair pinned up on her head. She waved her hands, trying to dry her long purple nails. "Yes? My son said you wanted to ask me some questions."

I opened my mouth to start, but she talked right over me.

"My husband told the police everything he knows. I don't appreciate you coming here and bothering us. We've lived in this house for almost five years now. I remember the day we first saw it. We were out driving around, and I told my husband—well, he wasn't my husband then—I said Jack, this is my dream house. This is the place—"

"Mrs. Thompson, I'm not with the police. I'm a private investigator." She stopped waving her nails, and I knew now that I had her attention, I had to keep talking and not come up for air until I was finished.

After my brief chat with Mrs. Thompson, I realized there was nothing for me to uncover at 329 Oak. And when Mr. Thompson came to the door looking for his wife, I was more convinced than ever.

Jack Thompson must have stood all of five feet five inches tall and weighed in at considerably less than I did. No way could he have been the Edward Blevins Skye had described.

Driving back toward Omaha, I caught sight of the gas station I had stopped at on my way through. Suddenly craving a candy bar, I thought it wouldn't be a bad idea to call the police.

While I waited for the phone to be answered, I peeled back the silver paper covering the Hershey bar. Its dark brown texture brightened my spirits. The detective who had given me his card after he'd cuffed Skye picked up on the fifth ring. After inquiring about the case, I was told she had been released.

"What about the blood in her hair?" I asked.

"There was a deep gash right at the hairline, over her left eye."

"And the gun?"

"It was registered in her name—she had all the papers with her. There was no sign of it having been fired," he added.

"You checked out the address she gave you?" I asked, already knowing the answer.

"Yes." A heavy sigh. "Yes, Miss Stanton, we checked it all out."

"So where is Ms. Cahill now?"

"She was escorted to Douglas County to have her wound stitched up, and then she'll be evaluated."

I knew he couldn't tell me how long any of it would take. "Thanks."

He hung up.

A breeze came up; I felt a chill on the back of my neck and along my arms. Wishing I'd thrown on a jacket, I was again struck with another inconsistency in Skye's tape. She'd said how dry and hot it had been outside the trailer. Even inside. I remembered thinking how it sounded like she was somewhere in the desert. Maybe she had become disoriented and was talking about an Oak Street in California; that's where she'd said she was from. And the sun shining so brightly had rung a false note. The closer I'd gotten to Elkhorn, the wetter the ground had appeared. It had obviously rained earlier that day.

I tossed the candy bar wrapper into a trash can, licked my fingers clean and brushed a few stray slivers from the front of my khakis. Before getting back into my car, I scanned the directory chained to the phone for the name Blevins. There was no listing.

As I shifted into third gear, I slid the tape into the player to listen to Skye Cahill's story another time.

When I was first released from the state psychiatric facility, I lived in a hotel. Being surrounded by generic paintings, lamps and furniture, I could logically assess my situation while not being influenced by anything familiar. My sister had put my things in storage, and I didn't even know if I wanted to remain in Omaha after the tabloids got through with me.

But the public does indeed have a short memory, and I managed to lay low, finally settling into a small apartment on Q Street. I found comfort in once again having my own things in my own place.

I made a cup of tea and was wondering what to do next, or even if I should do something, when the phone rang.

"Miss Stanton? This is Dr. Paige at Douglas County. Miss Cahill asked me to call to let you know we'll be keeping her overnight for observation."

"How's she's doing, Doctor?"

"Well, calmer than her previous visits. I think she's finally starting to resolve some issues."

Now I was surprised. "You've seen her before?"

"Oh yes, I was working with her in group until we found Ann."

"Who's she?" I held my breath.

"Her second personality. Why, I assumed you knew. Aren't you Roberta Stanton? The one from TV?"

"Yes. But I don't understand what that has to do with this."

"Miss Stanton, I was under the impression you were somehow related to Miss Cahill." I could hear him shuffling papers. "Yes, here it is. She has you listed as her next of kin, a cousin . . . on your father's side."

It took me a minute to mentally climb up and down my family tree. "I think there's been a mistake here, Dr. Paige. And even if it were true, why haven't you notified me before this if you thought I was a relative?"

"Miss Cahill has sessions twice a week with me. She is well over the age of twenty-one, and there have never been any problems. Besides, if I remember correctly, you were 'out of town' for about a year?"

He was diplomatic, I gave Dr. Paige credit for that. "Sorry, Doctor, but Ms. Cahill and I just met this morning. We are not related in any way. And the only reason we met at all is because she came to hire me. . . ." Suddenly I decided I was saying too much about a woman I hardly knew to a man I wasn't sure actually was who he claimed to be.

"Hired you to do what?" he calmly asked.

"That's confidential. Sorry."

"Well, Skye asked me to give you a message and I've delivered it. I guess that's it, then. Have a good evening."

"You, too." I hung up before he could. That always made me feel just a little superior, and after getting the runaround all day, I needed the boost.

Walking back into the living room, I propped myself on the couch. Holding the hot cup of tea between my hands, I studied the mug painted with tiny brown teddy bears, then stared at the blank screen of the television, and I started planning what I would do tomorrow.

* * *

Maybe it's true what they say. That if you think about a problem before going to bed, you'll wake up with the solution. Because while I brushed my teeth, I suddenly knew. I had to go to Ardmore, Oklahoma.

Skye Cahill had mentioned being born in Ardmore. No mention of where she was raised. I could have gone on-line, I guess. But no matter how proficient I became on my new computer, it was still a piece of plastic. Like the phone, I considered it just an impersonal tool. Something told me that if I looked up Skye's past, actually smelled the Oklahoma air, I'd learn something.

After checking my trusty Rand McNally, I figured it was about 570 miles from my front door to Ardmore. With the two hundred-dollar bills my client had paid me still folded in my wallet, I stuffed clean underwear and a few T-shirts into a small suitcase and felt excited at the idea of a road trip.

My Toyota was starting to show its age. A tire on the passenger's side was missing its hubcap. The faux leather interior was split in spots where the sun had baked it during last summer's excruciating heat. But for now I couldn't even think about replacing the blue Tercel. Besides, it ran like it had just glided off the showroom floor. And the best part—it was paid for.

Before heading out of town, I stopped by the hospital. It took awhile, but I managed to snag a nurse.

"It's very important Ms. Cahill gets this," I said for the second time and then handed her the letter I'd written that morning.

"She'll get it, don't worry." She looked at me with such pity. "We're all professionals here; we operate very efficiently."

It took every bit of self-control I could muster not to respond sarcastically. From clerks who couldn't make change to doctors who prescribed the wrong medication even after I told them repeatedly about my allergy to penicillin. The older I got, the more it became clear to me that very few "professionals" did their job the way I thought it should be done.

"Okay then, I guess I'll be going." I started to walk away, knowing in my gut that something would happen to my letter. "Remember . . ." I started.

"I know, I know. I'll give this to Miss Cahill." The nurse shoved it deep into her pocket and waved me good-bye.

My first impulse had been to distance myself from Skye, at least until I knew a little more about her situation. That went for Dr. Paige, too. In the letter I assured her I was working on her behalf and would return in a few days. Attached was my card with all sorts of numbers where I could be reached. I then pulled out of the hospital parking lot and got on the highway with a clear conscience.

The trip was an easy, uneventful one. Turning on the radio, I caught up on world events, switching stations as soon as one faded out and another came in clearer. Country music and sermons seemed easiest to find the farther south I got. It was technically winter, mid January. But other than the trees looking scratchy and bare, that day was a clone for one in early spring or fall. I had gotten by for months with a light fleece jacket, and now had to pull my sunglasses out of the glove compartment as the glare from other cars reflected into my eyes.

After hearing the tinny twang of one too many soulful guitars, I slipped Skye's cassette into the tape deck and listened to it for the fifth time in two days.

It took about eight hours to get to Ardmore, and I was pooped when I crashed onto my bed in the Okay Motel off Highway 35.

I slept for ten hours straight. Waking up early the next morning, I walked next door for breakfast and got into an easy conversation with the waitress. Between snapping her gum and scratching her head, Fern finally remembered the Blevins family.

"Lived here my whole life. But can't say as how I remember an Edward. There was Doreen, her twin boys Joe and Beau. Over to the other side of town was Fat Gator and his mama, Beatrice.

"Fat Gator?" I asked, trying not to be rude.

"Called him that on account of his summer jobs down at Disney . . . on the Jungle Ride. An' him also bein' a bit . . . oversized."

I stirred the grits around on my plate, wondering who ever thought to serve the white mush like it was real food. "What was Gator's legal name?" I asked.

"How 'bout that. I don't know. Hey, Dot!" she shouted to the hostess with the sixties hairdo. "You know what Fat Gator's Christian name might be?"

"Edward," she shouted back.

I couldn't believe my luck. What were the odds of coming up with a hit first time out? I quickly thanked the cosmos and pushed for a little more. "I don't suppose you'd know where he lives." When she cocked a suspicious eyebrow at me, I added, "I'm a friend of his daughter's."

"That man did have a passel of kids. But you're not gonna find ole Gator home, I'm afraid."

"Oh?" I looked up from my breakfast.

"He got hisself killed 'bout ten years back. Yeah, it was right about the time I started workin' here."

I had dreaded a day schlepping myself around from newspaper office to library to county records, and here all had been eliminated while I talked to Fern. She knew everybody's business and wasn't afraid to tell what she knew. Praise the Lord and pass the information!

By the time the lunch crowd started showing up, I had a map sketched on a paper napkin giving me detailed directions to the murder scene. Fern couldn't remember ever meeting Skye. But as she told me many times, Fat Gator was a "genuine lady's man." When I smirked, she assured me, "Gator could get real ornery, 'specially when he was drinkin'. But when that man was sober, he was a real sweetheart. He made a lady feel special, know what I mean?"

Blevins and Fern had gone all through grammar school together until Gator dropped out in the seventh grade. She wasn't sure what had become of his trailer or even if it was still hooked up on the lot outside town close to Enville, near Lake Murray. Fern had also been kind enough to give me the

name of the chief of police, his age, marital status
and year of graduation. She warned me he was a
snot at eleven years of age and was still one. That
I shouldn't expect much more out of him than a
grunt. I checked in with him before driving the ten
miles south toward the lake.

When I had heard the word "lake," my brain
did a free association: speedboats, skiers, cottages,
wooded areas, concession stands, motels. But those
were summer images and this was winter, a week-
day. The skiers were in school or at offices. The
only thing lit up in front of motels were their va-
cancy signs.

After finding the dirt road, I drove for a few
minutes hoping my tires wouldn't blow out. My
body jiggled up and down on the seat while I held
tightly to the steering wheel, forcing my car to stay
in the deep ruts. Just when I was getting ready to
find a clearing to turn around in, I saw a large silver
mailbox leaning to one side from too many side
swipes. The name, painted sloppily in red paint,
read: BLEVINS. I made a hard left.

There was the trailer exactly the way Skye had
described it. The only discrepancy was the rusted
lawn chair sitting in front of the single step. I didn't
see any vehicles parked in the area, and as I got
out of my car I reexamined the copy of the newspaper story Chief Jackson had given me. Contrary to
what Fern had said, the chief had been gracious
and very helpful. I could tell the unsolved murder
had haunted him for years.

As I put my hand on the dirty knob, the door
was yanked out of my hand.

"What the hell do you think you're doin'?" a frightened woman wearing a floral printed house dress asked. "This here's private property. You cain't go prancin' up to someone's private home and walk in pretty as you please."

"I'm sorry." I fumbled in my purse. Flashing the suspended license, I said, "I'm a private investigator working for Miss Skye Cahill."

"Let me see that." The woman grabbed my ID and brought it closer to her face. "This here's no good, missy." After looking me up and down, she finally said, "But if you say Skye sent you, I guess I can hear ya out. Come on in here." She stood back and motioned impatiently for me to enter.

The inside of the trailer wasn't anything like Skye had described. But then, if Blevins had been murdered ten years ago, there had to be some changes made. Chief Jackson had gone on and on about what a bloody scene the trailer had been after the murder. My eyes scanned the floor for traces of scarlet. But, in sharp contrast to the disheveled woman wearing grimy tennis shoes, the interior was immaculate.

"Can I offer you a cup of coffee?" she asked.

"That would be nice."

While she filled two cups she asked my name.

"Roberta Stanton, I'm from Omaha."

"So how would you hook up with Skye, her livin' out in Los Angeles?"

I took the cup she handed me and seated myself on the leather sofa.

"Well, that's kind of a long story, Mrs. . . . ?"

"Sorry, I'm Beatrice."

I sat a little straighter. "Edward's mother?"

She slowly lowered herself onto a folding chair. "My only child."

"I'm so sorry; you have my sympathy."

"Honey"—she blew on the hot coffee—"it was the best thing for all of us. I only wish I'd never brought him into the world is all." She waited for my reaction. When it was obvious I didn't know what to say, she asked, "Ain't that a terrible thing for a mother to say?"

"A few years ago I would have said it was. But not now. Being related to someone doesn't mean you automatically love them."

"Amen!" She smiled at me, and I could see she didn't have any teeth. "Now, Miss Stanton, tell me what it is you came all this way to find out."

"Well, I understand your son fathered several children with various partners."

She cackled at my civility. "You're bein' very polite, but there ain't no need. Eddie was a pig. He poked anything and anybody. I know what they says about him havin' all these children, but the only one I ever seen was Skye. She was a beautiful baby . . . a real Kewpie doll."

"You saw her? I was under the impression your son never met his daughter."

"Far as I know, he never did."

"Mrs. Blevins, the reason Skye hired me was to find out if Edward Blevins was in fact her real father."

"Oh, he surely was."

"You're absolutely positive?" I asked.

"It took some convincin'. Even after I got a letter from Helena—that bitch. Thought she was just stirrin' up the shit like she always done. She said she wanted money for the baby and didn't care if it come from the family or some stranger in the gutter. She was gonna sell the poor little thing. There was a picture stuck inside the envelope. 'Course, I had to be sure if it was true or not. Called me a lawyer, the one in them TV commercials. He said he'd check it out."

"And you never told your son?"

The old woman seemed weary at the memory. "I tried. Brought the letter for him to see. I was livin' up at the house back then, it's 'bout a mile from here. That way he never got wind of my mail, liked to keep my private affairs away from him. But when I told Eddie, he didn't wanna hear nothin' 'bout no kid. He just laughed, went on how I should be proud that the ladies loved him so much. That kinda talk always made me sick."

"So what did the lawyer find out?"

"Took 'bout ten days, but they said it was all true. My grandbaby was livin' in back of some bar in El Paso. Said that the place was a real hole and I should try to get her outta there. But I was too old to care for a baby myself. An' I certainly did fear for her if Eddie got wind of the situation.

"So I cleaned out my savin's. All twenty thousand of it. Mr. Blevins left me a little and there was government checks. It took everything I had."

"What happened to Skye?"

"The lawyer gave Helena the money and arranged for the poor child to be adopted."

"Did you have any idea where she was living?"

Beatrice Blevins looked at me for a long moment, studied my brown boots, then the hems of my jeans. "I knew all along. I fixed it so the pastor and his wife down at the Methodist church who had just moved to California got her. What better people for parents than those God-fearin' Cahills? They was such a sweet couple."

"Did they turn out to be the perfect parents you thought they'd be?" I wondered out loud, not expecting an answer.

"I figured they was till some woman called me one day—oh, it must have been 'bout five years ago. She told me Skye was in danger and asked me to help."

"What kind of danger?" I asked.

"That's what I wanted to know. But she just kept goin' on, like she was a doctor or somethin'—real quiet and listin' off how she had been beat up an' hurt."

I did the math. "Five years ago Skye would have been twenty."

Beatrice scrunched up her face while she did her own calculations. "She was married by then. To some important guy in the movies. Not anyone famous, some big cheese that did all the dealin'. I thought for sure she struck it rich."

"Apparently not." I could hear Skye's own words replaying as she told her father about her unhappy marriage. That poor kid never had a chance, and I wondered how much worse off she would have been if Beatrice hadn't tried so hard to save her. "Did you help?"

"There wasn't nothin' I could do. She was an adult, with her own life to live, and I was stone broke. Had to sell the house an' move down here. Eddie was long gone, but even if he was still around, he wouldn't of done nothin'."

"You did your best." I leaned across and patted her hand.

"Don't stop me from feelin' bad. But now ya say Skye come to see you? How did she look?"

I remembered those turquoise eyes. "Beautiful," I told her.

I stood to leave. Beatrice walked me out to my car and asked that I give her granddaughter her regards.

I was buckling myself into the front seat when something made me ask, "Do you happen to remember the name of the woman who called you about Skye?"

"Sure. Have a hard time with faces, but names stick in there pretty good." She tapped her right temple. "It was Ann. Never did give me a last name."

Dr. Paige wouldn't give me Skye's home address, and since there was no message from her when I returned home, I was forced to plant myself in his waiting room.

"The doctor only sees patients with appointments," his pretentious receptionist told me. "And he *never* sees investigators. If you have a legal matter, we advise you to take it up with the police. In turn, we will be more than happy to cooperate with them."

After that speech I went out to get a hamburger, bringing it back to eat, loudly and slowly, while I waited. I was slurping at the bottom of the ice in my plastic cup when the doctor came out.

"Five minutes," Dr. Paige said as I slid into the

chair across from his desk. "Please remember I'm seeing you only out of respect for Miss Cahill."

I checked my watch before asking, "When you called me the other evening, you said you've been seeing Skye for two years."

The jerk just stared at me and nodded.

"I assume that means she lives here, in Omaha?"

"Elkhorn."

Now it made sense why she'd sent me out there. Maybe seeing the street name had triggered off a repressed memory. "According to her grand-mother, Skye was raised in Los Angeles?"

"Yes."

"Would it be breaking any great ethical code to tell me the last address you have for her in California?"

He rolled his eyes in such a way that made me want to harm him. "Miss Stanton . . ."

"Look, you can either cooperate with me now or later. Now will only take up"—I checked my watch again—"four minutes and thirty seconds. Later could take days. I'm a bullheaded German with free hours to spend haunting your office."

He pounded his fist down on the date book in front of him. "Yes! Of course I know her address!" He swiveled his chair angrily around and started punching numbers into his computer. When the screen was lit up with Skye Cahill's history, he read the address: "Three-twenty-nine Oak Street. She lived there with her husband for three and a half years." Then he closed the file and defiantly turned toward me. "What else?"

"Three minutes left for you to listen to a theory of mine."

He sat back nodding, at first bored and then stunned to hear that I suspected Skye Cahill of murdering her father, Edward Blevins, when she was sixteen years old.

"Miss Cahill is incapable of such a violent act."

"What about Ann?"

The doctor's ears perked up then. "Now, that's an interesting thought." I must have struck a nerve; all of a sudden he wanted to talk. I leaned back and listened.

"The personality of Ann is the idealized mother figure. She protects and loves Skye, unconditionally. I would suspect she is capable of doing whatever it takes to keep Skye safe. But if that was the case, why hadn't she struck out sooner, try to harm the unstable parent or abusive husband?"

"When was Ann . . . born?"

"As far back as Skye can remember," he said.

"Then wouldn't it make sense that the mother would blame the father for putting the child in danger?"

"Very good, Miss Stanton."

"How long did Skye know she was adopted?"

"As far back as she could remember. Yes, it all makes sense."

I picked up my purse and pulled out a copy of the original cassette Skye had given me. I started to stand, and the doctor looked disappointed. "You're not going so soon? Look, I apologize for my bad manners."

I tossed the tape at him. "Listen to this and see if you agree with me that Skye was confessing to protect Ann, the personality who actually pulled the trigger."

He was excited now. "Sit, we can listen together."

I started for the door. "Dr. Paige, I'm really not interested in helping you make a name for yourself by exploiting this young woman. The chief of police from Ardmore, Oklahoma, has also received a copy of that tape and will be contacting you, as will the detective who booked Skye here, in Omaha. I have no interest in the outcome of this case. That will be left to the three of you."

I hurried out of the door before he could say anything else. When the elevator doors opened, I thought I was home free until I saw those frightened eyes.

"Miss Stanton." Skye grabbed my arm and nudged me to a corner in the hall. "I've been waiting outside your apartment for hours. Where have you been?"

"Working on your case," I told her gently.

"So? What did you find out? Was that man my father?"

"Yes, Skye, he was." I watched her expression and it never changed. I wasn't sure if I was talking to Skye or Ann. I felt so sorry for her.

"I need to see Dr. Paige," she said, and walked away as if I had suddenly gone invisible.

"And I need to make a call," I said to myself, dialing the police.

Someone once told me that the second most important thing about doing a job is knowing when you are finished. As I forced myself back into my car, I kept telling myself I'd done only what Skye

Cahill had hired me to do. My job was done. What happened to her as a result of my investigation was of no concern to me.

But still I felt guilty.